JORIS OF THE ROCK

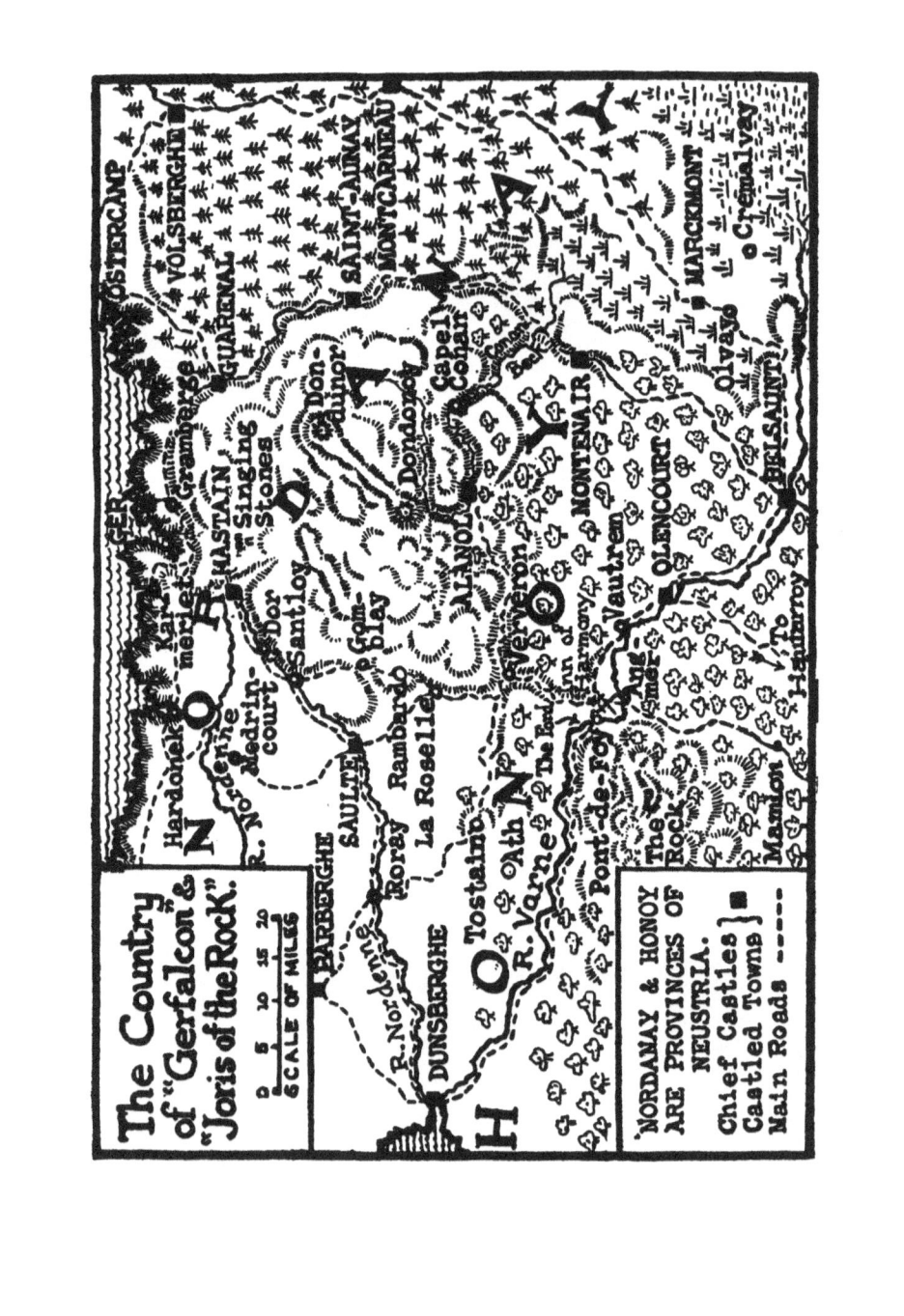

The Country of "Gerfalcon" & "Joris of the Rock".

SCALE OF MILES
0 5 10 15 20

NORDANAY & HONOY ARE PROVINCES OF NEUSTRIA.
Chief Castles ∎
Castled Towns ∎
Main Roads -----

OSTERCAMP
VOLSBERGHM
GUARENAL
SAINT-AINAY
MONTCARNEAU
MARCKMONT
Cremelvay
Olvexo
BELSAINT
Capel Cohair
Don-Amor
Dondonot
MONTENAIR
OLENCOURT
Karlmerle
Gramperge
HASTAIN
The Singing Stones
Hardonek
Nordenne
Medrin-court
Dor
Santloy
Gom-blay
ALANOL
Vautren
Harmony
Vereron
Hambarroy
To
Mamlon
The Rock
Pont-de-Foy
Inn of The Bird
SAULTE
Rambard
La Roselle
Rorey
R. Nordenne
BARBERGHE
Tostain
R. Varne
Ath
R. Nordenne
DUNSBERGHE

NORDANAY
HONOY

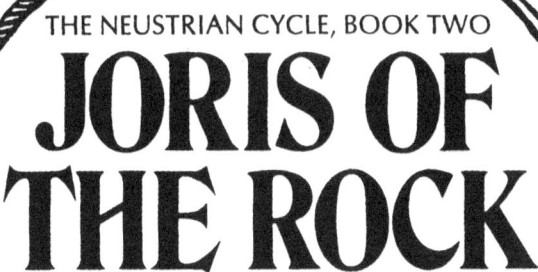

THE NEUSTRIAN CYCLE, BOOK TWO

JORIS OF THE ROCK

BY

LESLIE BARRINGER

R. REGINALD
The Borgo Press
San Bernardino, California ▫ MCMXCII

Published by
Wildside Press LLC.
www.wildsidebooks.com

CONTENTS

I. THE WAY OF JORIS OF THE ROCK

M Y BIRTHDAY," grumbled Tiphaine de Ath. "My birthday, and I may not even buy me a brooch with my own money."

Eighteen-year-old Tiphaine was brown-eyed, dark and comely, plump as a partridge, and stubborn as a mule. About her roared the Olencourt Midsummer Fair; before her, on the counter of a booth, glittered the brooch of lapis lazuli and silver; beside her, in the gray habit of the Friars Minor, her father's brother smiled with anxious kindliness.

"Come now, Tiphaine," he coaxed. "This purse I hold as it were in trust for you; we must not squander your gold at idle inclination. We should press on; it is already near the hour of nones. And I entreat you, pull up your hood; we are all God's creatures, made in His image, but Satan waits to peer from unregenerate eyes in such an hour and place as this."

Satan—or maybe his lieutenant Momus, fiend of mockery—peered from the solitary unregenerate eye of the wizened stall keeper; gnarled fingers beat a whimsical tattoo on either side of the bright gaud, and a wisp of beard wagged knowingly toward the girl's ear.

"I yield to none in admiration of the Rule of Blessed Francis," wheezed the stall keeper, "but it is very bad for trade."

"Uncle Blaise," began Tiphaine, but the friar lifted a thin hand to check her speech.

"Brother Eugenius," he amended gently. "Brother in God."

"*Uncle Blaise,*" repeated the girl with emphasis, turning from the counter to confront her companion. "I will *not* call

you Brother Eugenius; you are my uncle now and always. And
I will *not* pull up my hood; I believe you wish me marked with
smallpox, that no man should look twice at me. Besides, it is
too hot. And I will not pass by the pretty booths as though
they were dungheaps; I am no Poor Clare, nor mean to be one.
Is it a sin to be young and—and proud of the face and form that
were given me by the Sieur God?"

"It is no sin to be content with them, Tiphaine."

"Oh, you can twist my every word to put me in the wrong
and make me angry and ashamed. I have listened for leagues
to tales of saints and miracles and swift conversions and dread
pilgrimages; can you not bide an hour to let me look my fill?
I do not want the brooch any more; if I wore it now I should
think Saint Francis wept each time I looked upon it."

"Tiphaine!"

The remonstrance came in little more than a whisper;
beneath his long sleeves the friar clasped his hands in grief,
but his mild weather-beaten visage set a strange blot of calm
amid the thrust and uproar of a peasantry half crazed with
annual license. Blue eyes met brown—the man's frank and
tender, the maid's flickering and sullen—and Tiphaine
shrugged unrepentant shoulders and made to move aside.

"Tiphaine!"

She collided with a bulky figure, and the Franciscan's
mournful tenor exclamation was echoed above her head in a
comical bass. Tiphaine looked up past a gold-studded belt and
a broad blue velvet chest; the tall young man who blocked
her path stared greedily down at her, cocking his pointed
hunting hat awry on his thick auburn hair.

"A lovely name for a lovely demoiselle," he said; and the
girl was shyly aware of his bold hazel-coloured eyes, of the
pale full lips above his formidable chin.

"I pray you, lording, let us pass," chirped the little friar.
"We must reach Vautrem by sundown, and may not tarry
longer. Of your kindness do not delay us."

"Vautrem, eh?—bravely cackled, gray goose," muttered the

young man derisively; but he stood back, and Tiphaine shrank from him as his big thumb and finger nipped her arm above the elbow.

She heard the laugh deep in his throat; then, shocked and sobered, with *beast* on her tongue and fury in her heart, she caught at her kinsman's girdle of white cord and followed it through the throng as best she could.

"Who is blue Goliath?" asked one man of another as she passed them.

"Blue whataway?" came the amused response. "Why, blockhead, do you not know *him?* Gaston de Volsberghe, and no other."

Gaston de Volsberghe had pinched *her* arm and grinned into *her* face! Tiphaine's blush burned less wrathfully as distance grew between herself and the son of the great northern duke; for in the lists the Sieur Gaston was likened to a lion, although in the streets his name might oftener be linked with others of the brute creation.

Nevertheless, it was not until her companion had led her clear of the last fringes of the crowd that Tiphaine recovered curiosity to pause and look back. From where she stood, on the dusty road that mounted toward the forest, the whole tumultuous fair ground sprawled in view; meadow and river bank were patched and barred with multi-coloured booths and huts and tents that shaped an immobile core for the shifting swarms of purchasers and merrymakers round them.

Below the eating sheds the press was thickest; there they were bloodily baiting bears, and at moments the barking and yelling dominated every other sound. Closer at hand the archery butts gave off sharp intermittent cheers, and here and there a troupe of minstrels or musicians was ringed with onlookers or dancers. Hoarse-voiced jugglers and acrobats and farmers of monstrosity, beggars and fortune-tellers and cheap-jacks of every kind, were charming bronze and silver from peasant pouches; beyond the rim of the great pool of sound and colour the gateway of the Olencourt barbican stood open for men-at-arms and grooms and serving maids to come and go between the fair ground and the machicolated sheer of Count Fulk's great castle behind it.

Swans preened themselves along the water-lilied moat that was a broad dike cut across the neck of a horseshoe bend of river; hawk-eyed Tiphaine watched a gay-clad group of the count's family and guests move slowly across the lowered drawbridge. Gaston de Volsberghe, too, must have come that way to laugh at the crude pleasures of the commonalty.

"But he called *me* 'demoiselle,' " reflected Tiphaine. "He knew I was not just a peasant wench, in spite of this old dusty cloak and kirtle. I wish I had my samite *côte-hardi* and the headdress with silver filigree on it. . . . Oh, if my father had to be a knave, why could he not be skilful in his knavery?"

For Tiphaine was born of the lesser nobility; her father, a vavasor's second son, had abused his post of comptroller to the Duke of Ahun. He and his artless peculation being finished by the tusks of a wild boar, his motherless and solitary daughter had cause to weep before a vindictive duke and a revealing roll of household charges. Thrust forth from castle gates in the clothes she wore—with a little purse of gold nobles which the kindly duchess had crammed down between her breasts in the moment of farewell—Tiphaine sought out her younger uncle, the Franciscan, whom chance had brought to the Ahun house of his Order a month before. Until that day she had seen him seldom enough, for the friar had offended her father by refusing to eat good food in a good tavern with a duke's comptroller; but he had readily obtained permission to take charge of her, and uncle and niece passed northward together, aiming for the Tower of Ath in Basse Honoy, where the late comptroller's elder brother bore sway over a strip of cornland and a wedge of forest.

Castle-bred Tiphaine had hoped to ride thither upon a horse, or at the least upon an ass; but in giving her purse into the keeping of Brother Eugenius she reckoned without his share of the family obstinacy. Inflexible adhesion to the Franciscan

Rule she could respect, but after a day or two of the friar's meek company Tiphaine believed his valid reason for her travelling on foot to mask an oblique attack upon what she called her self-respect, and he, her worldly vanity.

"Hoofs bespeak money," he had pointed out. "The safest armour of the wayfarer is poverty."

And since Tiphaine had too much regard for her kinsman to grab at his hood and recover her purse by force, she had trudged five leagues a day with him for three days on end. Her fair skin freckled, her muscles hardened, and her exasperation grew; for Brother Eugenius lost no chance of inveigling a soul from the way of Nature into the way of Grace. Alternately adroit and simple in his use of holy violence, he drove Tiphaine at last into a half-day's silence; and it was with a real desire to ease her load of inarticulate wrath that he led her into the midst of the Olencourt Fair.

"I must stop staring before he reminds me of the Sin of Sloth, Lot's Wife, and the Foolish Virgins," mused Tiphaine; and she turned and set her face toward the Forest of Honoy.

"The peasants think us mad to be coming away from a fair that is just begun," she remarked a little later, as raucous comment drifted back from descending groups of farm and forest folk. "And so we are," she added sulkily beneath her breath.

"See how the willows droop in the stream," said the friar cheerfully. "Varne runs high for the season, and only the aspens stir. Do you know why? When the Sieur Jesus walked in the woods near Jerusalem, all the trees trembled for grief at what had to come, save only the aspen. And the Sieur Jesus looked sadly at the aspen; and the unhappy tree has trembled ever since."

Presently the pair of them were climbing slowly through sun-flecked shadow of oaks and beeches; alder blossom was dense that year, and its sickly odour hung heavy along the river bank. Dragon flies glittered above the murmuring brown water; Tiphaine fell into a reverie, went daintily clad and softly shod, wore jewels bright as dragon fly's mail, and with her beauty plagued great lords to madness and despair.

None of *them* dared look on her as Gaston lately looked; for one, the bravest and most courteous of all, was infallibly her slave, sworn to her service through all peril and despite. The Duke of Ahun himself would shift uneasily in his chair to know that she commanded the arm of such a paladin; the Duke of Volsberghe would claw at his coppery beard when his tall son hurtled athwart the tilting barrier at shock of the lance of the lover of Tiphaine.

"I shall know him when I see him," she told herself, "and he will know me—ay, though he find me tired and shabby, shamed by my father, angered by this feckless uncle who dreams himself brother to all mankind. Saint Catherine send my kinsman of Ath is shrewder than his brethren."

That kinsman had a son who was already a chevalier. Was it he who would right her before the world? If not, there were nobles and gentles enough in Basse Honoy.

Tiphaine smiled at herself; but behind the smile was a conviction that the Blessed Virgin, and the saints whose names had starred her prayers since she could speak, would not fail to guard and cherish so exceptional a maiden as Tiphaine de Ath.

Meanwhile, the din of the Olencourt Fair died out behind the travellers; in its stead were only the piping of birds, the hum of insects, and the lightest stir of wind in the dense forest. For miles of their way Tiphaine and Brother Eugenius had not been out of sight or hearing of their kind, but now they were alone. The girl drew closer to her companion, and he, as though divining a first nervousness in her, spoke tranquilly of the Count Fulk de Olencourt as keeper of roads and upholder of strict justice.

"They say patrols of mounted archers ride each day between his castles and his marches," added Brother Eugenius, peering ahead as though by sheer good will to conjure green coats, sown with silver lilies, from the gray trunks that palisaded all the western view. "Saw you how underbrush was razed as we drew near his ploughlands? I doubt not he aims to trim this track in a like manner."

"I would he had done so already," confessed Tiphaine. "Last night, in the abbey guest house yonder, the woman who served the broken meats was talking of this grim murderer and robber whom they call Joris of the Rock."

"Ay, me!" said the friar sadly—as though loth to admit that, Christ being fourteen centuries risen and Francis eight-score years a saint, some shreds of cruelty and rapine yet persisted upon earth. "A grievous worker of ill, if truth be told of him. I have heard that he first fell into sin through some injustice of the monks of Medrincourt. . . ."

For the first time that day a dimple started in the pink cheek of Tiphaine.

"The monks might call this Joris rogue enough to be a friar," she murmured slyly. Then: "Tell me, uncle mine—had you the power, would you betray him into the gyves of the Count Fulk?"

The Franciscan's mild blue eye accused her of mockery, but his scrupulous mind accepted the challenge, and his face grew more than ordinarily worried.

"That would depend," came his hesitant reply, "upon what—what possibility of repentance and amendment I discovered in him. It is vain to judge by hearsay."

Tiphaine groaned in humorous vexation; but before she had time to rebuke such dangerous charity a measured beat of horse hoofs woke and grew along the rearward road. Friar and maiden halted and turned at gaze.

"Count Fulk has sent a man at arms to be our escort," said Tiphaine drolly. "It was discourteous in him not to have allotted us a troop. He shall be roundly chidden when I——"

The mild pleasantry was slain upon her lips. Round a sharp leafy angle of the way, astride a gaunt black mare that swerved obedient to a jagged azure bridle, Gaston de Voisberghe breasted the sun-dappled gloom and bore unhastily toward the watchers.

Instinctively they drew together. Brother Eugenius fingered his beads; Tiphaine felt a curious stir along her spine, a sudden shortening of the breath. Dark hoofs wrought havoc in the wayside bracken; the mare came pounding to a halt. Thick lips twitched in a friendly grin; the Sieur Gaston opened a great brown hand to show a brooch of gold, supporting amethysts that gave a violet flame against the shadows of summer foliage.

"Pity if one so dainty went altogether giftless from the fair," boomed the assured young voice. "Come, Demoiselle Tiphaine, for a ride upon my saddlebow. Your friar may spend an hour in prayer and meditation, while we seek out a higher glade for the improvement of acquaintance. Give me your hand—come!"

Tiphaine stood white and motionless, with shoulders and hands set flatly to a beech bole; she shifted a fascinated gaze from greedy hazel eyes to gold-girt gems and back again, finding no word for this abrupt and smiling invitation. But Brother Eugenius stepped between his niece and the stirrup of the Sieur Gaston; his lifted face was no longer worried, but calm and unafraid.

"Lording," he said bluntly, "you speak very evilly, with purpose most unworthy of your rank and blood. I entreat you, turn aside and go your way, setting your heel upon temptation of your youth and strength, shaming the Fiend who would destroy your hope of Paradise."

"Likelier my heel will land upon your foolish face," came the serene response. "Down yonder I stood aside for you; stand you now aside for me, with no more parley."

The little friar looked steadfastly into commanding eyes whose pleasantry was fled; then, dropping on his knees, he joined his palms together and prayed aloud to the blue lane of sky above him.

"Sieur God, dear Jesu, Saviour of mankind, soften the

heart of this proud man, for pity on Thine Own Mother and on the mother that bore him! Let him slay me so that he spare the innocence of this Thine handmaid. . . ."

And over his shoulder he shot an urgent groan: "Run, Tiphaine!"

"No need," said a jovial resonant voice across the way; and a red hand, large as Gaston's own, came strongly on the azure bridle.

Gaston with one foot out of stirrup and sword hand whipped to his hilt, Brother Eugenius kneeling in the dusty grass, Tiphaine half poised to leap into the alders—each scanned the fawn-clad archer who had come so suddenly and silently upon them.

The archer was taller even than Gaston, but looser-limbed and narrower of build, his eagle's face was the colour of red sand, his blue eyes were frosty beneath bushy golden brows, and his moustache and curly pointed beard seemed spun of bristles of gold. There was insolence and menace in the drag of his heavy eyelids, in the cautionary snap of thumb and finger of his weaponless hand.

"Sit still, lording," he advised. "Both my comrades here bear prizes from the butts."

De Volsberghe glanced this way and that; two other fawn-clad men had slipped from cover, and sunlight touched their bended bows to sparkle on the arrowheads thereby. One was a fat greasy rogue with a broken nose, the other a little dark knave, hatchet-faced and bandy-legged; and each stared calmly and with relish at a chosen spot in the broad anatomy of the Sieur Gaston.

"Whose men are you?" growled that nobleman, setting his hand disdainfully upon his hip.

"These are my men, but I am no man's man," replied the golden-bearded leader crisply. "Down yonder we passed for foresters of the Duke of Hastain, but here that shift is needless. I am called Joris of the Rock. Come off your horse."

For a second the Sieur Gaston hesitated. Tiphaine's brown

eyes grew wide with apprehension, and Brother Eugenius—
now squatting on his heels—flung out a quick restraining
hand.

"Spare him, friend!" he whinnied. "God sent you to aid us,
but not to slay a man unshriven!"

"Come off your horse," rasped the outlaw, still intent upon
the brooding Gaston. "I will count six and no more. One, two,
three—ay, I thought as much."

The Volsberghe knew when he was beaten. Silently he
swung a foot across the mare's neck and dropped to earth,
and soberly he watched Tiphaine as the other turned to her.

"Your brave friar counsels mercy, demoiselle," said Joris
roundly; and again his voice held jovial contrast with his
mien. "The judgment is in your gift. Do we kill, or do we
send this lording hence on foot, unharmed?"

A miracle vouchsafed! Did Joris wink at her? No, his
left eyelid had a natural droop; and even at that moment
Tiphaine found it strange to be incuriously regarded as if
she were a man. But in one sweet indrawn breath she savoured
power; her sunburned fingers clenched and her colour flooded
back. Then her gaze fell on the kneeling friar, whose features
were aglow with saintly expectation.

Tiphaine giggled; to disappoint her kinsman seemed a kind
of duty, and yet she had no real mind to loose the shafts of
murder. Huskily she spoke.

"Uncle, I pray you rise up. One would say you adored the
steed of this—this gallant here. But——"

She turned again to Joris of the Rock, and her voice
sharpened.

"But I pray *you* let him go. The memory of this hour should
jog his pride forever."

Gaston de Volsberghe made a little sound of laughter
behind resolute lips, and the outlaw fixed him with a not
unfriendly stare.

"You hear that gentle doom?" he said. "Lording, I keep

your horse, lest you boast of standing scatheless in my power. But for yourself, begone in peace."

This time the pointed hunting hat was swept from the auburn thatch; the Sieur Gaston bowed to flushed Tiphaine and to unsmiling Joris. Thereafter, with no glance at friar or bowmen, he turned on his heel and sauntered off along the road.

Five pairs of eyes watched sunlight stripe and slide from head to foot of him as he receded; and when the blue-clad figure had passed from sight, the broken-nosed outlaw snorted and spat and thrust his arrow back into its quiver.

"Plague on that clemency," he growled. "A lordly ransom thrown away. And now he will raise the fair on us."

"Not he," muttered the little dark man, showing white canines in a mirthless grin. "The—the demoiselle has the truth of it; Gaston will keep a close tongue on this day's encounter."

"Ay, ay," said Joris softly in his beard. Then he turned to the friar and spoke with a certain rough courtesy.

"Madoc here is right, and Herbrand wrong," he said. "Nevertheless it were not wise to tarry. If you will, the demoiselle and you shall come with us; we can give you a night's lodging and set you on your road again past Ververon, beyond the Olencourt domain. If not, then plod along this track to your next misadventure. Choose."

"I—I cannot thank you, Master Joris, for I have no words," fluted Tiphaine before the friar could speak. "But we will come with you; and every night henceforth I shall pray to the Blessed Virgin, and to good Saints Michael and Christopher, that—that you may abide in honour and escape all danger of man or beast."

"That is fair hearing, demoiselle," was the outlaw's laconic rejoinder as he turned to shorten the mare's near stirrup; but Tiphaine saw that the fine lines at the corners of his eyes could on occasion deepen as with silent kindly laughter.

"Come now," he said to her a moment later. "Ride in his place who has made you free of the forest."

Clumsily he swept her aloft, depositing her in the saddle somewhat as though she were a live coal; and Tiphaine, with perception sharpened by the blast of her late danger, could have sworn that his nostrils twitched as with pain above the set line of his bearded mouth. She sat astride and tugged at her caught-up gown, praying to sweet Saint Catherine that any holes in her stockings were above the knee; for Joris moved round to shorten the off stirrup, and the long pheasant's feather in his high fawn hat danced at her shoulder as she lifted rein. Presently he glanced up, and the girl smiled a reply to his unspoken question. But his eyes were grave—and *tired,* she decided—beneath their heavy sunburned lids; and then Tiphaine became aware of Brother Eugenius, standing apart with sorrow in his face and with hands clasped in the nervous gesture hatefully familiar to her.

"Eh, some new holy agony," was her impatient thought, and as Joris motioned to his men to take the lead the friar broke into quick speech.

"May the Sieur God requite you, friend," he cried. "He in His wisdom grows the nettle and the dock together; so in the path of yonder lawless man stood *you,* to vindicate God's mercy on the innocent and helpless. Nevertheless I may not rightly hold my peace. . . ."

"I see the sting of this discourse is in its tail," said Joris blandly. "Nevertheless, what now?"

"Nevertheless this is a stolen horse."

"Uncle Blaise, for shame!" cried Tiphaine; but the outlaw only turned a quizzical glance upon the painful truth-speaker, while his comrades stared in dumb derision.

"Nay, now," protested Joris solemnly. "I honour you for that word, Friar; but surely God's requital may take the form of a horse. In any case——"

Brother Eugenius blushed, but his gaze was steady.

"You mock me and would make me seem ungrateful," he

retorted. "But God is not mocked, and no good deed ever justified a deed of evil. I spoke of spiritual requital."

"I also, if you had not interrupted me," went on the outlaw quietly. "The safety of this maid is my reward. I ask no other, save it may be the prayers she has promised."

"That you deserved, oh stupid Uncle," thought Tiphaine, coldly surveying her kinsman's confusion and distress.

"Stop his fool's chatter, Joris, and let us go!" begged the fat archer, grunting as his comrade's elbow took him in the ribs.

"Courtesy, Herbrand!" said Joris softly, eyeing the surly rogue from head to foot.

The golden beard was tilted away from Tiphaine, who only saw the effect of that scrutiny. Herbrand backed a pace, turned clumsily, and began to climb from the road.

"Well, Friar," demanded the outlaw chief, "are you coming with us and our stolen horse? Or can you not see God's dock leaf for God's mire upon it?"

Brother Eugenius sighed and bowed his head. He had made his protest and would contend no further.

And presently contentment fell upon Tiphaine as she swayed at ease through sunlight-shafted aisles of the high forest. Already she could scarcely credit, much less recapture, that moment of sick dread when the shape of the Sieur Gaston darkened all the day. Joris, the infamous outlaw, paced beside or behind her with his hunter's easy stride—his scabbard tip agleam, his longbow swaying backward from the feather-crested quiver at his hip. His sword hilt was of plain bone, but the mouthpiece of his hunting horn seemed silver bright and chased; men said he was a bastard of the great house of Montcarneau . . . and he had lifted her as though he were afraid. Plainly this Joris was not so black as he was painted; Tiphaine felt even a little disappointment, since the wickeder he, the stranger was his rescue of Tiphaine de Ath. Yet that was strange enough to justify her silliest dream.

"At the Tower they might not believe this tale," she reflected, "but that Uncle Blaise will establish the fact with copious dissertation, with examples from the Fathers, and many references to Holy Writ . . . so that in a day or two my lord my uncle and his family will all be tired to death of rescue, and of Joris, and of me."

*   *   *

Dusk fell early in the heathery ravine where Joris had his camp. Some thirty men, diversely clad and armed, sprawled upon gorse-strewn sand above a brawling stream, or stood to watch their chief's incoming by huts of logs and turf. And if Joris himself was no boor, these his followers were crows of carrion kind; their evil hairy faces twitched and leered at sight of girl and friar, and murmurs of gross comment threaded the still air that smelled of wood smoke, cooking meat, and wine.

"Plump goods," chuckled one ruffian as the mare stalked past him. "If they are peddling these at Olencourt I am for the fair to-morrow. I wonder is the nag thrown in?"

Tiphaine's contentment was already jarred, but at that she shivered and pulled up her hood, finding herself tired and hungry and forlorn.

"Are all men brutes or fools," she wondered, "excepting only Joris of the Rock?"

But at the end of half an hour, when a first blue star hung straight above the darkening lip of the ravine, and when she had dug her teeth into juicy venison smoked over pine cones, Tiphaine recovered a joy in life which she had not known since her father's death a week before. The main encampment was thirty yards away, cut off from the chief's own hut by a steep sandstone crag and a sharp bend of the stream; laughter and reckless speech were blurred by monotone of water and of wind, and all was peaceful round the new-lit fire, whereby the girl sat between Joris and Brother Eugenius, with three of the outlaw's lieutenants to complete their circle.

True, the Franciscan's scruples ruffled her tranquillity once

more when he begged their host to serve him last; but Joris
seemed to have the measure of that mild recalcitrance.

"Come, Master Friar," he said, "seek not to make *me* slave
to your humility. Here none eats last who has stood between
a Volsberghe and his quarry. Will you drink wine?"

"Water, I thank you," came the flustered answer, as Brother
Eugenius accepted the meat held out to him on the point of the
outlaw's knife, and scrabbled in the sand as if to rise.

"Madoc, serve our guest," commanded Joris; and the little
bandy-legged rogue snatched up a drinking horn and vaulted
over a shelf of rock to the water's edge before the protesting
friar was on his feet.

Tiphaine laughed ruefully; Joris actually smiled, and with
him the fourth outlaw, a haggard youth named Gandulf.
Madoc grinned as he swung the dripping horn to the
Franciscan's hand, and only Herbrand's prominent eyes held
a ferocious sneer.

"Holy Mary," prayed Tiphaine, "let not the folly of my
Uncle Blaise bring too much scorn upon his gentleness."

"In the name of the Pope, be seated," urged Joris; and the
friar obeyed, spilling half his hornful in the act.

Thereupon hunger was appeased and thirst quenched in
silence, or at least without speech. Tiphaine stared happily
about her at the bleak and pensive mask of Joris, at the starting
flames and the dark munching faces on their further side, at
the white smoke curling aloft against pine-crested heather,
and at a heap of yellow sand that gleamed beside the rocks
like sunlight spilled and forgotten at the end of the strange
day.

"Uncle Blaise said no grace," she reflected, "because the
meat and drink were doubtless stolen. Oh, but that bitter wine
was good! Let Joris plunder the rich, say I, so be it he does
such courtesy to the poor. How fierce and sad he is grown—
or is it only the trick of firelight? I wonder, has he ever loved
a woman? Small place for women here; how could any but
the baser sort companion him, who may not marry, lacking

benefit of clergy, lacking house and land and peace for all his days? He drinks and drinks, and yet is only sadder than before."

But then the outlaw chief laid down an empty flask, tore up a handful of coarse grass, and fell to cleansing the meat-stained blade of his long hunting knife. Presently he glanced aside, so that Tiphaine prepared another shy smile for him; yet his gaze went past her as though she were not there.

"Friar!" he said suddenly.

Brother Eugenius was nodding, but his shaven head came up, and his sleepy eyes quickened with good will.

"At your service, Master Joris," he responded.

Joris was staring into the heart of the fire when his bright beard moved again.

"Setting apart your vows, which I find more forbidding than inspiring—setting apart your rule, and short of heavenly aid or hope of Paradise—what is your first intention of the day?"

The Franciscan was wide awake now; his thin face glowed with confidence as he made reply.

"Set apart God's aid, my rule, my hope of Paradise, and there is not much left. But I take it you mean—what is my own first step to bring these weapons into play against the Devil?"

"Ay, put it so."

"Each day to behave as though it were my last; each year to root out of my life another sin."

Joris pointed his knife blade at the flames and squinted lovingly along it.

"You are not now at confession," he went on, "but it would please me mightily to hear against what sin you at present contend."

Brother Eugenius considered the grass between his san-dalled feet; a sidelong and uncertain grin passed between Madoc and Gandulf, and at sight of it double perception awoke in Tiphaine. Joris might or might not mock her kins-man, and his followers might or might not know the mind of Joris; but she was lulled by wine and comfort, and cared not greatly where the truth might lie. She listened idly when the friar looked up and spoke.

"A sin insidious enough," he promised gravely. "A daughter sin of pride. When rich men stalk abroad I find it in me to despise them; their gait and gear and clattering steel betray their desolate ignorance of all that makes for a true joy and a right liberty. But it is very evil for me, who profess humility, to itch with scorn of any man; not only by the reason of the Rule of Blessed Francis, but also because there dwells in every soul—be it of king or prelate or commander—the seed of a great saintliness, which if it come to flower must rightly abash me before the throne of the Sieur God."

Joris laughed abruptly, but his laugh was not of the kind to infect his lieutenants with mirth. None of them stirred or responded; and after a moment Joris slid his knife into its sheath, propped elbows on his knees, and cupped his bearded chin in his strong hands, as though he offered tribute of golden bristles to some exacting spirit of the fire.

"Eh, Friar," he commented, "I find your sin elaborate, and so maybe will Father Adam; but perhaps it will serve as evidence of his paternity. Myself, I am glad of the rich, and so are these my men. And in your way of life and mine I find a sameness and a difference; I, too, must live as though each day were my last . . . but for the rest, my only rule is to be supreme in all that befits my station. Of my following, Herbrand is stoutest wrestler, Madoc truest archer, and Gandulf fleetest runner; but I can throw Herbrand, outshoot Madoc, and pass Gandulf. Is it not so?"

"It is so, Joris," answered Gandulf smoothly, while Madoc nodded and Herbrand grunted assent.

"I am indeed as good as a king, though my writ run only a bowshot from my furthest man. Nay, no king can say more than that."

"There is a King of kings," the friar reminded him. "Yourself has served Him well this day."

Joris hiccoughed, and Tiphaine knew not if the sound

were chance or blasphemy; but she felt that Joris was not given to idle boasting. Indeed, his tone was so reflective that he might have been alone before his hut.

"I warrant," he added a moment later, "that even Ishmael found much to do besides the breaking of the Ten Commandments."

"When Ishmael set his hand against mankind," murmured Brother Eugenius, "the Commandments were not given. He erred in blindness."

Joris chuckled, and caught up the other's words.

"*He* erred in blindness. Well, take it thus. *I* have found much to do besides. Plague on it, Friar, may not the very Devil have his holiday?"

"Nay, that he may not," came the spirited rejoinder. "He is damned to wrongdoing till the sound of the Doom Trumpet."

"All work and no play, eh? Grant him at least a savour of delight."

"I pray you, Master Joris, jest no more in this wise. He is the Adversary, and his delight is in his labour."

Joris spat loudly into the heart of the flames, and for a space there was no word spoken. Tiphaine began to drowse, and the noise from the other campfires dwindled in her ears until it seemed a great way off and powerless to disturb her. Dimly she heard the voices of Madoc and Gandulf; then someone threw a log upon the reddening pile, and she started fully awake to catch the key words *peasants* and *Olencourt Fair.*

"To me," said Brother Eugenius, "it seemed they were content as ever I knew them. Theirs is a hard life, well we know; yet there was money in their pockets, and joy of a sort in their faces."

"Oh, ay," admitted Gandulf. "The hay was good, the corn is like to be better, the murrain has held off these three years past. Nevertheless there is much enslavement of freemen holding land by servile tenures; and for some reason hidden from my understanding, hinds will slave forever so be it they are not called serfs. Then there are those who go about the country stirring up unrest, saying the lords and bishops are not like Christ—and well for them they are not, or the hinds would nail them up as He was nailed. And again, those lords and bishops are all at feud with each other or with the communes. Saulte and Barberghe remember their old quarrel. . . ."

Name after haughty name the outlaw quoted, with swift malicious comment to adorn his tale; and the friar's face grew reproachful of this loose chatter.

"And so, across the north, there is strife brewing," finished Gandulf. "When the cats fight, the mouse shall preen his whiskers. *I* had rather sit in the forest with my captain Joris."

"Ay," snickered Madoc, "I wager an equal crown with any man that the next new year brings bloodshed to Honoy or Nordanay or both together."

"How say *you*, Master Joris?" asked the friar sadly. "Are the serfs so deluded as to rise in time of plenty?"

Joris looked blankly round at the last speaker, and again it seemed to Tiphaine that his eyes went through as much as past her. She stirred, resentful of this slight upon a beauty not often overlooked by men; half consciously she jerked back her cloak and twisted up a strand of straying hair, turning big eyes attentively upon the shining golden beard.

"I have heard sermons in my time," drawled Joris. "Was there not one in Holy Writ who waxed fat and kicked? An empty belly drives a poor pike, Friar. Lend Jacques an ear and he will shout in it. Treat him better than a dog and he feels himself good as his master. Rot him, say I, if he scare away the merchants; for I lose more than any by disturbance of the twined strands of hatred of which this life is woven."

"Life woven of hatreds?" faltered the friar. "What riddle is that?"

"No riddle at all. Have you not listened to Gandulf? Do not nobles, clergy, townsmen, and serfs hate each the rest? Ay, and the king away in Hautarroy—each fears him a little, and hates him just as much."

"Now that is truth," said Tiphaine boldly; and she loved herself for sitting by an outlaw's campfire and facing harsh realities of life beneath the starlit forest sky.

The five men looked at her, but she regarded Joris only. Behind her the Franciscan's shocked voice cleft a momentary pause.

"God pity you, child, you know not what you say. Master Joris is in error. Only as we are intent upon this miserable and corruptible life do we find occasion for hatred of one another. There are those content to be esteemed fools in this world, who humble themselves beneath the mighty hand of God and carry His Word from generation to generation. Charity is yet fruitful, and many a heart holds kindliness beneath a biting tongue. At Santloy, a year ago, I saw a man-at-arms, half drunken and very foul of speech, who broke into a burning house and saved a child and a kitten, himself being grievously burned about the hands and shoulders. . . ."

But Joris interrupted, staring glassily into the fire, deepening his tone until it checked and whelmed the mild flow of edification.

"So *you* were at Santloy that midsummer eve? We stood together in a strange hour, Friar."

Brother Eugenius had paused politely; for a few seconds he waited. Then, meekly acquiescing in the sudden end of his own discourse, he eased the curiosity of Tiphaine by putting a question.

"How so, Master Joris?"

"Heard you aught of . . . a strange rapid fray that evening?"

"Why, yes. I was at vespers and heard a tumult from the fair ground. Some of those in the church ran out, preferring a vain curiosity to their souls' welfare . . . and one, so I heard, got a death wound from an arrow in the very porch . . . but I held my place until the priest had done, and when I went forth the fray was over, and there was only a strange green band of afterglow above the houses, and two dead men in the nearest alley of the fair. For everyone but the stall keepers had run off to a burning barn beside the lodge of the Prior of Dor, and it was long before I understood what had come to pass."

"Which was, in fine?"

"As I remember it, some strange wench had lately been found in witchcraft"—Brother Eugenius crossed himself—"and was hastily tried and condemned to burning, that the people might not disperse before example was made of her; for there was grievous talk of magical ill-doing along the river there. And there was muttering among the townsfolk, for the wench was fair and known to many. Her given name was Anne, but she was chiefly called Red Anne, because of her hair, which she wore uncovered like any peasant, although her speech and clothing were burgher at the least—and she, being kept in ward at the prior's lodge, corrupted her warders and broke out, and was taken again, twice-wounded with arrows as she swam the river. . . ."

"And then?"

The outlaw's voice was even, and Tiphaine read nothing certain in his still face and stony firelit eye.

"And then, having cast off much of her clothing to enter the water, she was driven half-naked through the fair ground. But the Devil, her master, defiled and entangled the hearts of many with sight of her body, so that the prior's archers were encompassed and set upon by men of riotous temper—and while they fought around her on the river bank armed horsemen spurred across the shallows and broke through the press, trampling alike her guards and those who would have rescued her; and the leader caught her up on his saddle, and they wheeled about and drove off like the wind, not a rider among them being lost. But by their black coats and their silver lions men knew them; one who had fought in the Franconian wars told me he saw the leader lower his visor as he charged; and it was Lorin de Campscapel himself."

"Ay, it was Butcher Lorin," said Joris sombrely. "And she

rode off with him to his great hold above Alanol, and there abides, his mistress to this day."

"Better for her if the flames had destroyed her body," piped the friar, "for wantonness may be expiated, but commerce with the Fiend may not; it is of all things most foul and shameful and accursed."

Tiphaine saw no change in the face of Joris, but a change was there, for Madoc licked his lips and veiled his quick dark eyes, while Gandulf shuffled uneasily and Herbrand turned a dull incredulous stare on the Franciscan. Then Joris dropped both hands from his chin and bared his left arm to the elbow, showing a great white scar; and when the startled girl glanced higher she saw that his features were inflamed with drink or with some overmastering emotion.

"Look, Friar," he broke out, in the tone he used to bring the Sieur Gaston out of saddle. "This mark I won from Butcher Lorin's sword in the heart of that three-cornered combat; for I and mine were leaders of your 'men of riotous temper.' Now tell me, did *you* see this strange wench that occasioned it?"

"God send he did not," prayed Tiphaine, afraid of traps for holy folly.

"I saw her on that day's morning," said Brother Eugenius calmly.

"What thought you of her?"

"Naught, save that woe is upon them that know not their own misery; for nothing ensnares the soul so much as an impure love of the corruptible body. Also I heard her singing; and indeed her voice in speech or song was wonderfully rich and sweet."

"You are a brave man, Friar," rasped Joris. "Now tell me, where lay the judgment of your God in that past skirmish? Who was punished, and why, when Lorin de Campscapel rode through the river?"

"Master Joris, I know not. The judgments of God—your God as well as mine—are to be feared, not to be discussed

by men who lack the power to understand them. But I perceive
I have in some sort offended you; tell me how, and if I may
I will ask your pardon."

The outlaw beat his clenched fist in the sand beside him,
and seemed to bridle his wrath an instant before it broke
from him.

"A truce to these chirped homilies and godly little courtesies,
half-witted eunuch that you are! An hour of your long-suffer-
ing company would rouse the fiend in a dead rabbit. Are you
God's beater, who would scare the prey from cover for His
hunting? Look up, fool; this is the Forest of Honoy and
I am Joris of the Rock! Why, by the chimes of hell you are
more at ease when I revile you. Praise God for wicked men
in that they test the meekness of the good! Nay, without
wicked men you would have naught to forgive. Say, Friar,
would you forgive me if I named the Blessed Virgin witch and
strumpet?"

"No—but——"

"What, still a mitigation? Out with it!"

"But I should pray God and Herself that you might come
to know the horror you have spoken. Doubt not it rings
through Paradise and wakes a dreadful tumult of applause in
hell! *Sieur Jesu, through Thee I discern the misery of this
man's state . . . ay, by those words it is revealed to me . . .*"

"In God's name, Uncle Blaise, be still!" groaned Tiphaine,
clutching the gray frock as the friar stumbled up and signed
the Cross between himself and Joris.

"In God's name I will *not* be still!" he cried in a voice
deeper than the girl had ever heard from him, while his thin
face glowed and his left hand twitched aloft the crucifix that
hung amid his beads. "I *may* not be still! Outlaw, you are
bewitched—rise up and kneel, for it is written *Auferam
maleficia de manu tua . . .*"

"Put no Latin upon *me!*" snarled Joris; and in her fright
Tiphaine swung round toward him, eyes aghast, hands clasped
in supplication.

"Please you, Master Joris," she began, but her kinsman's voice bore down her own.

"Ay, by the grace of Him who said to the dumb spirit, *Ego præcipio tibi, exi ab eo* . . ."

"*Stop his damned Latin, one of you!*" roared Joris, groping as though for a missile in the gloom behind him.

Gandulf bounded to his feet, but Herbrand's upflung hand and skilfully turned wrist were quicker. A hatchet streaked through the thin smoke, with whirl of haft and flash of well-ground edge; and its head thudded hammerwise between the eyebrows of Brother Eugenius.

Tiphaine, who cowered as the weapon flew, saw her kinsman's face and throat lurch stiffly from the firelight; then his frocked body jarred the sand beside her, and her wild scream went up with Madoc's crackling laugh and a deep oath from Joris of the Rock.

"Bah, Herbrand, by the bones of Goliath of Gath you are a fool!" he grumbled. "I did not want the man destroyed, at least until——*Drop that, you!*"

The last three words he spat at Tiphaine as he bunched himself up and sprang; for the girl had clutched the hatchet and risen with murder in her face. Then she was gripped and overborne; one great hand locked her fingers helplessly upon the haft, while the other twisted her left arm behind her back.

So for an instant Joris held her, his stiff beard brushing her ear, his great ribs bruising her breast; then he tore the hatchet from her numbed grasp, half loosed her, and caught her to him again with a sound betwixt a grunt and a laugh that turned her fury to an agony of dread. When he spoke it was between clenched teeth, while amid his words he sniffed like a dog at her hair, at her straining neck and white averted face.

"Hey, demoiselle—look up. I meant no harm to that poor magpie—but *you* were a fool to make me touch you twice— that is, unless——"

For a moment Tiphaine bit and fought like a wildcat, wasting no breath on outcry; but when she was flung into the darkness of the turf-and-timber hut she began to shriek. And although there were many to hear, there was none to save; the girl grew aware that all her prayers had gone astray, that God had seen her worthlessness, and that her kind saints slept. Her hands that searched for a weapon found nothing but clothes and a blanket, and when the bulk of Joris darkened the doorway her shrieking was cut off by a dumb horror that was half a swoon.

In the blackest moment of all, when against her will her body responded to its defilement, four strange words were torn from the ravening bearded mouth beside her ear.

"Red Anne, my love!" groaned Joris of the Rock.

*   *   *

In the early morning, with no word spoken, Joris rose and saddled the stolen mare. Striding back to the hut, he stooped with unconcern into the narrow doorway.

"Come here," he said.

Tiphaine had kneeled to watch him, her fingers busy with torn clothing and disordered hair. Beneath eyelids weighted with fatigue and shame and misery she shot a glance at him, and realized that she was not to be thrown to his men. Dully she got to her feet and emerged into dewy air, while Joris picked up his unstrung bow and drew with one end of it upon the sand.

"Ride thus and thus," he bade her. "Here is food and a flask—and here your purse, with the ring and money, that fell from the friar's hood. *He* is buried these seven hours."

Tiphaine's fingers flinched from contact with his own, and the gold thumb ring fell to the ground. Joris glanced down at its device—a dagger bendwise between two stars, intaglio in a big cornelian—and curved his lip in loathing as the girl's plump turf-grimed arm and hand reached down to recover it.

"Mount and begone," he continued. "You should make Ververon in two hours at the most."

Unaided, she got to the saddle; and Joris led the mare up a

tortuous path to the head of the ravine, halting among the pines and loosing the bridle with a gesture of dismissal. When she had ridden a dozen yards alone Tiphaine reined in and gave him a steady venomous stare.

"*God curse you as I curse you,*" she called thickly. "*Your hag of hell betray you as you have betrayed me.*"

Then she shook the bridle and fled away; and Joris stood till the faint crash and drumming of her progress faded into the rush of wind-stirred leaves and morning tumult of the birds.

"Bah!" he muttered, turning toward his encampment, and fingering the lumps beneath his clothes that were swung amulets of iron against enchantment, of silver against cramps and rheumatism, of loadstone against poison, and of turquoise against steel. "That for my mercy! But the silly pigeon's curse is empty of bane, as her prayer of blessing. At least *her* maiden scorn is quenched. Anne, I would rape and slay until none dared to slur your name from Belsaunt to the sea."

As he descended the gorge Joris marked his two camp guards of the last watch standing at gaze beyond the smoke of a forest fire. They had seen him release his captive; and a grin twitched the leader's lips, for he knew that none of his band would dare to question any quirk of his behaviour.

Nevertheless he was faintly ashamed of failure to play through his rescuer's part. Of pity for his victims he had none; rather he blamed them for rousing passions which his strong man's pride would not suffer to go unappeased. Tiphaine owed her release to the spirit with which she had fought him; but after her curse she owed her life to the fact that the outlaw's bow stood by the door of his hut. His shame was self-regardant; that slight lapse from self-mastery was not quite of the way of Joris of the Rock.

II. THE TOWER OF ATH

THE son of Joris and Tiphaine was born upon a wild
March day when blown rain puddled the flagged passage-
ways and hissed on smoky hearths in the Tower of Ath; and as
she laid him first against the breast the ancient midwife
chuckled a heartening word in the mother's ear.

"This lusty rogue would make a pair of my lady's," the
midwife said.

Thereat Tiphaine smiled feebly; for the young châtelaine
of Ath, her uncle's second wife, had risen from childbed only
a week before. And from the moment of Tiphaine's first entry
into the tower the older girl had championed her against the
discomfited Sieur de Ath and his loutish son.

"But Aveline has everything, and I nothing save this ill-
fathered imp," she told herself in excuse for that ingratitude;
and anxiously, in the months that followed, she scanned the
baby's face to find therein a sign of the blond outlaw's share
in it.

What she saw reassured her, for Gilles (as she named him)
grew plump and dark-haired and brown-eyed, an Ath of Ath.
And Gilles was sullen and intractable, a very child of rape; he
had night terrors, and bursts of rage wherein he stiffened at
touch of Tiphaine's hand; and sometimes he bit the breast
as though he knew his mother's earliest desperate shame of
him. In Tiphaine's new home, indeed, that shame was past
before the child was born, for none gainsaid the word of the
little châtelaine; but outside was another matter, and sometimes when the infant's wail was stilled Tiphaine would lie
awake and ponder not his future, but her own.

27

"What shall I do when my imp is weaned?" she wondered. "Aveline cannot protect me forever, for her hand brought more honour than gold to my kinsmen. And *they* would have me wedded or thrust into the Church. A fair nun I, whom an outlaw thief dishonoured because he might not possess a witch! I was a fool to tell my tale outright, and a fool to yield the name of Joris; for thanks to my dolt of a cousin I am cried for stinking fish throughout Basse Honoy. Oh, yes, I am fair, but what proud chevalier will speak for me while dastard Gold-beard is alive to laugh at him? Sieur God, I pray you, blast with leprosy or levin Joris of the Rock."

Then, rigid in her bed, Tiphaine would send an impulse of black hatred questing through the forest; she would have had her curse batlike to ride above the outlaw's head in chase and foray—batlike to stoop and flick a blinding wing between the fierce blue eye and arrow mark or leap of hostile steel.

And in dark days of autumn—when round the Tower of Ath the poplars volleyed leaves along the wind, so that the moat was strewn with yellow, while the creaking windmill sails trapped gusty loads and tossed them aloft again in minor whirls of gold—Tiphaine made a little waxen man whom she capped and clothed with shreds of the old garments torn by the hands of Joris. And although she knew no spell to activate her rite, she stabbed the manikin through with pins and set him to melt before her fire, while the baby watched and bubbled his approval, stretching forth a pink and pudgy hand as though to help in this queer silent game.

"Ha, imp, you are your mother's son," exclaimed the brooding girl; and she caught Gilles up, and closed the tiny wavering fist upon a bodkin, and guided a slow thrust into the manikin's body.

"Be mine the blame, fat little parricide," she muttered, aghast and pleased at her boy's first stricken blow. "Let the Sieur God witness, mine the blame; I have had much to bear, but will bear this also. How the good Prior of Ath would goggle if he saw such doings in his neighbour's tower! Belike it would mean the stake. . . . Eh, Gilles, that were to set another and a darker seal upon you. What, you are pleased? *You* shall not lack for a living; Aveline will have you as playmate for her Juhel. Besides, a man is a sword, and there is always room for another sword . . . but what shall *I* do when you are weaned?"

The waxen image drooped, the flames leaped cheerfully upon the bedroom hearth, the baby crowed, and the wind sang shrill in the chimney; but there came as yet no answer to the question of Tiphaine.

Nevertheless the answer was preparing; and on the following day she encountered a first word of it. Riding abroad at the forest edge, alone save for her uncle's solitary page, Tiphaine came near the ovens of turf wherein the serfs boiled tar from their lord's pine logs; and as she sniffed the resinous reek a sudden whistling cackle broke from amid the trees.

"So that is she who would rear bastards to rule over you!"

Tiphaine drew rein; behind her, Briot the page went red and wheeled his mount upon the peasants. Some backed and cowered at sight of his lifted lash; but among the rest stood squatly forth the hooded woman who had spoken.

"Lay on, lording!" she jeered, with strange and difficult speech. "Your lady would prove your valour—this time by daylight, hey? Nay, never heed the mark of Barberghe; one day yourself shall be as brave as he!"

But Briot's hand had fallen, and Briot's fair shocked face was turned toward Tiphaine. The hooded head came round, and Tiphaine shuddered; the creature's upper lip had been cut to a ragged inverted V, baring red gums to the nasal septum above.

"Let be, Briot," she commanded sickly; and the pair rode on, while behind them a gust of ugly words and laughter stirred amid the trees.

"It is mad Yvonne," grumbled the vexed page.

Tiphaine looked round at him; she knew he pitied and admired her, and saw he was ashamed of his late clemency.

"I am glad you spared her," she said. "But who is she, with her harlot's mark and her scold's tongue?"

Briot's face cleared as he drew level with Tiphaine.

"She followed her lord for a month, claiming some justice for her husband's death at hands of a Barberghe man-at-arms. The foxy count—you know his avarice—would neither pay nor listen, and she importuned him in his hall and at his gates, and like a fool she even trailed behind him when he rode in state to Ger. So then he dealt with her as a drab who plagued his men."

"Foul justice; but what does she here?"

"I know not. Maybe, now that Barberghe is at open war with Saulte, she would have had short shrift on the count's own land."

"Men must forever be fighting," thought Tiphaine. "Poor Uncle Blaise—he was wide of the mark when he called us all God's creatures. That Barberghe Fox—wherein is he better than an outlaw murderer, save that the woman was his serf? It is true the peasants grow insolent . . . and *I* will not be mocked by them. I will tell Aveline; this hag Yvonne shall not stir up resistance in my lord's domain. There is already stubbornness enough."

For the Sieur de Ath was engaged in that noble task of which the outlaw Gandulf spoke beside the fire of Joris of the Rock; that is to say, the claiming as serfs of a handful of freemen who at stated times must leave their holdings to work on their lord's land; and many were the black looks lately cast from cot and furrow and ditch at the five-turreted tower above the confines of the forest.

"Death of my life!" snarled the nobleman, when upon that same night a kitchen boy was haled before him by the steward. "You laugh to hear what beggar women mutter in the woods? See now, a whip shall move your hinder end to glee, and then you may chew acorns for your keep. Give him a dozen lashes, swiftly."

So the howls of the kitchen boy went up as incense for the

wounded dignity of Ath; and when next she rode abroad
Tiphaine sought out the miller's wife and gave her one crown
for the outcast serving lad and another for herself. Tiphaine's
was a life of fury and compunction, of suspicions which she
thought were mean and of generosities which she felt were
foolish.

*   *   *

Throughout November of that year the Saultes and Barberghes harried each other's fiefs; across and across the deep
Nordenne went flame and sword and lamentation. But when
autumn turned to winter Lorin de Campscapel, the Butcher
Count of Alanol, swept out of his hill fastnesses and fell upon
the flank of the Duchy of Saulte. With such assistance the
Fox of Barberghe brought his foe to terms; but the gains of
four years past, the hopes of gain for another year to come,
were ashes and corruption in the wintry fields.

And then the Fox of Barberghe, blinded by his greed, levied
a first tallage in the land wrested from his rival. His tax
collectors, having ridden down an idiot boy who cursed them
on the bridge of Roray, were found next day as a trio of
corpses, stuck head downward in the thinly frozen river.
Barberghe himself spurred out to punish that impudence, and
barely escaped with his life; a blacksmith of the hamlet headed
the sudden wild uprising. In three days thirty thousand
peasants were afield; in a week eleven lesser holds were taken,
and by the midmost depth of winter the great revolt had run
from end to end of Honoy and Nordanay.

In Nordanay were few towns to complicate the shock of
sword and scythe; but in Honoy the communes had their say
in the quick strife. Some stood by the great lords, with hope
of chartered gains to follow; some fed the Jacques and marched
with them against the castles; some sat aloof with lifted bridges
and manned parapets, whence men cast stones and stirred with
scaffold poles that the moats might never freeze. Among these
last were Tostain and Hastain, whose caution the Duke of

Saulte mocked in a couplet destined to endure beyond the
Jacquerie and the reprisal that came after.

> Hastain by the river, Tostain on the hill,
> Shut gate and shiver when the war horns thrill.

Thus the great duke, when Tostain men refused him aid.
Some days later a force of peasants was similarly baffled of
assistance; turning their backs upon Tostain ramparts, the
hardy Jacques bound boards beneath their feet, and, crossing
woodland snowdrifts that would have whelmed a charger to
his girths, came swiftly and before the dawn about the Tower
of Ath.

*   *   *

Fast being broken, Tiphaine sat in her chamber, watching
her baby encourage his first teeth upon the great gold thumb
ring that had been her father's. She had given him an ivory
bangle clasped with silver, but new-weaned Gilles preferred
the taste and glitter of the gold; so that Tiphaine laughed—
amused yet pleased that he should abide by the device not
lawfully his own—and hung the thumb ring on the bangle that
he might not try to swallow it, and tied the bangle on a silken
cord to lie around his neck.

Outside her window snowpacks, loosened and sliding from
a slope of roof, fell *thump* and *flump* upon the wooden lean-to
sheds in the little courtyard. Somewhere below, a kitchen wench
was singing; horses snorted and stamped in the dark stables,
where the grooms tended them by lantern light. Presently
came the steward's squeak and an obedient sound of brooms;
rattle of well chain, rasp of grindstone, hungry yawn of a
sentinel just relieved—Tiphaine took little heed of them, for
in the muted wintry days she had heard them all so many
times.

"Imp, we are risen in favour," she said, twitching the cover
of black velvet from her mirror of polished steel. "Cousin Leu,
having nothing better to do, has promised us a game of chess.

Indeed, he thaws inversely with the weather; but that is
because we broidered a saddlebag to carry his fine new helm.
Miserrime, another gray hair! How many more before you
put on hose? And imp, our noses are too flat . . . but our
hands are prettier than Aunt Aveline's . . . *your* hands are
rosebuds, imp, but only a duke, or maybe a prince of the blood,
may dribble as mightily as do you. . . .

"Now it is time to go spinning in the solar. Where are my
tweezers? *So.* And if we are good, Aunt Aveline will play
upon her lute. Oh, hearken, imp, the silly men-at-arms are
quarrelling again . . . small blame to them, cooped up this
week or more . . . but my lord my uncle will be angry. . . .

"Now, who comes running here? Briot, what ails you?
What is that shouting below?"

The white-faced page leaned gasping against the door, shaking a sword too big for him as he summoned desperate speech.

"It is the Jacques, the bloody Jacques," he sobbed. *"They
are in at the postern . . . someone has let them in . . .
come, for your dear life, come!"*

Fiercely Tiphaine swept Gilles from his cradle; dreadful
tumult shocked on her ears as she fled in Briot's wake. It was
a flight nowhither; twice they recoiled from eddies of furious
combat, and the girl's breath was whooping in her throat when
at length she broke into the gloom of the little chapel.

"Stay there!" hissed Briot. "Someone holds them beside
the solar door. We are not yet spent!"

Then he was gone; and Tiphaine laid her little whimper-
ing son on the floor beside the altar and hung aghast by a
window that gave on the courtyard.

There below, in an angle of stable and curtain walls, her
cousin Leu had found a wilder game than chess; hemmed in by
baying serfs, he fought until he was hewn in pieces. And when
she saw the bleeding head of the Sieur de Ath borne proudly
on a pike by his one-time kitchen boy, Tiphaine turned moan-
ing to the altar; hardly conscious of her craft, she swept the
table clear of crucifix and candlesticks, rifled the chest thereby

of thurible and pyx, of patens and chalices; binding the clashing silvery heap in the altar cloth, she staggered to the door and hurled her load into the passage. A candlestick rang on the opposite wall and rolled back to her feet; stooping, she gripped it as once she had gripped a hatchet in the Forest of Honoy.

Out of her sight, a score of yards away, a fight was raging on a narrow stair; but as she paused irresolute, with fingers on the latch of the chapel door, the din died down to a receding yelling and stamp of feet. Silence hovered again above the Tower of Ath, a silence grim as any uproar of assault; and Tiphaine wheeled about and gnawed her hand in terror.

"Jesu in heaven," she wailed, "what comes next?"

Briot the page came next, dragging himself round the corner on hands and knees. As the girl started forward he collapsed, twisting a gray face upward when she knelt by him.

"All sped save me," he whispered. "They run to sack the priory. Flee if you may . . . I am done . . . see, take my dagger . . . oh, God!"

His stricken gaze went past her arm; Tiphaine rose dumbly, and from the far end of the passage came a fiendish whistling cackle.

"Lo, here is love's last greeting! Here is she who would rear bastards to rule over you!"

Side by side in the vaulted way stood mad Yvonne and a burly serf who carried a great ax. The man eyed tumbled silver, but the beggar woman peered as if for something else. Tiphaine's heart turned to stone within her, and as the pair stole forward she moved to meet them.

"Now play the man," urged Yvonne, as she paused by the door of the chapel. "Wipe out another score or two in sight of broken Cupid yonder . . . for me, I think to find in here . . . whoa, hell-cat!"

But the heavy candlestick flew true as if outlaw Herbrand had flung it. Full in the face of mad Yvonne it crashed, ending the ruin begun by the Barberghe headsman. Back reeled the beggar woman, battering her skull upon the limestone mouldings of the doorway. Tiphaine's last earthly glimpse was of her happiest handiwork; for then the growling peasant brought his ax blade whirling down upon her head.

Sated with slaughter, heedless of dim-eyed Briot who watched him, the murderer snatched his plunder and made off by the way he had come. Presently the page stirred and began to drag himself forward, groaning the *Ave Maria* between clenched teeth. At length he sank his face between the breasts of Tiphaine, that yet were round and warm; and then he, too, lay still.

*   *   *

The first to pass thereafter along that corridor of death were the black-a-vised miller of Ath and his gaunt wife. Trembling and crossing themselves—for they had no part in the killing—they crept into the tower to see if anything was left worth picking up; and in the chapel they leaped back upon each other at a low wail from the altar side.

"God save us!" cried the woman. "A child . . . living . . . unhurt."

"It is the little bastard," muttered her husband. "See, the ring is gold. Now, it were best perhaps to——"

"Nicholas, you are a fool. How long, think you, before this rabble is broken? Just so long as the foul weather lasts. What then? Great trampling men-at-arms, and hangings by the hundred. But if *we* have hidden away and preserved the heir of Ath——"

"I tell you it is the other. You saw the little Sieur Juhel—what was left of him."

The miller's wife set a gnarled finger on her lip, and winked a wink not altogether ghastly. The miller stared, and grinned, and nodded.

"If any hear him wail within the mill, we say it is our Dodart," whispered the woman. "Praise God our Dodart is a quiet baby."

"Ay, if they yell together we must drop this lording in the meal bin. See, wrap him in your cloak—and come, before they have done with the wretched monks. And when you praise God, praise him also in that Jacques need bread as well as noblemen. Else were we sped ourselves. I tell you, wife, I shall sweat through all this bitter weather until the day when we can hand *him* on."

"Take heart, Nichol; I will save our heads."

So, for the last six weeks of the terrible winter, little Gilles-Juhel lay by baby Dodart in the mill across the fields from the gutted Tower of Ath. At the end of that time he was Gilles no more, for events befell as the miller's wife foretold them; the grim Prior of Saint-Eloy-over-Hardonek rode in with a troop of men-at-arms to learn the fate of his friend the Prior of Ath. Having buried what noble and clerkly bones he could find, and having hung what serfs were taken skulking in the woods, he gave ear to the cringing miller and to the miller's sturdy wife. Their horse and half their goods he confiscated at their own prayer, secretly giving them gold in payment and reward; and no scared eye from the forest margin saw the bundle borne away upon the saddlebow of the prior's chaplain.

In this way the child thereafter known as Juhel passed from desolate Ath to Hardonek beside the northern sea.

*   *   *

"Ploughing again, friend," said the fair-haired peddler, leaning upon his iron-shod staff and staring from under heavy eyelids along the path which fringed the thickets near the mill.

"Ay," growled the serf. "They left enough of us to plough."

"This is Barberghe land, then?" asked the second peddler, glancing across the tilth to where a banner bearing counterchanged chevrons of red and black flapped from the top of a turret.

"No, but the Fox—the count—has it in ward these days,

and he has sent a rascally chevalier to keep the tower. He says the little Sieur de Ath escaped; I know not how. But look you, wayfarers—if your packs hold aught that came from castle or convent, go not near that gateway. One of your kind swings yonder, with crows to kiss and admire him. This cursed Chevalier de Medrincourt deals hard."

"De Medrincourt?" repeated the tall stranger, thumbing his bare chin thoughtfully. "Hum . . . I am glad of that admonition, brother; we will not tarry here. Ploughman, I wish you well."

The peasant grunted, raising his ox goad with the air of one who knew the value of well-wishing; and the lanky peddler moved away with his slim haggard comrade.

"Was it he pronounced your outlawry?" demanded the latter presently, with a jerk of his head toward the Tower of Ath.

"Eh? No, his father. But some there might remember me, even without my beard. Nevertheless, I will look at that scutcheon over the gate."

"Praise God the bridge is up," muttered Gandulf a few minutes later.

Joris chuckled and glanced aside.

"Never saw I one so scared of danger until danger came," he said. "Yet that is why I brought you, and not Madoc, to spy out this wasted land. See . . . a dagger bendwise between stars . . . ay, ay, it is the same."

"As how?"

"You mind the friar and his plump pigeon whom we took from Gaston de Volsberghe on the road from the Olencourt Fair?"

"Ha, yes, that prosy half-wit. I had clean forgotten him."

"So had not I," breathed Joris. "This was their journey's aim. Now come away; that pikeman grows inquisitive."

Gandulf gave a reminiscent snigger, but neither he nor his chief found more to say of Tiphaine.

Yet the girl's curse was fast in the mind of Joris; and that

was not for any mischance thereafter befallen him, but because
Tiphaine alone of all his ill-wishers had flung the witchhood of
Red Anne in his face without immediately suffering death or
injury.

"Last word to the woman that time," he mused. "Well, she is
dead, and the brat with her; or so I had it from that fled serf
of Ath a month ago."

That there had been a child meant nothing to Joris; animals
knew his kindlier moments, but children stood in awe of him.
Nor was Tiphaine the first to make him a father.

"Why, now," he said aloud, coming out of his reverie at a
hail from a swineherd's hut. "What has this scarecrow for
such as we are?"

Thrusting aside a press of lean gray pigs, the serf came
hobbling toward them, pausing to look behind him before he
spoke his business.

"Give you good-morrow, masters," he whined. "Do you
buy as well as sell?"

"Ay, if the gear be of worth," replied Joris.

"And honestly come by," added Gandulf, salting his words
with a wink.

"Ah, you are traders such as poor men look for in these
latter days," the other croaked. "No, it is not in the hut; it is
up in the woods. I have a mirror of steel in a velvet case, and a
pair of silver tweezers; ay, and a lady's shoes of good soft
leather, and other things besides. But I must be paid in silver—
you swear to do me right?"

"Too small for Anne," thought Joris when he beheld the
shoes. *"She* is no mincing châtelaine."

"A little stained," the serf confessed, with a harsh chuckle.
"Yet come by this time as honestly as before. *My* sweat went
to their first purchase; that I know."

"I will take the mirror," said Joris aloud.

And in the polished surface he saw sunlight of the cold
March afternoon break over the forest edges and gild the ban-
nered summit of the Tower of Ath.

III. HERODIAS AT HASTAIN

*T*A-*RAT, ta-rat, ta-rattle-ta-plat—ta-rattle-ta-plat, ta-rat, ta-rat! ta-rat.* . . .

The kettledrum held its own beneath market converse and loud bellowing of cattle; across the windy square the red-and-yellow canvas of a tall booth promised mirth—for townsmen still had money for a show, however desolate lay the land beyond their ramparts. Joris and Gandulf, hard-bitten though they were, lined up to pay market dues with ease they had not felt for days.

"What is the drumming yonder?" asked the man in front of them of another beyond him.

"Puppets," came the reply. "Herod and Saint Jehan Baptist, better than at Michaelmas. It is Guelf Reinager, that daft apothecary. They say he fled from Dunsberghe, suspect of violating graves."

"What is he, with that name?"

"His father was Easterling, his mother a Dunsberghe woman. He was accounted a great wrestler; deadly quick, too, with his dagger. Wenches flocked to him for salves and potions, but now he is turned showman and brews no more, unless in secret. The warden was not for his setting up in ordinary market, but that Guelf pled such hardship in the winter."

"Truly enough, belike. Small audience for puppets this late Christmas. Too many have danced puppet-wise themselves."

"Ay, on the never-green tree. But touching those hides of which we spoke at the gate——"

Gandulf nudged Joris in the ribs and nodded toward a side street, where the rising curve of rain-wet cobbles took on, beneath widening patches of clear sky, a blue reflected gleam;

in the midst of the gleam stood a crone with one hand cupped behind an ear. She, too, was listening to the drum; and presently, all alone as she was, she cackled and plucked up her ragged skirts. Skinny gray shanks and worn wooden shoes essayed the ghost of a jig; Joris roared out approval, and abruptly the antic ceased. The old dame showed her empty gums and wagged a reproving forefinger; then she sidled into an alley and disappeared.

"Granny has danced in her time," said Gandulf approvingly; but Joris was watching a younger woman's face, which gleamed half hidden by the shutter of an upper window near them. That face stared out toward the puppet show with a strange half-haggard glee; and Joris chuckled in derision.

"Poor shrew," he thought, "who gleans on market day the topics for a week of senseless chatter. Blood of the Pope, she takes her pleasures hard! But softly, my turn next. . . ."

Ten minutes later Gandulf and he stood almost alone by the puppet show; it was already near noon, and all the eloquence of dark Guelf Reinager could not compete with ale and puddings of the Hastain inns. Nevertheless the showman plied his drumsticks valiantly, shaking his cockscomb crest that was of stiff red leather sown with tiny bells; and at sight of Guelf's stature, at hint of the muscles which harlequin's gear could not mask, Joris instinctively straightened his own shoulders.

Guelf had a blue-black jowl, stern features, brown commanding eyes set too close for beauty; he drummed and wheeled as though a thousand watched him, and above, in the red maw of the puppet stage, little Salome swayed her hips and pouted scarlet mouth and nipples toward the market cross. From within the booth rose the mellow monotone of a gong, that was suddenly cleft and whelmed by a torrent of words in Guelf's sonorous voice.

"Here, gallants, you will learn why Saint Jehan Baptist lost his head, which will presently be conveyed before you, *by* a Nubian slave, *on* a charger of pure gold, *with* a blast of trumpets that shall stir each worm in King Herod's body. The whole as played before the King's own Majesty at Hautarroy, before His Eminence the Cardinal Count at Estragon, before the noble Dukes of Saulte, Camors, Ahun, Baraine, and Volsberghe, each in their several duchies, and—passing beyond the borders of this realm—before the Archduke Adalbert in his great hold of Harenheim. Here on my finger you see a ring, set with an opal rainbow-tinted, cast to me by the Archduke's self; who being fallen into a grievous melancholy whereby his life was endangered, had not smiled for the space of three months, *until* beholding these my puppets in the Mystery of the Flood he stirred in his chair, voided a mighty hiccough, and laughed until he wept. *Whereupon* he would have retained my services, but that I replied after this wise: Most renowned and puissant Prince, whose sword has shattered the Muscovite heathen to the great contentment and admiration of all Christian men, I who was born in Basse Honoy must return thither, now that rebellion of a black-hearted and ungrateful peasantry has drowned in its own recreant blood, so that roads are once more safe for honest wayfarers and valuable puppets; press not upon me the discomfort of refusal of an offer so unlooked for and magnanimous! *Whereat* the archduchess applauded me, casting with her own dainty hand a purse of gold which I in part expended on new spiked crowns for Herod and Herodias, presently to be revealed. . . ."

"A dreary wind bag—but the ring has merit," said Gandulf under his breath.

Joris made no reply; he glanced at the smooth horn hilt of the showman's formidable dagger, and raised his heavy-lidded eyes again in time to see Herodias swim out beside her daughter. The showman's rousing periods were cut off; up against silence went the first squeak of Salome.

"There is a fire in all my veins. I think, dame, I could dance forever."

"A truce to folly, girl; stand still and listen. Know you this Jehan of the asses' skins, this beautiful mad prophet who dips men in water of Jordan?"

Salome stood still and listened; so did Joris, with face gone white and chill beneath its sunburn. Herodias gestured to a voice that even dead Brother Eugenius had found marvellously rich and sweet; for Joris there could be no two such voices in the realm or in the world.

"What is amiss?" came Gandulf's curious whisper.

"Nothing," growled Joris. "Put off your tray—go and bring wine and pasties. Go!"

Gandulf went. On his return he found the play broken off; Joris was now sole audience, and Guelf Reinager was not disposed to tire his troupe for delectation of one lounging peddler. Four shapes emerged from the back of the red-and-yellow booth: a fat old harridan, a thin sickly looking girl, a bearded crook-backed dwarf—and last of all a graceful prowling figure in dove-gray hooded cape, with tunic, hose, and shoes of the same colour.

Gandulf saw Joris stride across tumbled wares. The gray-clad player had a woman's hips, and laid a woman's hand upon the arm of the forward-stepping showman.

"Stuff me with stones and bake me dry," said Gandulf to himself, "if that pink-faced man-woman be not Red Anne. What now?"

He tightened grip on a bottle neck, and padded up to his chieftain's side in time to hear the first words of that greeting.

"Stand back, Guelf," commanded the rare voice. "This is my friend—or was, in peril two years past. But I do not know his name."

Steadfastly Joris and Anne regarded one another; their companions looked from face to face and were aware of mystery in the encounter.

"Tell me," asked Joris blandly, "tell me, since you know me—are all these, too, your friends?"

"Friends proven," said Red Anne. "But who are you?"

"That you shall learn if you bid them step aside."

Tall Anne stood pondering. Beneath level auburn brows her eyes were pansy-blue; set far apart, they focussed with startling directness. Joris they almost disembodied, yet somewhere his craft sustained him. He even had time to learn how needless to Anne's loveliness was that wild splendour of hair now hidden by the close-drawn hood.

"Such a dire secret, is it?" she intoned. "What if I told the market warden?"

"One thing only would delight him more."

"And that?"

"If any should betray *your* presence here."

Red Anne grinned boyishly, with a snap of strong white teeth. Her hands were linked behind her, and her feet widely planted; Joris grew dreadfully aware of the charm beyond her beauty—the charm half comradely and half maternal, that lulled the madness of the Butcher Count and ruled his savage riders, that stilled brutality and spread good will wherever this red-haired creature spoke and moved.

"No need to wait for stake and gallows before this confession be made," Anne murmured. "Will it keep till nightfall?"

"Gladly."

"Then come to the Sign of the Leopard when compline rings; ask at the courtyard entry for Guelf Reinager's niece."

"Niece!" exclaimed Joris softly; but his eyes never left the rosy enchanting face, and only Gandulf marked the humorous twitch of the showman's bitten lips.

"Ay, *niece,*" repeated the girl, with mischief in a dimple. "By that style am I known there. Will you come?"

"By God, I will. Gramercy, Lady Anne."

"Ill-chosen oath—but no oath can contend with such a mystery. See, folks are coming again to jeer at Herod. Farewell, and do not doff your hat."

"You will be welcome—then," growled Guelf Reinager. "Meanwhile——"

Red Anne slipped round the corner of the booth; Joris and

Guelf exchanged a steady stare. Each made his face a mask; the showman's eyelids were first to fall, but Joris felt that he had not compelled their falling.

"Success to Herod and Salome, friend," he said. "Gandulf, we eat elsewhere."

And as the pair of them moved slowly off, Joris increased his comrade's bewilderment.

"Come to the well," he said blithely. "No wine for Joris this afternoon."

Behind them Guelf Reinager's lifted voice was suddenly blurred by the lilt of his drum: *to-rat, ta-rat, ta-rattle-ta-plat —ta-rattle-ta-plat, ta-rat, ta-rat . . . ta-RAT!*

*   *   *

Throughout the hours of afternoon tall Joris peddled his wares in a half dream; sometimes when his voice was silent his lips moved, but neither Gandulf nor any other of his men had heard him speak of the runes bought two years earlier in that same market square—runes which had captured and held his heart and now marched bravely through his head.

By birth a serf, by mingled blood deprived of servile resignation, Joris had grown to his eighteenth year in a forester's hut a mile from the great hold of Montcarneau, that guarded flat and fertile lands amid the Forest of Nordanay. There as a boy he throve on scraps and kicks and curses, until the day when his mother's husband chased him down the clearing with a flail, so that stripling Joris rounded a corner and ran his chin against the silver stirrup of a nobleman whose horse trod softly upon sand amid the gorse and pines. The furious serf arrived to find horseman and lad regarding with some interest each other's aquiline fairness and pale blue heavy-lidded eyes.

"Whose son are you?" asked the brother of the Count of Montcarneau.

"Morgain's-by-the-Ford."

"How old?"

"Twelve years, my lord."

"Eh, is it thirteen years since? What can you do?"

"Cut and carry wood and turf and bracken. Gather the dung from the priest's dovecote. Drive the cattle to water, and the swine to food. Scare the birds from the crops. Last winter I slung a stone at a wolf, and stunned her, and slew her with a hatchet."

"Enough, Briareus of the hundred hands. Why does *he* chase you?"

"To beat me. Every morning he beats me, and at night as well if the bailiff has beaten him. To-day I flung my broth at him."

"His jowl bears witness to it. Why?"

"He calls my mother 'witch.' "

"H'm. She could enchant upon a time. Come here, soup face."

The serf shambled miserably forward.

"Hearken to me. Beat you this lad in future no more than once a month. He will keep tally for you. Cut him a yew bow, four feet long at the most, and send him to the butts with it to-morrow. When he is fifteen bring him before me again. By then he should be beating you, so you have no incentive to forget. Boy, this coin to your mother; tell her as years go by we may find something in you."

As years went by they found in Joris a very skilful archer, a conjuror with horse and hound, a verderer sage and apt and fleet. In his care hunted elderly churchmen and high-born youths, the guests and pages of Montcarneau; a hard-riding abbot taught him to read and write, and a duke's barber trimmed his first beard to its point. When Joris was twenty-one the count's brother died, and the count gambled his verderer away to the dour Chevalier de Medrincourt, throwing in the person of widowed Morgain that Joris might not leave his mother behind him.

So Joris entered Basse Honoy, to find a stricter clergy and irksome restraint of pleasure in matters of wine and women. Coming first to commanding stature and then to iron strength,

and conscious always of servitude, he became a notable bully;
to elbow freemen into the gutter ministered to his pride, and
any tavern about Medrincourt would fill when news went
round that Joris was baiting some luckless stranger with deft
throws of his heavy hunting knives.

One joint he had in his strong man's armour, and that was
love for his mother. She, torn from her ford, found little joy
among strangers; also she missed the sound of weirs that had
grown into part of the forest silence around the hut where
Joris was born. Joris knew no homesickness, and sought by
gifts to hearten her. So, when the chevalier sent him to buy
prick-spurs and hunting harness at a Hastain Midsummer
Fair, Joris lounged somewhat sheepishly between booths
decked to tempt the burghers' womankind.

There he first saw Red Anne—her face alight with argument, her hair a blot of blinding hue against the sun-bitten
limestone of the market cross. He was then twenty-two, and
she seventeen; across a flame of orange silk the pansy-col-
oured eyes worked their prime havoc in the heart of Joris.

"Indeed," the girl confessed, "I have not much to show a
gallant fairing for his mother. Your kind is scarce—though
none the worse therefor. See, here is gray and tawny. I count
your mother fortunate."

Her calm and smiling friendliness bore down the man's
first swaggering impulse, and somehow foiled his second swift
intention to ensnare her interest by talking of his mother.
Lastly it broke his reserve, so that he leaned forward, fingering the stuff where Anne's brown fingers had warmed it,
mumbling a confidence before he was aware.

"Nay, she has food and shelter, but she is sick at heart.
Shy of her rougher speech, belike, and too old to outgrow it.
And now she wanders alone in the woods, talking aloud to
the birds and little beasts. Sometimes they follow her in at our
door. Why, even a weasel——"

Red Anne's gaze sank to the Medrincourt device—*lozengy,
argent and sable*—sewn in shape of a shield on the breast of the

verderer's green tunic; then she looked gravely up again, and
Joris cut off his speech as though with a knife. Glancing to left
and right, he leaned further across the counter; his voice
roughened with anger and sank in self-disgust.

"Four crowns for the gray? Take four and a half, and forget what I have said."

Anne, too, looked about them; none could have overheard.
Then her gaze came full against his own, and somewhere in
him Joris quailed. This was not woman to man, but mind to
mind.

"Fool!" she said, softly yet stormily. "*I* tell no tales."

Joris summoned his wonted hardihood and stared at her
unwinkingly for a moment.

"By God," he exclaimed, "I believe you do not. And I am
not one to believe what I cannot test. Your pardon."

"It is nothing," returned the girl, "but bid your mother
take heed."

When Joris had gathered up his roll of silk she looked at
him merrily enough, but the raillery natural between his sort
and hers died curiously upon his lips. He doffed his peaked
and pointed hat, glad of its silver medal and pheasant's tail
feather; and as he moved away he wished confusedly that
half the pleasures of his earliest manhood had never been.

That night he mocked at himself and her, drowning his un-
accustomed emotion in wine. A bargain of spurs put the first
drink in him; others followed, and Joris became stern and
sad, a man unmoved by all the red hair in the world. Until
the following noon he slept dead drunk in a stable; when next
he sought the fair ground Red Anne and her booth had vanished. None of those whom he questioned knew—or if they
knew they would not tell—why the red-haired girl should
vanish on the first night of a three-day fair; nor did Joris care
to press his queries very far. Of Anne he found no trace, and
of his need to see her no immediate surcease; for the first time
in his life he knew the agony of a frustration not to be
avenged by muscle or by steel. All he could learn amounted

to this—that Red Anne came and went with silks between the greater fairs of Basse Honoy.

While Joris stared at the cobbles that Anne had lately trodden, there came a tug at his cloak and a gentle hail beside him. Turning, he recognized Ingolard—the one-legged glee-man Ingolard, whose silvery voice and silvery hair were part of all festivities at Hastain. Ingolard sat on the steps of the market cross, smiling shyly all over his brown and wrinkled face, raising a dirty forefinger from an open scroll on his knee to point as with accusation at the bright hair of Joris.

"Stranger, you bear true gold," piped Ingolard most civilly. "Buy these strange runes that treat of gold and red. Ay, red and gold and black."

"What is it?" demanded the verderer, bending to snatch aloft the tattered skin. "What is this foolery?"

"No foolery indeed," rose Ingolard's shocked tenor. "It is honest prophecy of doom to be accomplished in these parts by one who shall come to rule therein."

Joris listened and sneered and read; and midway in his reading he spun round and searched the faces of those near him. His hard eyes widened, and his free hand fell to his dagger hilt; for he seemed to have heard close by him the deep laugh of Red Anne. Baffled and scowling, he turned again, and his thin lips moved delicately to the swing of couplets in faded purple ink.

> "Black and gold
> Red shall hold.
>
> "Gold and red
> At hand are led,
>
> "Yet separatèd
> Till years be sped.
>
> "Red shall sin
> For black to grin;

"Black and red
In the same bed.

"Gold shall sunder
And black shall blunder.

"Red shall run
Ere all be done.

"Black shall be riven
And gold given
To red new-shriven."

Thrice Joris read the runes from beginning to end; then he looked down into the bright and confident and tranquil face of Gleeman Ingolard.

"Whence had you these?" he growled.

"From the ancient who taught me my lore. He was afflicted with swooning fits and hours of strange prevision; and in a swooning fit he lately died. But he told me concerning these runes that glory awaited bright red and bright gold in Basse Honoy; and never have I seen so bright a gold as yours. Your name I know not, stranger; but I think you are one of the men for whom the world was made."

Stirring and elfin-shrill the words assailed bold Joris. He who feared no man living, and spared for God and Devil alike an occasional shrug or grimace, felt self-assurance blossom into faith—faith in the sword of Joris, who being a serf might not yet bear a sword at all.

The Chevalier de Medrincourt brooked scant delay in even a favourite servant, and that mid-afternoon saw Joris eating up the leagues of Basse Honoy with his long huntsman's stride; but the parchment lay in his bosom, and the blood of a great house sang in his ears of bastard's luck in the dark game of life. What if the runes were obscure, with their promises of rivalry and separation? Joris felt in his bones that some strange power of events, a power apart from God or Devil as priest and warlock knew them, had linked his life with Anne's and marked him for power and glory.

And from that first awareness of devotion Joris bore a sense of Red Anne's voice and form and movement that shaped a fragrant core amid the stress and turbulence of his new life. That new life came swiftly upon him, for Anne's warning at Hastain was not pointless; Morgain, derided by her neighbours because she was foreign and slow of speech, answered their jeers with mutterings of hatred. Tales of her converse with bird and beast ran through the village of Medrincourt; cattle plague brought priest and mob to her door, and Joris was trapped and bound and guarded while they tried his mother for witchcraft. Chevalier and men-at-arms were sorry for him; they drugged his wine and laid him senseless at the hour when Morgain was strangled at the stake.

For a week the verderer moved among his kind with civil manners and face like carven sandstone. Then, by accident or design, he met the fat sub-prior who had condemned her. Rage marred the handling of his hatchet; the churchman had time to moan the first words of a *Paternoster,* and thereafter Joris could not abide the speaking of Latin. For long enough, indeed, no Latin troubled his ears; nothing was left but flight across country before the dogs he had tended were set upon his trail.

Outlawed and excommunicate, he skulked in the uplands and wildwood of Honoy, knowing faintness of hunger and sweat of peril and hatred of all mankind, save only the Red Anne who came to haunt his dreams. During his first six months of solitude he found, three leagues southwest of Pont-de-Foy, a crag whose grassy lip gave a view of twenty miles of rugged moor and forest. Thereby a limestone chasm held caves and water; in such upflung country the winds were never still, and smoke of fires kindled in the depth was easily scattered and lost. Of that grim fastness Joris made a base, and by ones and twos he drew about him a band of outlaws and broken men; so that presently they began to say of northern Neustria that it had many rocks but only one Rock.

Chevaliers and merchants, and more than one churchman,

came to wait their ransom at that Rock's edge. Some waited in vain and were thrust blithely over; gorges and bogs so ringed the place around that noblemen suspicious of each other made no concerted move to find and cleanse of its brood that nest of brigandage. Lesser fry of the forest fled from the domain of Joris, or slunk to swell his power; and since he never robbed within leagues of his lair, travellers passing to and fro between Belsaunt and Dunsberghe could not dream how closely their track approached it. Prisoners entered and left the chasm blindfolded; only the doomed might stare a moment at ominous steeps and rugged skylines while clothing was stripped from their bound or hamstrung limbs.

Joris, then, dealt with the world as the world would have dealt with him; and near the end of his first year of sojourn in the wilds he shaved off his beard and put his life and the lives of three of his men in jeopardy by wandering down into Basse Honoy at the time of midsummer fairs.

Fortune rewarded his daring in her own cruel fashion; at Santloy, south of Hastain, he came on news of Anne. Taken in witchcraft, they said; so that Joris saw his love a second time amid the grounded pikes of the Prior of Dor. That was the evening remembered by mild Brother Eugenius; Joris was lightly armed, and to aim at a rescue seemed madness, but only for an instant did the shape of her half-bared dripping body sear his vision. Then he yelled and charged, alone for all he knew or cared, at the mailed men who grinned as they pawed and hustled her. But with him were half a hundred; and in the heart of that stubborn fray Red Anne saw and knew him. Alert and unafraid, with sunset light in her face, with the whirl and clash of steel around the draggled splendour of her hair, she smiled at Joris; but even that benediction availed him nothing thereafter. Through the blurred shouting broke thunder of hoofs; a dozen barded destriers shocked into the struggling mass of men. To Joris, as he stabbed and cursed, that onset seemed an earthquake; down he went in the heap, and a stamping horseshoe scattered fire from a stone six

inches beyond his face. Then he was up and clawing at a
bridle; vaguely he marked a white lion rampant on a sable
shield, clearly the dark and savage eyes in the visor slit above
it. A chopped stroke over the saddlebow laid open his left
forearm; a lance drove past his breast, and a dying man was
flung against him like a sack of flour. Over he went once more,
saved by the wretch upon him from the pounding hoofs above;
and as he gasped and cowered he saw Red Anne again. Bleeding and mired, fast-cramped in a shining solleret, her naked
foot swung high; amid torn clothing her shoulder and side
gleamed white against dark steel and surcoat, for the leader
had wheeled his mount and tossed his sword to his shield
hand and caught the girl aloft in the crook of his plated arm.
Her face was flushed and glad, and her eyes were stars; poised,
breathless, strangely small in her rocking turret of tall steeds
and armoured riders, she was swept from the sight of Joris
of the Rock. There came a gleeful roar and a great tumult
of splashing; Red Anne was safe and away with Lorin the
Butcher Count, leaving a litter of dead and a gaping crowd of
living on the bank of the shallows behind them.

With fingers clenched on his bleeding arm, the outlaw
loped and stumbled a mile along the river margin; and when
he paused for Gandulf to bind up the wound he gritted his
teeth for no pain of the flesh. "Black and gold red shall hold"
—if "red" were Anne and "gold" Joris, "black" was Lorin de
Campscapel, and the runes were coming true. Tidings of Red
Anne's witchcraft had chilled the heart of Joris; "red shall
sin for black to grin" was a promise dark enough, but "black
and red in the same bed" rang so foully in his mind that
he was almost grateful to the Butcher for supplying an alternative interpretation. If Black must for a space hold Red, let
Black be of earth, not of hell; but jealous misery clawed the
outlaw's vitals as he headed again for his Rock.

Then, for a space, he led his raids with a fury that startled
even his men. Farms blazed to the midnight sky, foresters
died on their thresholds, travellers dropped to the arrows be-

fore they could sign the Cross; in snows of winter the peasants sprang up at the bellowing of kine—sprang up, and heard the scratching and sniffing beyond their mud-and-wattle walls, and said to each other: "No, it is only the wolves."

Gandulf and two or three others guessed at the cause of their chief's new blood lust; but the bulk of the growing band knew nothing and cared less for the hidden motives of Joris, until that day when one among them called Anne a rampant whore and envied the Butcher aloud with outlaw frankness.

"Ursin, attend!" drawled Joris, and roared for all to cease their tasks and gather upon the Rock. When they were grouped before him he spoke his mind without heat, letting his hard gaze linger amid their evil faces.

"Ursin here," he announced, "has provided the day's diversion. All of you now take heed. Do I make rules without reason?"

"Nay, never," they shouted, wondering what should befall.

"Hearken then to a new rule. Save to myself with tidings, no man of you shall speak aloud the name of that girl Red Anne who dwells with Butcher Lorin. If any complain of another, the two shall fight it out. But upon that name our Ursin has voided the filth of his mind; therefore he leaps from the Rock or battles me to a finish. Ursin, which shall it be?"

Ursin looked at his friends, and saw they were all for sport. Stoutly enough he armed himself, cursing Joris and Anne in terms that brought sharp silence. Sword in right hand, buckler in left, chief and subaltern fronted each other, sliding and foining across and across a patch of coarse grass thirty feet long and twenty broad above the verge of the abyss.

Animal murmurs arose as the bright blades whirled and rasped; Joris in brown and Ursin in green moved starkly against blue sky, striving each to bring the red ball of the setting sun against the other's eyes. Ursin was bulky and first to sweat, but he wounded his leader's thigh before he stumbled; awhile he fought on one knee, his florid face grown gray.

Blood sprang out on his shoulder, blood channelled his cheek;
when his sword was jarred from his hand he flung his buckler
at Joris and plunged as though to grapple. Joris ducked and
laughed, backing and stabbing daintily; then he advanced with
buffeting flat-bladed strokes, driving the beaten wretch to
the Rock's edge to kick him screaming over.

"Do you abide by my rule?" he thundered, turning on
those who watched him.

"Yes, Captain," they chorused. "Yes, you have sealed it
fairly with Ursin's blood and your own."

Joris sheathed his sword with a flourish; the crossbar
kissed the plates of his belt with a faint sweet ring of steel.
Glancing over his shoulder at the uplands of Honoy, he
offered his late extravagance as incense to Red Anne.

"*I* abide by my runes," he thought, "*I* am one of the men,
Red Anne, for whom the world was made."

Thereafter her name was safe enough amid the outlaw
throng; but Joris had bitter moods of doubt in which he
thought himself bewitched, who knew his love so darkly and
maybe doubly bound, and yet found in her image the glory of
his day. Sometimes he sought relief in arms of other women;
comely Tiphaine de Ath was only one of several doubly outraged by his lust and his indifference. But although Joris was
sometimes a slave to his passions, no woman except Red
Anne could enslave him with grace of the flesh.

Sternly he restrained himself from haunting the Butcher's
marches; tales were blown to his ears of Anne's strange rule
above Alanol, and sometimes he pondered lying in wait to see
her when she hunted. Now her reputed witchcraft troubled
him little; Lorin de Campscapel seemed not the man to share
his mistress with the Devil. Yet there were rumours of Anne's
night-riding; some said she vanished from the towering hold
at times when gates stood shut, next to be seen by the
sentries when she shouted for the drawbridge to be lowered in
the dawn. And Joris chafed to think of her alone in the wild
hills or—worse—at play with comrades not of earth in some

ill-famed assembly hidden from men. Nevertheless he held away from danger of the Butcher's watch towers; the Butcher had bouts of madness in spring, the Butcher's brother Red Jehan was mad all year, their infamous riders were counted by hundreds, their hounds knew human flesh, and this their motto ran like cold fog over the moors: *Face Campscapel, Face Death.*

The caution of Joris was justified when the Butcher sided with Barberghe against the Duke of Saulte. When the Jacquerie burst over Normandy the outlaw was hugging his Rock; scurrying north for plunder, he found there was not much left. Peasants who once would have fled at his name now turned and fought him valiantly; the midwinter of rebellion found his diminished band again in their caves, living on cattle and corn and wine that had changed hands twice or thrice before it reached them. Some of the men would have had Joris set up in a castle when castles were easily won, but Joris, like the miller's wife at Ath, foresaw the end of that grim business, and let no lure of runes distort his judgment. When the constable marched into Nordanay and made a final slaughter of the Jacques, Joris shaved off his beard again; instead of adorning wall or stake with his shrivelled carcass, he took young Gandulf with him, and doucely peddled a pack amid relics of oppression, revolt, and revenge in Basse Honoy.

So he came to the Tower of Ath and purchased a mirror; so, on that windy market day, he slouched into Hastain and heard Guelf Reinager's drum, and looked again into the eyes that mocked him through the clang of his cherished runes.

*　　　*　　　*

The march wind died at sunset; by the hour of compline a full moon swam above Hastain housetops, silvering all the northwest corner of the market square. Joris and Gandulf trod quietly out of shadow, passing the ghostly puppet booth to pause beneath the iron tavern sign. On market days peaceable folk had license of late hours; watchmen observed the pair go by without motion of pike or lantern, and Gandulf shivered to think how pikes would flash and lanterns bob if their names were cried aloud across the cobbles.

Joris, too, shivered, but his fear lay beyond his comrade's understanding, and very near the confines of his own.

"What are they singing?" asked Gandulf, as jovial tumult swelled behind the shuttered windows.

"The jape of the Duke of Saulte," said Joris when he had listened. "But Hastain wits have been at work upon it."

Indeed, the rhymes was sturdily altered and enlarged; Duke Godfrey might have grimaced to hear the townsmen's version.

> "Hastain by the river, Tostain on the hill,
>   Stout hearts deliver when the war-horns thrill!
>   Pleasant limbs the lords lop,
>   Scythe-struck the steeds stop,
>   Shields split and swords drop
>   And swift shafts quiver,
>   But Tostain holds the hilltop, hilltop, hilltop,
>   Tostain holds the hilltop and Hastain guards the river!"

"God save us all!" sneered Gandulf. "The chirping of the communes . . . Saulte could starve either to surrender in a month!"

But Joris had rapped on the heavy gate of the courtyard, and was already muttering to the man who opened the wicket. Smells of stable and dunghill and damp stone, of torch smoke and peat smoke, of wine and cheese and roasting meat, assailed his nose in turn; thrusting of laden servants, blast of song and laughter, creak of rotting stair treads, and candle glow golden on the dark face of Guelf Reinager, brought him at length to the threshold of an inner room.

"Red Anne is there," said the showman, pointing grimly. "As for your comrade, I have not much to risk, but if he cares to throw awhile at dice——"

"That will I," Gandulf muttered; and when he sat down at Guelf's rickety table he gave a hitch to his belt.

"No need to bring your hilt beneath your hand," mocked the other. "*Her* friends are mine, until I prove the contrary."

Even Guelf Reinager, then, was fallen beneath the spell. The inner door stood ajar, and Joris, setting hand against it, stepped into the firelit gloom. Behind him his fingers shook on the clumsy latch.

"I was alone, but bar it if you will," belled she whom he sought. "Men have been brought to death this way, no doubt, though never yet by me."

The outlaw's hand came down as though the latch had stung it. Across the flame-bright floor Red Anne regarded him; she sat against the wall at the head of the bed, that was a broad plank set on three low trestles and covered by blankets. Beside her lay cloak and purse and dagger; spurs glittered in the rushes near a pair of trim thigh boots. The chamber was hung with rotting arras, and held, beyond the bed, no more than a battered chest and two three-legged stools, with saddlebags and earthenware behind the pile of fire logs in a corner. Moonlight gave form to the crisscrossed wicker lattice of the window, and spattered luminous gray on the motionless rags of Joris; otherwise only the fire showed gold and red to each other—for Joris had uncovered, and the girl's hood was down.

"Greeting," he whispered—and bowed, who had not bowed for years.

"Sit, friend," commanded Anne. "Ay, over there. Who *are* you?"

The outlaw bent his long limbs to a stool across the glowing hearthstone from the bed, and clasped cold hands around his patched and bony knees.

"Joris of the Rock," he said, and watched her steadily.

Red Anne made no movement, but her rosy face grew intent. Above high cheek bones, under the calm brow and the divided sweep of glowing hair, her shadowed gaze took measure of this ill-conditioned guest. Followed a twitch of the ripe generous mouth above her fighting chin; firelight defined a dimple in either firm round cheek.

"Eh, the poor warden!" mourned Red Anne. "Wolf's head and witch in his net, and he does not know!"

The heavy-lidded eyes of Joris puckered at the corner, but his hushed voice was hard and his sand-brown jaw set forward.

"So Red Anne *is* a witch. Herself has said it."

"Surely I am a witch. Raise you no Cross against me?"

"Neither Cross nor cold iron, rowan nor relic nor medal."

"Valorous Joris, why?"

"Nothing that witch can do to me you have not done as a woman."

"Fairly spoken if meant; but do not be too sure of that."

"Have not your arts told you something concerning Joris?"

"Why should I seek to know what matters nothing to me? This indeed I heard, that your mother perished for witchcraft, and that the fat sub-prior had thirteen wounds upon him."

"In faith I did not count them."

"Others did. Some who doubted her witchhood were thereby assured of it."

"You mean that there are thirteen witches in a coven?"

"Ay. And then you were outlawed. And this also I know, that you rob Count Lorin of cattle."

"Two or three head here and there; but his go very well guarded. You know it is not cattle I grudge the Butcher of Alanol."

"What do you grudge him, then?"

"*You* for his comrade and love."

"Joris, I think you are mad."

"Then there is glory in madness. Your uttering of my name goes through me like a javelin. Thought of you has been flame in me since I bought gray silk at your booth. Sometimes I see you as then, when I drowned in wine my anger that any girl should unman me. Sometimes I see you as at Santloy, when steel endangered you and it seemed that only steel

could save. Then I ponder tales of your sway over the Butcher
—how his roaring ravishing half-wit of a brother hides in
one tower for fear of you—how the Riders of Campscapel are
your slaves, and the peasants wax for your fingers. I have
thought you an elemental, framed of earth and air and fire; or
one of the race of the old gods, like that great white naked
image they dug from the mound at Dor, and by the prior's
command brake up and cast into the river. I know not how the
Butcher endures your commerce with the Fiend; I know not
how you can divide your favours between grim lovers such
as they; but I know I would draw steel on either—ay, on
both—if you so willed it. Maybe you paralyze the devil in the
Devil, as in Lorin, as in me. Red Anne, you were born to rule,
and not by terror; to me you are more than my own mother—
and if I were given to prayer and churchcraft, to me you
would rank above the Mother of God."

"Mystical lore in a wolf's head," said the hushed marvellous voice. Still-faced, attentive, glorious, Red Anne
crouched on her bed; now she lifted her chin a little, shaking
the glistening ropes of hair that had bunched on her shoulders.
Fire glow attained the blue of her eyes and gilded the round
of her throat.

"Nay, it is not too mystical," breathed Joris, leaning forward. "I am no fantastical chevalier, content with a scarf or
a rose. I would love you as a man loves, or a fiend, for aught I
know. When first we spoke I was bond; now I am free as air,
commanding many skilful blades, ruling the lonelier hills and
roads more surely than any count or baron. When you tire
of the Butcher, or the Butcher tires of you, come to me in
the forest; you shall not lack for comfort, and I have faith in
my sword."

"I doubt not you have gold and gear beside the Rock, wheresoever that may be. How many women have dwelt there-
under?"

"None. I have dealt heedlessly with women, but never
there. You only will have queened it at the Rock."

"Rising from cast-off mistress of a count to be an out-law's whore? Joris, you do not know me well; nor do you know my Lorin. Your words betray your unknowing."

"Yet I believe you will come to me in the end."

"Strange man! Why?"

"It is written."

"Written? Where?"

"Once upon runes. Now *here*."

Joris touched his breast. Anne's teeth set sharply, and her brooding face grew stern. Bringing her feet to the floor, she sat upright with hands on the edge of the bed and breasts defined beneath her dove-gray tunic; and her eyes, set wide apart, were again focussed with that directness startling as a squint.

"Tell me your runes," she commanded.

"No. Not until their prophecy is accomplished."

"Strange man again, and stranger wooing!"

"No stranger than your other—than your others. Can mortal still surprise you, who know the witches' ritual and govern the keep of Campscapel?"

"Ay, so it seems. But if I meant to come to the Rock, how should I find it?"

"What is your witchcraft worth, if it cannot discover Rock and runes?"

Anne's face lightened and grew merry. After a moment's pause she chuckled, and the little disarming sound drove Joris back on his stool, lest losing command of himself he should suddenly spoil all. Plainly enough he understood that she mocked him and his runes, finding in the latter small peril to her lover and her life above distant Alanol.

"Joris, I like you well," she crooned. "Guard your runes and your Rock, then; I shall maybe arrive at both when you least expect it."

"Either is ready for you when you trust yourself to me. We might be happy together in the moors—and not always in the moors."

"It will require grim turmoil to make *your* peace with Church and State."

"Ay, turmoil I thrive on. But hearken to this, Red Anne—if you need me you shall find me, so be it I am alive. Do you know Imbert, the dealer in hides, who dwells across the square?"

"Only by sight, but I know him."

"He knows *me,* but not by my own name. Go to him any time, draw him apart, and ask him how many clubs are in the pack this morning. If he say thirteen, he will add the name of an approaching day; on that day one of my men will be with him. If he say fourteen, then a man is there at the time. Only my trustiest pass between me and Imbert; any of them will convey you safely and secretly with him to the Rock."

"Phoo! What a cardinal's coil of precaution!"

"I am not done yet. Do not seek to have your guide ambushed by Riders of Campscapel, for you will be sadly disappointed in the attempt."

"What if I bewitched him?" the girl demanded softly.

"That I am willing to risk," said Joris, with a bleak grin. "Make your cause one with mine, and I shall trust you utterly. Many a man must have knelt for a word of hope from your lips; I will stand upright instead, with faith in my good fortune."

And he rose to his full height and fumbled in his wallet, cursing his heart that pounded to plead and his hands that tingled to plunder. He meant that he, not she, should end this queer encounter; and Anne's tilted regard was curious rather than friendly.

There came a silvery flash in her face; Joris half drew the mirror of steel from its velvet cover, holding it out to her through fire gleam and riddled moonlight.

"Look on your beauty in this," he growled, "and know it bought, not stolen."

"Harsh words, and mystery, and a gift," murmured Red

Anne as she took the mirror. "Is it art or nature in a wolf's head thus to snare attention? Men say that in foray you strike and are gone like a hailstorm on the heather. But indeed you have more of the Montcarneaux than their stature and golden hair . . . Gramercy, Joris."

"Harsh words for a foreman's lady, mystery for one well versed in mysteries, the gift for Red Anne whose bright company I covet as a priest should covet Paradise. Farewell, now that you know my mind. Love your Lorin while you may, romp with the Devil if you must, but remember I wait in the hills."

"How long will you wait?"

"As long as need be. How long was that old city in the taking?"

"Do you mean Troy? Ten years."

"I will wait ten years," said Joris.

And wait ten years he did.

IV.   THE PATIENCE OF JORIS OF THE ROCK

DURING the ten years of that second period of waiting Joris saw Anne four times. Boast to himself as he
might of being one of the men for whom the world was
made, the others held the castles, while he skulked in the
hills; his band grew with his fame, and a price of five hundred
golden nobles was set on his golden head, but as time went
on and turned the edge of his exalted expectation there was
often little enough to distinguish his own life from the
ratlike lives of his men. The touch of imagination in him found
outlet chiefly in generalship, although it also kept the lice
from his beard and sometimes clouded with sadness the hours
of his achievement. Wine that once had lost him his Anne now
brought her image before him; other women he would not
permit by the Rock, caring little for them himself and knowing what quarrels they would arouse among the rest. Apart
from his raids he found content enough in hunting and crude
sports, and no one knew from his face and bearing the moments when the runes stirred in his mind their manifold
snakelike gleam.

*   *   *

The first time was at Alanol itself, in the sloping market
place beneath the very sheer of the Butcher's barbican. Instead
of shaving his beard, he had let it grow rough and dyed it, with
the hair above it, a dark disguising brown; then, with Madoc
for companion, he drove a score of stolen sheep to the pens
that lined the pavement, and leaned on his iron-shod crook
to chaffer with the best.

Awhile he listened to a Hastain drover cursing old King

63

René; it seemed a royal castle was rising to overlook Hastain ramparts.

"He is within his rights, too," growled the drover reflectively. "It is royal forest up to the town moat, and a hunting lodge stood where the keep now stands. But we in Hastain have the Jacquerie to thank for that. Also the king has made his little nephew, Thorismund, our duke; but that is so that he can set a seneschal to spy on the lords of Honoy, for the princeling Thorismund is only eight years old."

"Ay," agreed Joris profoundly. "Well, there is gain and loss. Alanol has the Jacquerie to thank for *this*."

He swept the market place with a shrewd eye; for the Butcher had granted his town a charter because it stood by him against the peasants, and one of the chartered privileges was right of free market.

"Yes," growled the drover, "for all his reputation the Butcher deals as faithfully as our dear lord the king. But they say he was moved to it by the wonderful woman . . . hey, by the Mass, there she is!"

Deliberately Joris wheeled. There was doffing of caps by the gateway; the crowd divided respectfully, yielding a narrow path that passed the mock-shepherd's pen; and down the path, with only an elderly waiting-woman behind her, Red Anne moved leisurely toward the mercers' shops at the far corner of the square.

Here was no player in a puppet boot, thought Joris amid his awareness of danger. Madoc plucked at his chief's sleeve, but Joris stood fast, his sunburned face a little lowering, his great red hands tight-locked on the crook handle. Come what might, he would see her again, and be seen if she looked his way; outlaw's caution, fighter's craft, gave way before the overmastering impulse.

To-day Red Anne wore a white steepled headdress with a frontlet of green velvet. Her sleeveless gown, of purple cloth, revealed bosom and sleeves of a green velvet *côte-hardi;* a *tau* cross of amethyst hung on her heavy golden necklet, a little cloisonné pomander of gold was chained to her wrist, and girdle and shoes and purse and dagger sheath were of leather dyed purple and stitched with yellow thread. Her auburn eyebrows, narrowed by artifice, were drawn in a sun-dazzled frown, but the blue eyes were tranquilly amused; men stared and lifted hats and sighed, and even muttering women looked not unkindly on Red Anne, knowing that she checked her lord's ferocity and spent his money in the town and gave no wife deliberate cause for jealousy.

"Eh, she is fair," said one, and another: "The king's own court has none to set beside her." But for the most part the onlookers were silent, and Joris heard the rare rich voice greet one or two among them. Madoc drew a deep breath and waited; the eyes of Anne and of Joris met. The girl contracted her red mouth in a just perceptible *moue,* glanced at the huddled sheep behind the outlaw's motionless figure, and focussed gaze well past him as he bared his darkened head.

"At least she remembers and does not betray me," he thought.

The white steeple passed and was gone, the crowd closed in once more, and cheerful uproar reawoke around him; sudden rage stirred in the breast of Joris that he should slink disguised to peep at her. He glanced up and aside at the piled stone of the great hold beyond the bridged ravine, and there was that in his pale regard which, if it could, had laid the grim machicolated towers as flat as walls of Jericho; but if he lacked the faith of Joshua in seven circles widdershins and rending blast of trumpets, he hugged the simple and peculiar faith of Joris of the Rock.

Ten minutes later his body grew rigid again; someone other than Madoc plucked at his sleeve and spoke to him. Turning slowly, he stared down at the bearded humpbacked dwarf who had worked Guelf Reinager's puppets that other market day at Hastain thirty months before.

"Follow me," croaked the manikin, and sidled away with speed.

Pausing only to mutter a word in frowning Madoc's ear,
Joris lounged discreetly in rear of his guide, presently finding
himself at a fellmonger's dingy door. Pausing, he scratched
his powerful chest, sliding a hand between soiled tunic and
ragged shirt; then, having loosened the hilt of the broad
dagger whose pommel fronted his armpit, he stepped into a
gloom that smelled of sheepskins and greasy wool.

"Pass through," said a voice from behind a piled counter;
and Joris, with one glance behind to measure space and footing, passed through to the smoky kitchen behind the darkling
shop.

Red Anne stood waiting beside the brick hearth place; her
level voice struck at him through the noise of a simmering stew-
pot. Only the dwarf and her woman were with her in the
room.

"Why are you in Alanol?" she demanded, as Joris swung
the door to and grounded his shepherd's staff.

"To catch a glimpse or hear a word of you," he answered
simply. "I had not hoped for speech with you. I am well paid."

"*Now* tell me your runes."

"No."

"You withstand me here?"

"Ay. If you want me destroyed it is simple enough. Not
that I should be taken, but you may see a pretty fray if you
so please. There are worse weapons than a crook and a caldron of boiling stew. And if I am deceived in runes and you
alike, this is for me a comely finish; for I will kiss you hard
before I fall."

Red Anne regarded him silently, sniffing the while at her
pretty pomander; and Joris knew that his life hung on a hair.
If she dismissed him, it meant that she still mocked his runes
and any meaning they bore for him; and behind his headlong joy of encounter there spread a blackness of baffled fury,
a desolate foretaste of futile doom.

But Anne let the scented bauble drop the length of its fine
gold chain, so that Joris inhaled a drift of myrrhine perfume

amid the homely smell of the fellmonger's kitchen. Then he caught his breath, for the tall girl took a step forward, and another, and another, until she stood within a yard of him, looking up into his stony face.

"Go in peace," she said sternly, "but *go,* and come to Alanol no more. You promise not to come?"

"No. I will go now, but you grow too dear for such a promise."

"Then take heed—this pays for Santloy. If I see you here again, be sure you are sped. You and your runes disturb me not, and I honour valour in my lord's foemen, but do not believe I am lightly thwarted."

"That I have never believed," responded Joris thickly. "May I kiss your hand, Red Anne?"

For a moment, as her strong smooth fingers lay on the bony knuckles raised to receive them, Joris felt his wolfishness fall from him. His kiss was shy as a boy's, and when he stood upright again his eyes were young and pleasant.

"That pays for all," he said, "until—until——"

"Until ten years be past? Two of them are already spent—take heart, for you will need it—and now begone, you madman."

Joris turned and went. Within an hour he and Madoc were away with their unsold mutton, while Red Anne maybe tuned her great lute in the keep of Campscapel.

* * *

The second time was in the high moors westward from the mountain Domdonoy. Lingering far behind a party of his men, Joris lounged amid bracken above a stream that threaded the forest's northern limit; far along the ravine a gap disclosed remoter skylines, fretted on one blue hump by the towers of Red Anne's home. Joris chewed a stalk of feather grass and eyed the trim shape calmly; autumn came kindlier than spring to his body, and even the Butcher's hold was not unsightly because of the yellowing oak leaves between. Joris had no self-pity; rather he saw himself as a fate stalking the fells. He went no more into Alanol, but events had turned his attention toward the Butcher's marches.

René the king had lately lost his only lawful son, so that his little nephew Thorismund was now heir to the throne. Among the lands of the dead young prince was the county of Montenair, of which the central hold guarded the shortest road from Balsaunt to the northern sea; and René, suspicious of northern lords, had made Count Fulk of Olencourt his Castellan of Montenair. This touched Joris, for Fulk was no roystering pippin of a prince; Fulk's own domain marched with the royal county thus given into his keeping, and Fulk's extended power meant sad curtailment of outlaw's work in a wide angle of the Forest of Honoy.

"Prosper the madness of Campscapel," said Joris to himself, "for now a civil Count of Alanol could drive me south of Varne for good and all. 'Gold shall sunder and black shall blunder . . .' I would I could embroil the Butcher with this damned castellan. But maybe Lorin will blunder without my assistance. 'Red shall run ere all be done.' Patience, Joris, and . . . *ha!*"

No longer drowsing where he lay, the outlaw lifted his head. Mellow and sweet in the distance rang out the notes of a bugle horn, starting valiant echoes amid the rocks of the glen. Up-valley and up-wind went the eagle gaze of Joris; then he rose to his feet, aware of a travelling speck on a distant heathery slope.

"Headed this way," said Joris, and laughed as he snatched up his bow.

Bounding into the sunlit ravine, he gained the bank of the swelling beck and stood for a moment to listen. Muted by rushing of water, the voice of the horn rang faintly; but under it now was another note, a baying not to be mistaken.

Joris held his bow aloft and leaped into the whirl of cream and amber. For several furious minutes he battled his way upstream, now whelmed to the waist, now clear from the knees, treading always on drowned stones and cursing when he stumbled. Then he caught at the branch of a lordly oak that all but spanned the flood, and heaved himself aloft with a grunt, swinging the strung bow from his arm before standing to climb.

Presently he was twenty feet up, seated in a stout fork and well screened by foliage. Twigs and leaves dislodged in his scramble danced downstream and vanished; only the drip of his gear still moved, runnelling down gray bark or flashing to mossed brown earth amid the writhen oak roots.

The next gust of wind was quick with approaching clamour, but Joris had time to settle his bow in the branches and hug himself to stillness. Then the stag hoofs crackled in hearing and drummed along the further bank; full dark eye and cream-gray antlers, black nose and ruddy satin flank, ripped through a gap in the groundward leaves and hurtled out of sight beneath him.

Quiet now, save for a padding rush, and only a hundred yards behind, umber and black and brindled hounds flowed by; fire at his heart and ice in his spine gave Joris a second's kinship with the quarry straining ahead. Then he was Joris again, for a horn blast heralded horse hoofs; deeper drumming resounded, with curt shouts and hallooing. He grew rigid as his guardian tree, except that his fingers crisped on the friendly cord-bound grip of the six-foot bow beside him; and for his second and last time he saw the Butcher of Alanol. . . .

Stark upright in the saddle of a pounding chestnut stallion, with crimson bonnet blown awry and ravaged yellow features half concealed by coal-black masses of hair and beard, Lorin de Campscapel rode first of all his hunt. Blaze of dark eyes and pressure of pale mouth revealed the spirit coiling behind that ominous mask; the fame earned in Franconian wars and evilly upheld by tyranny at home seemed to the tranced watcher to smoke around his going.

All the stranger, therefore, the woman who came after—

that fury with the rosy face, with the uncovered plaits of flaming hair and the strong hand that once an outlaw kissed with reverence. Joris had heard of the Valkyries; in that glimpse Anne seemed one of them, whirling riot and death along the startled valley. *That* he had dared to love. Half blind to the thundering household, he clung in his place and blasphemed.

When the full din had passed he felt sweat on his forehead; humility curved near his spirit and shadowed its wonted haughtiness.

Far away in the uplands swelled the tumult of the kill, and still he sat in his place. A hunt at such a speed might well have shed half its following; but those who rode with Lorin and Red Anne seemed cut to worthy pattern. No further hoof beats shattered the rearward stillness; birds began to twitter again, and the stream sang untroubled beneath the whispering oaks.

Joris recovered his usual calm and lowered himself to the ground, loping away from danger as straightly as he was able.

"Hounds travel well," he reflected, "but arrows travel better. When next I come this way, I will not come alone. 'Red shall run ere all be done'—it has an idle sound to-day, when Gold runs tail between legs whilst Red rides like a whirlwind. But 'black and gold red shall hold'—*shall* hold, by the chimes of hell!"

*   *   *

The third time he lay in a gorse thicket above a dark hill tarn, watching Red Anne and her party half a mile beneath him. Now there were no dogs, and two of the six riders wore hawk hoops round their bodies; there was a girl beside Anne —a slim little thing in gray, on a white mount large as the other horses.

"That will be the wench called Lys," said Joris to himself. "A rank witch, they say, and very faithful to Anne. I would I knew the use of fern seed to make myself invisible—yet to follow my love through her day might destroy me with frenzy."

He thought of his voice, a shriek from nowhere, stilling the Butcher's hands upon Anne's body—of countercraft that might reveal him, of snickering laughter and glowing irons in the keep of Campscapel. A dull rage burned his breast, that twenty of his men should lie at hand in line, each of them knowing his chieftain somehow thwarted by that distant shape with its blot of brilliant hair. Vainly he sought to drag to light the love root in his mind, that robbed its neighbour weeds of life and throve on no more than a sprinkling of runes; but the strange plant was earthed beyond his delving, and although he tore at its flowers in wrath, he knew they would blossom again in an hour or a day or a week, shedding perfume that made him glad and afraid.

Nevertheless, for a space he trod them foully; this time the spell of Red Anne's face was lacking, and sullenly Joris swore to himself to ravish the first comely woman he met.

"If I had my way with Anne," he raged, "I should find her the same as the rest from shoulder to knee. Fiend fly off with this madness . . . let her go free this time, but if I meet her again she shall not outface me. It has been Joris for Anne thus far; next time it is Anne for Joris, though Heaven and Hell unite to defend her."

That night he raided one of the Butcher's hamlets, telling his strength with tongues of fire above the collapsing hovels. Yet when he had the chance to honour his oath he set it bleakly aside; outrage befell as usual, but Joris watched with no more than a sneer and turned away to direct the loading of plundered fodder.

A week or two later, when he returned to winter quarters beneath the Rock, he was met by Madoc and Herbrand, who had controlled the main force in his absence.

"We have a new recruit," said Madoc softly. "One Rufin, a cutthroat of repute from Ververon. He cut a throat too many, shook off the hue and cry, fled across Varne, and blundered half-starved into my hands in the forest. He says he is by-blow to Jehan de Campscapel, and by his voice and bearing speaks the truth."

"Bring him to me," commanded Joris; and presently a grinning ruffian with a shock of sandy hair strode confidently up to him.

"Your servant, Captain," boomed the newcomer. "May I touch your sword and remain?"

"You would in any case remain," said Joris coldly. "Give me that dagger of yours; in a month, if you show merit, you shall have it again."

Rufin stared, half aware that his manner had earned him indignity; for Joris began to keep state of a sort, allowing no equality save that of danger.

"Is this your custom?" Rufin asked, flicking a bright blade out of its sheath.

"No," replied Joris, who had not ceased to gaze at him.

"Here it is, then," rejoined the cheerful recruit, presenting a silver hilt. "Maybe you do well to make an exception."

"Do I so?" queried Joris blandly. "And why?"

"Eh, a wolf's head is always a wolf's head, but half a lion needs time for transformation."

Joris smiled as he took the dagger and proffered his sword point, for the device of Montcarneau was *quarterly or and gules, four wolves' heads erased counterchanged*, and that of Campscapel *sable, a lion rampant argent*. The outlaw chieftain thought too much of his own half-noble birth to grudge this villain a similar pride, but as Rufin nipped the blade and swore to serve its bearer, Joris contrived to drop the dagger and stood looking calmly down at it.

Rufin's grin broadened as he stooped and recovered the weapon; he thrust it deftly behind the leader's belt buckle before stepping back.

"I think we shall agree," said Joris, choosing to disregard that quick familiarity. But in his mind he added: "You are a dead man, Rufin, if ever we do not."

*　　　　*　　　　*

The fourth time was famous wherever the names of Joris or Red Anne were known. A long-smouldering feud had quickened between the Butcher of Alanol and his nearest eastward neighbour, the quarrelsome Count of Saint-Aunay; of such strife Joris was swift to avail himself, falling on each lord's villages with the war shout of the other, and once dodging from between black surcoats and white to leave them at blows behind him. Then wintry weather intervened, swelling the bogs and rendering trackless the gorges; in the first softness of spring Joris rounded the mountain Dondunor and hurled his full power into a renewal of that little moorland war.

That day an east wind drummed and thundered in the leafless elms by Capel Conan. Now and again cloud shadows swept blue-gray across the fells, but mostly the sunlight cut sharp shade amid the cottages and barns and remnant stacks, between the stone huts where the Butcher's serfs baked tiles of yellow clay, and in the rain-filled gully of the Conan Beck. Joris turned on the narrow road that linked the village with Alanol, and mustered his fourscore ragged wolves in shelter of rowan and thorn and pine.

"Cattle and gear we want," he told them, raising his voice against the headlong clamour of wind. "Use steel if you must, and fire before you finish, but remember these hinds are more use to us living than dead. Herbrand holds the path behind us; Gandulf leads the flanking party, falling on when I reach the church. Cattle must be driven through the village, not this way; Madoc goes straight ahead to wait at the turn and guide the beasts uphill to the left. No quean comes with us; wooers, be swift or refrain."

A laugh that was barely a laugh ran gutturally down the ranks. Presently Gandulf and his file had slipped away to the right, while Joris faced about and led the main attack downhill.

Mirth of action was in him after the winter's dullness; this was his way of life, the life of a man for whom the world was made. Brain, nerve, and muscle were turned to the sharp note of his swinging sword; to left and right behind him he felt his men break forward, almost as though they were wings that swept from his own strong shoulders. At the edge of the woodland he laughed and bayed his deep *Haro!*—and with a disorderly roar his followers repeated it.

Blind panic awoke in Capel Conan; a dreadful wavering squeal went up from forge and oven and byre and from the first long furrows of the fields. Lorin de Campscapel needed nothing from his serfs save unremitting toil and idiot fecundity; since the Jacquerie he had seen to it that they lacked weapons and spirit to wield them. Nevertheless some snatched up spade and scythe, waiting gray-faced to sell their lives as they might; the rest ran, tumbled, leaped, caught up their own children and trampled on each other's, or cowered and hid, to weep and whine and slaver till steel should find them out.

But never a blow was struck when Joris halted. Midway upstreet to the church he flung aloft his sword point and roared, "Stand fast!" With oath and stamp and clattering collision his rogues obeyed him, staring as Joris stared at the riders galloping furiously upon them round that curve ❧of road where Madoc was to turn the driven kine.

The riders were three, and foremost came Red Anne. Astride a mettlesome gray mare, with silver bells a-jingle on the bridle, with knee boots under her green frock and purple riding hood blown back, she bore a hooded falcon on her gauntleted left wrist. Behind, her servants' swords were out, and their faces set for death, but Anne herself was smiling when she reined in a score of yards ahead of the outlaw throng.

"*Hola,* Joris!" she belled. "Give me a moment's parley!" And to her men: "Back—back a dozen paces!"

"Gladly," said Joris, unmoved, with a rearward sweep of his blade to hold the gaping horde in place.

Then, as he stepped out alone, his left hand stole to his bonnet. Bareheaded, stony-faced, he strode to Red Anne's silver stirrup, exulting that at last she found him red-eyed in act of rapine.

"Flourish your runes to-day?" asked the woman, nowise abashed by his fighting mien; and added, before he could answer: "I like you better with your own colour of beard."

"That is as well," said Joris, looking her straight in the face. "You have mocked me too long, Red Anne. My runes go well enough. To-night at least you are mine."

Something leaped in the pansy-blue eyes that met his own so steadily; but Joris could not read its meaning.

"So be it—on one condition," Anne rejoined, glancing over his head at the muttering men.

"So be it on no condition," amended Joris. "We are not now in Alanol. What bargain would you drive?"

"This. Leave Capel Conan at peace, and I will come with you and give you what joy I may."

"But by the chimes of hell, what else can you do than come?"

His words and gaze were harsh enough, but behind them the iron seemed thinned in his blood. Red Anne smiled again, at this rogue and that behind him. Silence fell in the road and spread across the village; only the rooks, disturbed by the shout of attack, came wheeling back to their elms in a raucous flight. And lest the hush betray the bale of her coming words, the Butcher's lovely mistress leaned from her saddle.

"Talking of old Troy Town," she whispered, "more than patience went to its fall. What if I offer your joy to that man who lays his captain dead in my sight?"

Joris, still staring at her, grew white with controlled rage.

"Offer it, then," he growled, as she sat upright again. "Offer it now, and I lay *you* dead as you speak. But think you I cannot deal with any man behind me?"

"Ay, with one. Not with seven or seventeen. You wonder how I should fare? Well enough, maybe—and if ill, no matter to you, who by then were carrion."

"Are you so sure?" rasped Joris.

"We are always so sure, you and I," Red Anne responded; and Joris saw her eyes lift calmly to the hill track winding toward Alanol.

A chill struck through his fury and fascination.

"What is Capel Conan to you?" he demanded. Then, giving no time for reply, he went on: "No matter, you shall not save it. Bid your servants drop sword and dismount, or I fill them with arrows."

"Wooers be swift or refrain!" mocked an oaf well back in the press, but Joris paid no heed to gibe or following laughter, for Red Anne let fall her bridle and plucked at the lace knot of her hunting frock. Meeting his eyes with her own, she parted the green cloth and plucked at link mail gleaming blue beneath it; behind him oaths and sniggering died down to little startled beast noises, and Joris was starkly aware that Anne dared more than he did.

"Hold, tiger cat!" he grated, as a flap of mail fell forward and showed white tunic linen. "Have you then no——"

"Shame" was the word he wanted, and shame the sickness he felt; but instead of ending that speech he caught at the mare's bit and wheeled her in the track. Anne's knee jostled his shoulder; Anne chuckled deep in her throat and caught up the jingling bridle.

"In faith," she jeered quietly, "are you only brave in the dark? I but made way for your sword point—sometimes I wear mail in the hills. See now, your men are impatient—you must not disappoint them, Joris. Where is all your greatness gone, if you do not cleave your enemy? Will you hold me captive here while they sack Capel Conan? Indeed you are not so different from those who shuffle in rear!"

"Am I not, then?" breathed Joris, glancing before and backward and lifting a sudden grin; for vanity leaped to his rescue in this emergency. "Am I not? You shall see. Ride you and your men out of bowshot, and watch what shall befall."

"But if instead we fled?"

"I think you will wait to see."

"By Mahound you are right . . . yet if we fled there-after?"

"Flee, then, and farewell. Rot your terms and conditions; there shall be no harm done in Capel Conan—at least to those who dwell there. Go—go to the Devil!"

He dropped the bit chain and stepped back. Red Anne reached out with the riding switch that dangled from her right wrist and tapped him on the shoulder.

"Accolade for Chevalier Joris," she jested imperturbably. "This time I will not wait to hear the runes. Be what they may I have now a respect for them. Fare you well—and not too slowly."

With a stamp and a clatter she was away. Her servants reined about and spurred after, and Joris turned to confront a score of bended bows.

"Ai, Captain, let us shoot!"

"By God's bones, three good horses lost, to say nothing of —er—hum!"

"Ach, *now,* before it is too late!"

"But what the foul fiend ails him?"

"The foul fiend himself, I say. He is bewitched or——"

"Who but a half-wit would allow——"

"Down bows and silence!" roared Joris in their faces. "Madoc, bear *so* across the fields and bring back Gandulf and his party. Let the rest of you face about and return the way we came. For once *I* follow behind. No plunder here this day. Out of it—move—*Haro!*"

Shufflings and stirrings, evil regards askance, grimy paws lifted to hung charms—Joris observed them steadily, hands crossed on his sword pommel. Many might have braved him if one had given a lead, but the boldest among them re-membered Ursin's death scream on the Rock, and none ached to be first or even second or third to cross steel with his leader. Also the men had seen Red Anne; and the gesture of Joris in sending trusted Madoc from his side bore some weight. At all events they moved, with bewildered oaths and growling;

Joris, pacing last of all, turned and saw the riders halted just in sight.

Red Anne waved a hand above her head.

Half an hour later he paused, far up on a heathery lip of the moors, and summoned by name three or four who had scowled the blackest at losing sport and booty.

"Look there," he bade them briefly, pointing to where the hill road wandered beyond the ravine.

They looked, and their faces altered. Hundreds of feet below in the windy sunlight, three-score horsemen were spurring eastward upon Capel Conan—horsemen in black and steel, the dauntless and infamous Riders of Campscapel.

"Perish my beard," said one hairy ruffian, blowing a gap-toothed guffaw. "Why did you not tell us, Joris? We thought you moonstruck in daylight—but there was sense in that!"

Joris turned on his heel, vouchsafing no answer. He, no more than his men, had known the cost of delay; and his warrior's mind, that half-despised witchcraft as well as priest-craft, wrestled uneasily with the problem of Red Anne's searching westward glance and casual warning of danger.

"A strange name *I* shall henceforth bear in Capel Conan," he reflected.

And he led his chastened band to burn two farms of the Count of Saint-Aunay instead.

*   *   *

But the ten years went by. The last of them found Joris with more than a hundred men, raiding ever farther southward, returning from time to time to the moors of Nordanay to profit by the dragging strife of Saint-Aunay and Campscapel. Joris himself looked much the same as on the day when he flouted Gaston de Volsberghe and offered up murder and rape at the altar of his love. True, there was gray in his golden beard, but his powers were if anything greater; still he outshot his surest bowmen and winded his sturdiest runners. In foray his life seemed charmed, and the outlaws

believed in his luck and craft. Herbrand was slain in a forest
scuffle soon after the encounter at Capel Conan, but Gandulf
and Madoc were still his chief lieutenants; and to them was
presently added Rufin, whose dagger had long been returned to its scabbard according to the promise made by
Joris.

Rufin proved brave and discreet, and Rufin it was who
skulked on the crags and watched Saint-Aunay outwit red
Jehan de Campscapel in a galloping fray beneath the shoulder
of the mountain Dondunor.

"Sore snouts above Alanol to-night," chuckled Rufin,
gulping his ale. "And my daddy's among the sorest. His visor
point was flattened like the heel of an empty wine skin. A
score of the Riders were down—short shrift *they* had, you
may be sure. The Butcher lies sick, they say; he would never
have risked such a charge."

Joris grunted assent and then was silent. Presently he was
alone on the flat of the Rock; it was the sunset hour, and fires
glowed in the limestone chasm. By one of them a man was
playing on a little reed pipe; the thin inconsequent sound of
it drifted up to the chieftain as he sat humped and brooding
in face of tranquil sky and many-coloured hills. When he was
twelve Joris played on such a pipe, gazing over treetops at
the towers of Montcarneau, wondering what it was like to
live in a castle. Now he was thirty-five, and still he wondered;
for the moated grange of Medrincourt, whose hall and kitchen
and stables he once knew well, could not compare with the
great holds of Montenair and Olencourt, of Hastain and
Guarenal and Ger. Campscapel, too, that sat above frightened
Alanol . . . the thoughts of Joris slanted heavily along
pain-darkened ways, and his runes, once so comforting,
clacked idly in his mind against the cheerful folly of the
piper's airs beneath the blood-stained Rock.

Joris, as has been earlier said, knew no self-pity, but he
was conscious of talent in him that outlawry had wasted. Set
in a frontier tower, with lands of his own to guard, he would

soon bring credit on his banner—that banner he sometimes pictured in fancy, with its silver baton sinister across the red-and-yellow wolves' heads in quarters yellow and red.

"A frontier would suit me best," he mused, with a twitch of his firm lips. "I doubt not I should find some irk in having an overlord again. But only a war will right me now, and there is none in sight save these blind skirmishes of counts among their villages. Give me a war, a real war, wherein men may find their worth. Then, with a hundred swords to sell, there might be amnesty and reversal. And Anne's mock title of 'chevalier' could yet belong to me in truth. The Church, too, should have its say—oh, I would kneel till my marrow bones ached, and drone what folly they asked of me. If any of these rats below bear crimes beyond absolution, let them stay in the hills; they would be very welcome to this my twelve years' home."

After a while he stirred and exclaimed aloud:

" 'Black shall be riven, and gold given to red new-shriven,' " he quoted. "By the blood of the Pope, I have said the words a thousand times and never seen that gold, not red, might be the shriven one. Likelier outlaw than witch, indeed, to gain a bishop's blessing. 'And gold given (to red) new-shriven.' "

And for some minutes longer he sat dreaming in face of tranquil hills and many-coloured sky. At length he yawned, and stretched his powerful limbs, and rose to descend from his eyrie.

"It is long since my runes gave me relish for supper," said Joris of the Rock.

*　　　*　　　*

Saint-Aunay pressed his advantage, and in the following June his raiders nearly captured Red Anne in Capel Conan; but the villagers fought like men-at-arms, having her in their midst, and the Butcher himself got wind of the leaguer in time to rise from a sick bed and spur to the rescue. Joris, hearing of that fray, altered his plans for summer raiding; if the Butcher were out again it was safer to plunder the southern edges of the Forest of Honoy.

Yet summer passed into autumn, and the Butcher seemed holding his hand. Joris sent Gandulf northward alone, and thought mischance had befallen him; for dry October dwindled and dull November came, and the forests filled with mist and gloom and yielded up no Gandulf. Finally, Joris assumed his old disguise as a peddler and haunted the wayside taverns on the roads to Hautarroy; and there, on a noon of drizzling rain, he held a merchant's bridle at the door of an abbey guest house, and heard the direful rumour that shook down from the north.

The Butcher had taken his enemy hunting, to eastward of the hold of Saint-Aunay. Count and countess and half their household were prisoners; by setting the lady on horseback in front of them, and holding lances to her back, the laughing Riders of Campscapel had ridden across the lowered drawbridge and made a dreadful slaughter, leaving the dark towers belching smoke before they rioted westward. That was all the merchant knew, and when he had told it he stared, for the hulking peddler dropped his bridle and made off through the abbey hamlet without a glance behind him.

Tossing his pack aside, Joris struck out for his base; for two days he covered the ground as though he knew wolves had wind of him. Saint-Aunay was grumpy neighbour enough, but his countess was an Olencourt; there would be stirring doings betimes if Fulk the castellan moved against Alanol.

"Is Gandulf home?" he snapped, when on the morning of the third day his camp guard stepped from lair in the fog-bound limestone defile.

"Not yet, Chief."

"Has Madoc news from northward these six days?"

"Ay, that he has. The Saultes and Olencourts are mustering along the Butcher's marches . . . you know Saint-Aunay taken?"

"Yes. No more?"

"Not that I know."

So Joris sat and cursed the weather; and while he cursed, slim Gandulf entered the far end of the gorge, for Gandulf was skilful as an animal in tracking across moor and forest.

"Ay, it is all as you say and Madoc hears," croaked Gandulf, flinging himself down by the chieftain's fire. "But you have not the half of it. Saint-Aunay, his lady, and twoscore more were haled to the hold above Alanol, and there they were bloodily tortured to death . . . and then the story goes mad. I waited two days in Montenair to hear some sense in it, but not a shred could I find. Men gaped and goggled, and the new young Count of Montcarneau came flying to the castellan, and as I came away I saw him riding northward again, bound for the warden at Ger. But from Alanol blew *this* tidings—that the morning after the torturing they f-found the Butcher dead. . . ."

"Dead? *The Butcher dead?*"

"Ay, dead in front of chained and dead Saint-Aunay. And his body servant was dead behind him, and none knows how they were slain. Red Anne swears it was Red Jehan; Red Jehan accuses Red Anne; and both deny it roundly. Some have it the Devil came in person and slew the Butcher himself —being jealous, maybe, of the doings in Lorin's hall. The Riders of Campscapel are divided, but most hold with the Lady Anne, and some of the townsfolk openly call her their countess, whilst others come riding daily to Saulte and the castellan, bawling to them in the king's name to come and—and end the business *their* way. . . ."

"Death to Red Anne and Jehan alike?" demanded Joris harshly.

"Ay," finished Gandulf shortly, with a flicker of red-rimmed eyelids; and in the one word Joris heard compressed the tumultuous menace of a thousand voices.

"Fiend swallow this fog," he growled in his golden beard; for Rufin and a score of men were absent, raiding westward, and Joris needed his full power and clear weather for action.

Black had blundered, Black was riven; place must be found
for Gold in this strange coil to northward.

"Pile up the fires," he commanded. "To-night we will have
sport and feasting."

Sport and feasting they had to curb their leader's impatience. Fog forbade archery and crag climbing, but there
was wrestling and tug-of-war, and a kind of cock-fighting in
which men were seated and bound sole to sole to batter each
other with quarter staves until one of the pair fainted. Also
there was sword dancing to the groan and squeal of bagpipes;
and when the fog was thickened with smoke the shadows of
the dancers danced beside them, writhing across the gold-shot
murk like spectres from the slovenly mounds beneath the dark
foot of the Rock.

Joris sat by the mouth of his cave, drinking deeply, swearing gaily by the bones of Goliath of Gath and by the chimes
of hell. After supper came roaring songs; he himself sang
"The Lay of Fastingal," beating time with a dinging war
hammer on gyve chains formerly stricken from one of his men.

> "This is he on the gallows tree
>   Whom shadows long befriended,
> Stiff and stark at the edge of dark
>   With all his cantrips ended.
>
> "Body and limb and heart of him
>   His strength hath now forsaken;
> Every crow in the vill doth know
>   That Fastingal is taken.
>
> "Bonny and tall was Fastingal,
>   And blithe and free he wandered;
> He could slit your purse and help you curse
>   To find good silver squandered.
>
> "He mocked at the priest, at man and beast
>   And flood and flame and thunder;
> He tumbled a wench on the blacksmith's bench
>   With the blacksmith dead thereunder.

"For a crimson rose he tore his hose
  On a wall of the bailiff's garden,
But he stood to die for a pigeon pie
  Before the crust could harden.

"So here spins he by the gallows tree
  Whom fortune long befriended;
And his eyes and his nose are torn by crows
  And all his cantrips ended."

The multiple clink of the down-flung chain was drowned in a shout of applause; Joris was not so often genial that his men should fail to play up to his humour.

"Nay, now," protested Madoc, grinning half ruefully, "that I call a death's head of a song."

Joris drained a wine skin and threw it at the other's head.

"Take heart, Madoc," he laughed. "You and I shall fall in battle or die never; by potency of that last draught it is revealed to me."

"Die never?" demanded Osmund, one of the oldest of the band, whose piglike eyes were drunken-dull above the red blob of his nose. "How mean you, Joris, 'die never'?"

"Why, never die, man," shouted Joris. "Dry up and blow away instead, after the manner of wood ash. Madoc, your turn—give us the *Dies Irae!*"

But Madoc grinned again and struck up "Huon's Hunting," whereof fourscore outlaw voices proclaimed the thunderous chorus.

"'No,' she said, and 'No,' she said,
  'I tell what I have seen.
Werewolf's eyes are ravening-red,
  But Huon's eyes are green!'"

Soon after midnight, when fires sank low and the chasm grew silent, a cold wind stirred from the southwest, shredding the wreaths of fog and whining with rising force through the deep forest. By dawn the first November gale was tearing leaf wrack from the trees and hurling shower after icy shower against the gray flank of the Rock; by lowering noon the half-drowned Rufin and his men had struggled back to shelter, and Joris knew that no lord or league of lords could make effective any threat against Red Jehan de Campscapel until the spring should come.

At the first lull in a month of storm he slipped out with a dozen men and ranged the bank of swollen Varne. His usual crossing place—a disused ford near Pont-de-Foy—was quite impassable, and half his men could not swim; while the bridge was newly guarded by a barricade of timber covering either end. Dejected-looking men-at-arms splashed to and fro in the village, and the priest's house flew a pennon showing the red and yellow bars of the great house of Saulte, charged with the crescent "difference" of a younger son.

"There you are stuck, my Chevalier," said Joris when he saw it. "And here, by the chimes of hell, am I stuck also. For months ahead Red Anne and roaring Jehan stand in peril only of each other."

But Anne's danger from Count Jehan troubled Joris very seldom. He felt her to be easily a match for the strange monster who for years had cowered in his corner tower for fear of her arts. It was said that Red Jehan's peculiar dread was to be turned into the shape of some wild animal—although no man knew of an animal wilder than Jehan himself when a fighting mood was on him.

And because of his runes, that now seemed near fulfilment, Joris was not too savage during that cold winter by the Rock. The element of reverence in his love for Anne excluded all pity; Red Anne pitiable was a thing unthinkable. Yet to Joris life as a whole seemed an affair of fists and belly and loins; not without pleasure he counted Anne's loss as favouring his own cause with her. After all (so he told himself), she was a woman, needing her man like another; witch or goddess or elemental could not escape the call of the prisoning body. And Anne was born to rule, as he once told her; to Joris it seemed that a woman could never rule alone.

*   *   *

"It is a man," said Gandulf, checking his shambling gait to pucker face against the bitter wind that roared in the iron-gray woods and drove down the white hillside beneath them.

"More like the stump of a tree," growled Rufin, shifting the long stag-weighted spear shaft that lay on Gandulf's shoulder and his own, and dropping the point of his own shorter spear to break the lumps of impacted snow from the boards nailed under his wooden shoes.

"It moved them; I tell you it is a man."

"Well, leave it there. It will not be a man long after sundown."

"Gracefully said," boomed Joris as he strode up behind them. "Unburden yourselves and come with me."

The stag's brown body sprawled in the track, with black hooves crossed on the spear, pink tongue lolling, and wonder and reproach fast-frozen in the jelly of an upturned eye. Behind, the little procession of trudging hunters and game-laden sledges slackened to a halt; Joris and his two lieutenants creaked and rustled forward, leaving a furrowed and flattened wake on the slope of virgin snow.

The wind hacked at their fur-clad limbs and whipped the hood of the fallen wanderer across his blue-white face. When they bent above him his stiff lips chopped at faltering words impossible of comprehension; Joris squatted down, swung a mittened hand to his girdle, and stemmed the muttering with the mouth of an uncorked flask.

"Who are you, and whence come you?" he demanded shortly.

"I am called Flar . . . a smith of Alanol . . . fugitive these three days. . . . I brained a Rider of Campscapel with a roof tile, praised be God . . . Help me or slay me, whosoever you be, for I starve and my feet are frost-black, and I have said what prayers I know."

"We could do with another smith," muttered Gandulf.

"Especially a smith from Alanol," added Rufin with a grin.

Joris stood upright and bellowed downhill. The first sledge, swept of its heaped furry load of deer and hare and coney, rasped from the trail and mounted toward them.

"Come to our hospice by the Rock," jeered Rufin aside.

"Ay," added Joris smoothly, "and be drawn thither by a son of Jehan of Campscapel."

The lifted gaze of Flar the smith was dull and stupid enough, but the sound of the dreaded name, and perhaps the face of Rufin, seemed working in his head; for later, clinging to the blood-fouled sledge, he talked feebly but clearly to Joris, who strode beside him.

Count Jehan was master of Alanol, and nothing of life or honour or gear was safe from his drunken fury. There had been armed resistance to one more than ordinarily savage edict; the result was fire and pillage through a quarter of the town.

"The place is hell since Red Anne fled," said Flar, as Joris shaped a question.

"Fled? When did she flee?" growled Joris, lurching closer.

"Nearly two months gone by—late in November it was. With her, they say, fled the Demoiselle Lys and a page whose name I know not."

"Why did they flee?"

"Some bloody household brawl, I heard. Jehan too drunk at last to heed his old terror."

"You are sure? Red Anne is fled, not slain?"

"Ay, sure enough. Red Jehan would have mounted her head on a pike, and maybe her body as well, for all to admire his power. And now, next time God has a thunderbolt to spare, He well might use it on that accursed keep."

Joris laughed in the wind's teeth and slapped his belted sword hilt, staring ahead across white desolation where the tumbled woods receded to the first sharp sun-kissed rampart of the uplands of Honoy. "Red shall run ere all be done"; the shock of this news, the offence of his own ignorance, the sudden emptiness of that quarter of the sky and hills which in his heart belonged to Anne—these could not deaden the runic clang in his exultant breast.

His memory held Flar's latest words through that stir of emotion; and presently, slanting a not unkindly regard upon the supine refugee, Joris spoke from his outlaw's store of experience.

"No thunderbolts to spare for Jehan de Campscapel. God wastes too many on that little ironstone hump, between the limestone and the grit, northwest of Dondonoy. It is no place for priests up there—else we should have a tidy tale of why the hump is damned. Belike some wandering Apostle stubbed a toe on it."

Flar grinned in answer, forgetting the groaning panicky prayers that had lately broken from him. Devotion to Heaven soon wearied the hardy little smith; when his feet were cured he transferred his worship to Joris of the Rock.

*   *   *

So Red Anne had vanished into the gales of that wild autumn, and Joris heard no more of her until full summer came again. Her earthly paramour being dead, it might be that she dwelt more evilly than before; the outlaw pondered old tales of the Kingdom of Elfin, and once, in a gust of sudden rage, let fly a yard-long arrow into one of the round hummocks that lay in groups about the eastern uplands and were accounted the dwellings of gnomes. The shaft sank feather-deep in the peaty mound, and Joris strode up and drove feathers and all from sight with one impatient prod of his foot.

"The Butcher is swept away," he mused, "and maybe by the Devil's self. Must I now contend with Satan for my love? Then may some elf take my arrowhead in his rump and scuttle howling to his master with tidings of Joris of the Rock."

But the mound was silent beneath his stout oiléd brogues; only the spring wind stirred in the quickening heather, and a pewit screamed as he whirled between the brooding eyes of

Joris and the helm cloud darkening the distant slopes of Dondonoy.

For a desolate moment the man saw his love affair as a grotesque and slipshod folly, lacking all true relation to a life of valiant turbulence. Then again the faith of his runes struck outward from the core of him; remembered events fell into rank, marching to ordered music of destiny that gathered and rang to a cymbal clash at each bygone encounter with Red Anne.

"Ten years or a little over—it is all one to me," he told himself. "I have waited so long I make no task of waiting longer. Nevertheless, jade Fortune shall yield me my uttermost due in the end."

In darkened hours of his own frustration he still could summon a smile at the news of frustration befallen others. In Hautarroy old René's queen was dead, and shadowy factions were shaping behind Thorismund of Hastain, the lawful heir, and Conrad, a bastard son of the king. The youths themselves were firm friends; but old feuds and rivalries gathered force along the lines of the new cleavage. Saulte and the castellan were props of young Thorismund; by machination of their foes at court those two great lords were forced to stay their movements in the hill parts about Alanol. So that Joris was free once more of tracks into Nordanay, and Red Jehan ruled scatheless till the dry heat of June.

Corpus Christi came and went; in his great hold of Ger the Count Warden of the Coast March lay stricken by an apoplexy, while an untried boy, a nephew scorned and obscure, sat uneasily in his place. For a week or two the dark hulls of Easterling pirates had crept this way and that along the northern coasts; on the octave of Corpus Christi they launched a great concerted raid on seaward towns and villages of Nordanay.

That octave, and its anniversary for long years afterward, was known in the north of Neustria as Raoul's Day; for in its morning the Viscount Raoul, that untried boy from Ger, led

horsemen through a rising tide to fall upon and utterly destroy
four ships and crews of the raiders—and then drove straightway southward over the moors to keep tryst with the desperate
men of Alanol. By means of a secret stairway he and his
falcon surcoats climbed into the keep of Campscapel; the town
rose at his signal, and in a furious midnight fray the red
Count Jehan died with four fifths of his ill-famed garrison.

"God's thunderbolts are not all of one kind," said awestruck
Flar the smith to brooding Joris when they heard of it.

"Do you wish to return to Alanol?" Joris demanded.

The little smith shook his head.

"What life I had there is broken," he muttered, "but it is
good to know Red Jehan in hell and townsmen in the wards
of that accursed castle. The little viscount must be crazed
himself, to hand its keeping over to the burghers. Also they
say he protected the women."

Other words were on Flar's lips, but the darkened face of
Joris restrained their utterance. Flar, too, thought of bruited
witch flights explained by a secret stair, and wondered whence
Raoul of Ger learned of that entry.

"Get to your anvil, Flar," commanded the chieftain, tossing
a belt across the floor of his cave. "Mend me that buckle
swiftly. To-morrow we make for dead Jehan's marches.
Townsmen should prove poor lords of a countryside."

*   *   *

Over the brow of a steep ridge appeared a cluster of black
surcoats, only five hundred yards away from the uptoiling
outlaw horde. Joris caught glimpse of a score before they
vanished; and they were plainly soldiers, led by a soldier, for
in a second all but one of them seemed nothing but steel caps
and tilted buckler tops glinting here and there amid deep
bracken and gorse.

In front of Joris was a single striding outlaw scout; and
on the very skyline one tall half-armoured figure stood regarding them. The scout looked up and back, saw Joris halt, saw his

comrades straggling to a standstill, looked up again at the black-surcoated watcher, and lost his head. His longbow rose, and a shaft streaked up the hill crest, quivering in the black shield lifted to meet it. Joris heard no word of command, but one went forth, for the scout collapsed like a sack emptied of sand, and lay huddled with seven feathered butts sticking from face and body.

"Fool," said Joris between his teeth, and wheeled to shout "No more!"—for one of his bowmen yelled with rage and let fly a long shot, the arrow falling short by fifty yards. Now the man on the hilltop had his empty sword hand in air; a faint hail broke across the bracken.

"Parley, whosoever you be. We seek no fray with you."

"Have parley, then," bellowed the outlaw chief. "Come forward alone and meet me. I am Joris of the Rock."

And in a waiting silence the leaders approached each other. The stranger's pallid feathers were vulturine but fleshy; his hard gray eyes and cruel mouth, with the soiled white lion that ramped across his sable surcoat, set the bleak danger smile upon the lips of Joris.

"I am Adelgar, late troop captain of the Count of Alanol," said the stranger when they came face to face above the tumbled corpse.

"Leading the last of the unhorsed Riders of Campscapel?"

"Yes."

"How many of you are there?"

Adelgar looked past Joris at the five-score outlaws below.

"Twenty-seven," he answered, meeting the outlaw's stare. "Twenty-seven, well-armed, and half of us veterans of the Franconian wars."

Each man saw the other's mind. The black surcoats were outlawed as surely as Joris himself, and they must either join him or be straightway cut in pieces. The first course held various risks, but the second would prove expensive; Joris might well lose half his followers in pulling these trained war dogs down.

"Seek you a new troop?" demanded Adelgar harshly.

"Not I, Captain Adelgar," was the blithe answer of Joris, "but I am very willing to welcome twenty-seven hardy fighting men."

Adelgar took the point with a grim nod, and appeared to consider it.

"Your fame is enough for me," he said after a moment. "A live wolf's head is better than a pack of dead counts. I will engage your best swordsman for the honour of becoming your chief lieutenant."

"I am my own best swordsman."

"Your second-best, then, or any you appoint to try me."

"That is well spoken. Summon your men, and I will summon mine. We will stand back to back, and when I give the word let each bid his crew sheathe bow or sword; our confidence shall quicken theirs."

Strangely enough, on the windy hill slope, followed the drawing-together; presently uniformed rogues and motley gazed on each other with curiosity. One outlaw only seemed to resent the truce; he it was who had loosed the second upward arrow, and now he stepped to confront his chieftain, pointing aside at the slain man in the bracken.

"Make what terms amuse you," he shouted, "but give me blood for my blood."

Adelgar turned beside Joris, and necks were craned around them.

"Your brother was a half-wit, and you are another, to shoot without my word," rasped Joris in reply. "Gain what quittance you can on the person of Adelgar here."

Five minutes later Adelgar laid the complainant dead beside his brother, and Joris counted a clear gain of twenty-five stout blades.

"Wear your sable surcoats till they fall to pieces," he bade the newcomers, "but pick the silver lions from off them before to-morrow morning. And the first of you who says in my hearing, 'We did not *this* under Lorin or Jehan,' runs the gauntlet down a ravine, with rocks for pebbles. I warrant you did not *that* either. The same shall befall any man of mine who flings old enmity at you; henceforth you are all my men, and our foes are around, not among us. Adelgar leads those I shall give to him, and no more. Flar, have you understood?"

For the little smith from Alanol stood scowling at the badges of Campscapel. And although at the time he jumped and blushed and grinned, Flar only of all the outlaw throng found courage to defy that union; for on a night soon afterward he slipped away and was no more seen by the Rock or among the hills.

But Joris wished again for war, his band being now far stronger than ever before, and its immediate employment the easy task of rounding up strayed cattle or stealing them in scores from defenceless farms in sight of the dead Butcher's empty march towers, and even in sight of the ramparts of Alanol itself. Many hides and horns were stored in sandy caves under Dondunor before the outlaws scented autumn airs and turned their faces to southward; Joris moved his power in five parties, of which the middle three alone were plunder-laden. Madoc led the advance guard, and Joris himself the rear guard; between them the convoys of ponies and kine were in charge of Adelgar, Rufin, and Gandulf—each hating the others and jealous of his own success in slinking across Varne and past the borders of the vigilant castellan.

V. DIANA IN THE FOREST

SO CAME a September day when Joris picked and ate the
late wild strawberries in a derelict sandstone quarry,
peering the while between thorns and ragwort at an approaching cavalcade.

"Some reverend father has been getting in his rents," he
muttered to old Osmund beside him; for four men-at-arms
rode first, and behind them a fat church dignitary, followed
by two monks, a banner bearer, and a dozen laden pack
ponies piloted by armed servants, with four more mounted
men-at-arms in rear.

"What is the banner?" asked Joris; and the whispered
query went down the line of sprawling men.

"The good saint was a martyr," he reflected. "He holds
his heart and liver, or maybe his kidneys, and regards them
with no loving countenance. No doubt they savour too much
of the world for his liking—eh?"

"Saint-Eloy's-over-Hardonek," came the low-voiced reply,
passed by the man on his other side.

"A wealthy house, and famed for generosity," said Joris,
plucking at the cord of his slung horn to bring the mouthpiece
into place.

At the single harsh note his score of outlaws bounded up
and crashed through undergrowth upon the startled wayfarers. The fat cleric had courage; he reined in, snatched up
his crucifix, and bayed a deep threat of damnation at the
attackers, but an arrow aimed at himself sank into the neck
of his rearing mare, and in a second he was groaning at the
wayside. Behind was wild confusion; Osmund tore the banner
from its wounded keeper and flung it across the pack of the

first led animal; three men-at-arms were unhorsed, and half
the servants had run yelling down the road, but the rest stood
firm, and for two or three minutes the thieves got nearly as
good as they gave. One of the monks was young, and bore a
heavy staff heeled in a bucket at his stirrup; with this for a
weapon he laid about him, shielding his superior and the older
monks beside him, but Joris cut the staff in two and stayed
his blade to laugh at the fury in the other's face.

"Carry a mace next time, you man of God!" he jeered. "By
the bones of Goliath of Gath you mistook your vocation!"

"Slay me, you hound of hell," returned the young monk
fiercely, "but spare the old sub-prior, for he never harmed
living creature!"

"Nay, I slay neither; I like a lad of spirit. Keep your mare
to mount the old man; his girth proclaims him slow to sin. In
Purgatory you both may thank me for relieving you of the
balance of your worldly dross . . . *no Latin, Brother!*"

The last words were barked at the older monk, who, dazed
and white with fear, strove yet to bless his enemy before the
latter could slay him; he raised a trembling hand toward Joris,
understanding neither the outlaw's reassurance nor his own
new peril.

"God, Who hears me, forgive you your sins, and bring you
at last to grace!" he piped, staring with dark fanatic eyes at
the mocking face of Joris.

"Praise Him if it please you for setting Neustrian language
on your tongue," rasped the outlaw, "but for me, my skin is
oiled with sin against such watery benediction. Farewell, and
a blithe journey . . . and tell your saint that Joris is beholden
to him."

Five minutes after their onslaught the outlaws were streaming away from the track—every pack pony with them, and
three good horses besides—while behind them five of their
number lay slain or abandoned among Saint Eloy's fallen.
One rogue had the sub-prior's cloak that was trimmed with
black lamb's wool; others bore new weapons torn from dying

men-at-arms, and red-nosed Osmund pawed his captive banner with amusement, while Joris eyed the heavy little chests that lurched to the scrambling mule pace over red earth and between red pine trunks of the Forest of Honoy.

That night he sank his fingers deep in gold. Ten pieces went to each of the men who had helped him to win it, and sternly he forbade gambling until they reached the Rock, for gambling meant cheating, and cheating meant knives, and knives meant another corpse or two when eyes and muscles were needed. One little coffer he took for a twilight stroll beneath his cloak, and buried it secretly amid oak roots on a slope, and marked the spot by hasty dagger-carvings on two trunks near by. Only old Osmund counted the coffers left, and winked and said nothing; for Osmund was of the loyal sort whose leaders rise to fame.

But Joris lay long awake that night, his mind roused by his new fortune in matters of men and gear.

"Six-score swords to sell now, and trouble brewing to southward," he mused. "Since the king exalts his bastard, the princeling must look to his chances. . . ."

For during that summer old René had married again, taking to wife the Countess of Burias who nineteen years before had borne him a son. And at their royal wedding the young Conrad stood with his parents under the crimson pall, in token of formal legitimization; care was taken to proclaim him outside the succession, but the same afternoon saw Conrad created Duke of Burias and richly endowed with lands to south and west of Hautarroy. And even Joris in the northern hills smiled to think of that proclamation.

"Six-score swords for the highest bidder, be it Thorismund or Conrad or this strange little lord of Ger . . . though I doubt *his* humour would not march with mine for long. Still, I am ready. Good health to the sub-prior of Saint-Eloy-over-Hardonek. I would I might hear his tale to his prior up yonder. I warrant I gave him the wildest, strangest day of his saintly life. Alas, my reverend father in God, the peaceful soul gains goodlier savour from adventure than does he whose daily fare it is, such as that plaguy outlaw Joris of the Rock."

Gold of his coffers stirred thought of gold of his runes; Joris opened his eyes and blinked at the stars.

"'And gold given—to red—new-shriven,'" he murmured. "That scared old shaveling on the road . . . by the chimes of hell, am I shriven at last?"

And, as it happened, the following day was among the strangest, if not among the wildest, days of his own tempestuous life.

*   *   *

It was quiet beneath the spreading beech boughs, there on the bank of the gliding forest stream. Joris had sat for an hour in the sun-splashed gloom. Squirrel and trout and water ousel flashed and flitted about their business near him, and his trained eye marked their stir amid first yellows of the turning leaves or amber of sunken boulders; but his long limbs barely moved, and his eagle's face might have been carved from the sandstone bluffs across the whispering water.

Dozing, he thought he dreamed, but started awake to know that he had caught a sudden unlikely sound—the elfin chirrup of a flute among the dense alders. A startled pheasant got up from bracken high above him; followed a stir of voices and a deliberate *clop-clop* of approaching hoofs.

"Bold vagrants these," thought the outlaw. "Bold, or very innocent to stray so far from the road. Minstrels travelling northward to the autumn fairs. The sub-prior's gold inclines me to mercy; slugs shall creep in the wolf's path. Besides, I warrant they have nothing worth a second glance, save their pipes and tabor and maybe a florin between them, to keep them until Michaelmas."

Then a green-clad youth appeared, leading a laden pack horse; and behind him, in short kirtles of green, came a slender girl and a tall woman. All three wore hooded capes, and stout boots to the knees; each carried a bow and quiver, and the lad a sword as well. The girl had a flute to her lips;

her slim fingers were stilled on the stops as she saw Joris ahead.

The flute slid into a sheath at her belt as she caught the bridle to halt the plodding nag. The youth plucked out his strung bow and whisked a shaft into place. Beyond him the woman stood at gaze, shading her eyes with a brown hand against the morning sunlight; her hood fell back, and the flame of her hair leaped out against gray writhen beech trunks and brown gloom of the forest glade.

Joris sat still as the roots at his flank, but for a moment his head was dizzied as with the fumes of wine. Over moss and beech mast Red Anne trod catlike and alone toward him—a Red Anne thinner, browner, fiercer than he could remember her, with head a little bent and blue eyes steadily aware in the rose and sunburn of her face.

Joris got grimly to his feet, churning heel in the ground to stay himself from stepping forward. If this was the hour for which he had waited, it should not startle him beyond self-mastery; he swung his bonnet off and stood with head erect and hand on hilt, while sunlight mailed the gray of his tunic with shivering disks of gold.

"Greeting once more," he growled—and his heart leaped, for Anne's regard came up the length of him with a sombre appraisement. Yet her eyes held a sullen aloofness new to his senses; and something in him ached to find her tired, a little haggard, coarsened by what had befallen her since that last meeting at Capel Conan.

"Greeting, Joris," she returned, with a sudden half-friendly grimace which shook his purpose. "In all my paths you only seem unchanged. I should perhaps have paid more heed to you and your runes."

"Whither are you bound?" demanded Joris simply.

"Nowhither, save that we aim for the Singing Stones before November Eve."

"Ah, you hold to that loyalty . . . and who are these behind you?"

"Ivo and Lys," said Anne. "They served me in Lorin's hold. We have taken a leaf from your missal and peddled packs to Hautarroy and back again. My face is too well known beyond Varne, but we have friends here and there, and gear for the winter—unless you mean to rob us."

"Friends there and *here*," amended Joris. "Stay or press on as you please; a party of my men lies yonder, and there is fire and food and shelter without danger or compulsion."

Red Anne considered him gravely, and raised her shoulders with ever so slight a shrug that somehow daunted him.

"Gramercy, Joris," she whispered; and over her shoulder she called to her companions.

"Lys, Ivo, come here. Give greeting to our night's host, Joris of the Rock."

Lys was slender, with ivory pallor of health and light blue indifferent eyes; her hair was mouse-brown and abundant, her mouth clear-cut and fine above a delicate pointed chin. Ivo, too, was slim to wiriness, and little taller than the girl; his eyes were hostile, dark blue with long lashes, and there was pink on the nose and cheek bones of his thin freckled countenance. They answered with composure the bluff hail of Joris, and the latter sustained a second faint shock to find in both young faces a sullen depth of expression resembling Red Anne's own.

For a moment he felt baffled, as though he were a dog and they three cats, observant and unafraid; then he looked again at Anne and gestured along the stream.

"My men shall build another shelter for the night," he said.

*   *   *

"Joris, you drink no wine?"

"Not now. Wine has been for when you were not here."

Only Red Anne could hear the murmured words; Joris, sprawling beside her, saw her smile faintly in the twilight. She and the others had slept all afternoon—Anne and Lys in their own rough bower, and Ivo in the ramshackle tent of

Joris—and supper round the fire had eased the harshness of their weathered faces. Lys was gravely mute, but Ivo talked with old Osmund; the rest of the men had a fire of their own a score of yards away. Joris and his party sat near the shelters on a grassy ledge above the darkling stream; across the water rose a short steep of heather, crowned by a group of firs that cut black ragged shapes out of the fading rose and yellow of a wide clear afterglow. Only the zenith was blue enough to show a first few stars; eastward was high still cloud, and the gold blur of the mounting moon. The air, although not yet chill, was sad with autumn; the heavy scent of heather warred with the fragrance of burning pine logs and the odours of roasted grouse and venison. A faint breeze stirred above the camp, for the smoke of the two fires rose straightly for a space and then was slanted away toward the east; and owls called to each other amid the nearer woods.

Red Anne grew less severe as the wine went round; Joris sat by her half-tranced, yet acutely aware of her body. The grasp and slide of her fingers on knife or cup or manchet, the turn of her warm rosy throat, the poise and slant of her round arms beneath tight-fitting sleeves, seemed spinning ghostly webs through all his flesh; the fire glow on the near rope of her marvellous hair seared through old bitterness and welded to one sweet consuming need the promise of a thousand forest twilights.

And from their noontide encounter until she noticed that his drinking horn held water, Red Anne had not spoken apart with Joris. Glancing past her shoulder, he saw young Ivo scowl across the fire, and leaned nearer to mutter an idle question.

"What ails your page boy, now?"

"Ivo? He is mortally jealous of anyone who speaks to me. But he is only a lad—faithful, and brave to folly if need be."

"So I perceive; no man has thus regarded me for a period. Can he sing?"

"Ay—Ivo, where is the little harp? Find it and sing to us."

Silently Ivo reached out for the canvas-covered gear on
the pack saddle behind him; presently he was nursing the
instrument, screwing the keys and plucking sad and dainty
sound from tautening strings.

"What will please you, my lady?" he asked, with eyes
half sulky, half appealing.

"A song," replied Red Anne, in a voice grown harder and
deeper.

Ivo lifted his chin, and stared at the blur of the moon, and
sang a triolet in a clear untroubled tenor.

> "An elf I met in Santloy Wood
>   Where rowans flame beside the river.
> When evening on the hilltops stood
> I met an elf in Santloy Wood.
> He looked too happy to be good,
>   His eyes were red, his ears a-quiver,
> That elf I met in Santloy Wood
>   Where rowans flame beside the river!"

"Enough of that," said Anne when he would have sung a
second verse; and Joris caught a gleam of amusement in the
pale eyes of Lys that looked from Anne to Ivo and back again.

"Sing one of Herluin's songs," commanded Anne; and Lys
stared into the fire.

"Who is Herluin?" asked Joris, resentful of standing outside the secrets that these queer creatures shared with his love.

"He paged it with Ivo yonder," was the woman's moody
reply. "Lys, too, remembers him," she added dryly.

"I remember him well," declared Lys in her cool high tones.
"He fled on the night when the Sieur Jehan slew my lord
Count, his brother. Poor Herluin—he should have been a
monk. By now I think he may be. Too sensitive a soul for
this bleak world."

"You did not always mock him," snapped Ivo; and Joris
saw that boy and girl plagued each other with memories.

"Who, I?" responded Lys, with an edge to her delicate
voice. "Oh, no. He kissed me once—or rather thrice—in the

name of his Holy Trinity. But it is true he made good songs."

"This one among them," said Ivo, watching her grimly as he began to sing.

"A score of spears he led that day,
    For strength can woo if prayer be vain,
And smiled when o'er the mailed array
    His banner took the wind again,
    Remembering, as he tightened rein,
        A song she sang of old Provence,
    A ballad with a strange refrain
        Plus faict douceur que violenz.

"When sank the sun on flame and death
    He held her on the saddle's bow;
She cried Our Lady 'neath her breath
    And snatched at steel; he foiled the blow
    And kissed her pallid face aglow,
        But silent scorn was her response;
    The winds of twilight whispered low
        Plus faict douceur que violenz.

"In carven chair before the fire
    Alone and grim he sate all night,
But tore his soul from out the mire
    And freed her in the growing light.
    Yet ere her troop had spurred from sight
        He saw the maid look backward once
    And heard the gale cry down the height
        Plus faict douceur que violenz.

"Lady, yourself the tale shall end.
    Lied that old singer of Provence
Down the long years this word to send:
        Plus faict douceur que violenz."

"A fitting song for the occasion," mocked Lys when it was done.

"As fitting here as in the keep of Campscapel," retorted Ivo.

"Yet not entirely out of place in either," muttered Red Anne, so low that only Joris caught the words.

Then, in a moment, his world changed; Anne's right hand, that had lain in her cross-kneed lap, came down upon his own left hand in a gesture hidden from their companions. The fingers of Joris closed in a mighty clasp; the blood throbbed in his ears, and all that was left of his boyhood leaped in him. He scarcely heard Anne's voice as she bade Lys and Ivo play together; the plaints of harp and flute were joined beyond the fire, and Anne leaned a little toward him, whispering under the lonely sounding music.

"Joris, are you still of your old mind concerning me?"

"Yes."

"And if I give you my love, will you rage if I leave you at times?"

"No, if it be not too often."

"Tell me, is there a pool to bathe in below the camp? I saw none deep enough when I doused my face at noon."

"Not in the stream," breathed Joris. "But up the slope behind, and down the other side, beyond the larches and under the oaks, there is a pool where deer drink. It is over my head in the middle. There is deep grass about it, but the edge is sand. Shall—shall I show you?"

"No. I will find my way. Give me the quarter of an hour and then come if you will."

"*If I will.* When?"

"Oh, let the fire burn low, and your men finish their drinking. And I must find me a towel; I am not yet altogether a savage, though I saw in your face that I have changed."

"Not—not in my heart."

"Eh, have you fashioned an Anne that does not change?"

"*No.*"

Harp and flute were silent; Osmund, with wine in his gray beard, was stuttering maudlin approval, but the deepened tone of his chief put a period to his words. Anne recaptured her hand and raised it in air.

"Ivo, bring me the harp," she commanded; and then, taking the instrument from him, she looked up at the boy's grim face.

"What will please *you*, Ivo?" she inquired, half smiling.

"Your own pleasure, my lady," responded Ivo smoothly.

"Spoken like a courtier. Lys, what will you choose?"

" 'Brisingamen,' my lady," came the cool high answer.

" 'Brisingamen?' Spoken like a nun. Have your will, though it be dreary."

Joris lay stark and enchanted, bound by the first deep note of a "discord," a song almost rhymeless and of a rhythm strange to him.

"Between the timeless roots of Ygdrasil
  Where seven metals hissed in shining veins
  From gloom to vaulted gloom around their dinging anvils,
  Laboured the four swart gnomes.
  In fume and sweat, with rage of craft and cunning
  Deep, deep in the Kingdom of Stone,
  They wrought Brisingamen.

"Brisingamen, the god-desirèd necklace,
  A chain of burning and melodious diamonds
  Compact of stolen rainbow-shards and sunbeams,
  Foam from the moon-path on the midnight sea,
  Ice from the splintered helm of the Frost King.

"Athwart the fields in airs of windy evening,
  Over the murmuring grass from the world's rim,
  Bruising the clover that kissed them
  Moved to the smoking earth-cleft,
  The cream-white feet of Freya.

"Freya, Odin's golden daughter,
  Calm with doom-wise calm of Asgard,
  Deep, deep in the Kingdom of Stone,
  Bought Brisingamen.

"Athwart the fields in mist of windless morning,
  Over the silent grass to the world's rim,
  Brushing tears of dew from the shamed clover,
  Wandered the bruised feet of Odin's daughter.

"Four times looped around her golden shoulders,
  Hiding the earth-stains on her shining shoulders,
  Freya bore with grave greed
  The chain of burning and melodious diamonds,
  A fourfold fury of frozen fire,
  Smiting with white light
  The groaning gates of Asgard.

"When her eyes, proud and haunted,
Bright above the earthling splendour,
Glowed in sight of the hero-kindred,
Age withered the brow of Odin.
Hœnir hushed the Harp-lilt,
Tyr gnashed his Sword-hilt;
Thor let the Hammer fall
And Earth trembled to the shock;
Doom-wind yelped in the high hall
With fore-blast of Ragnarok."

Vaguely Joris knew names and stories of the old Northland
gods; no fret of ignorance disturbed his hearing of the
ancient song. But indeed the words barely mattered, save for
the shapes they lent to Red Anne's marvellous voice.

Once he glanced away from her glowing head; the gloom
between the two fires was patched with the stricken faces
of his men as they stood or crouched to listen. No sound of
breath or steel or leather invaded the hearkening trance of the
ravine; the plash and murmur of the stream seemed muted,
and the owls had ceased to call amid the woods. Old Osmund's
mouth was open, and his pig's cheeks were creased as with
pain. Ivo's staring eyes were alive with worshipping torment.
Beyond Ivo the girl Lys had lost her shrewish mask; if
malice prompted the choice of that song it had recoiled upon
her, for tears spilled slowly into the hollows beneath her
downcast lashes.

"The Kingdom of Elfin," thought Joris, "is wheresoever
Anne sings. Anne, Anna, Diana—Diana Queen of Elfin—
and now none other can lift voice when she has ended. This
is the wedding song of Joris of the Rock."

Half an hour later he sat in his tent, that was made of
stakes and boughs and tarred felt bound with strips of hide
and weighted with stones. A star winked through a gap in
the wall; Joris tugged at his beard and groaned, and bit one
hand to stem the sudden shivering of his body. Of all things he
had deemed himself readiest for this; yet twice he reached

to the felt door flap before he jerked himself to his feet and gained the tranquil outer air.

A sharp ring of metal on stone told him his camp guard stirred beside the ashes of the further fire; far along the lonely valley a stag belled faintly. As Joris turned to the steep larch-crested slope the moon slid slowly from a pallid bar of cloud; three paces, and he was checked by a strange sound from the second shelter a dozen yards from his own. The boy Ivo had lain down at its entrance, but he was not to be seen; and presently Joris knew that Ivo lay weeping within. Lys was there with him, and pity and impatience blended in her voice.

"Why do you stay to be tortured?" she demanded. "Have you not arts enough to make a living alone? Go to, you know you have. Do you think by dwelling in fire to become a salamander?"

The choked reply was unintelligible. Joris curled a contemptuous lip and soundlessly strode uphill.

At the top was a breath of wind that drowsed among the larches. Moonlight played softly golden on smooth boles and sound-deadening carpet of needles; autumn odours assailed the outlaw, and pallid mists defined the nearer hollows, while in the east the blue-black sky was fretted by jet-black rocky heights above the limits of the Forest of Honoy.

Joris inhaled deeply; the night air was wine of triumph, the hand that had trembled was firm on his belted sword. Below was a gleam as of a gold, sharp-cut by goblin oak boughs; Joris trod swiftly downhill, godlike in strength and desire. Beneath his feet the whisper of larch needles gave place to the driven rustle of grass; trunks of the oaks seemed shifting to impede him, and his eyes dazzled at the shaken glitter of the moon's reflection in the pool. Red Anne's name began to hammer in his head, with such long-buried foolish words as his mother had used before he grew too tall to run to her for comfort.

And suddenly he saw the witch—the faint sheen of her shoulders, the white pride of her lifted arms as she loosed from around her head the tight-coiled hair that still warred faintly with the all-silvering moonlight.

"*Hola,* Joris!" she chanted quietly, turning toward him so that he saw her body very pale gold and barred with shadows of leaves and branches.

"Joris," she said again as he stumbled forward, "take me and make me forget for a while."

"Forget what?" he muttered, pausing with nothing alive in him save eyes and heart and breath.

"All that has gone before," she replied more strongly; and the shadows slid and altered and fled as she moved a pace forward, ankle-deep in the autumn grasses beside her tumbled clothing.

"Are you not cold?" whispered Joris; as she shook her head and the down-rippling coils of her heavy hair, he laughed and fell on one knee and spoke again.

"Said I not you came of the line of the old gods? Where are your dogs to tear me, Diana by the Pool?"

But Red Anne only smiled, bending above him to kiss his brow and lips, standing arrow-straight again to draw his bearded face against her cool body. And then at length the blood rose up in Joris; he gasped and reeled to his feet and lifted her from the ground, gripping her so that she smiled and swore as he carried her under the trees.

"Line of all gods or no," she murmured after a time, "I still am chiefly a woman. Joris, gold-bearded Joris, must *I* next be cast in a river, as was my marble sister whom they dug from the mound at Dor?"

"A river of sleep, maybe," breathed Joris in her ear. "But you have called me gold-beard; listen at last to my runes."

So Red Anne listened at last; and when he had told them and given his interpretation, she chuckled and tightened her arm across his breast.

"You do not admire my runes?" demanded Joris, surprised.

"Ah, yes—but I have heard them before."

"*Where?*"

"In Hastain as a child."

"And what was said of them?"

"Only what Ingolard said—that they foretold a doom to be accomplished in those parts by one to rule therein. Are *you* the one, think you?"

"Maybe, if war were upon us, and my thieves a free company."

"Am I then but a milestone in this lord's path?" mocked Anne softly. "The witch is mastered by the pool—another period in the progress of the Chevalier Joris."

"*You!*" came a dire loverlike growl. "You are . . . a woman who shall see what things her man can do."

"Great things, I swear, if your exploits be all to one measure. So shall we soar together, you and I? Eh, Joris, it is long since I was happy as I am to-night."

"But you make light of my runes?"

For a second of time Red Anne was silent; then she chuckled again, and after chuckling sighed.

"No, not I," she responded. "Red is content with its new-shriven Gold. Yet there was nothing in your runes of three trees on a hill and a great shadow beside."

"What trees are those? What shadow?"

"I know not. Think you a witch does not seek to read her own future? Only another can read it, never one's self; and all upon whom I have worked have seen me pass into such shadow. And some have seen me happy beyond, but most have failed through terror. Do you remember the dwarf who was at Hastain with our puppets, the dwarf who brought you to me up in Alanol?"

"Ay. What of him?"

"He died striving to see for me. He prayed me to press him beyond the veil with all my powers; and I so pressed him, and he died."

Joris was silent, tasting the first thin lees of triumph; flesh that had made them one cried out on spirit that mocked at unity.

"I have not made you forget," he growled; and suddenly old curiosity stirred angrily within him.

"Since you speak of your craft," he went on, "tell me how you knew that the Riders of Camp'scapel were coming upon us that day at Capel Conan."

"One of my falconers bore a carrier pigeon."

"Ha! secret stairs and carrier pigeons . . ."

"Ay, I read your mind. You think the most of my magic is adroitness? There is more than that in it, Joris."

"And also . . . you aim to go on November Eve . . ."

"Yes. To the Singing Stones. To meet the Devil."

"Even so. Sometimes I have wondered if the 'black' of my runes was indeed the—the Count Lorin."

"Do not speak of Lorin any more. We loved each other, he and I. The day he died I had betrayed our love—no, I had no hand in his death; I gave myself in pity to another, and later stood apart from all that night's doings. Or Lorin might not have died. So speak no more of him. But since you, too, have loved me long and well, I tell you this: I am the mistress of my coven, Joris. I meet the Devil as an equal. *I* kiss him on the shoulder, and not often. You think of witches as a pack of snivelling outcast whores; many such there may be, but there are others, too. Little enough has our Devil had from me for what I have learned of him. Little enough save gold; ay, devils need gold, for I know of none who can make it."

"But—but in the rites, do you not give this—all this glory beneath my fingers . . ."

"There comes a moment in the dance when that is the right, the only thing to do. It is a ritual woven very long ago. Strange powers rise from the ground while we dance it—powers of earth and night and fire. I do not often dance that dance; and when I do, my yielding is of ritual, not of lust."

"But surely *he*—he delights in you above all others?"

"Our devil gets his fill of women, Joris. I am only a part of his rites to him."

"And, Anne . . . *your* devil . . . are there many devils of equal rank?"

"Many and many, each to his coven. But ours is Grand Master of the Covens of Nordanay. And he has taught me subtle things . . . and has promised me one thing I lack, and still I lack that thing, so that I know not now if it be withheld by feebleness or malice."

"What thing is that?"

"A child."

Joris sat stunned and silent; his hands, that beneath Anne's cloak had plagued her lovely body, grew motionless on that warm tragic flesh.

"But L—Lorin de Campscapel——" he stammered at length, and broke off in sullen vexation at having uttered the name.

"Ay, Lorin never fathered any child," Anne murmured. "I laboured long enough to lift that enchantment from him. For *that* he bade me wander at will, knowing I strove to give him a son. But I myself am barren, Joris; oh, I am sure by now. I have eaten mandrake root enough and chanted a legion of spells. And for *that* I stayed your hand when we met in Capel Conan; no man hurts a child when I have power to prevent him. And no witch of my coven dares openly to cross me in that matter—or indeed in any other matter. No fat of babes at the Singing Stones—so purge your mind of that folly. And now, once more, Lorin is dead—and the others never counted. But you are here and alive; make me a duchess if it please *you,* but make me a mother to please myself, fierce Joris of the Rock!"

*   *   *

"Give you good day, friend Adelgar," called Red Anne, when first she came into the limestone chasm; and Adelgar grew stiff and saluted, his pasty vulturine face going red at this recognition. A dozen others she remembered in the hold above Alanol; Ivo nodded easily at this man and that

among them, and even Lys smiled faintly as they touched their
steel caps a second time. But Joris felt for a moment that he
had set foot on a quagmire; it angered him that these his followers should have seen Anne daily while he moved ob-
scurely beyond her furthest skyline.

Then he shrugged the emotion aside, and made for his comrade and love a lordly welcome to her new home beneath the
Rock. Henceforth their cause should be one if he could so in-
sure it; yet on a morning some weeks later he learned that
his qualm was not without foundation.

He slept in his rush-strewn cave, although it was near midday; for he had journeyed through a calm October night and
reached the chasm at sunrise. Outside, by the frowning entry,
Red Anne hummed a tune as she spread his shirts and her
own to dry on bushes or boulders. White smoke rose thinly
from the chieftain's own fire close at hand; farther down
the ravine was thicker smoke from the ovens, and farther
away again, beyond the tethered hill ponies, a score of men
were playing a kind of football on the flat reach of sand and
peat at the foot of the great crag. Close to them were mounds
that hid the shattered bones of the unransomed dead; the
core of their football was, indeed, a skull, and its cover un-
tanned cowhide stitched with hempen string. Some as they
played swore loudly that ghosts were siding with their op-
ponents, although even the hardiest jester avoided the place
in the dark; now that the mists had gone the autumn sunlight
was pleasant in that ominous cleft of the hills.

So thought the viper that crawled near the highest fire, until its blunt black nose encountered a crumble of hot ash;
then, to a wrathful hiss, the gleaming body twirled about and
drove for the dark cave mouth.

Red Anne, seeing it, uttered a deep and wordless cry and
snatched up the club with which she had beaten the linen.
Joris started awake and heard the viper's death blow; voices
and rapid footsteps approached as he dived into the sunshine
and found the reptile's body with Anne bent grimly above it.

Beyond Red Anne, as by magic, a dozen figures were gathering—Lys with arrow on half-drawn bow, Ivo clutching a dagger, Rufin and Adelgar and others, most of them poising ax or sword or guisarme.

Joris stood to his height, reading the threat in their eyes; Red Anne had once cried out, and these sprang up to defend her. Only Rufin among them could Joris count his own—but Rufin was unarmed, and already grinning aside at Lys whom he greatly admired.

Anne turned and chuckled, showing the snake to her friends; weapons sank to earth, and laughter and words broke out around the cave mouth. Joris, too, summoned a laugh, and clipped his saviour around the body to kiss her in sight of all.

Presently they were alone again, and then he was very thoughtful. Anne had been with him less than a month, and only the sorriest brutes of his following did not respond to her presence. She had dressed wounds and an injured limb or two, making her patients slaves for life; three of them, sitting about in the sunshine, had carved her a dozen skittles of bone with lopsided wooden balls to throw at them. There was scrambling to gather her arrows when she shot at the crude butts; and she knew half the men by name before her first week by the Rock was done. Her coming had buttressed the power of Joris, but not all his lover's pride could deaden the chieftain's instinct which told him that at Anne's word that power might also be sorely imperilled. And as though she read his mind, the woman made an end of her task and knelt beside her mate.

"Joris, you are glum," she said. "Go in again and sleep."

"Nay, I have slept enough," he replied, eased by her tone and her nearness. "But what should I have done had the viper waited a week?"

For the time of Allhallows drew near, when Anne might be straying again; and reminder of her ungrudged liberty brought a faint unusual shyness to the witch's rosy face.

"This time I stay with you," she promised—adding after a moment: "Unless you whip me forth because your men admire what here is yours alone."

Joris caught at her hand and crushed it in his grip.

"Gramercy, reptile," he growled to the dark dead shape in the dust.

"Mother Eve will be angry to hear you thank her enemy," mocked Anne, tugging her hand away from him to nurse it.

"Mother Eve and her daughters are little enough to me," affirmed Joris. "You are a daughter of Lilith, if ever there was one. Ay, and your Lys is another."

"Your Rufin finds her one at least, although he might not say it so. Bid him take heed how he frets her; it is a dangerous slut in the sulks. She has pined for that strange lad Herluin who fled from the hold of Campscapel. She is most formidably chaste these days—ay, and when last we went to the Singing Stones she stuck steel in one of the covens who mocked her."

A prospect of Rufin's early demise held no distaste for Joris, for the braggart tired him at times; but such an affair might lead to disastrous quarrelling. Winter beside the Rock was often a time of tension; fog-bound, sleet-bound, snow-bound, outlaw tempers grew short and outlaw weapons loose.

"I will douse our Rufin's fire for a space," he promised. "I would not lose him yet—or you your sister in Lilith."

"My little sister in Lilith . . . bah, Ivo should serve her turn," said Anne with the sudden brutality which sometimes darkened her beauty. "They are limp comrades now, the pair of them. Sometimes I wish . . ."

"Wish what?"

But Red Anne shook her head and would say no more.

And limp comrades or no, Lys and Ivo were something of a problem during that cold season. Sometimes they quarrelled like cats; but unlike cats they came to heel at one lash of Red Anne's voice. Sometimes they were friendly, and then Joris felt a strain on their leashed hatred of himself. He had so long gauged the motives of his followers that it irked him a little to dwell in sight of those two comely heads whose thoughts eluded him; and only their joint devotion to Red Anne restrained him from gross experiment with girl and boy.

Yet for the most part he lived in a contentment far exceeding any he had previously known; the tenuous golden thread of his love, that had held through so many dark and violent years, was now spun to a bright tapestry about him. Red Anne hallooed to her man across the frozen hills, knelt beside him above the stricken red deer, plunged in his wake through icy moor streams, and netted the stars in her unbound hair as she half unmanned him with artful wild caresses. How these were learned he cared not; he gleaned from them a fury of joy that slew all other emotions.

In the sports which filled the finer days Anne took her part with a skill that delighted him. When they made a snow man far up the ravine, she stood two hundred and fifty yards away and drove four arrows in succession into the white lumpish face and body; only Joris himself, and a dozen of his men, did better than that. Rolling great snowballs to the cliff edges to floor the men who raced and dodged beneath—flying on the rough game sledges down white steeps of the frozen hills—curling with flat stones, or swaying on crude bone skates, across the dark ice of the lonely tarns—the witch who had ruled as a countess romped like a carefree boy. Sometimes, after the evening meal, she sang to the whole throng; but oftener, in the cave of Joris, she played to him and a few others, crooning strange airs against monotonous choruses hummed by Ivo and Lys. Also she worked mild magic for his diversion—making a puppet talk, and conjuring with knives and coins and kerchiefs; so that the winter seemed half gone before Joris was aware.

Then, on a still night about the time of Christmas, he drank more deeply than he intended, and overstepped restraint of his old curiosity.

"Tell *my* fortune," he said, "if you cannot achieve clear vision of your own. The two must interlock; and my runes have served only thus far. Rufin, another log; and Gandulf, another wine skin. What do you say, Anne?"

Red Anne set her drinking horn aside and looked levelly at him. Beneath that gaze he grew restive, aware that never before had he challenged her witchcraft in presence of others.

"Do you really ask it of me?" she demanded curiously.

Joris was silent for a second or two; then he roughened his voice to efface that hesitation.

"Ay, that I do," he replied. "A fortune not of the fair-ground sort."

"The other is not easily done," rejoined the woman deeply. "But what I can I will achieve. Lys?"

Lys shook her head, and it seemed to Joris that the cheeks of Lys grew paler in the lights of torch and pine logs.

"Ivo, are *you* willing?"

The boy nodded, blushing, and then stared into the fire.

"But——" began Lys, and checked her words, for Anne turned sharply upon her.

"Hold your craven tongue," she commanded. "The thing can but be tried again. Once more, Joris—you wish it?"

Joris peered at her face and the faces of her companions; and again it was as though he were a dog, and they three cats who watched him. Resentment of mystery fretted him, and he grinned at the startled interest of his sprawling lieutenants. Adelgar was not there, but Gandulf and Madoc and Rufin sat awaiting what might befall.

"Yes," he growled sharply; and Red Anne shrugged her shoulders.

Then she lifted an iron spit and gathered the peats and logs to one bright central blaze. Facets of limestone gleamed through the murk, eyes red-rimmed with the stinging smoke shone in bronzed faces; at Anne's imperious gesture Ivo got to his feet, his shadow spreading and dwindling as he rounded the fire and sank to a sitting posture with back to the glow and face toward Red Anne. An expectant silence fell, and from the outer darkness drifted the faint noise of the stream and the thin clamour of song from caves below.

"A candle," said Red Anne to Joris, "and let the torches be quenched. Lys, will you hold the flame at least?"

"As you please," replied the girl, her face a mask of indifference as she sidled behind her lady. Joris passed her the lighted candle, and folded his hands round his knees; when all was set he found he could see the features of Anne and Ivo in profile. Red witch and haggard boy sat cross-legged and close together but not quite opposite, so that Ivo's left knee lay on Anne's, while Lys crouched on her heels behind Anne's left shoulder, holding the flame out of Anne's sight but full in Ivo's face.

"Joris, your sheathed sword hither," belled Anne. "Lay it beside me—so. Now silent and motionless all, whatsoever betide us; a word or a cough may spoil the whole. Ivo, are you ready?"

"Ready, my lady," croaked the lad.

"Then look at me for a moment."

Ivo shivered and looked; Red Anne twitched a hand to the strings of her tunic and swiftly laid bare the curve of her left shoulder.

"Take my right hand in yours, and watch the flame," she bade him. "Set your left hand on my shoulder, and stop trembling, fool. Empty your soul of sadness, your mind of present knowledge, your heart and loins of desire. What do your hands feel now?"

"Your flesh," muttered Ivo flatly.

"Forget I am Red Anne. Forget you are Ivo. Forget the joy you had of me, the shame and tears I brought you, the first hour in the keep of Campscapel, the last hour in the forest. Forget the time and place and season. . . ."

Joris stirred and swallowed hard, but none paid heed; he was no longer master in his own cave. Suddenly quite sober, he bit on his new knowledge; Ivo, that glum-faced rat—the

thing was flung in his face, so that before his lieutenants he
must pretend he had known.

Then Joris saw the youth's face, dead-white beneath wind
burn and candle glow, with eyes whose pupils were unnaturally
large and mouth that twitched with a queer repeated spasm.
Anne made long stroking passes with her free arm.

"What do your hands feel now?" she murmured at the end
of silent minutes.

"Nothing," came the reply, in a dull whisper.

Anne's chin was shadowed from the fire by Ivo's body,
but Joris saw a sparkle of sweat steal down the triangle of
rosy brow between the masses of shining hair.

"She looks like a fallen angel," he thought, and then: "I
have loved her from head to heel and know not a tithe of
her secret thoughts. I am only one of a daft procession . . .
no, by the chimes of hell, she was right. Lorin she loved, and me
she loves, and the rest were nothing, Ivo among them. It is *my*
child she looks to bear."

In each month since her coming to him Anne had one day
pulled a faint particular grimace, and Joris loved deeply
enough to grieve awhile in her grief, although any sign of a
child would soon enough have irked him. And now the fire
of Anne was expended on craft that daunted him; fallen angel
or no, she was grown to a deadly stranger.

"What do you feel *now?*" she demanded a third time; and
Ivo's answer was stronger, but toneless and slighghtly gasping
as though with shortened breath.

"A coming in the left hand, a going in the right."

"Ay, and what do you see?"

"Nothing. Black nothing that whirls to a standstill. . . .
Now it is still and very deep."

"Is there a light in the blackness?"

"No—yes—a star low down, and greenish blue. It grows.
It is not a star, but a ball of luminous mist. It fills the darkness up."

"Look in the mist for this cave," said Anne, and lifted her

left hand to touch Ivo between the eyes with its extended thumb.

"*See!*" she muttered fiercely; and then: "What do you see?"

"I see the cave, and those therein, and my own body like a doll's. Round all the heads save yours and mine are cloudy trails of imagining, waving this way and that like drowned weeds in a stream. Some thoughts are plain, and some very dim. *Your* head is set in a sharp orange glow; sometimes it fades a little, and then you fan it up with a shiver of will. A thought breaks loose from the glow, and stabs round the cave like a comet, weaving a pattern of light in its going."

"Ay. What thinks Lys?"

"That this stress slays Ivo's body, unless you loose it soon, for Ivo loves you dearly and love impedes the vision."

"What thinks Joris?"

"The thought of Joris leaped sideways when he heard it was known. The backward-fading swirl holds Gandulf and Madoc his friends and all others here his foes. Now he bears on the runes that brought him to this pass, and quests the future with an anxious greed."

"Ay. And Gandulf?"

"Gandulf is cursing witchcraft. His thought blurs and writhes with shame, because since you began he has three times secretly signed the Cross."

"And Madoc?"

"Madoc pities Ivo, and thinks you truly a succubus born of——"

"And Rufin?"

"Rufin's mind also has leaped and twirled like a wounded weasel. But he bears stoutly on the thought that it would be good to bite the dainty neck of Lys. Also he is afraid; and he damns a louse in his left armpit."

"So," and Anne groped at and caught up the sword beside her, drawing the hilt beneath her hand that clasped Ivo's.

"Whose sword is this?" she asked quickly.

"Joris of the Rock's."

"Withdraw your sight from the present. What shall befall in a year's time?"

Ivo's shape was silent for a moment, and Joris saw that Ivo's eyes had now a dreadful inward squint. At length the gray lips moved.

"Many things . . . hidden turmoil in the realm . . . the king in—in danger of sickness . . . lords in council, and a name on all their lips."

"Whose name?"

"Joris of the Rock's."

The body of Joris grew rigid; his mind quailed to a flare of triumph.

"What shall befall Joris?"

"The realm shall wait on his word: he holds great power in the moors; only you could break him, and you wish him never any harm, but where you move with him it is very dark."

Lys nodded slowly behind the candle flame, so that the shadows fled and returned above her cheek bones and chin; her pale eyes glittered strangely, and only she seemed aloof from the moment's absorption.

"Can you see beyond the darkness?"

"Yes—yes—Joris laughing amain at the end of a great battle. Thousands of slain in the meadows, and the royal standard taken. . . . Ay, and ten thousand men shall follow Joris. No, it is blurred and lost; but there will be a boy in the hills, the son of Joris of the Rock."

Joris gasped and began an oath; Red Anne humped her shoulders a little and bent a blazing stare on her victim.

"What of myself?" she breathed. "Myself apart from Joris? Is that son *mine?*"

"I cannot see. I am bound and blinded by the mercy you once showed me. Ah—*ah*—a great pain severs us, and I see you pass into shadow. Shadow immense and dreadful, like nothing in the world. Your hair is quenched and lost to me; over the shadow stand three trees, very still among rocks against clear sky. *No,* they are not trees; they are—— I dare not look. Turn me away or I perish."

"Do I move beyond that shadow?" demanded Anne abruptly.

"Ay, I see you again—spent and bloodless, but very happy."

"Loose him," whispered Lys. "*He* is spent!"

"Ivo," said Anne, paying no heed to her flame bearer, "what of yourself in a year from now?"

"Nothing. I cannot see. There is uttermost blackness."

"And of Lys?"

"Blackness again; no, starlight, and foam of heaving waters. But—Lys too is not unhappy; no, it flashes away from me."

"And—and——"

Red Anne's voice grew hoarse; she was losing some grip of power, but still she drove on her way.

"Ivo, cast your mind *back* to the slaying of Count Lorin. How was that deed accomplished?"

Ivo's face was contorted, and Ivo's body drooped, yet words began to crackle in his throat. Red Anne leaned forward to catch them, but behind her Lys snarled softly and blew out the flame of the candle.

Ivo collapsed against Anne's outstretched arm. Bundling the limp figure roughly sideways, Anne turned on the girl and struck her full in the face with a clenched fist.

"Bitch!" she belled in a fury. "Why have I borne so long with your accursed meddling!"

Lys raised one hand to her smitten cheek but gestured calmly with the other at the foam on Ivo's lips.

"Slay us both, then," she mocked, "and on to your sacred grove. If Joris has two friends here I have only one, and he dying."

But Anne turned back to Ivo and took him in her arms, calling him softly by name and chafing his thin body from pit of stomach to throat. Presently the boy stirred and spluttered; Anne whipped a kerchief from her bosom and wiped the foam

away. Ivo came back into Ivo's eyes, and, finding himself thus
held, drooped lids and turned his face against Anne's shoulder; and at that the staring Joris got to his feet and spoke into
the shadows.

"Rufin, attend," he rasped. "If any word of this night's doings spreads beyond the seven of us, it will be yours, in wine
or heedlessness or mischief. Let me hear a murmur or see a
sign of betrayal and you are trussed and rolled from the
Rock. Tell me you understand me!"

"I understand you, Captain," responded jaunty Rufin. "But
I shall not stand easily by to see harm done to the demoiselle,
for it seems to me that she has ended a very beastly business."

Lys shot a venomous glance at the speaker, and shrilled response to his chivalry.

"Red-eyed hog of the forest, I give myself for my lady to
cut in pieces before I take *you* for my champion!"

"Lys goes unharmed," said Anne from the cave floor. "Joris,
turn your men out—Ivo, go you with Lys—Lys, give him a
cordial, the bittersweet and briony. And child, I did wrong
to strike you, and you right to thwart me. And now, until
morning, begone."

Red Anne turned and threw herself flat on her cloak, with
face buried against her forearms; and Lys, before she rose,
bent forward and kissed the bowed resplendent head. Joris
saw the cave emptied save for Anne and himself, and drew
the felt and canvas door flap across its frame of wood. Then
he turned to the prone and exhausted figure beside the fire.

"Are you content?" came her deep voice, with an edge of
something like scorn to its weight of weariness.

"Yes," said Joris simply. "Even to know how greatly you
pitied your Ivo. But I have tried you sorely; I shall ask such
things no more. Yet some time I would see you rule beside
the Singing Stones. And some time else, in this place or in a
castle solar, I would see you nursing our son."

Anne made a little sound between a laugh and a sigh, and

presently Joris set the curtain open again to draw the smoke from the cave. Then he covered his love with blankets, and sat awhile beside her, listening to her quiet breathing as she lay flat and helpless in sleep. Once he touched a thick wide-flung rope of her hair; once he almost laughed aloud, foretasting the future half revealed to him. Then he shut and secured the door flap, and wrapped himself up to lie down by Red Anne, and in a while was dreaming of power and battle, and of a strange gnome who came to him in the hills and said, "I am the son of Diana and Joris of the Rock."

VI. SAINT–ELOY–OVER–HARDONEK

"BRING me the cedarwood box with the goldbeaters' skin," said Brother Leo, shutting his tired eyes and leaning back in the stone seat, that was cushioned because he was old and racked with rheumatism.

Juhel leaped to obey, for Brother Leo let him watch the painting and gilding of the great capital V that had been three months in the doing; also Juhel had learned to puddle the colours in their little dishes, and to change the water pots and cleanse the dainty brushes. For the sake of the beautiful work he endured the fusty smell of Brother Leo and his furs; and presently white head and black were bent again above the vellum.

There, in the whirls of crimson and green, Michal sneered from her window at capering David, whose harp was now to be embellished; Juhel felt strange squirms of satisfaction in throat and body as magic grew beneath the aged blue-veined hands, that only ceased from trembling when thus employed. But to-day, indeed, they began to tremble even now, so that Brother Leo had perforce to lay down his little knife; and tears furrowed his withered cheeks, because he did not want to die before his lovely V was perfected. Then Juhel's heart turned over in him for pity and for anger against he knew not what, and he leaned against the mouldy furs and ventured a choked whisper.

"Brother, let me try—I will not spoil it."

The old monk blinked with quick hostility; but the brown chubby face, the big dark eyes and quivering childish mouth, gave him to smile as he shook his bowed head.

"No, boy," he murmured gently. "You are how old?—

eleven, too young yet awhile. But Saint Eloy heard your offer, and the ungracious answer in my soul. *Vana gloria* indeed; I am chidden by my own handiwork. See, I will draw you a little shrine of the good saint, and you shall colour it as you please; and it shall be your offering on Holy Innocents' Day."

Juhel understood only the second half of that speech, but his face glowed at the promise; the low humming of autumn sea wind, the twilit sheer of Saint Eloy's towers, the pallid sheen of the moon in the eastern sky beyond them—these joined to stamp the moment in his memory, filling him with the peace of ancient buildings founded and shaped in love.

Half an hour later he echoed Brother Leo's sigh at the iron boom of the compline bell, that summoned the monk to holy office and drove the boy to supper and bed. Juhel scuttled away down the west walk of the splendid cloister, paused at the lavatory entry to glance at his hands, decided that this evening they would pass Brother Adrian's scrutiny by the refectory door—and jumped at the eldritch whoop of Folquin de Forne by the long stone trough within.

"Juhel! hi, Juhel!" called tow-haired fair-skinned Folquin, bounding out upon the smaller boy. "Have you heard? The sub-prior is come home again. Hamo is killed, and five of the men, and the great banner and all the money and horses were stolen. They were set upon in the forest by Joris of the Rock!"

At Folquin's first word Juhel had become a different creature. Rapture, and even candour, vanished from his face; the cherub became an elf, and his questioning voice harboured derision.

"Who is Joris of the Rock?" he demanded, as the pair of them made for the refectory; for he liked to ruin the enthusiastic declamations of Folquin; and Folquin snorted, his eagerness stemmed by scorn.

"Joris of the Rock? Why, a great murdering forest thief who eats two Juhels for supper every night—did you not know *that?*"

"Do I ever know anything until you have told me it?"
asked Juhel, demurely ogling his companion beneath bent
brows.

"You *are* a fool," said Folquin angrily, and flung away from
him.

Juhel grinned and followed, knowing that he would hear
the news at table; for the only silent meals were dinner and
collation, which the boys took with their elders. Had he treated
Folquin thus a month ago, Juhel would have been well
thumped; that sideways ogle had constantly provoked the older
boy, and many a rapid flight had Juhel taken, only to writhe
and squeal at last in his captor's merciless grasp. But somehow beautiful Folquin discovered that half his victim's anguish
was enjoyment; abruptly the torturings ceased, and for a
time each boy was ashamed to notice the other. Now they were
on speaking terms, but Folquin did not know that Juhel loved
him, and Juhel clung to his method of irritation lest Folquin
find out and grow shy once more.

That night, besides rye bread and "souse" or onion pottage,
there was a treat of raisins, given by the prior because the
good sub-prior's life was spared to them; and the buzzing
voices of thirty boys discussed the robbery and killing and the
exploits of Brother Matthias and his iron-shod staff.

"It is a shame he might not bear a sword," cried Folquin.
"He would have slain Joris with a sword. What is a staff against
a sword? They were cowards, the servants who ran away. I
hope my lord Prior has them flogged. If they had all stood
together they might have beaten the robbers off."

"Folquin should have been there," said Juhel indistinctly,
his mouth being full of bread. "With a sword," he added more
clearly, addressing the tall pewter salt cellar. "What are twenty
great robbers to Folquin and a sword?"

"Bang his head afterward, Folquin," said somebody else.

Folquin's angry blue eyes gave Juhel a pleasant thrill.

"Bah!" exclaimed Folquin. "*He* would have run roaring
down the road."

Juhel nodded cheerfully, and a moment later thrust an uncomfortable remark into a lull of talk.

"If we have raisins because the sub-prior was saved," he observed, "we should have no bread because Hamo and the rest were killed."

"Juhel, you *are* a fool!" exploded Folquin again.

Juhel said nothing more, but that night he prayed to the Sieur Jesus and to the Blessed Virgin not only for the souls of the dead servants, and for Brother Matthias who was so brave, but also for the men who ran away from Joris, because they now must feel so sorry and ashamed. Then he prayed as usual that Jesus and Mary would help Brother Leo's V; but again as usual he said nothing to the Sieur God, for of Him Juhel was mortally afraid. And as for the Holy Ghost, It seemed to the small boy not a shining Dove, but a tall hooded Terror without a face.

*   *   *

Either horn of the cliff that protected the harbour of Hardonek was crowned with a great monastery—Saint Eloy on the east, Saint Remigius on the west. Behind them the gray stone wharves and houses fringed the southern arc of the little bay; between them, and hundreds of feet below, rode in and out the bright brown sails of fishing vessels, or wider canvas of a cog or galley laden with wine or wood or onions or quarried stone. Juhel could never remember a time when the chimes of Saint Eloy had not been echoed or forestalled, faintly or sharply as the wind decreed, by the chimes of Saint Remigius across the deep green water; and only on the days of All Souls and of Holy Innocents was he purposely reminded of the dark times before his coming to the coast.

Vaguely he thought of the Sieur de Ath and of the Lady Aveline as his father and mother; some time, he knew, he would meet them, with Leu, his half-brother, and the cousin called Tiphaine. That would be in the dreadful hour of which he sang in the Mass for the Dead:

"Tuba mirum spargens sonum,
Per sepulcra regionum
Coget omnes ante thronum."

But he was baffled when he tried to think what he should say to them. Only the Virgin Mary let herself be loved without question; in Juhel a customary reserve was sometimes shattered by artless greed for affection—a greed which generally shamed him before its force was spent. Thus, when once he contrived to hold a fistful of Brother Odo's robe through some five minutes of a grammar lesson, he was not surprised when Brother Odo cuffed him soundly and deliberately. Juhel wept as in duty bound, yet something in him triumphed over Brother Odo's contempt; for the young monk's gentle face had lit before it hardened, and Juhel knew that he was nearly hugged instead of clouted. Then there was Folquin, the lad of spirit, the born leader and tormentor, whose armour Juhel had somehow breached; but the rest of his schoolfellows held little interest for his questing and secretive mind.

And from those of his own size Juhel brooked no violence; he often cried as he fought, and always gave rather more than he got, so that he was generally left to his own devices. Rough comradeship he really did not understand; he was seldom truly happy save with a monk or two in cloister, library, or garden. Reading he liked, and feeding the goldfish in the little fountain pool of the herbarium, and above all, singing in the choir; the last was an accomplishment which saved him many sullen hours at games for which he had no wit or aptitude. Nevertheless he swam well, climbed rocks skilfully, and shot a goodly arrow; for in none of those arts had he to work with others or others to depend on him.

Until he was over twelve this was the daily plan of Juhel's cloistered life.

At half-past five in summer and half-past six in winter Brother Adrian marched down the long dorter ringing a little hand bell pitched to rouse the woefullest sluggard. Followed a donning of clothes, a wash in the stony trough, a scuffle round the three great towels whose increasing wetness made for early rising; then a sedate procession, two and two into the great dim church for prime and the Mass of the Blessed Virgin, and sometimes Chapter Mass as well. Thereafter the boys broke fast alone with Brother Adrian, for the monks ate nothing before noon.

When the convent was at chapter the boys played; terce rang them into school in the sheltered north walk of the cloister. On greater feast days the morning's work—or, if holiday were granted, the morning's play—was broken by High Mass; otherwise they sat till after sext, the midday office, and then dined with the monks. While the latter enjoyed their "meridian" or after-dinner nap, Juhel and his companions were turned loose within bounds for two hours or more on end. At nones their whooping ceased; no sound from the fields might disturb the slow march of their elders from the great dorter. Next, the boys must be washed and sobered for the light meal called collation, and for reading or quiet games in the cloister, or choir practice for the dozen chosen voices, or the steam and repressed din of the weekly bath. At sunset two-and-two again to vespers; then learning of lessons for the morrow, and play when the lessons were thought to be learned; and lastly, at the hour of compline, supper and evening prayer and bed.

For Juhel bed did not invariably mean sound sleep. Sometimes he woke the half of his roommates with a scream of terror; that was when wild beasts chased him through a dream forest. Sometimes he had a waking nightmare of unutterable loneliness, when the blue-gray window shapes dwindled and grew remote, while he, too, shrank until he felt no bigger than his morning's finger nail; then to cry out seemed entirely useless, for any noise he made must be no louder than the singing of a gnat. But on stormy evenings the gales would get into his blood and excite him, so that he tossed for hours and heard strange voices in the war of wind and sea, and when the outer dark grew full of demons and too menacing to be

borne, with what relief would Juhel see dim lights slant
through the shutter slats, and hear the friendly organ blast
and the brave steady choiring of the monks at nocturnes—
the answer of Michael and the heavenly host to all the powers
of air and night and evil! Juhel sometimes dropped into exhausted sleep in the ten midnight minutes which elapsed before the burst of matin song; and more than one of the monks
sang better and more lustily because he knew that a small
boy had listened and found comfort in the sound.

Nobody blamed Juhel for his nightmares; there were several orphans of the Jacquerie among the other boys, but all
had relatives of a sort to visit them and send them clothes
and toys and comfits, and none was sole survivor of such a
massacre as that in the Tower of Ath. Sulkiness by day was
another matter; the solitude which might have cured it formed
no part of the boys' conventual life save as punishment.
Hence Juhel had his share of bread and water, and an
occasional encounter with the birch rod of the lean third-prior.
Yet on the whole he fared contentedly as those of happier
begetting; and after his seventh year he grew comely and
plump and strong.

Vaguely he knew himself legal ward to the Count of
Barberghe, that foxy lord whose greed provoked the out-
break of the Jacquerie; vaguely he thought of the tower and
lands which he would one day possess; but the outside world
meant little to Juhel, even when it came so close as to rob the
good sub-prior and kill the convent servants. True, on the
octave of Corpus Christi in that same year Juhel had leaned
from a window and watched with staring eyes six galleys of
the Easterlings stand in toward the harbour mouth, only to
put about and sail off to the westward in search of plunder
worse defended; then, indeed, he had added a squeal to the
great roar of triumph and derision which went up from the
cliff tops, where monks, lay brethren, and men-at-arms waited
with slings and bows, with lime and pitch and smoking torches,
to defend the harbour entrance. And later in that strange

day he, too, had laughed and cheered to hear how at Karmeriet up the coast the Viscount Raoul of Ger had dealt with four more pirate ships and crews. In another twenty-four hours came news of the death of Red Jehan de Campscapel, and the young Viscount Raoul rubbed shoulders in Juhel's mind with Roland and Olivier and Amadis and Arthur; but for the most part the boy preferred to forget that he was Sieur de Ath, and that some day soon he must leave this beloved home to enter the household of the Count of Barberghe, to learn to be page and squire and to earn the spurs of chivalry.

Some of his schoolfellows were already destined for the cloister; these Juhel rather pitied, since they must more and more be encompassed by iron restriction of monkish life as ordered by the stern prior. Folquin de Forne and a dozen others, besides Juhel himself, were orphan wards or heirs of noblemen; and sometimes they talked among themselves of the wicked peasants whom one day they would rule.

"They will not rise against *me*," promised Folquin on one occasion.

Folquin was perched on the cloister wall, his bright determined face the fairest thing in all that expanse of sky and sward and sunlit carven stone. Juhel looked up from a game of fox-and-geese; the squares were deeply scored in the cloister pavement, and he sat cross-legged on the rushes beside them.

"What will you do if they try?" asked Hugolin, another of Folquin's admirers.

"Ride them down as my father did. No, I shall bid my archers fill them with arrows; it is folly to waste a charger among their scythes. A pack of idle vermin! What are you grinning at, Juhel?"

"You, wasting your archers' time pulling arrows out of peasants. Why not starve them all dead? Then your archers can scythe the corn, and you can glean behind them."

"Gomeril!" shouted Folquin. "What would *you* do, then?"

"Keep them on my side if I could," said Juhel.

"Ho! Little Jacques-Juhel! A lot *you* know about your peasant friends! Will you give them comfits and sing to them in the solar? Peasants are made to be kicked, and I shall kick them."

"You might kick Juhel, too," suggested Hugolin.

"Him!" snorted Folquin, meeting Juhel's eyes and looking away.

"*You* come and kick me, Hugolin," Juhel advised. "Come on, greedy-guts, and see what will happen."

But Hugolin only scowled, for he knew what would happen.

*   *   *

Folquin it was in the end who brought to Juhel the news that the Count of Barberghe had come to visit the prior.

"He wants to see you," said Folquin. "Brother Adrian sent me to say you were to wash and to go at once to the prior's parlour."

"*Oh!*" breathed Juhel blankly, staring down from the ledge of a cut haystack into the lifted face of Folquin. Folquin was excited, a little envious that the world clutched Juhel before it clutched himself, and even, perhaps . . .

Panic in front of Folquin was unthinkable; Juhel crushed it down in his heart and got soberly to the ground. If this was the last time he would tread his way between the familiar farm buildings, at least he had Folquin beside him. Cattle lowed in the tilted fields, poultry clucked in the shadow of barns, and apple blossom filled the orchard; ahead was the landward slope of the cliff ridge and the bulk of the gray monastery, and east and west were shards of sea—pale-green and jaggedly shaped by the slant and sheer of dark cliff faces, or curved and fringed with surf along sunlit reaches of sand.

"Do you not *want* to go with the count?" asked Folquin curiously.

"No," replied Juhel. "He—it is he they call the Fox."

Folquin nodded, accepting Barberghe's reputation as reason for reluctance.

"You will do well enough," he remarked; and then: "I wish I was coming too."

"With *me?*" breathed incredulous Juhel, glancing at him.

"With anyone," said Folquin absently. "I am tired of this place, and besides, I am thirteen now."

Then he saw that Juhel was flushed and somehow hurt, and a queer smile touched his carven lips. When Juhel had parted from him he dived up the stair of the boys' dorter.

"So you are Juhel de Ath," snapped the sly-featured bulky Count of Barberghe when the boy stood before him.

"Yes, my lord Count."

"My lord Prior tells me you have in you the makings of a man. It is time to test you in saddle and hall. Ay, I can see the Ath in you. Be ready after meat—and look me in the face when I address you."

"Attend me later, Juhel," commanded the prior; and so the boy came at length to receive the gold signet ring which Tiphaine his mother had first hung round his neck twelve years before.

Juhel looked down at his device, the dagger between stars; and when he knelt to receive the prior's blessing he set the ring on his thumb.

"This is my very own," he thought. "It is the only thing besides my clothes that I can take away."

But as the boys flocked out of the refectory Folquin pounced upon Juhel, drawing him deftly aside, and at the same time fumbling mightily beneath his own tunic, from which he presently drew a flat leather-backed book with a tarnished silver clasp.

"You—your ballad book——" stammered the younger boy, finding the soft and pleasant-smelling leather in his hand.

"Keep it," said Folquin hurriedly. "You always liked it better than I did."

Juhel gulped; a golden glory suffused the moment, to fade with the flash of Folquin's tow-bright hair across the trim sward of the cloister garth. But he had caught at

Folquin's fingers, squeezing them hard; and then he turned away, hiding the gift as Folquin had hidden it, and wondering if the two of them would ever meet agagin.

"*He* will go as page to the Count of Montcarneau," mused Juhel. "Barberghe and Montcarneau are friends. I hope——"

Then he came shyly out among the Barberghe surcoats, and presently he sat on a patient gelding that was more at ease than himself among the trampling destriers. For a moment Juhel wished he could have seen the completion of Brother Leo's V; then he squared his shoulders and set his teeth and waved gaily enough to kind old Brother Adrian who stood by the outer gateway.

The cavalcade moved forward. Immediately in front of Juhel flapped and bellied the great chevron banner; at times it seemed to hide the half of his familiar world. And indeed the red-and-black device hid most of Juhel's joys from him for many days to come.

Once he turned in his saddle, and caught a farewell glimpse of the priory towers. Then the gelding stumbled and nearly threw him, and the man-at-arms behind laughed loudly at his fright.

The ballad book slipped down over his stomach, and had no power to stay an inner sinking behind it. Yet somewhere in him Juhel knew there were good things far beyond the range of life in the gray-walled enclosure of Saint-Eloy-over-Hardonek.

VII. GRAMBERGE AND THE SINGING STONES

ON THE day when Juhel rode out into the world, Joris moved from winter quarters, determined to collect the hides and horns hidden during the previous summer in sandy caves beneath the mountain Dondunor. The winter had been bitter; Easter drew near, but snow still flecked the topmost ridges of the hills. Gandulf, with twenty chosen men, was left to hold the Rock and its approaches; so that just over a hundred sturdy outlaws, with forty pack ponies, followed Joris and Red Anne across the secret ford near Pont-de-Foy.

They made their passage in dawnlight, when Varne ran like dim steel between the blur of the misted woods, that were brown at hand and blue-gray in the distance; and Joris, glancing aside at Anne's untroubled profile, felt a swift stir of exultation that he strode thus companioned on his first venture of the new year.

"Will you and Lys," he growled to his love, "ride ponies over the water—over the running water?"

"Ay, that we will," said Anne, setting her hand on his sword hilt. "But once across we are men, Joris, asking no further privilege."

"You will ride to the Singing Stones at least?"

"No. This time it is in my mind to walk. Will *you* come to the Sabbath on Good Friday night? The council on Good Friday Eve we must attend alone."

"As you will. And my men?"

"No more than one or two, and of the trustiest. We want no brawling. Madoc, Adelgar, old Osmund . . ."

"Madoc must stay in charge by Dondunor. Adelgar had best

second him. I will bring Osmund and Rufin and Romarec, un-less——"

"Rufin?" repeated Red Anne; and she rounded on Lys with a face grown suddenly cruel.

"There comes a merry Sabbath," she told the girl. "Joris and Rufin will dance with us; are you content?"

Ivo grinned; Lys raised her ivory face, and her pale blue eyes flashed surprise before they hardened to recklessness.

"That will be merry indeed," said Lys composedly; and Joris wondered for a moment why Red Anne should abate the displeasure which had hitherto guarded Lys from Rufin. In the riot of a Sabbath the sandy-haired rogue would no doubt have his way; but Joris saw no harm in that. Lys he disliked and rather despised; if her dagger parted Rufin's ribs he would forgive her, but her private woes meant nothing to one for whom the world was made.

Yet that night in the forest, and on the following morning when he took a two-day farewell of Red Anne, Joris noted a change in Lys. She showed more liveliness and colour than he had before found in her; and she sang and jested blithely, no longer avoiding Rufin, so that Joris shared the mild surprise which Ivo expressed in his hearing.

"What ails you, Lys?" demanded the boy as they made ready to leave the camp. "You are strangely glad."

Lys put her pretty head on one side and pouted lips to her flute.

Tirra-lirra-loo, she played, and smiled across at Ivo where he sat cleaning his sword.

"It is spring," said Lys, with a tremor as of laughter in her clear, high voice. "The spring, when lambs leap and buds thrust; the spring, when youths lose their hearts and maidens lose their heads; the spring, when all the world goes kissing, even to Judas Iscariot."

Ivo laughed, but Lys somehow reminded Joris of a fine dagger blade perilously bent. When Red Anne and her two companions had disappeared toward the northwest, Joris

struck camp and drove straight westward with his file of
laden pack ponies. His intention was to halt ten miles from
the Singing Stones, and to slip away from his men on the
afternoon of Holy Thursday; but Holy Thursday at mid-
morning brought him Red Anne again.

*   *   *

On foot, in green cloth, she left him; in soft black leather,
astride a foaming sweating mare, she returned. Horse and
rider burst so suddenly into sight over the crest of a near
grassy ridge that lounging men cried out and snatched at
their weapons. Joris, inspecting his ill-cured hides, stood as
though frozen; this was the Valkyr who once had hunted with
Lorin de Campscapel.

"Come with me, Joris," she called, resplendent in fury.
"Bring all your men and sack Gramberge; pluck Lys from
the priest's house and halve the jewels she stole from me."

"Gramberge? Lys? Jewels?" growled Joris of the Rock.

"Yes and yes and yes. Last night she fled from the Stones,
leaving my wallet empty. We hunted her across heather; in
the dawn we tracked her down the moor's edge and saw the
priest of Gramberge drag her into his dwelling. The jewels are
the last of the jewels of Campscapel. I took them when we
fled—rubies and diamonds, too. The bailiff we slew, and two
others; but the little priest withstood us, and I gave him a
period to yield up my little sister in Lilith, promising that if he
did not *you* should come by noon and put the place to pillage.
Three hinds set off to Ger for help; them we finished with
arrows. The rest I bade hide in the church, giving them surety
of safety there. Ivo and four of the coven have bows, and surround the hamlet. This is the bailiff's horse. Will you come?"

A score of the outlaws heard the first appeal, and two-score
—so quickly they gathered—listened to the second. Joris had
not moved, except to take one pace aside when the trembling
mare drooped head and slavered on his booted instep.

To gratify Anne's private vengeance; to recover for her the

jewels whose very existence she had hidden from him; to let her pledge his sword as though he were her servant; to feel the disadvantage at which she held him in face of his following—four separate reluctances gripped coldly at his spirit. Then Rufin spoke.

"Gramberge is a scant three miles from Ger," said Rufin. "That warlock count——"

For the Viscount Raoul had succeeded his uncle, and men went very warily within his jurisdiction; but Anne beat with clenched fist upon the pommel of her saddle, and her figure, trim and sturdy in its strange costume, stiffened against the windy upland sky.

"Leave Rufin with the hides, since he is afraid!" she cried.

"*I* will come with you, Lady Anne!" promised Adelgar, standing close to the woman's stirrup.

"And I—and I—and I," added other voices.

"The word is with Joris only," said Madoc, softly but clearly.

"Tell me one thing," demanded Joris, as though Red Anne and he were alone. "Why did you not break in yourselves and drag that little hell-cat forth?"

He had his leader's moment then; for the first time since he knew her, Red Anne's eyes darkened with diffidence.

"To each his power," came her sullen response; and Joris learned at last the limit of her courage. Immediately she was his woman again—his woman, turning to him for her own justification—and faint scorn edged the laugh with which he spun on his heel.

"Unload saddles and packs together!" he roared. "Pile them here and leave them; we shall have more gear by nightfall. I am no Easterling or Campscapel, and to-day I tweak the tail of the new Count of Ger!"

A cheer resounded from the ranges; ten minutes later the outlaw throng was streaming swiftly northward, those on foot gripping belt or scabbard of those who rode the bare-backed ponies. This was a country unfamiliar to Joris, but

Anne knew it thoroughly; sometimes mounted, sometimes leading her mare, she guided the human wolf pack to end what her coven began.

Joris and she barely spoke throughout that three-hour scramble, but once she turned to the man and smiled to see his long legs trailing in bracken.

"Do not grudge me my jewels," she said. "I kept them in case you tired of me; but now it is less the jewels I seek than the blood of that thieving vixen yonder."

"You plagued her soundly before she fled," grunted the man in his beard.

"Ay. She would have it I disgraced myself by taking you for a lover."

"Now did she, by the chimes of hell?" laughed Joris of the Rock.

*   *   *

Sea wind salted the outlaws' lips as they tethered the ponies among twisted thorns to leeward of the northernmost crest of the moors of Nordanay. Red Anne alone kept hold of her bridle, leading the mare to the hummocky edge of the eight-hundred-foot incline of screes and ling and brushwood. Clear in the gray noon lay Gramberge; something fluttered on the roof of the squat belfry tower that stood apart from the little church, but otherwise the hamlet seemed deserted.

"The hinds have dragged their gear to the altar," called Anne, "but I warrant they left the new count's sheep and corn outside."

"To-day I tweak his tail, that valiant little lording," said Joris once more, eyeing the towers of Ger which rose, against steel-coloured sea, above the swell of gorse-strewn pasture that hid cliff edge and town and castled promontory. "There are some here will gladly brand my name in his parchment rolls. Madoc, is all secure?"

"All tethered and secure," said dark Madoc, unslinging a bow with glee in his hatchet face.

"Then hearken!" bellowed Joris, turning to face his horde. "Any man taking the girl Lys renders her first to Red Anne or to me. Then she is Rufin's and no other's. And now let none outpace me till I bid him. No harm to the church or those therein; all else is for your sport. Upon Gramberge, *Haro!*"

"*Haro!*" came the hundredfold echo; and the outlaws poured downhill.

"Horses in the priest's orchard," gasped Anne, as she guided the stumbling mare. "They were not there when I left to find you."

"Guests at the wedding of Lys," boomed Joris, happy in rapid action. "Now who comes running here?"

For as the shouting, laughing throng swarmed on the breathless slope, a figure black as Red Anne's own danced from the thickets below them.

"Ivo, with tidings," said Anne. But even then Joris was startled to see the cloven cut of Ivo's shoes, the tufted tail tucked up in Ivo's belt, and, strangest of all, the helmet that swung by a strap at Ivo's shoulder—a helmet of sable leather, camailed with cloth and vizored with the dried and eyeless mask of a great mastiff.

Ivo was flushed with climbing and running; his eyes were grimly amused as he stared uphill at that armed avalanche.

"The belfry is held," he cried, "and Lys well guarded within. Barely the quarter of an hour ago four men—two of rank, two squires—and a crimson-clad woman spurred in as if from Guarenal. They paused at the priest's house, took him and Lys therefrom, and await your coming—all but the squires, who rode for Ger, but were ambushed by Rioc and Blanche on the hill brow *there*."

"You saw them fall?" snapped Joris, halting to listen.

"Both of them!"

"And their horses?"

"Caught and somewhere hidden," Ivo responded, grinning hardily up at him. "We have seen none else attempt to get through since those we slew after dawn. The serfs are barred

in the church. Someone rang the peal of exorcism for nigh
on a full hour, but the hill and the wind are against its being
heard at Ger. If any come that way, Rioc will warn you."

With a wave of his hand Joris plunged forward and downward; the sloping woods grew full of oaths and crashing footfall, of foul jests loudly voiced and bump or rattle of steel.

Anne leaped to her saddle when undergrowth yielded to
pasture; first of them all she reached the church, reining the
mare back on her haunches to shout at the pallid faces crouching behind the windows. Joris ramped through the near
orchard, swinging his sword in response to her beckoning gesture; beneath black skullcap and bright braided hair Anne's
eyes were hard and joyful in a glowing face.

"By Mahound, man," she clamoured, "that little belfry
holds your fortune. There is the Count of Ger, with Reine, old
Guarenal's granddaughter, and Enguerrand du Véranger, his
march lieutenant. Carry *them* into the hills, and Nordanay
shall crawl to you. Only render me Lys—it is all the thank I
ask."

"You shall have your thanks," grated Joris, observing the
belfry shrewdly as the tail of his power came bounding across
the half-ploughed fields.

The building was thirty-five feet high, and reared with an
eye to defence, for the roof was stoutly battlemented, the
single door narrow and iron-studded, and no window more
than a slit impossible of entry. Joris laughed once, and wheeled
on his lieutenants.

"Hither axes!" he thundered. "This meat is tenderer raw
than roast! Rufin, a ram and ladders; Madoc, iron to break
the mortar out and pegs to mount upon; bowmen, rake the
slits and let no head show on the roof. Axes amain!"

Here and there they ran at his bidding; Osmund led the
ax party, and as they neared the entry the man behind Osmund
screamed and stamped to a burst of his comrades' laughter;
for a long arrow whizzed from the slit above the door and
pinned his foot to a grave mound.

All about the belfry swirled and bayed the outlaws; some stood on their comrades' shoulders to drive spears into the slits, but the latter were plugged with wood, and roof tiles skimmed the parapet to crash among the besiegers. Loud rang the ax blows on the door; presently Rufin and his party came staggering from the woodpile, bearing a great log that should reënforce the axes. Picks clinked at the mortar, and bowmen stood well back, drawing hard that their shafts might not injure comrades on the far side of the belfry. The one archer within was shooting with leisurely skill; three men were arrow-smitten to death before the seventh shock of the ram beat in the door and roused a yell of triumph.

Down thudded the log, its bearers scattering right and left to let their comrades pour close arrow sleet into the gloom beyond the wreckage. Feathered butts bristled in the doorway, revealing a crisscrossed fragment of a harrow that swung loosely within the opening. Axmen ran forward again to finish their work; pikes drove the dangling lumber upward and inward, and a first man dived beneath it—to stumble forward with a split skull and cumber the way with his body.

A dozen crowded to take his place, but the sheltered swordsmen made murderous play behind the narrow opening. Outlaws hindered each other, dancing and thrusting in vain; a second corpse sprawled on the first, a third fell back and was trodden beneath the shouting press.

"By the chimes of hell!" roared Joris. "Are two mad popinjays to hold you up forever? Scatter again for bowshot, and bring me a dozen bucklers!"

"Popinjays!" croaked old Osmund, nursing a bleeding arm as he turned to confront his chief. "Give you joy of such popinjays; they fight like fiends from—*hell!*"

Osmund shuddered and gestured oddly; above the fiery nose his pig's eyes grew hurt and astonished. Still mumbling at Joris, he swayed and fell flat on his face; between his shoulder blades stood up an arrow from the slit above the belfry door.

Joris gave an angry chuckle and stood aside out of range; Madoc, grasping his chief's intention, was already fixing the bucklers upon pike heads, that the defenders might be pushed bodily backward from the entry. And now Adelgar was binding three short ladders together; and still Red Anne sat her horse by the church porch, watching her lover's leaguer and guarding the serfs and their children.

Madoc's siege cat lurched forward, a blind eight-footed beast of wood and hide and steel. Decked with belfry arrows, its snout felt for the doorway; a long lunge and a great yell, and the casing of bucklers vanished within, the pike shafts splaying and crossing as the crew of four crushed forward among them. Madoc was close behind, setting his hands on the doorposts to check the hampering mob that would have followed too quickly.

Adelgar's ladder was laid to the western wall; Adelgar bounded up it, shouting something unheard amid the din. Quick as lightning a sword smote from between the merlons above him; Joris saw blood and brains on the fleshy hawk's face as Adelgar crashed backward. More than one problem, it seemed, was to be solved by this day's work.

But the second and third and fourth men up the ladder went the way of Adelgar. A dozen archers watched to trap the swordsman who held that parapet; but he dodged and fought like a maniac, with arrows whistling over his head and outlaw after outlaw dropping to his blows.

Madoc was gone inside now, and others with him, but Joris could see them still battling in the ground-floor space of the belfry. Maybe an inner door was held, or a winding stair had checked them where the cat could not be used. . . . The thing was growing ludicrous, and Joris halted only to choose which way he might show how a belfry should be stormed.

Then he chuckled again, for the defender of the roof had torn a guisarme from a falling man, but lost his own sword in the act; and a second ladder was going against the wall.

"Not *beside* the first, you fools!" roared Joris, starting forward; but already four men were loading the rungs, and the din was terrific. High over all soared a girl's shrieking; Joris, his victory half assured, halted in fascination to see the guisarme hook drive the topmost rung of the second ladder away from the crenel where it lodged. The first climber grabbed at the blade, but the ladder had already overbalanced; yelling and clinging, the four described their ghastly quarter circle, thudding hideously to the grass amid their dodging comrades.

"Set us again!" thundered Joris, marking an outlaw on the still-standing ladder grapple with the man beyond the parapet; but as he reached the broken bodies a hand fell roughly on his shoulder, and he found himself staring into Rufin's convulsed and villainous face.

"See there!" screeched Rufin, pointing. "See there, you tweaker of tails!"

Like a flash Rufin was gone. Joris looked over his own shoulder; the crest of pasture toward Ger was fretted by line after ragged line of horsemen, their short surcoats buttercup yellow as they charged fanwise over gorse and grass toward Gramberge.

Red Anne's voice came strongly to him: *"Joris, this way— there is yet time!"* Amid the rush of his shouting men he gained the gray mare's flank, gripping a stirrup leather as Anne tightened rein for flight. Away they raced together, Joris still swinging his sword; and before and behind and about them scurried the wrack of his power, while from beyond the hamlet swelled vengefully a continuous roar of *"Ger!"*

"Straight upslope if it kills her," said Joris between his teeth; and beyond the clinging ploughland loam the mare crashed into the thickets. Half-light enveloped the man; the world was shrunk to a steep hillside, where briers tripped him and alders buffeted him—where mud slipped beneath his feet, and the mare's sweating shoulder jarred his own. He was forced to sheathe his sword, to unsling his bow from his shoulder and carry it or use it as a staff; quiver and horn and scabbard hung awry, hampering him in that ungainly flight. From time to time he leaned perforce against Anne's sturdy thigh; and below them rang the sounds of pursuit, that if it were successful might turn the beauty of Anne to a charred horror, and would doubtless wrench to swollen hideousness the throat of Joris of the Rock.

*   *   *

"Better dismount," said the man an hour later. "Else she will die in her tracks and throw you. Well for us they did not pursue across open moor."

Red Anne awoke from sullen reverie to fling herself out of saddle and stamp away her stiffness in the sodden heather. Curiously she eyed her lover, for Joris was almost gay.

"Ivo in that hour of vision said only I could break you," she reminded him. "Only I, who wished you never any harm. By Mahound, Joris, I *have* nearly broken you. It is time you bought more runes, or parted from me in haste."

Joris glanced aside at her; it was strange to see Red Anne forlorn and savage in defeat.

"For this pass," he declared, "I have to thank not you but devilkin Ivo. Him we shall see no more, I warrant; I hope they caught and hanged him. Adelgar I could spare; for Osmund I am angry, and fiend knows how many more. When we reach that rock ahead I pause to hold a muster. But this I know and say—I have not yet done with that little fighting weasel of a count."

"It seems ill done to cross him. But *I* have not yet done with that renegade vixen Lys."

"You will not lightly reach her in the keep of Ger."

"Not lightly; but there are spells to move so mired a spirit as hers. Be sure she will know herself cursed by me; that is the best beginning. Give the count joy of his rescued beauty!"

"Why did you plague them so, these two who have turned and stung you?"

"Because their love was slavish. Because they were with

me above Alanol and too often reminded me thereof. Because I was known for kindness and hugged that one rich cruelty. Because I taught them witchcraft and they feared Christ less than I do."

For that strange self-indictment Joris found no easy words.

"Yet you purpose revenge on Lys?" he demanded at length.

"Ay, even so. She knew too much to desert me scatheless. Come to the Singing Stones to-night, as you had first intended."

"H'm. That depends."

"On what?"

"On Rufin, among other things. Observe him at the muster."

So saying, Joris unslung his bugle horn and blew a rousing rally. The stumbling men ahead stood fast, the laggards pulled themselves together; Madoc, astride a pony in the rear, assembled thirty mounted like himself and brought them swinging along to the hollow where Joris had chosen to halt.

Sixty-one they numbered in all, who at dawn had been a hundred and seven. Madoc grimaced at the figure, and then stepped swiftly to the side of Joris; for Rufin spat loudly and lounged to confront the latter.

"A word with you, Joris, in all men's hearing," brayed Rufin, jaunty no longer. "I say you were mad or bewitched to lead us upon Gramberge. Pledge us here and now to keep to honest thieving; mix no more with witchcraft and church-craft that defeats it. Or straightway release *me,* and as many as will come with me, from further obligation to serve Red Anne through you who are her mouthpiece. What was the demoiselle to you, that you strove to recapture her?"

"Here is a lover gallant but confused," mocked Joris, glad of an outlet for wrath. "Rufin would come to the Singing Stones, but Rufin's pretty one fails him; avaunt all damnable witchcraft, cries Rufin. Hearken, you oaf; if my band were reduced to the two of us, you should not leave me unbidden. Think you I want a ghost of myself botching raids in the hills?"

"Not yet a ghost," growled Rufin; and in one quick movement he ripped out his dagger and flung it at the heart of
Joris. Joris shrugged, but not quickly enough; the blade sank
into the outer side of his left upper arm, drooping beneath the
weight of its hilt before he tore it out and tossed it to earth.
A dozen swords were at Rufin's throat and breast, but the
leader waved them aside and plucked forth his own weapon.

"Not yet a ghost, by God, but soon to be one," he rasped.
"Stand back all, and keep a ring about us. Rufin, draw and
defend yourself! *Have at you, ape!*"

Steel flashed and kissed and sang; Rufin was a crafty
swordsman, and after a first fierce onslaught played to let the
dagger wound help him. But Joris attacked like a whirlwind;
backward and forward they stamped and slid in a sudden
wind-blown drizzle of rain. Rufin's mouth was first to open,
but he snicked the tip from the golden beard and cut Joris
below the knee before an upstroke found his armpit and
forced a breathless groan from him. He tossed his hilt to his
left hand and pierced the leader's jerkin at the right shoulder,
barely grazing the skin; the stiff leather gripped the sword
and gave him over to death. Into his undefended side went
the leaping point of Joris; Rufin grunted and staggered back,
clearing his blade and missing the golden head with a last
strong back-handed blow. Then he was down on flank and
elbow, with life soaking redly into the peat. For a moment
his fierce eyes held the laughing eyes above him; then they
dimmed, and Rufin spoke as though to the heather.

"Prosper your witch," he said clearly, "for I think she will
ruin you soon."

Then his head drooped and sank on his arm, and his eyes
shut and opened again.

Joris stood staring down at him; the words caught at a
fading memory—the memory of a girl who called down a curse
and fled on horseback through the forest. For a second the
threat weighed sharply; then Joris looked up at grave Red
Anne, and round at the eyes of his attentive men—*his* men

now, one and all, whatsoever had been in their minds when the fight began.

"We will go on," he announced, stabbing the earth with stained steel and sliding the latter, cleansed, into its scabbard.

As he turned his foot struck the dagger—the silver-hilted dagger which once he had borrowed from Rufin. Flicking his own from its sheath he dropped it and picked up the other; somehow it pleased him to claim that forfeit again at last.

"Let me bind up your wounds," said Anne, producing a kerchief; and presently all were in motion again save the shape that had been Rufin.

A raven sailed from nowhere, gigantic in the first spring dusk. Men averted their eyes and plodded swiftly away. Madoc whistled a little tune, and the weary horse of the bailiff of Gramberge whinnied as though in fear.

"By the bones of Goliath of Gath," said Joris to Anne beside him, "I feel as though I had left ill luck with that dead rogue behind us."

"Maybe," replied the woman absently; and, looking at her, Joris realized that for her the day was barely begun.

*   *   *

Toward midnight Anne parted from Joris in a cave three hundred yards upslope from the Singing Stones. Together they had crept from their camp, leaving Madoc in charge of the weary men; for two hours, with uncanny precision, the woman has guided her lover through wind and rain and glancing starlight—turning this way or that at the first squelch of a bog, choosing a path among rocks that seemed to bar all advance, tramping surely across jet-black peat or dim gray of gorse-encumbered sand.

"By my hilt, you know your parish," swore Joris, striding in rear. "I think you can go where the Devil cannot, between the oak and the rind."

The words were out before he found them grotesque by reason of his errand; then he laughed, to point or excuse them as Anne might please, but Anne's response was matter-of-fact.

"Wheresoever flesh can go the Devil has been before," she said. "Ay, even to Paradise; wherefore we pray in the Black Mass——"

She broke off with an ugly little sound of tongue and teeth, and Joris found nothing to say. Until the last possible moment he resisted the uneasiness which sundered him from this strange resolute companion who yet was his love of a hundred nights; but when the tops of the upright dolmens cut irregular shapes against a reach of sky swept momentarily clear, he set hand to his sword and scowled at the blur which was Red Anne's face.

"You hear the singing?" she asked, pausing beneath a low scarp where bushes hugged the boulders and little caves yawned drily to the thrust of an exploring longbow.

"Ay," said Joris gruffly. "Your stage is fairly set."

For amid a rustle of heather and a hiss of waving hawthorns went up the long, strange harmonies, the boom and whistle and mock-plangent humming, pressed and torn from the Singing Stones by the angry midnight wind.

"Now I go," came Anne's voice, with a note in it as of stifled laughter. "Wait until you hear the song of invocation; then, if it please you, creep forward to watch. You are sure you will not have me make you known?"

"Ay, that I am. This is no play of mine."

"Then farewell—and when all is done, you are still my Joris, and I am still your Anne."

They kissed strongly in the darkness; then she was gone, and Joris chose a rocky hole wherefrom he could observe the broken uprights towering three hundred yards away from him. Before his love had time to reach the dolmens, lights woke among them; Joris and she had come a more desolate way than any, meeting or overtaking none of the figures which seemed to spring to life in the sudden flickering radiance.

All in a moment the Singing Stones were a medley of black

and orange-gray, starred with waving torches that streamed
and sparkled and smoked, patterned with crazily changing
shadows along the planes of the great trilithons; the ruined
circle filled with a rumour of greeting and laughter that
blended with its own ghostly organ song. A confused welcom-
ing roar told Joris that the Mistress of the Coven had been
seen; immediately the mingled din died down, and the torches
appeared to assume a rough alignment—some being stuck in
holes and clefts of the uprights, others held aloft by hand.
A squall of thin rain swept across the ink-black ranges;
through the faint sheen of its wavering mist the outlaw saw
the shifting assembly clot to stillness amid the lesser stones
of the inner ring.

"By the chimes of hell," he swore, "I will not wait like a
slave."

The words of his apposite oath wrung a grin from him,
for as he pulled his hood down over his eyes the voice of Red
Anne chimed in the wind; and by the time he had gone a
dozen yards the whole throng was singing. Joris was not much
given to thrills along the spine, but the swell of that deep chant
raked him from loins to base of skull; breathing strongly,
using his unstrung bow as a staff, he trod with slackening
speed toward the bright and sounding mystery.

He had refused to let Anne show him to her friends, saying
that in Nordanay too many owed him a grudge for him to
trust his undefended back among the witches and their
acolytes. Then Anne had laughed and asked him if men
stabbed each other in church; and the implication of her
question only hardened his resolve to keep himself aloof in
spirit from whatsoever might take place that night. And now,
as he approached the eastern quarter of the stone circle and
saw more clearly the blur of facts, he was more than ever
glad of that refusal. For something of ancient hope and
sorrow and greatness, something old and true as the very
building of the Stones, streamed in the wavering torch glare
and groaned in the surging hymn.

"Bah!" he whispered against the wind. "The most part are what Anne called them—snivelling outcast whores, who creep here and endure a discipline for greed of assuagement only to be had of devils in the dark. Yet someone attends to their singing——"

Then he stopped still in his tracks; for at either end of the long low step before the massive altar stone leaped up strong blue-white flares. The kindlier torchlight paled before them; nor might the wind do more than slant the two strange little flowers of fire and whirl their thick sulphurous fume away into the dark. Between them stood Red Anne, her proud face sharply silvered; in front of her the crowd lurched solidly to its knees.

The new and ghastly glow beat strongly into the drizzling blackness, but no eye in face of it could hope to see tall Joris, standing in partial shadow thirty yards from the nearest tumbled megalith. He drew close in to a hawthorn bush, and watched Anne raise both hands to helm herself with a beast-head like that which had swung at Ivo's shoulder above Gramberge; but Ivo's mask had been a dog's, and Anne's was a horned cow's. With her movement the hymn rose to a crash and stopped; the wind and the Singing Stones together took up their soft forgotten parts, to be whelmed again the instant after by a new and rapid chorus. Joris, fascinated by the trim cow-headed figure that now beat time with a strange brazen-flashing rod, suddenly found that he understood the words; for the hymn had seemed to him gibberish. But this must be the song of invocation; its quickening quadruple beat set his pulses galloping.

"Ha! Ha! Sieur Yaan!
Sieur Yaan! Sieur Yaan!
Hear and find us—loose and bind us,
Rise and reach us—rule and teach us,
Fast enslave us—smite and save us,
Strike or spare, Yaan—help us dare, Yaan,
Only thou, Yaan—guid'st us now, Yaan.

Bread and wine, Yaan—ours but thine, Yaan!
  Bid us dance; let flesh and bone
  Wheel around the sacred Stone;
  Wheel and whirl and whirl and wheel
  Till the solid ground shall reel,
  Till the stars slip down the sky
  And the rooted hawthorne fly,
  Till in spate of furious glee
  Anguish all in praise of thee!
    Ha! Ha! Yaan! Yaan!
    Ya-aa-aa-aan!
    Ya-aa-aa-aan!
    YA-AA-AA. . . ."

The final chord seemed never ending; presently Joris realized that voices took it up in relays, for now one note and now another rang more strongly, but still the whole chord never died away. He choked down a snigger; the greater part of the singers were women—townsfolk and peasants mingled, so far as he could see—and for a moment he was reminded of a chorus of amorous cats. Yet after that moment amusement waned in him; and very soon the sustained sound was not amusing at all. There was too much ferocity in it; and suddenly Joris gasped and swore, for the chord laid a touch of power upon his body. The notes were somehow *spreading;* they began to ring from the cloud wrack hurtling overhead, from the black masses of the hills on either hand, from the cave-pocked slope behind him, and from the very ground beneath his feet. Each separate gust of light rain in his face was a stroke of added sound; and around his chill-struck forehead seemed set a tightening circlet of iron.

Again came a shock of silence, jarring him free; Red Anne half turned to the altar, and the blur of faces went weirdly out as cloaks or arms swung up and heads or hoods sank down. It seemed that none save Anne might look upon what came next—none save Anne and Joris, who stared in shaken curiosity from the last outskirts of the light.

Anne's voice went chanting up alone, in dreadful and sonorous prayer.

"Pater noster qui erat in coelis . . ."

Joris dropped his bow and clapped his hands to his ears. Holy Ratin was bad enough, but this . . .

The cow-faced Mistress of the Coven held out her left hand toward the altar; and a tall Thing skipped from the shadow of the great trilithon behind it, vaulting deftly upon the stone to sit cross-legged upon it.

Stag-headed, with tremendous antlers, the black and brooding shape of Evil lifted a paw in benediction as the kneeling crowd raised heads and shouted acclamation. The name of Yaan was a shrill defiance, a roar of earthling challenge to heaven that reënforced mailed temporal tyrannies with spiritual demands on patience and obedience and toil. Since alewives and farmers' daughters welcomed this Yaan, it was not in his aspect to daunt Joris of the Rock; nevertheless the outlaw's mouth was dry, and the hand that groped for the fallen longbow was less steady than when it let the life from raging Rufin.

The monster raised a hollow-sounding voice, thrusting himself backward until his tail hung down behind the altar; in a trice all were in motion, save Yaan himself and Red Anne, who bent to kiss the black shoulder and seated herself on the altar beyond him. A minor devil bearing a torch bounced round to their rear, standing to light the second act of that unseemly adoration. Stumbling, squealing, giggling, shoving, the file of figures circled the flares—one man to every two or three women—and Joris laughed an uncertain laugh, being loth to admit to himself a disgust that curved so near Red Anne.

Yet a man for whom the world was made will take the world as he finds it; and presently Joris felt an impatience for the end of that dreary rite. The greatness was gone from the play. Yaan and Red Anne wore dignity; not so that fawning rabble.

He squatted down on a boulder, glad of his cloak of frieze that Anne had borrowed and left with him. For a while it was hard to see what passed; Yaan spoke to this one and that in the press before him, his great voice booming praise and blame and laughter amid sharp bursts of applause from his audience. Recruits were thrust forward for rites of initiation, but Joris had no desire to see hysterical defilement of Crucifix and Wafer. He had killed a priest or two since that first revengeful slaying at Medrincourt in Basse Honoy, yet his quarrel was with the Church, not with the Sieur God. Once indeed, while a scared girl piped her responses, Joris yawned; but when Red Anne stood forth alone he got to his feet again.

The Mistress of the Coven pushed up her cow's mask like a visor; her anger against traitress Lys awoke a loud assenting outcry, but Joris heard therein little more than flattery and fevered expectation. Rioc and Blanche were present, it seemed—they and another had seized the horses of the Count of Ger and his companions that grazed in the priest's orchard at Gramberge, and had fled first of all, not trusting the outlaws to leave them their mounts should they give the alarm. So Ivo, too, was proved a traitor; yet Anne made nothing of that, for all her fury was turned against Lys.

"Lys betrayed *her,* and Ivo *me,*" thought Joris very grimly; and under his excitement crept a gray blur of fatigue. "Anne uses me," he muttered; and then: "She is made of iron as well as of earth and air and fire. Hey, what is that in her hands? A barnyard cock for sacrifice?"

One loud indignant squawk went up, and a gust of brutish applause. Then human sounds died down, and with them—as though by merest chance—ceased the light rain and lessened the eager wind, so that the blowing of the Stones sank to a murmur tremulous and forlorn.

Anne made wide passes over the reddened step, between the steadying blue-white flares, before the feet of humped and silent Yaan. Her voice broke suddenly forth again, grew hoarse with effort and command, compassed strange-sounding names:

"Aamon, Trimasel, Marbas, Agares . . . Sargatanas, Sidragrosam, Agaliarept . . .

"Shake her with wind and bellowing thunder . . . blast her with breath of furious flames . . . rot her with reek of poisonous marsh vapours . . . choke her with slime of foul worm-breeding waters . . . smite her with showering elf-shot from all the coasts of the world. . . ."

Joris had his wish at last; he saw Red Anne in power beside the Singging Stones. The dining curses shook his hardihood, vaguely he wondered why she called on elementals while one who was surely greater than they sat watching, but as the thought formed in his mind Yaan stirred and reached out for a rod—a spear—that had been stuck in earth beside the altar.

Yaan rose from his squatting posture with powerful ease; the shaggy blackness of him towered aloft, casting a grisly shadow on either upright of the easternmost trilithon behind him—and as he towered he shook the spear, stamped one long cloven hoof, and roared the name of Lys to the dark sky.

Then Joris felt the sweat start out on his temples; a wail of ecstatic dread ran sharply through the assembly, and Anne herself backed aghast against the altar.

Alone in face of that Satanic panoply, ignoring all who gaped and huddled beyond her, the slim untroubled shape of Lys outraged the smoky light and mocked the swirl of fury and terror that thickened between the Stones.

Fascinated, bereft even of unspoken oaths, Joris crept forward to the verge of darkness, his eyes fixed on that strange white-clad figure—for Lys was clad almost as if for penance, in nothing but a single robe of some fine stuff that clung wetly about her thin body. Her unbound hair was dragged to wisps and streaks by its own dripping weight; her queer pale eyes kept a spark of the old malice as steadfastly they looked upon Red Anne.

The Mistress of the Coven laughed a ringing laugh that hushed all other voices. Above and behind her Yaan hugged himself and the spear whose broad blade flashed at his

shoulder; each brutal detail of his ritual accoutrements glowed
and gleamed in the upflung light. Lys glanced from Anne to
Yaan and back again, and Yaan gave a harsh bray of merri-
ment.

"Traitress, you have well chosen!" he boomed. "Your body's
end shall now be swift that had else been lingering. You have
sought sanctuary beneath the emblem of my Enemies; did you
hope to escape *me* at the last?"

But Red Anne took a lurching stride from the altar step,
and her great golden voice clashed through the musical rumour
that still hung overhead.

"Why do you show your sickly rat's face here?" she belled.
"Who bade you come again, little renegade thieving whore?"

"None bade me come again," came in strange shrill reply
from the livid lips of Lys. *"I am beyond you and your power,
I think forever. Abate your bloodshed and cursing; they are
rites of vain observance. I am not so damned as I thought;
nor are you, Red Anne. Nor is any human creature, save those
who bloat and enfeeble their souls by preying on weaker souls
about them; they indeed, floating at last alone, burst like foul
bubbles and are lost in the Night of Unknowing. But those
who possess their souls apart earn choices stranger than
Paradise or Purgatory or Hell!"*

"'Possess their souls apart'!" rose the mocking roar of
Yaan. "Do *you* possess your soul apart, soused herring that
you are? Is there no Pact to steer your spirit when all those
runaway bones are broken?"

"Peace, fool," responded the elfin voice. *"Your pacts, your
threats, your visions, and your godhead are cobwebs in the
doom blast that shall whelm you. If you would break the bones
of Lys, go fish them from the falling tide along the Hardonek
sandbanks—by dawn they should be floating beyond
Capdelest."*

Yaan grunted, twitched up his spear, and drove it full at
the slender figure—that neither flinched, nor stayed the weapon
flight. The bright blade vanished in the peat, the haft quivered

and stilled; a shuddering groan swept the assembly, and Joris felt his knees clap unbidden together. The thing that bore the shape of Lys had not stirred; its greenish features were still turned calmly toward the furious rosy face that Lys had loved.

"Will no place then receive you?" cried Red Anne. "Are you condemned to blow about between the stars? At least if I cannot hurt you, you do not daunt *me;* if I hear a voice cry *'Herluin'* on the nightwind, I shall know it is you, poor misty monster, mourning those loveless nights in the hold above Alanol!"

"Red Anne, you have sorrow in you that anger cannot hide from me. I warn you, strive not with Herluin; power is sometimes given to him and to his kind that hope may never perish from the earth. If hope were gone, a jest is spoiled for always. How shall men dance, without a piping of hope?"

"You . . . *whose* jest . . . what power has Herluin?"

"Eh, but our little Herluin, who made sweet songs to you and blushed that we tended his pretty body—our little Herluin is the great new Count of Ger. I will tell you what Ivo could not when you thrust him half beyond the Veil—it was Herluin slew Lorin de Campscapel on the night our old life ended. I gave him a potion to bring him to me, but it sent him killing mad instead. I might not be his woman, but if I watch and wait I may yet be the child of his love. Farewell."

The cool high voice died out along the breath of the Singing Stones; brown hair and livid body, pale eyes and silken garment, one moment held their place and the next were gone.

Joris found himself on his knees in the soaked bracken that lipped the outer megalithic ring. Nothing was as it had been; the witch-play seemed an evil farce beside that unbidden apparition and the passionless inconsequence of its message. But Joris reckoned without Yaan.

Yaan laughed aloud again, and took a flying leap from the altar. The outlaw, ducking to scramble away, attained the shadow of his hawthorn before he turned to watch. The whole

throng was again in motion, and suddenly a drumbeat woke—
a drumbeat curiously familiar to Joris.

*Ta-rat, ta-rat, ta-rattle-ta-plat—ta-rattle-ta-plat, ta-rat,
ta-rat—ta-rat.*

"Hastain," the listener remembered. "The puppet show. The
old granny who capered alone. The woman who grinned behind
the shutter. There is shamming and juggling here, but there
is more than that. Ay, now they dance. . . ."

Between the outer and inner rings took shape a circle of
men and women, who linked hands and faced outward and
clumsily pranced widdershins to the quickening beat of the
drum. A flute woke a thread of melody amid the tapping and
shouts and laughter. A horn warbled throatily, and an eldritch
din of bagpipes broke out; Yaan was striding about the inner
ring, wielding now a little whip, but Red Anne sat alone on
the altar, her cow's mask pulled again over her face.

There was not room for all the crowd to dance in one circle;
presently Joris saw a second circle whirling within the first.
Four beast-headed members of the coven made the harsh
jigging music; others ran yelling to and fro to encourage
the dancers. One, dog-faced and slim as Ivo himself, shot out
from the leaping, staggering frieze and skipped and gambolled
all alone amid the half-lit heather; another squatted on a
fallen inner stone, diving first one way, then the other, to
clutch at the hair and clothes of the passing women.

This, rather than anything that went before, was what Joris
expected to see; but now the dance was well begun he found
it madder than the singing and stranger than the ghostly
visitation. His joints began to twitch; he swore, and gripped
his bow, and found his fingers tightening separately and to
rhythm. His head swayed on his shoulders, his teeth gnashed
softly in time as though of their own volition, his breathing
became involved with the beat of that mingled uproar that
presently surged in full swing around the motionless Mistress
of the Coven.

"What dreams Anne now?" wondered Joris—and then stood

aghast, for his very thought came only in quadruple lilt, and words being found, rang through his head in daft continuous iteration. *"What-dreams-Anne-now, what-dreams-Anne now, what dreams——"*

Swiftly and more swiftly throbbed the music and flew the dancing feet. Voices died breathlessly; a girl tripped and went hurtling against the base of a megalith, but those who loosed her hands only reached out to take each other's, and no one heeded her as she lay dazed and bleeding. Joris, battling with the mutinous body that bade him plunge into the riot, recalled the last words Anne had spoken to him—many hours ago it seemed—and felt a stir of rage against this lawlessness so different from his own. Joris, a skulking onlooker when great lords took the road, had come to skulk and look on in his own hills; he caught a moment at the possibility of staying such a scene with a quick hail of arrows from the surrounding gloom.

Quieter and more deadly grew the whirling double ring. Here and there sprawled those who had fallen out—some vomiting, some foaming at the mouth, some stark and still in a trance of exhaustion—but threescore at the least were still rapt and dancing when two dog-headed devilkins stood up beside the blue-white flares and lifted each a leathern water bucket.

Yaan thundered unintelligible words from his place at the hub of the flying wheels; the flares disappeared with a stench and a fierce hissing. Torches were flung down, trampled out, or beaten dead against the lichened grit; to a whirl of sparks the dance formation was shattered into a formless mob. The music died in a dreadful chorus of yells; darkness stormed the Singing Stones and utterly overwhelmed them.

The last that Joris saw was the cow-headed figure of Red Anne, still seated motionless upon the altar slab, with frantic couples reeling and falling about her on the trampled grass. Then, when the binding rhythm was gone, when only the thrum and whistle of wind remained to deaden the lecherous tumult, a panic of disgust and loathing caught the outlaw by the throat.

Killing and rape he understood as true prerogatives of men for whom the world was made; but this wild interweaving of song and dance and foul worship, of spectral admonition, of hatred and ravening lust, was too much even for Joris of the Rock.

If Anne's reserves and secret dreams centred around such beastliness, he felt his right to resent them. If she were mad with her childlessness, he could not cure her. And if she needed him in the dawn, she must seek him at his camp.

"It is against nature," snarled—and turned, and fled into the night.

VIII. COLLOQUY AT BELSAUNT

FOR eighteen months Juhel de Ath learned lessons of life
in the household of the Count of Barberghe. At first he
shared his tasks with half a dozen others; then he became
third page to the Viscount Robert, a sullen and spiteful young
man who halted in spirit between his father's avarice and his
mother's love of ostentation. Juhel served him deftly and well,
receiving in return an occasional well-placed kick and many
shrilled curses; it was hard to maintain the outward cheerful-
ness enjoined upon all junior gentlefolk in service of their
superiors.

"God speed you, my lord," said Juhel demurely each morning, when he brought Robin Barberghe's clothes to Robin
Barberghe's bedside; but except for that one sentence he never
opened his mouth in presence of the viscount unless the latter
spoke to him. And Juhel's real feeling for Robin Barberghe was
somewhere in the middle of the gradation of hatreds with
which he regarded those about the two of them.

He hated his guardian, the foxy count, with a desolate
realization of endless feudal contacts to come. He hated the
haughty countess for her prying eyes and nagging voice, for
the pride she took in her son, his immediate master. He hated
most of the castle women, especially those who crept along
the corridors to the viscount's bedchamber; sometimes they
were still there when he roused sleepy Robin in the morning,
and Juhel collected a queer little gallery of memories that
scared and depressed him. He hated the chiefs of the household, who pounced upon his brief leisure for help in their
several departments; only the chaplain and the master of the
minstrels were his friends, and among the other boys he found
it wise to pretend a dislike for the hours he spent in study of

books and music. But chiefest of all Juhel hated Gavin and Guy, his fellow pages, who stood a head taller than himself and plagued him soundly and often.

Boastful Gavin liked to make Juhel weep with pain, for it became a task that required some skill and perseverance; treacherous Guy preferred a chicane of trips and pinches and jeers timed for embarrassment. The chaplain kept Juhel's ballad book and ring for him; apart from these, his small possessions were at the mercy of his companions, for he slept in their room and was seldom apart from them during the day. Juhel learned how to dance naked on a stony floor in winter; how to sleep in a bed in which Guy had strewn breadcrumbs, cockroaches, or icicles; how to serve for half an hour in the hall with only one pair of points to hold up his plundered hose; and how to push a half-open door and step back to avoid the thigh boots or water bucket poised to drop on him. When the misdeeds of Gavin and Guy involved him in trouble with higher powers, Juhel blabbed without hesitation, thereby earning the name of "sneak" and providing his tormentors with moral justification for further violence.

"But they would torture me again anyway," Juhel reflected, "and there is always the chance of a beating for them."

He prayed for disasters to overtake Gavin and Guy, yet was not surprised when the pair of them throve; vaguely he felt that, given the prime stupidity of his relation to the House of Barberghe, a Providence so unreasonable could not be blamed for lesser misfortunes. By the eighteenth month of his life as a page, Juhel was an expert little liar, masking bitterness and bewilderment with an indifference demure or sullen or amused; he rode and ran, swam and wrestled, no better and no worse than others of his age, and found some comfort in two or three secret and long-continued fantasies.

In one of the latter he lived again with Folquin at Saint-Eloy-over-Hardonek; a flash of moonlight, an undertone of wind, could witch him from the dreary hold of Barberghe into the gray priory above the northern sea. In another and

stranger waking dream he lived in a silent castle whose sur-
roundings changed with his mood and with the season of the
year; armed and glittering he came to its kindly portal over
great hills, across dim marshes, or through the cathedral aisles
of a pine forest. He slew his dastard enemies of mornings,
hunted in the afternoons, and painted magnificent manu-
script decorations at night; at table he had the first cut of
the joint, and nowhere in that existence were any women.

His Tower of Ath took no place in those daydreams; it was
a reality as unpleasant as the rest, especially after Gavin told
him of the dishonour done to his family by Joris of the Rock.

"Unless you kill Joris," said Gavin gleefully, "no one will
ever dub you chevalier."

But Juhel scarcely heard him, and at sight of Juhel's horror-
stricken face even Guy was surprised and ashamed.

"*You* could not help it, Juhel," he pointed out, "and any-
how it is no honour to kill a villainous outlaw."

"Of course the child was your cousin," added Gavin. "But
after all, the Duke of Burias himself was a bastard until the
king married his mother."

Thenceforward a new and darker desolation clouded Juhel's
thoughts of his heritage; he wondered if the ghost of shamed
Tiphaine would carry the ghost of her murdered baby about
the gloomy tower until she was avenged by her sole surviving
kinsman. The years of squirehood ahead were suddenly lightened by contrast; for long enough yet the domain of Ath could
be forgotten.

Meanwhile Gavin and Guy constituted his chief problem;
and when at length they quarrelled, the fact of their quarrel
loomed larger in Juhel's eyes than the fact that they and he
were to ride south in the train of the Count of Barberghe on
a summer visit to the royal court at Hautarroy. Gavin half
strangled Guy at the cost of two loosened teeth and a black
eye; Juhel heaved with suppressed mirth when both were
flogged by the count's chamberlain.

"Curse him!" wailed Guy on the morning of departure.

"Here I must ride for four days at the least, as stiff as Lot's wife and as sore as Hamor the Hivite. And my lord Viscount will have capon roasted with syrup for his supper, if any innkeeper be slave enough to make the syrup—and *I* shall be roused at midnight by his bilious yelling. And at Hautarroy we shall have no sleep, any of us; once last year I slept for three hours out of forty-eight, and one of the three was in a gaming den."

Juhel, who then had stayed at Barberghe, now perceived that a little sober sympathy might gain him information undistorted by malice; he gave Guy some assistance in the last packing of Robin Barberghe's finery, and when at length the trumpets shrilled for the count's outgoing from his great hold, Guy and Juhel rode side by side near the head of the long procession. Gavin was somewhere behind them, having been detailed to watch the viscount's tilting armour, which went on a pack saddle of its own; and for the first time Juhel found equality with greedy brown-skinned Guy.

It was August, and long cloud shadows trailed over the ripening corn; abbey after lordly abbey spread its woods and vills and granges in the plain of Nordanay. Here and there was new building; sometimes a remnant of blackened stone roused whispers of the Jacquerie among the Barberghe men-at-arms. From the high-arched Bridge of Roray Juhel stared at the brown murmuring river; for at that place, thirteen years before, the great revolt had begun.

"A penny for my lord Count's thoughts," said Juhel very softly.

"Bah, much *he* cares," commented Guy, with eyes fixed on the plumed casque ahead of them. "There, on the left of the road, he had his row of gibbets. Seventy-two, they say, and some doubly loaded. That was his answer in the end."

"I suppose he enjoyed it," breathed Juhel after a pause.

Guy pulled a face.

"Yes," he muttered. "I want to fight when I am a man, but not against dirty serfs. *I* should not have enjoyed it."

"Nor I. Now . . . Gavin would."

Juhel spoke experimentally, with seeming innocence; his companion rose to the bait.

"Yes, rot him, he would. He is never content unless someone is being hurt; yesterday he dropped his work to run because two grooms were fighting in the stable. If he cannot set one dog on to another, or find a rat to pound to death, he will catch hover flies and put them into spiders' webs. . . . I should like to see him bewitched into a hare's shape and squeaking as he fled before our dogs!"

"I have made up a little poem about him," confessed Juhel with lofty carelessness.

"What? Tell it to me!"

"If you promise not to tell *him*."

"Go on! I promise!"

"This is it:

> "Listen to Gavin
>   And think of the thunder
> Of battle fronts closing,
>   Of panic and plunder,
> Of rape and of murder,
>   Of drowning and flame,
> Till, scared by the sound
>   Of his terrible name
>   You'll rhyme it with 'ravin.'

> "But lords, have no fear,
>   I doubt if he'll hurt you;
> And ladies, no need
>   To set guard on your virtue.
> Walk in his wake
>   Down the length of a street,
> And see the queer turn
>   Of his knees and his feet,
>   And you'll rhyme it with 'spavin.' "

Guy was impressed and amused; for some time afterward he memorized the poem with soundless movements of his lips, and during the whole of that journey Juhel and he were friends.

The first night they slept at an abbey. When on the following day they came near the river Varne the Count of Barberghe turned eastward at the Inn of Harmony instead of holding on his way south to cross at Angmer. Past the great hold of Olencourt he led his train in haste, for there was no love lost between him and the dour Castellan. And in the afternoon of the second day Juhel first laid eyes on a city—the fair city of Belsaunt, builded and walled with red and gray stone around the red palace of its bishop and the gray cathedral of Saint Austreberte, its patron.

The cynical page became again a flushed and wondering child; Juhel had not understood in what small space the burgher families dwelt above their crowded shops. Trim girls laughed at his absorbed face; one fair-haired minx leaned out of an upper window and flung a rose at it. Startled, he caught the flower as it fell, and most ungallantly hurled it back, missing the pink foolish maiden by inches only. Then the deepening sunlight flashed on the blue and silver-coloured sign of the Four Swords; Juhel must fling his bridle to Guy and leap to the cobbles, scuttling forward to hold the gilded bit chain of Robin Barberghe's bay.

Amid his careful duties he found time to note the thronging blazons of great lords—the gryphon, gold on blue, of the Constable Volsberghe, the red and yellow wolves' heads of Montcarneau, the silver fleurs-de-lis of Olencourt, the black bull of Ahun. He himself stood trimly enough in tunic and hose of black and red, with the three Barberghe chevrons counterchanged on his breast and a crow's feather in his red pointed hat.

"I believe it is going to be better now," he thought.

*　　　　*　　　　*

Supper was not at the Four Swords, but in the sombre machicolated mansion of the Duke of Ahun. There Juhel saw the Sieur Gaston de Volsberghe, lately returned from service in the Emperor's armies, with truth and legend like a cloud of evil bats around his banner; and among the mob of pages Juhel ate his fill of veal and mutton and wild goose, with puff-bread and *pynnonade,* a confection of almonds and pineapples which he particularly loved.

In a corner of the great hall he sat down on a bench and folded his hands over his stomach, praising Saints Christopher and Nicholas for his removal from the cheeseparing dominion of the Countess of Barberghe. He would have liked to talk to Guy, but Guy was drinking with the Volsberghe pages—no, horrors, Guy was maudlin drunk, with his arm about the neck of Gavin!

Gavin's prominent light eyes roved round the noisy crowd and came to rest on Juhel; Gavin's sleek rat-brown head was cocked attentively toward the grinning slobbering lips of Guy.

Something—perhaps the *pynnonade*—turned over in Juhel's inwards; he was betrayed, and knew it. Gavin nodded reflectively, and got up on his feet.

Juhel slipped past the dais screen and into a kitchen passage. Almost blindly he fled, with no intent but to flee; and in a moment his little flitting figure was swallowed up in the vast Hotel de Ahun.

"Little reptile, I will flay you!" raging Gavin sang into the gloom; and Juhel heard his pounding feet in the flagged passageway behind.

Smells of damp stone, lanterns hanging at corners, round-arched windows that gave glimpses of courtyards grassed or cobbled between dark sheers of masonry; once a group of poplars, feathery against opal afterglow, and once a silent reach of garden, shadowy blue and shining gray beneath the summer moon. . . .

Stairs and more stairs, with direction lost; an upper corridor, barred by faint lights here and there; a rumour of approaching words, waning only to wax sharply; a door ajar, a panic-stricken push and cautious entry, a queer smell of bees-wax. . . .

Juhel cowered on a shadowed wooden floor behind some sort of pierced wooden screen; he was near a yellow-coffered ceiling, pleasantly lighted by a great chandelier whose pulley ropes ran down out of his sight. Curious muffled shapes stood round him in the confined gloom; he had just time to realize that he was in the minstrel gallery of some small hall when deep voices resounded terrifyingly in the passage.

"Hamo, you will keep this door shut and stand on guard outside it until I send to dismiss you. No one is to enter, not my lady Duchess herself. See to it."

"Yes, my lord Duke."

There came the scrape of a drawn sword; Juhel held his breath in fright as a head came round the door. But the Duke of Ahun was hooded against the night air of his upper stories; one glance to left and right at the blanketed harp and viols, at the music stands and benches, could not show him the huddled boy in the deep shadow among them.

The head vanished, the door slammed; Hamo leaned against it with a cough, and when his lord had gone began to whistle softly to himself.

Juhel sat with triple terror knotting in his brain—terror of his present predicament, of Robin Barberghe who must shortly miss him, of Gavin when the two of them should meet again. Then a door grated open, this time out of his sight in the chamber below; and the great voice of Gaston de Volsberghe thrilled the listener's eardrums.

"In faith, my lords, I feared I was come home to rust awhile; but now it seems unlikely."

Laughter followed his words, and a setting and scraping of chairs; nearly a dozen men had entered and were placing themselves around a table. Through the patterned holes of his gallery screen Juhel saw gleaming silks and satins, the flash of a gemmed sword hilt, the flick of a ringed hand. He dared not move forward to press his eye to a chink in the carving, lest the boards groan or creak to his weight; instead he held himself very still.

"Be seated, my lords," came the request of the Duke of Ahun. "I have set seal on every entry; we may speak freely for a time."

There was a final stir and trampling, dying down into expectant silence. Then someone spoke in tones like the Sieur Gaston's, but more tired and hollow-sounding; and Juhel knew that it was Gaston's father, the old Duke of Volsberghe who was constable of the realm.

"The first news, my lords, is that our cock is game."

"I knew it," crowed a younger man, in a voice so aptly of the barnyard that a gust of laughter ringed the board.

"The Duke of Camors," thought Juhel, "and half-drunk, too. But the rest of them are marvellously sober."

Words and phrases, quietly spoken at first, becoming gradually more audible as the speakers warmed to their subject.

"He shall have no alternative, my lord Duke."

"The mischief is that all our northern holds are clean impregnable without protracted siege. . . ."

"Oh, ay, Barberghe, time is everything."

"And Montenair is hapless."

"Well, Marckmont at the crossing of the marshes . . ."

"But who knows what is in the head of Raoul of Ger?"

"Dreams, and a damnable quickness with steel."

That was Juhel's own master; so the Barberghes, foxy sire and spiteful son, were both in this coil, whatsoever it might prove to be. Gradually a sense of the scene formed in Juhel's mind. There was Gaston explaining, inviting, forestalling criticism; the constable seconding him with a flung word or two; Camors hiccoughing a little, but very sure that all was for the best; Barberghe moodily considering, objecting, temporizing; someone else scenting blood but still half dazed by an enormous supper. Ahun himself was all but silent; a few younger men confined their opinions to grunts and monosyllables.

Juhel's inexpert conjectures stabbed and recoiled amid the fragments of discussion; only gradually were his own fears forgotten in the realization that he listened to a planning of great treason.

At length he felt his eyes widen, and a shiver not of dread assailed his body. "Our cock" was Conrad of Burias; when old King René died his nephew Thorismund was to be set aside—and old King René was lying sick in Hautarroy.

"But why not wring the princely neck?" demanded some-one gruffly.

"Because his cousin of Franconia has next claim," said the Sieur Gaston smoothly. "Do you want Franconian armies to find us all at odds? Thorismund must be seized and—persuaded. Moreover, we must have Belsaunt; for this place is the key to all the north."

"I see. And my lord Count of Ger being also my lord Baron of Marckmont——"

"Holds coast road and marsh road, dividing my lord my father from my lord of Barberghe, and me from my greatly desired Belsaunt."

"My lord and my lord and my lord!" thought Juhel in the shadows, his natural disrespect at length reasserting itself. "Gaston must be set on his plan, since he keeps his temper so shrewdly. But it is a great baseness, and they are making of *me* a rebel and a traitor."

Juhel squirmed at the idea, thus first presented to him, that his own life was one of thousands to be staked by these noblemen. Thousands of people were living all round him; in Belsaunt, in Honoy, in Neustria, in Christendom, in Heathenesse that stretched to the ultimate sweep of ocean— and merely by living after their customs they compelled each other. War, and a reaching after power, were customs of great lords. For a moment existence was revealed to Juhel as a thing of hideous and unbearable complexity; if it came to a vote down there, the word of tipsy Camors or wily Barberghe might doom great rivers of blood and tears to flow. And yet—

Saint-Eloy-over-Hardonek had taught him so—he knew that
all that would be must accord with the rulings of the Sieur
God.

It was too difficult for Juhel, whose youthful heart still
quaked for signs of a great mercy beyond the dull horizons of
adversity; he sat spellbound and sick, half heedless of the
tense debate until Gaston de Volsberghe closed it with a fist
blow on the table.

"Then *I* will sound this prodigy of Ger whose name so
plagues you all. For the rest, each to his task, and say no word
to your ladies, for you know what that may mean."

The last gust of laughter had a reckless ring in it. Chairs
were thrust back; Camors belched joyfully. Voices thinned
and lessened, footfall and movement checked at the doorway
and receded beyond it. Behind Juhel, in the upper corridor,
someone hailed Hamo, who replied with alacrity and stumped
quickly away.

Juhel sat rigid for a moment, and then groaned and grimaced in a torment of pins and needles. Many seconds elapsed
before he could stand upright; then he slipped out into the
passage and scuttled unhappily off to find the way by which
he had come.

Corridors, corners, stairs, a brushing of dusty arras—once
the squeak of a rat that turned in a moonlit entry. Then a
covered way resembling one walk of a cloister, but with no
low wall between the outer columns; instead, you stepped
straight out upon gravelled paths, in a shadowed angle of a
garden where ghostly roses stared from the black web of their
bushes, where trim beds were pallid with ranked marigolds
and tulips.

The mingled breath of delight halted the boy in his tracks.
He sniffed, and choked down a sob; it was cruel that such
beauty should strike up between two miseries. Gavin would
roundly deny that he had chased Juhel from the hall; what,
then, could be said to the Viscount Robin?

Later Juhel wished that he had grasped more tightly the

splendour of his moment among the friendly flowers; for as he neared the steps that led up into the great hall, one of the Barberghe squires came out and looked around.

"What are *you* doing here?" he demanded, moonlight showing him the chevroned tunic and the still-chubby face.

"I got lost," was Juhel's truthful reply.

"Well, come with me. My lord Viscount wants one of you— *you* will do."

"Where is my lord?"

"Gone to the bear pits. They are to have a torchlight baiting."

Presently Juhel had to cling to the squire's sword belt, so thronged was the gallery round the sanded pit. In a strange war of costly perfumes and uprising animal stench he wormed his way through the press; once he was crushed against the fur-trimmed mantle of a slim and lovely lady. He embarked upon an apologetic stutter, but the lady looked down and smiled, her chin no more than a foot above his own. Her oval face was glorious in the red flicker of torchlight; she had green eyes and a pale skin and hair that gleamed like bronze beneath the rim of her yellow-horned headdress, and Juhel knew her for the Lady Yolande de Volsberghe, daughter of the constable, sister of the Sieur Gaston, and—some said— mistress of Prince Thorismund himself.

"Some day some maid will not expect apology for *that*," affirmed the Lady Yolande with critical good humour; and her soft scented hand came up and tickled Juhel under the angle of the jaw. The boy blushed painfully and struggled away; and later, crouching silently by the balustrade and beside the silken legs of Robin Bargerghe, he wondered if the many tales they told of her were true.

It was queer that her lovely remembered features, seen so close for a second or two, could blot out the noisy sport beneath for moments at a time. Not until blood began to spurt did Juhel succumb to the spell of the game; then he stopped wondering whether the Lady Yolande was really so fair as he believed, and watched with paling cheeks and quickened breath the grim death shuffle on the blotched brown sand.

Midnight found the Viscount Robin too drunk to retire to his inn; the household had followed the count thither and only Juhel was left with his young master. Robin Barberghe slept in a bed beside the Duke of Camors; Juhel lay on a mattress near them, glad that the night was warm, and the duke's page friendly, and the duke's great boarhound much less formidable than he first appeared. Weariness conquered his dread of coming retribution; the ducal snoring that lulled him to sleep seemed barely separated from the boarhound's morning sneeze that awakened him.

Then, indeed, sunlight and dew and twitter of birds could not redeem him from wretchedness. Like a criminal he slunk behind the sleepy Viscount into the courtyard of the Four Swords; sullenly he looked at Gavin and Guy, wondering how soon their chance would come.

It came just before breakfast, when Robin Barberghe went alone into his father's bedroom. Juhel, groping in his saddle-bag for a clean shirt, found his beloved ballad book gone and gave a yelp of dismay.

Three minutes later he was down in a small flagged court leading off the main inn yard. He struggled in Guy's skilful grasp, while Gavin lugged the book from a belt wallet.

"Let me alone, you big beasts!" he screeched. "Give me my ballad book and let me alone!"

"Get hold of his other hand, Guy."

"Ai, the little devil kicks—you would kick, would you?"

"Yes, I would kick you dead if I could. Oh, no, I did not mean it. Gavin, please, *please,* Gavin, do not throw it away!"

"You made a rhyme about me, little pig—now see where your book is going."

Up flew the slim brown leather-covered tome, curving downward again to lodge on a jut of crazy tiles.

"There, now the pigeons can read it. And that is only a beginning. I'll make you write your poem down and eat it. And now you will be late to breakfast. . . ."

Guy released Juhel, and the tormentors fled laughing. Juhel stood white and still, gnawing a knuckle and staring up at his treasure. A servant of the inn passed through the yard, and like a flash the boy turned to him.

"Will you get my book for me, please?" he demanded, pointing aloft. "I will give you a florin and three pennies, which is all I have."

"None of your games with me, young master," said the man, disappearing without an upward glance.

Juhel clasped his hands and stood considering. Two great tears stole down his smudged face; then he flew at a water butt, climbed up on its edge, and scrabbled with hands and foot at the leaden drainpipe above.

"If you fall in there, you will drown," said a quiet voice from nowhere. Juhel craned his neck, changed grip on the lead, felt his firm foot slip on the mossed edge of the butt, and half jumped, half fell to the flags, whence he did not attempt to rise or look for assistance.

Instead, he lay utterly hopeless, crying softly and rubbing his bruised behind; but when he found a young man bending over him he started up on an elbow with more of defiance than pain in his expression.

"Are you hurt?" demanded the same quiet voice "No? Or no more than usual? One moment, someone is coming. . . ."

The young man was of middle height, and wore thin leather garments of the sort used under armour. His uncovered hair was thick and light brown, his aquiline face brown-ivory, austerely yet sweetly carven; his wide pale mouth held a half smile at its chiselled corners, and his eyes were almost of faery, being green-gray flecked with amber. Juhel blinked at their friendly regard, and the stranger stood upright.

"I will get your book for you," he said, and suddenly raised his voice in a call: "Hey, fellow!"

The sleepy serving man had reappeared, and now came lumbering up to them.

"Fetch a ladder."

"Please you, worshipful sir, the master of the house has bidden me find for my lord Count of Barberghe . . . in fact, I am sent to bring . . ."

"I am the Count of Ger. Fetch a ladder."

"Oh—oh, good my lord, I crave your pardon—I was nowise aware——"

"You and your awareness be damned in one heap, but *fetch a ladder!*"

Like an unwieldy crossbow quarrel the man went hurtling into a doorway. The young count chuckled and looked down again; Juhel was kneeling now, with dark disordered hair framing a grubby face aglow with gratitude and half-incredulous worship.

"My—my lord Count, I—I—I——"

"It is nothing, boy. I once lost a ballad book myself. Come, stand up!"

"It was—I could not bear to lose it, my lord. I will pray God to guard you against all dangers forever—but——"

"But what?"

When Juhel was on his feet his head came above the count's shoulder; he looked the rescuer of his treasure up and down with a hungry, dazzled glare.

"But, my lord, you said you were the——"

"So I did. So I am."

"It was you who destroyed the Easterlings and took the great hold of Campscapel. . . ."

"I with a hundred brave men. But what is the use of taking the hold of Campscapel if I cannot have a ladder when I want one?"

"My lord Count . . ."

But the page's husky voice was interrupted; Gavin bounded into the courtyard, raising a derisive yell.

"Juhel, you fool, the comptroller wants you—and you are going to catch it hot!"

The Count Raoul of Ger in his plain leather garments made no better first impression on the page than on the serving man. Not until he was caught by the ear did sprightly Gavin connect Juhel's loitering with the handsome stranger.

"Ow, let go!" he squealed. "Who the devil are you?"

"Hush, you silly clown," spluttered Juhel, standing on one leg in shocked distress. "My lord is my lord Count of Ger!"

"Be off," said the count, loosing goggle-eyed Gavin with a box on the ear. "My compliments to my lord of Barberghe, and tell him his page shall follow with me."

As the end of a ladder came wildly through a doorway Juhel snorted and looked up at the count's face.

"And now," he said, "Gavin will boast forever that you, my lord, clouted his head for him."

"Fame indeed. But tell me, what is your name?"

"Juhel de Ath, my lord."

"How old?"

"Fourteen, my lord."

"Do the bigger pages bully you often?"

"N—not often, my lord."

"Tell me the rhyme you made about Gavin."

"My lord:

> "Listen to Gavin
> And think of the thunder . . ."

The Count of Ger smiled, and Juhel suffered bewitchment. The face of Yolande de Volsberghe fell to second place of honour in his heart; here seemed something more worshipful than all the ladies in the land.

Then he grabbed and pouched his ballad book, and caught at the count's hand to kiss it violently.

"Gavin has some reason for wrath," said the young nobleman reflectively.

"My lord, he—he keeps us awake until midnight with his

tales; he believes half the ladies are in love with him. It **was** mean of me to make fun of his legs, but——"

"Each to his weapon, hey? Can you arm a chevalier, and ride?"

"Yes, my lord."

"And serve at board, and stand still, and hold your tongue?"

"Yes, my lord."

"And swim, and read a blazon, and play the lute, and hit back with a quarterstaff, and blow your nose in season?"

"Y—yes, my lord."

"Well, follow me."

Juhel was pale and shivering with excitement, but when he followed Count Raoul into the chamber reserved for those of gentle blood his face went a proud crimson. Throughout the meal, when his duties allowed, he kept his dark eyes fixed on the face of the young war captain; the curious regard of Gavin and Guy could not disturb Juhel, for as Raoul of Ger seated himself he said to Barberghe beside him: "Excuse your page, my lord; he and I were delayed by a slight exchange of courtesy."

"The lad is Robin's," replied Barberghe, after one glance aside at Juhel, "but I am glad to hear of his behaviour."

"I also," added the Viscount Robin quickly; and he and his father set themselves to use great civility toward their fellow guest.

Toward the end of the meal they were talking of horses, and Robin complimented Count Raoul on his great dapple-gray destrier that stood in the stables below.

"That is Noureddin," said the count, "own brother to my Safadin. Sixteen hands high, and five years old, and trained as ever war horse could be. Robin, here is a bargain—take Noureddin as a gift, and lend me your brown owlet of a page until he be eighteen; I warrant you will then find him a trim squire."

Juhel paled and trembled again, scarcely believing his **ears;**

and he saw the Fox of Barberghe elbow his son gently in the ribs.

"Why, willingly, Raoul," cried the Viscount Robin. "I take it as great grace in you, for the bargain is more generous than just. Juhel, come hither; my lord Count of Ger has saved you from a drubbing, but I dare tell he knows how to administer one at need. Serve him as cleanly and well as is in you, and guard the honour of his choice. Raoul, I render you Juhel de Ath; Juhel, bow to my lord."

Juhel made the supreme bow of his fourteen years; and behind the backs of two counts and a viscount he stuck out a deliberate tongue at Gavin and Guy, plucking up the edge of the ballad book so that it showed for a moment at the square-cut neck of his tunic.

His tunic! Half an hour after breakfast Juhel tugged the garment off and danced on it, so that Piers du Véranger permitted himself a first smile as he laid his own best tunic out for Juhel to take up. Juhel was fellow page to Piers now; Piers was darker even than he, grave and gentle and self-contained; Juhel looked for jealousy in Piers and was slightly disturbed to find none.

"What is this?" he asked, pointing to the little silken escutcheon—azure charged with a golden swan—sewn on the left breast of the yellow cloth whose main device was a black gerfalcon with extended wings.

"The badge of Marckmont," replied Piers. "Marckmont is my lord Count's barony; there is a little castle which he loves more than the great hold of Ger. At Ger there are four pages; but *I* am the only page of Marckmont . . . yet . . . and only I have the Marckmont badge on my clothes; and only I came with my lord on this journey. What are you looking at?"

"Marckmont," repeated Juhel, wide-eyed and still-voiced. *"Marckmont at the crossing of the marshes."*

"Yes, that is right. There is a long causeway. But what do you mean?"

"Nothing," said Juhel. "That is—only something I heard

last night. But I hope my lord Count makes *me* a page of Marckmont."

"Hurry up," advised Piers; and a moment later he asked: "Are you glad to come from the Barberghes, then?"

"*Glad!*" grunted Juhel, involved with his black borrowed hose. "I hate the lot of them. But my lord Count—of Ger, that is—seems to me . . ."

He stopped, afraid of making himself ridiculous.

"Seems to you what?" inquired Piers, with tone suddenly edged.

Juhel plunged.

"The best and noblest lord and chevalier in Christendom," he muttered, flushing up to the roots of his hair.

"Of course," said the other, half surprised, but tranquil and good-natured as before, so that Juhel was emboldened to ask a question.

"The household," he began diffidently, "do they—are you often beaten?"

Piers stared.

"Tuck your shirt in at the back," he ordered, "and tie up those Barberghe clothes in a bundle. Why should I be beaten?"

"Well—*I* was," mumbled Juhel, stricken by the difference between life and life.

"Ah—the Barberghes," said Piers, as though the name explained everything. "And now come with me; there is a groom waiting to take your bundle back to the noble viscount."

"Curse you, clothes," whispered Juhel, as the bundle vanished from his sight. Then he caressed the silken badge of Marckmont on his breast, and twirled upon one finger the cap which Piers had lent him—a black-and-yellow cap, with a pheasant's tail feather clasped to the crown by a little bronze gerfalcon.

"Take care of that," commanded Piers, indicating the clasp. "It was a gift to me from Master Nino Chiostra, who fashioned it."

"Who is he?" inquired Juhel curiously. "An Italian smith?"

"Comptroller to my lord Count. They lived together in
Belsaunt once, before my lord was even viscount. Yes,
Master Nino is a Tuscan, and a graver of gems; it is mar-
vellous to watch him. Also he is a deadly swordsman.
Also . . ."

The two boys were advancing toward the door at the end
of a long upper passage. The door was ajar; from behind it
came a thrumming of lutestrings and a man's sweet tenor
voice.

> "Sing ho, six comely demoiselles,
>   Carim-cara, cara-carim.
> In each a differing charm excel,
> And each a partial love compels,
>   Carim, cara, carissima."

"That also," whispered Piers as he knocked on the door, "is
Master Nino Chiostra."

"Come in!" boomed a second and greater voice, so that
Juhel jumped before he followed Piers into the room.

"Now, by the harrowing of hell!" said the second voice in a
lower key. "It is not yet the hour of terce, and I have sipped
one scurvy half flagon, yet already our Piers goes double!"

The speaker sat half armoured on a truckle-bed; he was
barely above average height, but broader than any man Juhel
had seen, with straw-coloured hair and a pink square-jawed
slab of a face. The little tight-lipped mouth above his formidable chin went strangely with the laughter in his small
blue eyes; Juhel's glance flew over the great shoulder to the
big *estoc,* or two-handed sword, in the corner behind the bed.

"Master Nino, Captain John, Master Hubriton," piped
Piers evenly, "my lord Count bade me introduce to you his
new page, Juhel de Ath."

"Your servant, my masters," muttered Juhel, with a com-
prehensive bow that failed by only an inch or two to match
his other in the breakfast chamber. Timidly he straightened
up, to meet in turn the honey-coloured eyes of the handsome
comptroller and the black eyes of the gaunt secretary.

Master Nino Chiostra, too, wore half armour for the journey; his plum-red velvet cloak lay on the table at his elbow, and a pearl shone blandly on one of the fingers that danced up and down the strings of his great lute. Beneath black curly hair his face was very brown.

"Whence come you, Juhel?" he asked kindly; and while Juhel told him he looked the boy over.

"Serve my lord Count well," he said at length, "and all here are your friends. This is no Barberghe school of valour, where a blow resounds six times until it reaches a kitchen lad. Follow Piers carefully, and nothing will go amiss. Away now, the pair of you; while you are arming my lord Count we will find another horse."

"Straight in the back and full in the calf," growled fair-haired Captain John. "He will do."

And when Juhel slipped out with Piers the second verse of Nino's song pursued them down the passage.

> "A doleful doom I bear in mind,
>   *Carim-cara, cara-carim;*
> When that my true love I shall find,
> Six charms in her must go combin'd.
>   *Carim, cara, carissima."*

"Who—who is the great soldier?" asked Juhel as they went.

"Captain John Doust, the Englishman, who took the head off Jehan de Campscapel. No man in Neustria, I dare wager, would stand up in his best suit of plate for Captain John to take one blow at him with that grim double-handed sword. It is merry when they are together, my lord Count and he and Master Nino. Even Master Hubriton will enter into their jesting, and he is glum enough for the most part. Now, silence."

In a fever of hushed devotion Juhel helped Piers to buckle the bright armour upon Raoul of Ger.

"Easier with two of you," commented the young count absently. Then he turned his eyes from the thronged street beyond the slatted window to the two dark heads bobbing about him.

"Juhel, you are strange to cities," he observed. "Mark this—be courteous to the burgher folk as to any priest or chevalier. Their way of life is not a better way, or yet a worse way, than mine and yours; it is a different way. Up there, in Street of Anvils, I had upon a time great kindliness and comfort shown me. I would have all burghers know that my coats mark their friends. You understand?"

"Yes, my lord."

"Good boy. You are deft with the armour, but still you touch it with hot palms, which will not do. Piers works with fingers only, and so must you. Piers, take my shield to-day; Juhel, the helm and cloak. Follow on."

How different this sally and this mounting from every such occasion gone before! The great courtyard of the Four Swords was bright with yellow surcoats; men wearing other colours—among them chevrons red and black—formed a mere fringe of groundlings. A fringe admiring, sullen, critical . . . and, to Juhel, utterly negligible.

To-day Count Raoul sat his great iron-gray stallion Safadin; Juhel felt that he would like to whisper an apologetic explanation in the ear of dapple-gray Noureddin, parted from his more famous brother to make a page happy.

For Juhel felt that he was going to be happy. Dimly he knew that he had met with those who were gentle, and yet not fools or weaklings. In a world of bullies and clods and cowards he had inwardly mocked at the duties preached to him; amid the crowding sable falcons he suddenly saw those duties as proud and shining things. Serve and obey, yes—but first be sure that what you served was worthy.

The count's trumpets shrilled. Juhel tightened rein of the black gelding set apart for his use. Forward through the summer air, into the shadowed streets of Belsaunt—Gavin and Guy bareheaded and respectful at the great inn gateway; Juhel, with cap pulled tight on his curls, sparing them one contemptuous glance as he rode forth to Hautarroy.

IX. THE SPIRES OF HAUTARROY

NIGHT in the ancient city. The moon a glittering silver disk emerging from swift translucent cloud. Beyond the open doors the archbishop's terrace, flagged and dully gleaming, with shrubs in stone vases; beyond again, mysterious blackness of trees, where a nightingale had sung and fallen silent. Beneath each door and window the dainty shadows of clambering roses, dancing in shapes of moonlight that slanted across the floor.

Juhel, curled up in a window seat of the dim antechamber, paid dreamy heed to the wind song, sniffing the blown perfume as he dared not sniff its counterpart in Belsaunt hours before. For this was his third night with a strange household, and no one had yet made any attempt to kick him. All afternoon, since their arrival in the city, Piers had run and ridden on the count's errands; now Piers was in bed at the Sign of the Burning Bush, and Juhel all alone had followed their lord on his visit of respect to the aged prelate.

They—the tired old man and the grave young one—were in there, behind the purple-curtained door; on the other window seat in the antechamber dozed a page of the archbishop's household, and Juhel felt himself to be alone.

To-morrow his own clothes were to be ready—and with a swan upon the breast of each tunic, for Juhel was appointed second page of Marckmont. To-morrow he would see the Prince Thorismund at archery practice. To-morrow the lords who had met in conclave at Belsaunt would have followed to the capital; ah, he must tell the Count of Ger what he overheard in the Hotel de Ahun. So many things had crowded in his mind since then.

To-morrow, therefore, he might also see again the Lady Yolande de Volsberghe. He made a faint grimace at the thought: even here, in Hautarroy, you must come to the archbishop's palace before you escaped from women; at the Burning Bush the serving maids giggled and squeaked round corners, thrusting themselves in the way of men-at-arms, cursing roundly when the latter clipped and kissed them; at the Burning Bush, too, the fat wife of the tavern master had licked her lips and beckoned to him; but Juhel had pretended not to see. And although the Lady Yolande was so fair that it had hurt him to touch her, and almost hurt him to remember her, Juhel had that in his blood which recoiled from all reminder of fleshly violence.

"Great lords seem mightily pleased to be away from their ladies," he had sneered to Piers at noon, when they saw a painted but elderly nobleman stand in his stirrups to accost a grinning woman of the town at her window above him.

"H'mph," snorted Piers. "Wait until you see my lord Count ride again to Ger."

Juhel was silenced, and in part discomfited; already adoring his master, he had not faced the fact of a countess in the background. Vaguely he shrank from having to respect a side of life that hitherto had shown him nothing but ugliness.

Yet Ger was far away, and that new trouble very misty. Now, in the shadowy antechamber, his colourful daydreams of war and chase and delicate brushwork came coiling upon him; very quietly he began to croon the lilting verses of Master Nino Chiostra, that went with streaming banners and jingling spurs and bridles.

> "First to enchant me she must bear,
>   *Carim-cara, cara-carim,*
> The nimbus of Olivia's hair,
> But not Olivia's nose, I swear,
>   *Carim, cara, carissima.*

"Next must I claim, and she allow,
  Carim-cara, cara-carim,
Costanza's calm and steadfast brow,
Yet not Costanza's ears, I vow,
  Carim, cara, carissima.

"And by the Mustering of the Ships,
  Carim-cara, cara-carim,
My love must pout Elena's lips
Yet shame Elena's narrow hips,
  Carim, cara, carissima."

That, if any, was the way to sing about women. There was always something wrong about them . . . but here came the Sieur Count, escorted by the archbishop's chaplain.

Juhel leaped to his feet, shook the other page awake, and stood respectfully tendering the count's sword belt and rich cloak and feathered bonnet. Behind the shapely head of Raoul of Ger he caught a glimpse of the archbishop's black-and-orange hangings, of the great bronze candelabra and the high blue ceiling starred with bronze and gold. The count's wide eyes and aquiline nose and big well-carven mouth chimed in Juhel's heart, even as the great cathedral bells began in that same moment to chime upon his ear.

"Midnight," said Raoul of Ger; and when he was belted and cloaked the chaplain led him to a postern in the street wall of the gloomy palace. A gentleman-at-arms saluted; pikemen grounded their butts; Juhel flicked his own cloak round his shoulder in imitation of his master.

Outside was blinding moonlight and rushing wind. At the foot of an ink-black alley lay the darkling sheen of water; beyond were the dim island towers of Sanctalbastre, and beyond again the rock of Ingard, crowned by the great royal castle, loomed sable in cloud-shadow.

"My lord Count," asked the chaplain, "shall I call the link-men of the household to light you home?"

"I thank you, Father—no. I have only to round three sides

of Saint Andreas to reach the Burning Bush. It is nearly as plain as daylight."

A moment later Juhel was trotting behind his lord as the latter strode into the open space before the western end of the cathedral. From a street on their left came voices and a flickering of torchlight; a glance showed Juhel a perspective of shuttered houses, with a tall gateway open at the end of them, and a lighted courtyard filled with moving men. By twos and threes the torches passed into the warren of alleyways; it was Sunday morning, and the guests of the cardinal count were leaving the Hotel de Estragon.

Raoul of Ger turned away and aimed for the northwestern angle of Saint Andreas. Juhel, as he went, picked out the saint's own image above the doorway. Galilee porch and ranked kings and bishops in their niches, steps where the beggars sat by day, slender western turrets where the pigeons nested—all these, as moonlight flashed and passed, stood sharply cut in silver-gray and sable, or blurred and lost in one dark face of stone. Behind the soaring bulk of the great central tower dim masses of gray cloud went scudding; the plane trees and chestnut trees that lined two sides of the square kept up a constant hiss and roar, shifting and tossing their dark foliage against frowning stillness of blank-windowed palaces behind them.

There were houses of great noblemen—the Hotels de Lestembourg, du Fors, de Boqueron, and at the far end, coming close against cathedral outbuildings beside the northern transept, the Hotel de Hastain, the home of young Thorismund, heir to the sick and ancient king.

Count Raoul and Juhel passed the base of the northwestern tower; the boy glanced up at the buttressed bulk of the north nave aisle. The roof was invisible now, and only a line of crocketed finials cut into the stormy sky.

"Like a great ship riding at anchor," thought Juhel, "only safer, and kindlier, and more blessed, and very still."

He glanced across the windy square to taste the contrast of

the raging trees, and suddenly caught his breath. Then he
reached out and tugged at the count's flying cloak.

"My lord," he muttered, "my lord! We are followed!"

The count spun round.

"Where? By whom?"

"Two men, among the trees. They are still now. One, two,
three trees to the left of the turret with the shining vane."

"Over many people about for cutpurse dealings," commented the count. "See, torches all over the square behind."

"*They* have no torches," whispered Juhel, wishing he carried a dagger.

"Come along, boy, we are only five minutes from the inn."

The count's voice was amused, but he quickened his stride.
Ahead was a dark entry, leading through the buildings of the
choristers' school into the open space behind the cathedral
apse. From that passage branched a narrower alley, which
skirted the flank of the Hotel de Hastain and led into the
same open space a score of paces to the left of the other.
Gaining the mouth of the entry, the count paused; straight
ahead of him stretched the dark passage, with a wooden post
at the far end to restrict its use to foot passengers. Beyond
the post were cobbles, wall-shadowed, tree-shadowed, and at
length brightly moonlit, running to a gutter and a sheer house-
wall; and as Raoul of Ger stepped forward an owl's cry,
thrice repeated, rang from among the trees behind.

Juhel gasped. Along the branching alley something creaked.
The mystified count ripped out his sword and advanced up
the passage to the alley mouth, with his page shivering in
rear.

Darkness and emptiness in the alley; only the rushing of
wind in leaves to be heard. The count's left hand came groping backward, to find a hot clutching paw; the count trotted
down the covered way, dragging the scuttling Juhel behind
him.

In a flash they were clear of the building; a deep-toned
twang resounded from their left, and something whizzed to

thud into wood behind them. Over his shoulder Juhel saw
a swinging first-floor shutter in the building beside the mouth
of the alley; then he was hauled past the low wall of the
choristers' playground and flung into the black shadow of a
buttress of the cathedral apse.

The count knelt to peer round the arris, and a man broke
sword in hand out of the passageway, shouting something
unintelligible toward the window beyond him.

"Behind the buttress!" cried an answering voice.

The man turned; then, at a clash of steel in the passage,
turned again.

"Oh, God!" he squeaked, and ran like a rabbit across the
moonlit space to disappear in the mean streets beyond the
angle of the Hotel de Hastain.

The shutter clashed to in Thorismund's dark wall. A
second armed man, with a boy scampering behind him, broke
from the passage and stood glaring this way and that.

"Watch ho!" he roared at the top of his voice. "Come on,
you skulking knaves! Watch ho! this way!"

"Get into cover," called the count calmly. "They shot from
the window beyond you."

The count was out in the moonlight again, pointing with
his sword.

"Who the devil are you?" spat the other, striding up with
blade advanced; and then: "Why, Raoul, what the fiend is all
this?"

Juhel saw that the newcomer was the Sieur Brian de Saulte,
brother of the great duke and close friend of Prince Thorismund.

"I do not know," confessed Raoul of Ger. "For God's sake
come behind the buttress—and the lad, too. Now, what is
amiss? What happened to *you?*"

"I came from the cardinal count's and saw two knaves go
stealing along in front of me—after you, if it was you ahead
—and one of them hooted like an owl, and then they slipped
into the passage—and I after them, and one turned like a

stoat, but I had already drawn; and besides, I wear chain mail. *He* lies there at least. What befell you?"

The Count of Ger told him, while Juhel and the Saulte page grinned at each other in scared excitement.

"But that is the Hotel de Hastain," muttered the Sieur Brian, with a thunderous frown on his fair hawk's face.

"Well I know it. Was it a crossbow?"

"Was it—yes. The bolt sticks in that post. Hark, here is the watch."

Lights had appeared in windows across the way, but the Hotel de Hastain reared an unresponsive bulk against the stars. Torches guttered round a corner and came streaming down the wind; lanterns swung amid steel corselets and a glitter of guisarmes. In the passage someone stumbled and swore.

"Hell to pay," cried a clear voice. "Conrad, mind your feet; a dead man, I vow."

In a moment the space at the end of the passage was bright with torch and lantern; the bolt gleamed in the wooden post at the height of a man's heart. Backed by a gay-clad group of nobles, a beautiful youth with flame-red hair and cloak of emerald green stood staring at the count and the Sieur Brian, and at a saluting captain of the watch.

"What has passed here?" he demanded imperiously.

Brian de Saulte bowed low and gestured at the post. The Count of Ger lifted his chin and looked his royal cousin in the eye.

"My good lord Prince, I seem to have dodged a bolt intended for Brian—who, coming behind, slew one of those who followed and had given the signal to shoot."

"To shoot where from?"

"That window."

Thorismund turned, and in the haughty press behind him someone sniggered.

"Impossible," said the prince flatly.

"My lord Prince, I saw and heard it."

"Do you know what you are saying? That is my own house."

"I know what I am saying. That *is* your own house. I noticed it. The angle of the bolt confirms my words. It missed me by a yard only, and my page here by inches."

"Page? Here, stripling, *you* tell what happened."

Juhel, already sufficiently scared if only by the new tone in his master's quiet voice, now swallowed and stood forward to begin a faltering tale. The prince listened soberly, and beyond him in the unsteady light Juhel could now make out the dark impassive face of Conrad, Duke of Burias.

"Bring the corpse here," commanded Thorismund when Juhel had done. "Show a lantern, someone. Montdor, is this a man of my own following?"

The prince's chamberlain moved forward and bent low.

"I never saw the rogue before," he said after a moment. "Upon my oath he is none of yours, my lord."

"Nevertheless——" began Brian de Saulte harshly; but the young prince stepped forward and caught at Brian's hand.

"Montdor," he ordered sharply, "guard my honour and yours! Indoors at once and apprehend that crossbowman. Conrad, you and I will later see Brian to his door. Captain, dispose of this carrion; if another man be caught, bring him to me forthwith."

"One moment, Thorismund," said Conrad of Burias curiously. "May I ask my lord of Ger why he thought this foul blow aimed at Brian rather than at himself?"

Roaul of Ger flashed his charming grin full in the speaker's face.

"Why, then, Raoul?" inquired the prince, with one hand now on an arm of Brian and Conrad alike.

"Gramercy for that courteous query, my lord Duke," said Raoul of Ger. "But no one knew how or when I, with one follower or more, might leave my lord Archbishop; while many must have known that Brian, with one page only, might pass hereby soon after midnight."

"I am answered," replied Duke Conrad. "But also I say, the Sieur God be praised it missed you both."

"Amen to that!" cried the prince. "Now enter with me, all, and see what Montdor finds for us."

The Count of Ger bowed and begged to be excused. Thorismund of Hastain eyed him angrily, but made no objection. Juhel was suddenly aware that no man present respected the prince as he respected the Duke of Burias, or the Count of Ger, or fiery Brian de Saulte. And Juhel would have liked to know what happened next; but the count took a courteous farewell of the prince and his companions, and walked deliberately away.

Ten minutes later, when still on his knees after pulling off the count's elegant puce-coloured thigh boots, Juhel looked up into his master's face and gave a gasp of nervousness.

"What is it?" asked Raoul of Ger sharply.

"My—my lord, at Belsaunt, four nights since, I overheard a secret conclave . . ."

Raoul of Ger listened, sitting almost motionless on the great bed, with fingers of one slim strong hand twisting slowly amid Juhel's curly hair. Once or twice he stopped the boy to question him, but mostly he kept silence until the end. Then he bent the dark head backward and looked into Juhel's wide brown eyes, reaching out with his other hand for a crucifix that lay in the top of his open travelling chest.

"Have you spoken of this to anyone else?" he asked.

"No, my lord."

"Then take this crucifix and swear upon it that you will never tell again a word of that Belsaunt council to any human being unless I so bid you."

Juhel swore willingly, glad of the hand in his hair and proud of his great service—for such he guessed it to be. For the count's next question he was unprepared.

"If you were I, Juhel, what would you now do?"

"Accuse the traitor lords before the King's Majesty," replied Juhel promptly.

"It is not so easy as that," said the count, smiling. "The word of one small page, however honest, will not carry far. The mouth of one small page, however truthful, can all too soon be stopped in Hautarroy. This tale of yours will be accounted to you, but marvel not if you never hear of it again."

*   *   *

Noon in the great tilting ground beside the royal river. Banners listless on their striped staffs, paint blistering on the bright shields of parade beside the door of each trim silken pavilion. Master Nino Chiostra grimacing at his handiwork—for he himself had laid the gold ground and the black gerfalcon on the shield of Raoul of Ger. Juhel's hand sticky with heat on the black-studded yellow leather of Safadin's bridle; beyond Safadin's glittering chamfron, above the oval sweep of trampled grass, a perspective of red-draped barricades and gaily patterned awnings, holding between them a pink and gray-white sea of faces. Somewhere at the far end the fierce Count of Lestembourg, with a page adjusting his sword belt as Piers now adjusted the belt of the Count Raoul.

Juhel was desperately excited; his free hand shook as he raised it to beat the flies from Safadin's twitching nostril. The stallion's teeth clashed on his silver bit; a great hoof rose and stamped, raising a blur of dust. In the bright swell of steel that guarded Safadin's chest Juhel saw his own brown reflected face blob-nosed, with receding brow and chin, like the face of an idiot Jew.

The count appeared, a steel-and-yellow figure of unwonted breadth, with his curved shield slung at his left shoulder, and with a falcon "displayed," of black *cuir-bouilli,* rising from the morse-encircled crown of his great closed helm. A languid buzz of interest thickened along the lists; here and there a northern voice shouted a word of approval.

There came a throaty clamour of trumpets, and long-drawn shouting of the heralds. Piers swung the silver stirrup; Raoul of Ger hopped twice and clanked into his saddle. When the shield was in place Juhel let go of the bridle and stepped back. The count held out his right hand, in its steel-cased gauntlet, to receive the haft of a hornbeam lance thrust upward by a squire; the three-pronged plate at the lance tip flashed as it swung level and high again.

Safadin snorted and stamped anew, trampling a dozen paces into position. Raoul of Ger leaned slightly to his saddlebow and couched his lance. Two hundred yards away the dragon-crested helm of Lestembourg gave back the noonday light.

Once more the trumpets clamoured; the count's gilded spurs winked; and the great bulk of Safadin broke forward through the trembling sunlit air.

Juhel clenched his fists and stood erect; a little eager mooing sound escaped his lips before he tightened them. All the force of his boy's spirit bore down the lists with that bright receding avalanche of flesh and blood and bone and silk and steel.

Grimly out of the distance grew Lestembourg's blazon—lozengy azure and sable, charged with a golden dragon—rocking, hurtling, flashing above the red-draped tilting barrier.

Eight flying horsehoofs drummed to the crash of impact; both lance shafts cracked and shivered, the fragments flying in air. Juhel gave a gulp of relief, and Piers let out a long-held breath; either horseman straightened up and slanted his smashed weapon aloft before checking and wheeling his mount to repass at a canter.

Again the applause was feeble; three hours of jousting had cloyed the public taste for niceties of encounter. Only when a rider clanged to earth was there now any real shouting; the first moment for which Juhel waited was gone, and the second and third brought his heart into his mouth for no purpose, since Count Raoul and his opponent broke each three lances with a ferocious dullness, neither so much as losing a stirrup to tip the scales of honour.

Juhel had Safadin's bridle again almost before he was

aware; Piers vanished within silken doors to serve his dismounted master with wine. A groom led the destrier away;
another pair of noble horsemen fronted each other in the hot
lists.

"Next the mellay," thought Juhel; for at two o'clock the
jousting would become a tourney, and Thorismund of Hastain
and Gaston de Volsberghe would lead the two parties, each
containing thirty lords and chevaliers. And Juhel must dance
about between the outer and inner barriers, keeping as close
as he might to the black-and-yellow colours of the Count
Raoul. The combat was to be *à plaisance,* with blunt lances
and pointless swords; old King René himself had seen to that.
As it was, bad blood would no doubt show; when the jousting
barrier was removed the laziest burgher drained his ale and
opened his eyes to watch what might befall.

But division of tourney cut right across court faction; the
young prince and the constable's son had drawn the written
names of their followers from a tilting helm. Thorismund
found Conrad of Burias, Robin Barberghe, and the Duke of
Camors behind him; Gaston drew the Duke of Saulte and
the duke's brother Brian, with two great lords as yet politically
neutral—the youthful Counts of Montcarneau and Ger. Each
combatant flaunted a silken sash bound round his sword arm
above the gleaming elbow cop; Thorismund's men bore crimson, Gaston's white.

Juhel, with eyes so .ately opened to the underworld of in-
trigue, grinned at this mating of foes and sundering of
friends. He wished that he might watch the whole engage-
ment; and then, half ashamed of such idle desire to gape like a
townsman, he sent a quick prayer into the blue sky above
the opposite awnings—a prayer for the safety and achievement of his master. Save for the danger to Raoul of Ger, who
was of slighter stature than many of his peers, Juhel found
utmost satisfaction in the quick alternate din of kettledrums
and trumpets, in the drawled yells of the tilting marshals and
the formation of the two glittering lines of array.

Not a face of the contestants could be seen; only a close knowledge of blazons could help the spectator to accurate counting of gain or loss. But only a fool missed Thorismund's golden portcullis, or Gaston's golden gryphon, or the red boar of Burias—or, indeed, the chevrons of Barberghe and the gerfalcon of Ger. Juhel, priding himself on his skill in that side of his service, had a third of the noble names from their owners' brilliant shields before the signal was given for onset.

The constable, the old Duke of Volsberghe, bowed to King René and moved to the purple-hung rail of the royal balcony. Stiffly he raised a thick white truncheon; silence brushed the lists as with a down-swept wing. Loud in the hush fell the truncheon, clattering on the boards of the gallery; to one concerted stamp and jingle the raised lances sank to the charge, and a roar of cheering all but drowned the curt adopted battle cries of *Gules* and *Argent*.

Quick thunder of hoofs, a mingled crash of meeting, and across the centre of the lists writhed a turbulent blur of colour and flashing metal. Men unhorsed or unhelmed were vanquished; a dozen went hurtling from their saddles at the first crossing of spears. Squires and pages scuttled to succour them, braving the fury of flying hoofs; lances were shattered or cast aside, swords torn out and whirled amain. Argent bent Gules into a bow, strained its own formation, and broke into three fragments.

In a moment the contest was one of groups, crimson and white mixed and spinning, with riderless horses plunging around and between. Juhel lost the falcon surcoat, saw it again, lost it again; out he ran on to the dusty grass, heedless of Piers, heedless of solid uproar from the galleries and of a page in Hastain colours who reeled sobbing past him with hands pressed to his hip. . . .

It was all very well in the romaunts, where you could read slowly and note how this lord overthrew that lord; out here great deeds were doing and you had no time to mark them.

There, that was Gaston de Volsberghe, beating Camors from his saddle. Conrad of Burias unhelmed a fair-haired Saulte; Lestembourg split Prince Thorismund's shield and sailed clean over the neck of his own stumbling charger. Beyond him was my lord himself, his falcon surcoat in shreds; three dinging blows he dealt his royal cousin, woefully crumpling the coronet of Neustria. Robin Barberghe drove manfully between—oh, joy, my lord bowled Robin sideways across the prince's saddlebow. Ah, black damnation, my lord, avoid the Castellan of Montenair. . . .

But the grim castellan was not easily avoided. Aiming at Gaston de Volsberghe only, he sloped his green shield starred with silver lilies, downing a southern chevalier with one blow of his sword, and the Count of Ger with another. One—two—and Juhel squealed, bouncing forward at sight of his master's collapse. Safadin reared with loosened bridle; the count was over and hidden, and plate that protected might also stifle—praise God, a yellow-coated squire had dashed straight into the mellay, followed by another and another.

A surge of strife encompassed Juhel; he nipped between two destriers whose riders both bore crimson, and flung himself at Safadin's head, his feet flying free as the great brute caracoled. Down thumped the iron foreshoes, and Juhel banged his ribs against the steel bards that hid the stallion's shoulder; but Safadin seemed to know him, or at least to know his colours, for in another moment he was towing the boy away.

Trying to appear as though it were he who led the ponderous charger, Juhel bolted for the barriers; a groom ran to meet and relieve him, and five minutes later he stood aghast at the door of the yellow pavilion.

Raoul of Ger was a motionless figure of steel, sitting inertly in a rough high-backed chair. As Juhel moved into the warm colourful gloom, Piers lifted the great helm from their master's shoulders. The count was very pale, but he blinked and smiled; a great weight rose from somewhere about Juhel's middle.

"No bones broken," murmured Raoul. "But I am glad of excuse to leave that game for to-day. Fulk's arms is heavy."

"Never saw I such whacks given and received," grunted Nino Chiostra, plying pincers on the stained and battered plate armour. "Piers, Juhel, my lord's bath, quickly."

"Sip this," growled John Doust, proffering a cup of red wine of Estragon. "By the scabbard of Michael Archangel, it eased me to see you set about the prince and topple Robin Barberghe out of saddle."

"Robin was my second man," claimed Raoul with blood returning to his cheeks. "I have paid my shot. Let them all batter each other senseless. So half a dozen are spared, the realm were no worse."

"Which half dozen?" asked kneeling Nino, grinning up into his friend's face.

"Ah, let me not commit myself," laughed the count, turning his laugh into a groan as the squire who was assisting Nino lifted the dented thigh piece from a bruised leg.

Juhel, busy amid brass cans and steam, was soothed by an access of self-importance. *He* had enlightened his lord concerning the great plot; he was the count's retainer, not the king's, and in the eyes of Juhel the count could do no wrong.

Mute and solemn and armed with a towel, he ushered his lord into the bath tent behind the pavilion, vaguely aware of cessation of uproar in the lists; but not until nearly twenty minutes had passed did Nino Chiostra part the curtains and show a face alive with tidings.

"Some dunderheaded squire of Conrad's has put the fat into the fire," said Nino, advancing to squat on the edge of the great tub. "The first I saw of it was Prince Thorismund, unhelmed, riding up to the king's balcony, waving his sword and shouting in a tidy rage. The king nods to the constable, the constable lifts his truncheon, the marshals spur and bellow, the trumpets blow as if to burst, and all the hammer-and-anvil din goes tinkling down to silence. Conrad

comes riding slowly up, and there on his shield, for all to see, is
azure, a lion sejant argent."

"No baton sinister?" demanded Raoul of Ger, hugging his
knees amid floating aromatic herbs in the soapy water.

"Not a trace of it."

"But, by the Mass, go on."

For *azure, a lion sejant argent* was the royal device—King
René's own, which only Thorismund might bear beside;
and Thorismund himself must show in addition a label of
cadency to mark him as heir.

"Well, I was too far off to hear, but they say the king
was wroth with Conrad; and then and there he broke up the
day's tourney. The prince sat with a face like doom—so much
all men could see; and when the king bade heralds take the
offending shield from Conrad there went up a growl from
half those in the lists. And there was hissing in the crowd, and
someone shouted 'he is more worthy of it than the other.'
The pikemen tried to reach the shouter, but his companions
thrust him away between their legs, and he escaped.

"But the king rose up and bade Conrad ask pardon, first
of himself, then of his nephew. Conrad with no change of face
complied, dropping on one knee this way and that; and his
chamberlain stood forth and cried out how it happened. The
shield was finished, said the chamberlain, save only for that
all-important detail—as though men waste the silver paint
where the baton crosses the lion's body! But it seemed Duke
Conrad has to-day had three shields broken on his arm, three
shields bearing his own boar's head; and in his haste a
wretched squire, running to the duke's pavilion, caught up that
other and bore it out to his master in the mellay."

"H'm. And the king accepted the excuse?"

"Yes, and Thorismund also. Thorismund got off his horse
and went to Conrad, holding out his hand."

"Ay. He can be generous on occasion. And then?"

"Conrad bowed and clasped his hands behind him. And

Thorismund went white with rage, and turned his back and
stalked to his horse. And in the silence someone clapped—
men say it was the Duchess of Camors. And Gaston de Volsberghe sprang to earth and strode to hold Conrad's bridle;
and Alain de Montcarneau dismounted and picked up Conrad's
sword and gave it back to him. But Thorismund rode away—
and the Saultes and Olencourts wheeled mounts and followed
him, yet only a dozen others went with them. Many more
waited for Conrad. And there is rested—to the tune of such
a gabbling from the balconies as you can well imagine. But
now——"

"Now?"

"Now *you* are the chief of those whose sympathies are unknown and undeclared."

"Ay, since Alain holds with Conrad. I do not envy myself.
Juhel, the towels. Piers, I will wear the gray velvet and the
silver girdle garnished with opals. And Nino—touching that
same royal shield—what do *you* think?"

The young comptroller crossed his legs and pulled absently
at his straight brown nose.

"Why," he said after reflection, "I think that these full-
blooded wall-faced heroes like my lord Duke of Burias
cannot bottle up their deep lusts forever. I believe he kept that
blazon in his tent without a thought of marring the dainty
lion with any baton sinister. Even as you have sat brooding
on your old romaunts; even as Camors dotes on his wine
cup and Barberghe on his treasure chest, Thorismund on a
comely maid, and I—God help me—on the light in a well-
cut emerald; even so has Conrad dwelt upon his father's
shield, the emblem of the royalty he covets—poor fool that
he is."

"In faith, Nino, I believe you may be right. That brawl
beside the cathedral apse ten days ago—that marked an
attempt to embroil Thorismund with the Saultes. It failed,
although no crossbowman was found; and now, by this day's
misadventure, Conrad stands in the king's displeasure."

"Small moment, if half the realm stand with and for him."

"No, that is true. Nino, I would we were less in the eyes of men. Here there will be stout parts to play; that is, we must lie and cheat, and presently, perhaps, slay those with whom we have hunted and sung and feasted. I had rather turn a rondel, and you, I warrant, had rather carve a gem. Long life to King René, I say, for when he goes we are all at each other's throats."

"Amen to that," said Nino Chiostra softly.

Juhel regarded the pair of them doubtfully. Could they really deride Conrad for desire of sovereignty, or really prefer their toys of leisure to riding armed through an admiring land?

Suddenly Nino Chiostra chuckled.

"Ten thousand little fleeting devils!" he cried. "Let them beware of you, Raoul! The man who only fights to finish and go to sleep is often the wickedest fighter of all."

"Ay," observed John Doust, thrusting his fair hair and pink countenance round the canvas door flap. "Ay, it is well said as I say it: *Trust in God and mount your archers*. But if you aim to finish a campaign with men taken from towns and farms, send knaves among them who will point to your enemies and say: *Those misbegotten hell-spewn mandrakes hinder us from going home*."

"But what if some captain equally wise abide in the tents of wickedness?" demanded Nino Chiostra with a grin.

John Doust ruminated.

"Then it comes back to God and the archers," he decided. "But I will not be snared in subtleties. The only right side is the side I am on. Are we for Thorismund or Conrad?"

The Count of Ger rose, naked to the waist, and flung a wet towel at his war captain's head.

"Nay, I am all discretion," rumbled the Englishman, brushing the missile aside. "Truly a bath tent is no place for such confidences. Juhel has grown coney's ears, and Piers squints with impatience."

"At fourteen one is very ready to take sides," said Nino. John Doust regarded his friend askance.

"Graybeards of twenty-two," he grieved, "find it, alas, far otherwise. But Raoul is so quiet that you may hear the flap of vultures' wings. Let Conrad—or Thorismund—now take heed. By the harrowing of hell, I am like to be sorry for Thorismund—or Conrad. And after all, we fight for peace to follow."

"Out upon you, inveterate war dog," cried Nino. "*You* would fight for peace until no living thing remained in all the land."

"Ay," said Raoul of Ger. "And then might real peace begin."

*   *   *

Morning at Hautarroy. A cooing of doves, and the harsh cry of a peacock. Framed in the tall unshuttered window, and broken by the pink stone balusters of the balcony, a sweep of trim lawn, frosted with dew that sparkled in early sunlight. Beyond, a dark rigidity of cedars; in one corner the wavering flash of a fountain, in another the ordered blaze of gillyflowers and lilies.

This was the palace of the old archbishop, where now the Count of Ger stayed as a guest. The tourney was a week past; the king was already reconciled to his son, and Thorismund had left the city to seek his own castle overlooking Hastain—ostensibly in a huff at Conrad's regaining of favour, but actually by advice from leaders of his party; for Raoul of Ger had made his choice, although remaining outwardly aloof from either faction.

The aged prelate was no politician; Thorismund's and Conrad's men alike could seek the Count of Ger without remark. Juhel grew used to announcing those who eyed each other askance in his master's antechamber, and this morning he marched demurely upstairs to receive food for excitement.

"What is it, Juhel?" asked the count, turning in his carven chair beside the sunny window.

"My lord, a Franconian merchant waits below—Master Dietrich Halbern, with a casket of leather goods."

"Halbern? Oh, ay, Duke Conrad spoke of him. Bring him here. Juhel!"

"My lord?"

"One moment. Very shortly I expect a visit from the Sieur Gaston de Volsberghe. When the merchant is gone, and when I am well engaged with the Sieur Gaston, come you to me and say that a squire of the Duke of Saulte waits at the postern. Just that and nothing more. At the *postern,* remember. And now bring hither that Franconian leather seller."

Dietrich Halbern was very tall, but he stooped and leaned on a great staff that was shod with iron and topped with a grinning lion's head in beaten copper. His long gown was of good green cloth, unseasonably trimmed with fur; his little fur cap was turned up with red silk and adorned with a leaden image of Saint Christopher, patron of travellers. His sand-brown eagle's face was clean-shaven, and dark hair fell thickly upon his thrown-back tawny hood. And if Dietrich Halbern's appearance jarred somewhat with his modest manner, his voice held reassurance for mild folk who traded with him; he spoke slowly and gently, burring his hesitant words with Franconian manner.

His wares were dagger sheaths and purses, belts and pouches and wallets, of stamped and coloured leather. A scent of musk enveloped them; Juhel stood dutifully by the door, sniffing silently at the perfume, until the count waved him away.

Ten minutes later he was in the room again, very conscious of Gaston de Volsberghe towering behind him. The famous commander had gray in his auburn hair; his hazel-coloured eyes were bland, his thick lips smiled graciously above his great chin, his mighty blue-clad figure topped even that of Dietrich Halbern—but that was perhaps because of the merchant's stoop.

"*Ohé,* Sieur Gaston," called the count, rising to take the other's hand. "You are most welcome. I beg you will be seated; I entreat your indulgence while I choose a gift or two from Master Halbern's store."

"My business can well wait," said Gaston simply, lodging his trim bulk on a window seat; and again Juhel halted by the door, while the merchant took up his slow persuasive murmur.

"Eh, my lord count, this is best Austrasian stuff; I have seen none like it save at the emperor's court. The emperor himself, God save him, has hunted with such a sheath at such a girdle. See, it is very daintily sewn, yet very firmly weighted with lead at the tip, that you shall not reach for steel and find it tilted out and lost a mile behind you. Look now, at this my dagger; I house it, so. See, it slides sweetly as a priest's hand to a flagon—and to draw it, flick, flash, I am stoutly defended. And the purse to match, so handy, so mightily secure; there is linked steel behind the straps—no thief may sever that in a crowd, nay, not if he work with a razor. . . ."

Raoul of Ger paid little heed to the burred patter; he pulled and fingered the wares, buying at length a purse and a belt and a fine saddlebag with a pattern of gilded roses. Gaston de Volsberghe seemed struck by the outward contrast between slim count and giant tradesman; the latter he observed with more than ordinary attention, and when Dietrich Halbern snapped the catches of his little trunk the Sieur Gaston arrested him.

"Merchant, where have we met before?"

One flickering glance of bright blue eyes, and the Franconian's heavy eyelids were again discreetly lowered. Holding the casket by its straps with one hand, Master Dietrich bowed, and gestured with the other before picking up his cap and staff.

"My lord, it might be in many places. Harenheim, Harksburg, Brelstein, Bartsch—every year I am in each city. But also I wander far and far, seeing many and many noble blazons; into Lombardy and up again to Innsbruck, ay, and across to Avignon. Perhaps at the Emperor's court itself?"

Gaston did not reply for a moment. It was absurd that a noble should remember a merchant and not be remembered

again. Raoul of Ger spared the pair a second's amused wonder
before he motioned to Juhel to show the Franconian out.

"Plague me, Ger——" boomed the Sieur Gaston, as the door
closed behind Juhel; plainly the Volsbergh was puzzled, and
Juhel, glancing up at the eagle face as he held a curtain aside,
saw a deepening of the laughter wrinkles beside the heavy
eyelids. Master Dietrich Halbern seemed to have had his
little joke; he regarded Juhel aslant with a frosty good humour.

"Give you good day, my pippin," he growled, in a voice
almost devoid of accent; then he disappeared in the bustle of
the courtyard, and Juhel promptly forgot him and his musk
and his lion-headed staff. For now arose the peculiar duty laid
upon Juhel by his lord, demanding a smooth tongue and a
steady eye.

The count and the Sieur Gaston were not in the chamber
when after a quarter hour he returned to it. Through a window
he saw the pair pacing up and down a reach of lawn where
none could come unseen upon them. Ger barely came to the
Volsberghe's shoulder; he had his thumbs hooked in his belt,
which to Juhel bespoke a certain depth of meditation.

The boy marched soberly downstairs again and out into
the morning sunlight. Passing beneath the windows of the
wing allotted to the count's retainers, he heard Nino Chiostra
carolling a verse of the song about the six demoiselles:

> "Then by the dreadful Midnight Sword,
>   *Carim-cara, cara-carim,*
> Lucrezia's skin she must afford
> Without Lucrezia's whining word,
>   *Carim, cara, carissima.*"

Juhel frowned; he knew all about that midnight sword.
Master Nino probably used the first six trisyllabic names that
came into his head; two of them being his versions of Helen
and Lucrece, the classical allusions were inevitable. But Juhel
could never forget the black Tarquinian wrong in his own

family history; later he wondered if his faint anger had power to run before him over the dewy grass.

The ill-assorted couple paused to wait his approach. It was hard to keep chin up and confront the questioning glance of two such famous men, even though one were his own beloved master.

Juhel linked hands behind him and bowed, scared of the impatient Volsberghe stare.

"My—my lord Count, a squire of the Duke of Saulte waits at the postern."

"My regrets to my lord Duke," said the Count sternly, "but I cannot ride with him to-day."

"Name of God!" growled the Sieur Gaston, stepping forward to tower above the startled boy. "Ger, what is this lad's name?"

"Juhel de Ath," was the calm reply; Count Raoul's strange eyes were very much aware of the Volsberghe's face, but the Volsberghe regarded Juhel only.

"Boy, had you ever a sister named—rot me, what was her name?—*Tiphaine?*"

"No sister, my lord, but a c-cousin," stammered Juhel, crimson and aghast.

"I can believe it," boomed Gaston. "Ger, you were mightily fooled just now—and I more mightily still. Dietrich Halbern is no Franconian merchant. This boy's face has unlocked my memory—our fawning Dietrich Halbern is Joris of the Rock!"

Count and page stared at the Sieur Gaston. Juhel turned sick with mingled surprise and rage, but clenched his fists and stood upright to receive a rapid command.

"Run, boy, to my lord Archbishop's officer of the gate, and ask if my men saw which way the Franconian went with his fur cap and his casket. You to the Franconian Envoy, Sieur Gaston; I to the Provost of Hautarroy to have the gates shut and the city combed."

"Well said," barked Gaston de Volsberghe. "And as for our other business, I think we are agreed."

"We are agreed," said Raoul of Ger; and Juhel heard no
more, for he was already trotting away.

The few Franconian merchants who admitted to knowing
Dietrich Halbern swore that his eyes were brown and his hair
of a gingery shade. No sergeant or pikeman saw the mock-
Dietrich pass before the gates clanged fast; but no one bearing
his likeness could be found beneath the spires of Hautarroy.

X. THE GLORY OF JORIS OF THE ROCK

"BUT how did you win into and out of the city?" asked Red Anne.

"I came on this Dietrich Halbern in the forest," explained Joris, "and we slew him and his three men—fools to travel so few together—and from his letters of credit and introduction I learned that he was new to Hautarroy. What then? His clothes fitted me; no one noticed the sewn gash beneath the left armpit of his good green gown. Gandulf rigged himself up as my servant. I tell you, Anne, I had a tickling between the shoulder blades in those thronged streets, yet it was sport of a rare kind. And although I did not know how the devil to go about a leather-merchant's business, I was lucky to strike acquaintance with a gentleman of the Duke Conrad's household. Conrad himself bought a belt, only two days before the quarrel at the tourney."

"And coming out?"

"We bribed a lout who drove a wagon; I lay among piled hides, and faugh! they stank to heaven. Gandulf rode by the carter; no one remembered *him*."

"But why should Gaston de Volsberghe recall a meeting so many years gone by? A good thing your hair was dyed."

"He has not often been thwarted, that one. A maid *and* a horse

And Joris told Red Anne the tale of Tiphaine de Ath as he remembered it—even to the curse with which she fled from him.

The pair sat on the grass near the lip of the Rock; Anne listened in silence, gazing out into the quiet autumnal twilight. She herself seemed a sturdy Spirit of Autumn, with her flaming

hair and rosy face and man's clothes—this time of deep brown
beneath a faded purple cloak; for upon her were gathered more
brightly the hues of heather and bracken and falling leaves
that filled the forest and moors, and even the gray sheen of a
distant tarn found counterparts in the steel disk of her cloak
pin and the silver pommel of her broad dagger.

Since that night, eighteen months before, when Joris fled
from the Singing Stones, their relationship had undergone no
change; Red Anne had ignored the outlaw's midnight desertion, and once when Joris voiced a fighting man's impatient
doubt she startled him by a mild acquiescence. Also she went
less often to the devil-worshipping assemblies, and wandered
more quite solitary in the hills.

"I must believe your antics touch and wake strange powers,"
he had growled, "but I will not believe you govern any but the
least of them. *Your* deadliest force is in your voice and face
and under your clothes; and then in your arrow shot, and last
of all in drugs and spells and dancing. Is it not so?"

"It is so," Anne had answered deeply, turning to him the
invitation of her strong round arms. "And are you not afraid
of Rufin's last words to you? 'Prosper your witch, for I think
she will ruin you soon.'"

"Not I," said Joris joyfully. "The dying rat bites hard
until he stiffens. Who would not blast his slayer, if a threat
could achieve it? At the least I am not ruined for nothing—
hey?"

And now, as Red Anne listened to the tale of dead Tiphaine,
her eyes grew dark with brooding and decision, so that Joris
paused in his tale and looked a question.

"'Your hag of hell betray you,'" she quoted very softly;
then, rounding on the man, she smiled.

"Will you essay a bout with powers of darkness?" she
demanded, "knowing that if you fail I *have* betrayed you, who
yet would serve you very well? For now I would betray those
powers to *you;* I am very weary of being a witch. But if they
are too strong for you—for us—then I shall have led you to

your undoing. Will you risk a gruesome failure, and a very
ugly death, and maybe an after-death of the kind that blackens
the heart to imagine?"

Joris, stretched on his cloak in the dusk, took a stalk of red
sorrel between his strong white teeth.

"What for?" he demanded curiously, half scenting a jest.

"I will tell you. You know Prince Thorismund holds his
state at Hastain? On All Saints' Eve he comes to the Singing
Stones."

"By the chimes of hell! Why? And how?"

"Jaded with hunting, and also, I take it, with his new and
sobered way of life. At least I am told he is coming, secretly,
maybe disguised, to look on at the rites and taste a new
excitement."

"And how many with him?"

"I know not. Few, I should say; the thing would shake
from his party some who now abide by him."

"Then, Anne, if this be betrayal, send me more of it
quickly."

"Now I have told you, what do you purpose to do?"

"You know. And Yaan, who threw spear at a ghost, shall not
stay me—or think you he will?"

Red Anne was silent for a moment.

"I do not know," she confessed at length. "I have not seen
a profanation of the rites save when Lys stabbed one who
mocked at her; and Yaan let that pass, since I asked it of
him."

Joris held up his stalk of sorrel, bitten now in twain, and
laughed abruptly and low.

"I will earn me a shrine in Saint Andreas at Hautarroy,"
he said. "Saint Joris saves the young prince from the Devil.
There is red blood in the rip, for he took and gave shrewd
clouts in the mellay. I knew he sulked at Hastain—it is said,
because Conrad finds greater favour not only with old René,
but also with Yolande de Volsberghe, Gaston's sister."

"You saw her?"

"Oh, ay. A likely wench enough, but over-thin. She looked me in the face; yet by the beard of Goliath of Gath my pulses quickened more when I met Brother Gaston."

It was Anne's turn to laugh.

"Eh, man," she muttered, "you are nearly as doomed a husband as little Raoul of Ger."

"Perhaps. *His* lady would have shivered had she known how many fingers itched for his windpipe there in the archbishop's palace."

" 'I warn you, strive not with Herluin,' said Lys. And Joris, I think she was right. Until you must, pit not your luck against the luck of Raoul of Ger. He has served *your* turn in his time."

"In faith he has," agreed Joris. "But I would I had gutted him at Gramberge, and given his maid to my men. Yet I think my turn will come. . . . 'Make me a duchess,' you said. Ivo . . ."

He paused, and the woman smiled; this was the first time Joris had admitted memory of Ivo's halting prophecy.

"Ivo," Red Anne reminded him, "said only I could break you. His word added to the words of Lys and Rufin—again, are you not scared to sup and sleep beside one so charged with menace for you?"

Joris caught the strong nape of her sunburned neck in one hand, and shook her gently to and fro.

"Come down and see," he growled. "Herodias, Diana, jade, sorceress—come down and see."

*   *   *

More than a week before All Saints' Day Red Anne rode to the northward. She was to meet Joris and his men at a fixed point in the moors between the Singing Stones and Dondonoy. The outlaw chieftain watched her go with a frosty smile on his lips, and turned to make his own arrangements for so late an autumn expedition.

"Maybe my last," he told himself. "Princeling, I think you are set on a journey stranger than you look for."

The band had grown again to eighty stout ruffians; this time he took them all, breasting half-risen Varne at his old crossing place near Pont-de-Foy. The weather was cold and misty; it needed all of three days to reach his trysting place.

There, in the heart of the sullen and desolate moors, his love came to him again, but not as he expected. She stumbled on foot through wet bracken in an hour of cloudy morning, while the dark screes behind the outlaw bivouac echoed the sharp cry of the grouse and magnified the snarl of a stream in the deep ravine below. Joris strode forward to meet her, and saw she was somehow stricken; her eyes encountered his indeed, but presently seemed staring through him at a thing she loathed and yet must look upon.

"What is amiss?" he barked. "Is Thorismund away? Where is your pony?"

"Thorismund?" she replied, in the flat voice of one half awakened from sleep. "Why, no; all goes as you would have it in that affair."

"Then by the chimes of hell what ails you?"

"*Ivo——*" she wailed, in a manner very strange to Joris; then she pulled herself up, and brushed a mired hand over her forehead.

"Something to eat," she demanded brusquely; "then I will tell you. But now—something to eat."

And when she had eaten savagely, and drunken more than her wont, Joris drove Gandulf and Madoc away with a jerk of his head; and, alone with him in the lee of a grit crag, Anne twisted the string of her unbent bow between strong hands and told a halting tale in a hushed voice.

"I found him with a family of charcoal burners," she said. "Still wearing his black tunic; but the rest of his gear he had changed. He looked at me as ever—as though I had fallen from heaven. *And if I have, it is far as Lucifer's self. . . .*

"He pled to come with me again—fiends, how he pled! I told him you would wring his neck for those false tidings above Gramberge, and he begged at least to see me again on All

Saints' Eve at the Stones. I told him that assembly was like to end in a fashion unusually grim, and he swore that if there was danger to me he must be there himself. I said no danger threatened me, and he laughed as the damned laugh, vowing that he feared you not if I were by. Lastly he wept—and came away with me. *Ivo!*

"That night he slept in my arms—no, Joris, *no!* He might have been my son. He *was* my son between the dusk and the dawning. He seemed burned clean by suffering—not even a dirty little jest left in him. He was as strange and sweet as that young Herluin who was once his friend and now is Count of Ger. *What am I that such boys trust and worship me?*

"But Ivo, in the night, up in the heather—Ivo talked of a death in life, of visions of old merciless gods, of Christ more merciless than they. He talked of the stars, of the flight of birds, of wind song and tree blossom and of that ancient discord called 'Brisingamen.' I told him of Lys and her end, and of how she came once more among us. At what she had said he laughed, in a manner very weird to listen to. He tried to show me a mystery—a thing he had shaped in his heart alone in the hills and the forest. He claimed that Christ and God are at war with one another. That God created Christ and then grew old and afraid of Him. That Church and coven alike are nearer to God than Christ is. That Judas Iscariot was in truth a very godly man. But half of what he said I could not understand. . . .

"And in the morning we met with Blanche and Sabelle of the coven, and heard their news of Thorismund. Blanche is a tavern wench in Hastain, and she will lead the prince to our assembly—the prince, and with him only Guy de Saulte, young brother to the duke."

Joris grunted approval, but said no word; and the witch went on.

"Thereafter Ivo and I—I see you marvel that I bore with him, since he betrayed us by Gramberge. But you know my anger does not last as even I would sometimes have it last;

and, Joris, I have seen too many deeds of worth and villainy to blame men overmuch for anything they do. Besides—who passes from one way of life to another must always betray old comrades, if only by absence from them. Who am I to judge Ivo, I who play Judas to my coven?"

"It is not evil to betray evil," claimed the man; and then he laughed and caught up his own words. "Who but you, and myself, and my men behind there, would blame Ivo at all for the trick by which he broke us? Joris is evil, no doubt, and Yaan is evil incarnate; and the young prince is perched atop of a most glorious edifice of tyranny and greed and pride, which yields not to Yaan or Joris in the evil of its working. Say, Anne, then—where is good?"

"I do not know. At least I am not sure where it abides. I saw it two days since, as I am going to tell you. Ivo and I, the day being fair, held along the bank of Nordenne when we had better have taken to the hills. Several folk—farmers and foresters—saw us, and some knew me. Far away we heard the Prior of Dor hunting; and in the mid-afternoon, when we had reached heather, a man hallooed from a hilltop behind us— and when we turned to look at him we saw he held leashed hounds and wound a horn to companions behind him. Whereat we made swiftly away, but when he was joined by a dozen others we saw the leashes slipped, and half a score of hounds —a whole relay—broke down into the gorge between, as it might have been *there,* and *so.*"

Anne pointed and gestured, but Joris kept his gaze upon her tired face.

"Down they came, great hounds of chase, alaunts and mastiffs too; and away we went, Ivo running by the pony's head and plucking out the bow he carried. *I* had no bow, fool that I was. Joris, you have told me that twice men have chased you with hounds?"

"Yes, years gone by. Go on."

"Then you know—or if you do not know for yourself, you may guess—how the terror grows as it grows in a dream.

Someone must have told the prior that I who once escaped him was riding near; for a rout of horsemen crested the one rise as we fled over the next. Then it was up and down, up and down, athwart the silent ravines—who would have thought the prior hunted to east of the river that day? One dry bottom we crossed, and seemed to draw ahead, but after the next climb we dropped to ford a torrent and found the hounds gaining. . . . *Ivo!*

"Across the angry beck was a rocky shelf, along whose edge we must flee to reach a transverse cleft in the high moor. Only fear kept the pony going, but Ivo seemed made of iron; as we plunged into the water he said something to me which I heard but did not understand. We dragged the pony through and I mounted; the sleuth dogs gave tongue on the slope behind, and the little beast bounded away as Ivo called out again.

" 'Forward, I follow fast,' he shouted, and I was round a corner, and on a returning curve beyond it, before I looked back. And when I thought to hear Ivo behind there was only a great baying. And a hound's body whirled downstream below me, with an arrow in its throat. . . .

"Then I knew that Ivo had not followed at all, but was holding them at the crossing. And . . . *Ivo!*"

Until that moment Joris had never seen Red Anne in tears. The muscles of her face did not relax; but shining drops coursed down her cheeks and misted the pain in her eyes.

"I was afraid," she muttered. "More afraid than I have ever been. As I checked the pony I thought: *If I go back then Ivo dies for nothing.* So I drove the pony forward again, and could not forbear to look back.

"I saw, when the heather slope allowed, first three hounds still or kicking on the far bank, then another struggling in the water, then one that crawled and howled on the near side. Ivo had somehow crushed him with a stone. That made six dogs. Then—then I saw a rolling, thrashing heap that was Ivo and the four others, with Ivo's sword still feebly smiting and blood pouring free—*for he must have aimed to cripple all rather than kill one.* . . .

"Then I brayed like a mule in anguish and horror, and beat the pony forward, and rode and rode till twilight—and no hound came after, so it seemed the main hunt was headed some other way. Nor horse nor hound nor man I saw, and my pony dropped between my knees, and I fell and jarred my body into a daze. But when I got up I found blood on the pony's pastern; Ivo had pricked it with an arrow before he turned on the bank. And then, too, I remember what Ivo said before he last called out. It was this: 'I will not come again to mock you, Anne, beloved!' He meant that he still loved me more than Lys did; and that I believe is true. . . .

"So I travelled fasting all next day. And the Prior of Dor has lost ten dogs of value; and you have lost a pony. And Ivo's bones are stripped on the moor. And I am here—and by Mahound I know not who is the gainer."

"I for one," said Joris. "And you, when you have rested. Freely I forgive your Ivo; that was a very gallant finish. Take heart, Anne; there are great days to come."

Red Anne laid hand upon his arm, and he saw that her eyes were haunted.

"You do not understand," she said. "I am proved a coward, who was never a coward before."

"Pooh! Folly! *I* have run away a score of times, and skulked and sweated, and laughed at it thereafter. Plague take it, Anne, the lad was paid again—for who stands to be torn to shreds without sufficient reason?"

"*Ivo*," muttered Red Anne, shutting her eyes; and without opening them she spoke again to Joris: "Yet was his sacrifice like no other that I have heard of."

"Still," Joris reminded her, "there is on my sword arm a scar . . ."

"No, Joris, it is not like. *You* fought very bravely that day—but with thought of earthly reward, did you not?"

Joris made an impatient movement, regretting his choice of

example. Anne's eyes flew open, with tears still gemming lids
and lashes; Anne's lips smiled a wise and rather dreary smile.

"You man for whom the world was made," she whispered,
"*you* do not know what cowardice means, for you confound
it with robber's caution. *You* do not know the bitter fog beyond
the last dominion of striving gods."

"I do not," agreed Joris roundly. "But Herbrand and
Osmund and many another of my men have died, as it were,
for me, and do not haunt my memory; indeed when I think of
them it seems they were good for very little else. See, Anne,
both you and I were born to lead and to enjoy; what does it
profit an omelette to mourn the broken eggs?"

"Yes," said Anne to herself. "It is like one other that I
have heard of."

"Take my spare cloak," ordered Joris, "and sleep by the
fire there until you are rested. We must not have you falling
melancholy-sick two days before your assembly."

Anne obeyed silently, and Joris sat musing beside her body,
as once before he sat in his cave by the Rock. Overhead sang
the moor wind, reaching down an occasional gust to scatter the
white smoke of the campfires; rocks and heather and bracken
grew clear in the mild October afternoon.

"Rain to-morrow," said Joris, and greased his thigh boots
anew while waiting for supper.

Once he noticed the woman stirring, and bent above her to
watch her face. Anne made a little clucking noise deep in her
throat, and her mouth twitched open and shut on a sharply
murmured name.

"*Ivo!*"

"There is virtue up to a point," thought Joris grimly, "even
in the sleuth dogs of the Prior of Dor."

*   *   *

Holyrood Eve was almost sultry; at twilight a low solitary
peal of distant thunder checked outlaw ribaldry and dicing;
men looked up and around, as though the strangeness of their

errand were only now apparent. Joris had strung them in a line beneath a heather-crested sandy bluff to southwest of the Singing Stones; a mile behind, the ponies were tethered to hawthorns by a tarn. That was the quarter of uttermost desolation, where ridge after ridge of dusking purple swelled to the grisly cloud-helmed bulk of Dondunor; and Joris saw in the fading light a certain greenness colour one or two near faces. He noted with relief that no second peal came after, and that a breath of chilly wind played in his face from the seaward and the north.

A slight shower fell; the sprawled rank took hobgoblin shapes, huddling bodies and bows beneath frieze cloaks, munching food from greasy wallets and sipping coarse wine from battered flasks. A man roared out a jest, and Gandulf strode along under the bluff to curse him into sulky silence. Only Joris and Madoc stood in sight of the Stones; they had crept amid rocks and hawthorns to avoid breasting a skyline.

Red Anne came blackly toward them from the caves—a wallet corded to her belt, her cow headdress under one arm, her cow's tail looped over the other, her brazen ritual wand gleaming in the last light. Catlike she trod, so that sturdy Madoc backed a pace when first he found her by him. Gandulf joined the group, and as the wind gusts freshened up the slope the four of them heard the first faint thrilling of the dolmen ring.

Madoc shivered in his tunic of leathern leaf armour, Gandulf's hand rasped nervously across and across the rusty steel of his corselet. Anne stood with arms folded, the beast head swinging from her shoulder, the serpent-twined rod hugged carelessly against the blackness of her clothing. Joris, glancing aside, saw her face in profile against the faint pink cloud rents to westward; for him the hour grew timeless and enchanted. Princes of earth and hell should stand in the shadow of Joris; he might not surround the Stones, lest a late-comer stumble upon his men and give an alarm, but Madoc and Gandulf would lead the horns of creeping attack, and he himself in the centre would sound the call for onset.

"I shall go now," said Anne, low-voiced.

"Why now?" asked Joris. "We have hours to wait."

"I must watch alone among the Stones," she responded. "I must bid them farewell and make a kind of peace with them, for they have been my friends for twenty years."

"Go, then," muttered Joris, "but——"

Red Anne turned upon him in the twilight, catching him firmly by the beard that still bore traces of its dark disguise as the beard of Dietrich Halbern.

"Nay, man," she breathed, "do not doubt me to-night. Here in my wallet I have betony and motherwort and vervain, a bronze bell and a parchment. Certain spells I must cast to cramp the power of Yaan. You may not believe in them, but I must still make sure. Only keep your men in hand; if there are any overscared, it will maybe help them to hear me. And when the hymn of invocation ends, I will point my wand at the prince. . . . Kiss me, Joris."

Joris flung an arm around her and kissed the upturned mouth.

"If there be fighting," he murmured, "I would not fill your own friends with arrows. Can you not warn them or group them together for safety?"

Anne drew a deep breath and stiffened in his grasp.

"If there be fighting," she said, "you had best slay all who oppose you. But remember I cannot tell what Yaan may do; I have warned you he has deadly powders to cast into the flares, and for that you must be prepared. The rest is—as it will be. Fare you well."

"Farewell until midnight," growled Joris.

Something else she seemed to say, but her voice was lost in the rising wind. She strode away downhill, and darkness and the dolmens swallowed her up.

At the end of half an hour a light flickered among the fallen uprights of the inner ring. A pungent whiff of burning herbs assailed the nostrils of the hidden watchers, and suddenly men ceased their grumbling and shuffling and scratching—hearkening one and all to the sharp tinkling of the bell and the marvellous mingled voices of earth and air.

Red Anne was singing alone amid the Singing Stones.

*   *   *

Midnight was clear, with the waning moon just set. Joris let the lights flare, let the strange hymn begin, before he stood at the bluff's edge and motioned his men forward. With bows and pikes trailing in heather the long sickle of stooping crawling figures pushed forward down the rough incline; this time the chant failed to encircle the brow of Joris with iron. Instead, the hard glee of the fighting man possessed his crouched body; he marked the place of his intended entry into the inner ring, where now the blue of torchlit faces was veiled for the coming of Yaan.

Rasp and slither and grunt and creak, whelmed by the ringing din below. Thick bell heather caught at his cloak, yielded to his arms, sprang up and smote his face. A man immediately behind was swearing softly in amazement; Joris paused to hiss a threat at him, and the hiss startled himself, for the sudden ritual silence cut all other sound from about it.

Yaan leaped upon the slab between the blue-white fires; Joris rose to his feet, with sword in one hand and lifted horn in the other. The howl of joyous acclamation gave him another dozen yards; Red Anne's swift stride and pointing gesture showed him two cloak-muffled figures standing a little apart beyond the kneeling throng.

"Strangers, what do *you* here?" belled Anne; and from near the pair a woman leaped up to confront her.

"Mistress, that is not right!" she cried. "No question to guests of the coven! My—my friends wish us no harm; let them be, and on with the Sabbath!"

"Ay, let them be!" called others. "What ails you, Mistress, to-night?"

Red Anne tilted her cow's mask up like a vizor and lifted her chin; from her strong round throat went up a yell of tormented laughter as she raised the brazen rod like a sword and dashed it into the ground.

"Faithful, protect yourselves!" she shouted—and turned, and darted between the nearest megoliths to vanish in the shadows beyond.

Sharp and fierce brayed the horn of Joris; the assembly broke into rout and clamour at the thudding rush of his men. Madoc and half a dozen more were already beyond the Stones; the prince and his companion turned and blundered full into their arms. In a second each of the pair was the core of a kicking heap; Joris had time to see as much before he wheeled in the glow of the flares and pointed his blade toward Yaan— or toward the altar slab where Yaan had been the instant before.

"By God, the Devil has bolted!" he roared at the top of his voice; then, amid stampede and screaming of witches and laughing of his swarming followers, he saw the blackness of Yaan reappear—a bounding antlered mystery that thrust what looked like an iron casket flat upon the nearer blue-white star of fire, and collapsed as though into the earth at the end of the long altar.

There came a hiss and a red sparkling along one side of the casket; the casket vanished, the lit earth and the tall stones brightened and shuddered to a rayed burst of orange flame and a stunning thunderous crash. Joris dropped like a log, and heard his sturdy ruffians bleating as they broke and ran and tumbled. Stricken and dazed, but fighting-mad, with the stink of his own singed beard in his nostrils, he gathered himself together and lurched again to his feet; nothing mattered now but the black shape stealing upon him sword in hand.

Joris backed, blinking, keeping his point between him and that approaching figure of dread. Half the torches had been quenched by the explosion, and the near flare had vanished, but there was light enough to see that Yaan had doffed his stag's headpiece. Above the atrocious panoply lowered a human face—the mad face of Guelf Reinager, apothecary, showman, and Grand Master of the Covens of Nordanay.

"*Haro!*" croaked Joris, stiffening his sword arm; and like a whirled spear came the priest god's thrust. Craft of muscle, and stoutness of link mail, served the outlaw better than conscious skill in that extremity; but the familiar jar of steel cleared fog from between his strength and his fury.

The pair had the inner ring to themselves; they stamped and foined and hewed a moment before the arrows began to streak and strike around and upon Guelf's leathern armour. Gandulf and others had not run far; a devil at blows with Joris could not work further blasting magic upon the altar slab. But the long shafts stuck or rebounded; there was mail beneath the tough leather. Guelf ripped one out and dashed it at his enemy's face, tearing a wound in the cheek of Joris that presently bled inward and gave a taste of blood; and Joris pierced the leather gorget and saw the crafty mouth sag sideways with pain and effort.

But his own mail was cloven in three places; he had got the light of the remaining flare across the swords as he intended, yet Guelf knew the lie of the fallen stones, and Joris did not. And if the outlaws were rallying, the company of Yaan were not all cravens; a pair of bagpipes hurtled from the shadows and struck Joris above the knees. He lurched and overbalanced; Yaan's lightning stroke bruised his humped back, but his own desperate upward stab did more than all his craftiness.

Down on him sprawled the groaning, snarling blackness of Guelf Reinager; each grasped the other's throat, each dropped his sword and fumbled for his dagger. Joris felt his breath gone and his head bursting; he loosed the wet black gorget, groped for the iron wrist that choked him, gurgled to feel his left hand nailed to the peat, and poked wickedly upward with his dagger held like a sword.

Everything loosened and gave above him; the heavy head of Guelf crashed down on his own clutching hand and upon the

outlaw's battered mouth. The dagger of Guelf had found the
hand of Joris, but the dagger of Joris was fast through the
eye and in the crazy brain of Guelf.

"I perceive the Devil is dead," gasped Joris, writhing free
and releasing his wounded limb. Then he realized that others
had been fighting about him, and suddenly remembered the
first aim of that night's madness.

"Are they safe?" he shouted, stumbling to his feet, and
addressing the world at large with a sweep of recovered steel.

"Ay," said Gandulf beside him. "That is, the prince is bound
and sat upon. Guy de Saulte is yonder, having broken loose
and downed three men. Nay, Joris, you are half in pieces
yourself."

Despite his lieutenant's remonstrance, Joris reeled forward
to where Guy de Saulte stood with his back to a megalith,
with a half ring of laughing, thrusting men to dodge and parry
the furious strokes of his sword.

"Yield, monkey!" thundered Joris. "Have we not saved you
from hell fire?"

"*A Saulte—a Saulte!*" shrilled the exhausted boy, his fair
face set and ghastly. "I risk hell fire to make you certain of it,
filthy churl! *A Saulte!*"

"Assault be it," punned Joris thickly; and he shattered the
lad's sword at the hilt and split the blonde head to its eyebrows.

"Any more?" he demanded, shaking his reddened blade.

"All fled, save six who stayed for arrow shot," reported
Madoc, grinning with tongue outthrust like a dog's. "The
prince lies quietly, since we bound and gagged him."

Joris peered this way and that in the weird light; the
remaining altar flare was sputtering now, with none to tend it,
and the few lit torches burned smokily against the uprights
of the great trilithons. The dead were sprawled or huddled
here and there; and the ghostly music of the Stones hummed
softly overhead.

"Where is Red Anne?" he demanded harshly, when they

had shown him the fierce-eyed bundle that was captive Thoris-mund.

"Here, Joris," replied the woman, moving between two uprights behind him.

He turned, and saw that she had changed her ritual dress for the brown hunting gear of the previous day. Her face was set and still and tragical; she bent a steady look toward the still shape that had been Yaan's, and made with her un-strung longbow a little gesture of finality that was almost a salute.

"Now I will lead you to the ponies," she promised. "But first, your face and hand are torn. Were any of your men injured by that bursting fire box?"

"Three slain," said Gandulf blithely, and gave their names. "I dodged behind a pillar, or I had made a fourth. These rites are ruined between you, and I own I am not sorry; yet mountebank or no, yon Guelf had something of might in him."

"Madoc, blow a rally," commanded Joris thickly. "Pest, but my ears ring yet. Gandulf, guard the prince yourself. Bandage my hand first, Anne; I bleed there like a butchered sow. In faith, are all the lights going?"

"Whoa, chief," said one of his watching men, seeing the tall figure stagger. Joris felt himself caught and held; a veil of angry blackness swathed his senses. For the first time in his life he fainted.

The east was gray when they set him on a pony. Prince Thorismund was bound upon another, which Gandulf led in person. Red Anne rode by her man, and Madoc went to the head of the straggling half-mounted column.

When the Singing Stones were out of sight the sun got up in splendour. Brighter colours of earth were none than the red hair of Thorismund and the red hair of Anne; the outlaw chieftain glanced from one head to the other, and smiled to think that such a hue was often accounted unlucky.

"Here," he said within his heart, "begins the glory of Joris of the Rock."

*   *   *

Over the fading heather, down rock-walled, thorn-studded hollows, past amber tarns and the bright green of whispering bogs, swept that ragged and triumphant company, with the young prince bound in their midst. The flaming mop was dishevelled and matted, the beautiful face gray and dirty and strained; when Thorismund reeled and nearly fell they took the gag from his mouth and dosed him with thin sour wine. He blinked and coughed and grimaced, but spoke no word at first; his clear blue eyes grew calm and observant, and Joris regarded him narrowly and issued a curt command.

"Leave that gag out, but bandage my lord's eyes."

Thorismund licked his bruised lips and looked from Joris to Anne and back again.

"Faith, I have heard of you both," he said hoarsely, "but I thought not thus to make your acquaintance. Does Conrad promise good pay?"

"He may do when he hears of your plight," replied Joris, returning the royal stare with cold assurance. "Meanwhile Your Grace will excuse this rough precaution."

Thorismund's eyes vanished behind a grimy scarf; as Gandulf knotted the fabric, Thorismund's mouth twisted and grew grim.

"It was folly to kill Guy de Saulte," he remarked, and they heard his teeth snap shut.

"Your folly may be law in Hautarroy, mine here," drawled Joris, waving Gandulf forward and gathering up his own cord bridle into a swaddled hand.

Thorismund's cheeks and chin grew pink beneath the earth stains, but no further word escaped him throughout that strange morning. By noon the sun was hidden, and no one blindfolded could judge direction from the antics of gusty wind among the hills; when the outlaws halted to break their fast the captive was allowed to use his eyes and hands, and for the first time Joris felt a stress behind the long-continued silence of Red Anne.

"What ails you?" he grumbled suddenly. "Have you some new lofty grief I cannot share?"

"Maybe my coronet casts weight before its time," said Anne, spearing a gobbet of cold mutton on the point of her broad dagger.

Joris laughed abruptly, and Thorismund's haggard face grew intent as he eyed her and turned on Joris.

"What is your price?" he demanded sharply.

Joris took wine skin and drinking horn and carefully poured out a measure. Over the wine he regarded the unkempt prince, and coolly replied.

"Whatever Duke Conrad offers, and a little more."

Thorismund's eyelids drooped, and he nodded as though satisfied.

"Have you pen and ink and paper?" he asked after a pause.

"Not here, but at my Rock. And both Red Anne and I can read the vulgar tongue in which Your Grace will please to write. But I see no occasion yet for writing."

"You must convince the king that I am taken."

"The Duke of Saulte will do. The tunic of the Sieur Guy should convince *him*."

"You—you buried Guy?"

"We left him naked for the crows," replied Joris brutally, "as you or he or any man of rank might have left me. If the duke rides to the Singing Stones he will not know one skull from another. Two of my men who fell were tow-haired as any Saulte."

Deliberately Prince Thorismund crossed himself; his lips moved as though in silent prayer.

"Speak no Latin aloud," ordered Joris, "or you are struck on the mouth and gagged again."

"May no man then talk Latin in your hearing?" queried the captive.

"No, until and unless it be the bishop who shall reverse my excommunication."

"Ho!" exclaimed Thorismund; and for the first time Joris saw amusement in his face. "Now, save for that I might make a beginning of ransom by dubbing you chevalier, although my sword and spurs . . ."

"I hold them," Joris assured him. "But do not Castilian kings and lords dub Moorish chevaliers who are by birth and faith and breeding excommunicate?"

"You have me there," admitted the prince. "Besides, you have wrecked a coven, which must mightily please Holy Church. I think you must let me write to my lord archbishop."

"So long as I read the letters," said Joris blandly, "you shall write to all and sundry as you desire. But now it is time to move on: 'Gandulf, the mount for my lord Prince.'"

*　　　*　　　*

That night they slept in the Forest of Honoy, three men taking turns to watch beside the shivering prisoner. Thorismund made no complaint, although the morning found him pallid and wretched; he ate a morsel of black bread and drank water from a brook, and stood up for his eyes to be bandaged, casting a quick glance around him at the damp autumnal woods.

"Are the trees changed in their manner this day?" Red Anne suddenly asked him.

It was their first direct speech together, and Thorismund turned his bright head to regard her steadfastly before he made reply.

"Yes," he said. "How did you know?"

"Men took me once to burn me as a witch. I, too, looked at the trees I loved, and found them changed and heedless, whom I had thought to love me."

"What, even the trees?" murmured Thorismund, with a kind of haggard gentleness that mocked and slew the sneer on the woman's lovely face. "That was a treachery baser to you, who have ruled among them, than to me, who only hunt in their shadow."

"They live their own lives," responded Red Anne gravely. "All who do *that* must needs work treachery sometimes."

"By the Rood, I think you are right," said Thorismund, as Gandulf dropped the scarf over his eyes. "But breathe not such a heresy if ever you go to court; for there are treacheries enough without so glib an excuse for them."

"I have seen the Lady Yolande de Volsberghe," drawled Joris, feeling it time to intervene. "You lost a jewel, my lord Prince, when she left you for Duke Conrad."

"Talking of former loves," snapped the blindfolded youth, "I once saw Lorin de Campscapel. *You* lost a lover there, Lady Anne, when Raoul of Ger slew him."

Joris laughed harshly and drew his cloak about him.

"The speech of a prince is precious," he barked. "My lord, your last remark has cost you a thousand gold nobles beyond what else your carcass may be worth."

"Spoken like a churl," said Thorismund quietly.

"Gandulf," commanded Joris, "your boot toe to the princely rump."

Gandulf laughed and obeyed with a will; the captive, with hands tied behind him, lurched to the kick and fell awkwardly sideways. His full lips were clenched to a pale line, but he made no least outcry.

"My boot shall be embalmed when it grows old," cried Gandulf to the grinning onlookers. "For to-day it has broken stoutly into the story of the realm; nay, it has shaken as it were the very seat of royalty."

Red Anne stood silently by.

Throughout that day the company traversed the forest, zigzagging southward toward Pont-de-Foy. Twilight found them already near the secret ford, waiting for darkness to cover their crossing; and since the flat land by the bridge was out of sight beyond a bend of Varne, Joris had the prisoner's eyes again uncovered.

"Behold a river, Prince," he growled. "We cross it before moonrise. Your hands shall be loosed for the operation, and a man behind you shall carry a pike exceedingly sharp."

Thorismund was silent, watching the last light dying in the beech glades. Despite all stains and fatigue he was very fair; even in torn buff hunting clothes he seemed amid the outlaws a thing of spun and tinted glass contrasted with coarse shapes of earthenware and wood.

"And is this he," thought Joris, "who has cuckolded half the peers of Neustria? By the chimes of hell he looks no more than a silly maid himself."

The hard proud core of Joris was swollen with exultation. He sniffed the misty night air of the chill November woods, ground his heel into crackling twigs and yielding moss, and hummed a little tune, ignoring Thorismund beside him and even Anne behind them. When at length the prince spoke, it was to the woman; and his eyes were on stars above the sable masses of the trees.

"Lady Anne," he said civilly, "what is the shape in the northeast, between the Great Bear and the Bull?"

"That?" came Anne's indifferent reply. "That is the Charioteer."

"He who drew Elijah into heaven?"

"I do not know."

"Then there is the Dragon and the Little Bear, the Lyre, the Swan, the Flying Horse. *I* could do with a flying horse. . . ."

His levity jarred on Joris, but Anne herself snubbed it as she looked due east.

"There is also the Hunter rising to watch all runaways from over the edge of the world."

"Very true," sighed Thorismund, and thereafter held his peace.

When it came to urging his sturdy pony into the chill whispering water the prince glanced thoughtfully around him; but a man rode forward on either side, and the promised point

of a great pike head wavered a foot from his spine. Then he
shivered and exclaimed, for water poured over the tops of his
thigh boots, insuring an added misery for the rest of his
journey. In front and behind were grunts and oaths and
plashings; it was a soaked and dreary company that mustered
on the far bank amid the alders and willows. Vaguely beside
the climbing Hunter grew the herald glow of moon dawn; men
stamped and cursed, low-voiced, waiting for light on their way.
At length a first gold horn peeped behind slim distant pines,
and Madoc left the side of Joris to lead the trampling file
uphill. . . .

Before the hour of terce on the following day they saw the
Rock ride darkly blue above a sea of mist; the southern facet
of the crag took on a sudden red-gold gleam, and the chill
whiteness of the ravine became suffused with tones of tawny
and amber. But Thorismund drooped ghostlike where he sat,
with eyes uncovered but with no care for place or manner of
his journey's end; they had to haul him from the pony's back
and carry his stiff body to a cave next to the chieftain's own.
And there he lay, supine on a heap of sacking, with his own
cloak to cover him and a tall cross-eyed rogue named Romarec
to guard him, until fires were kindled and broth and wine
made hot.

By the hour of nones his abode was strewn with dried
heather and warmed by a little fire of its own; he had eaten
nothing, but drunk a deal of water, and presently a deep cough
set him on a rack of torment. In the first dusk Red Anne awoke
from her day's sleep and went to see him; and when she had
done so she pulled a lip at Joris.

"Your princeling begins to mutter nonsense," she said. "He
has a deadly fever. Lend me your wolf-skin coverlet, and
come to see."

Joris, himself newly awakened, growled a curse and followed
her. In the reek of the smaller cave the prisoner looked more
than ever like a doll; but when the outlaw bent he saw little
beads of sweat on the smooth brow and throat. The wide blue

eyes stared vacantly into firelit gloom; but now and again a
thin hand wavered to side or breastbone as though to check a
starting of pain. A spasm of coughing played havoc with the
beauty admired of many ladies; rusty-coloured spittle flecked
the white chin and the mean blanket under it.

"Leave him to me," murmured Anne. "Bid them set up a
tripod here, and a little caldron; and bring me my own saddlebags and the small chest of oils and powders."

Before Joris complied he knelt and possessed himself of the
great emerald ring that flashed on one damp princely finger.

"This must serve instead of a signature," he grunted in his
beard. "Take all the gear you need for nursing him; I would
prefer more than a corpse with which to bargain. Two men
shall watch all night by an outer fire. Gandulf shall bring you
lanterns and wine and water."

And presently Joris sat alone in his own sleeping place,
turning the emerald in torchlight and pondering the phrasing
of the message which Madoc must bear to the Duke of Saulte.
He spared a thought, too, for his own good fortune in having
at hand so skilful a leech as Anne. Dead or alive, indeed, this
sick boy should advantage him; but a prince able to sign his
name was needed for full flowering of the greatness of Joris
of the Rock.

*   *   *

So Madoc, grinning with wolfish importance, sought the
plain of Basse Honoy, knowing himself fairly safe, and
charged with a pack of dexterous lies. By night he came again
to meet Joris in the hills near Ververon—for Joris crossed the
river again, to keep the scene of parley from the neighbourhood
of the Rock. And with him Madoc brought Brian de Saulte,
brother to the duke and to that Guy whom Joris slew beside
the Singing Stones; and by night in a hollow of the hills they
came face to face—the nobleman in half armour, with a firm
rein upon his tongue, and Joris in his hunter's clothing, very
careful to hide the glee in his heart.

"The prince lies sick of a fever," said Joris roundly. "Your brother, the Sieur Guy, was slain by the mock Satan, as my man here doubtless told you. We had not time to prevent it— he gave his life for the prince. And the prince lies very well tended, and fast recovering."

Brian de Saulte said nothing at all to that, sitting his horse so stilly that the light of the dying moon seemed frozen on the curve of his plain helmet.

"Not to waste your time or my own," Joris continued, "these are my demands. First, release from excommunication, for me and for all those with me when the prince was— rescued. Second, the Prior of Dor to read the decree himself, and to shrive us, and to celebrate my marriage. Third, reversal of outlawry, again for me and my full company. Fourth, the king's full pardon, and amnesty against all claims arising from the way of life which has been forced upon me. Fifth, the prince's accolade for myself before he leaves my charge. Sixth, promise of employment as captain of a free company, signed by the constable and countersigned by three wardens of the marches. Seventh, a stronghold of my own, to be held of some tenant-in-chief, but *not* the Duke of Volsberghe or the Count of Ger. And eighth, three thousand gold nobles under my hand before the prince departs from among my men. . . .

"These, I say, are my demands. They are noted here on this skin, inscribed by a clerk of my following. Will you bear them to my lord Duke, your brother?"

"Yes," replied Brian de Saulte, reaching out a gauntleted hand for the grimy parchment. "But if these demands are made terms, what oath will bind you to deliver up the person of the prince unharmed?"

"Any oath I may honestly take when the ban is removed. I will gladly swear on the Rood or the Sacrament, or any relic brought to me by the prior."

"I will meet you again at this place in ten days' time," said the Saulte, pouching the document. "Until then, farewell, and God treat you as you treat the prince."

With that the colloquy ended, the Sieur Brian's solitary servant leading away the horse that Madoc had ridden; and Joris and his lieutenant strode off into the forest.

"Now may the weather last," thought the chieftain; but aloud he said: "That was strangely easy."

"Ay," returned Madoc softly. "Old René is sick again."

"Oho!" growled Joris, well pleased. "If our golden egg should hatch before it leave us, prices go up, my Madoc. But tell me how you fared."

As low-voiced Madoc talked, Joris remembered the words of Ivo: "Great turmoil in the realm . . . the king in danger of sickness . . . lords in council, and a name on all their lips . . . whose name?—Joris of the Rock's. The realm shall wait on his word. . . ."

It was good to be Joris that night. The keen smell of the woods, the flash of the moon's thin sickle amid the trees, meant more to him than he generally knew; but now a faint wonder came to him—would approaching success ring hollow sometimes, at memory of such black-and-silver mystery amid the beeches of the Forest of Honoy?

*　　　*　　　*

In six nights and six days Red Anne seldom left her patient. What sleep she had was taken in the prisoner's cave; barely a hand but her own touched the helpless thing that was heir to the Neustrian throne. And at noon on the sixth day Joris sought her with news, only to have it checked on his lips by the weariness in her face.

"By the beard of Goliath of Gath," he swore, "have you taken his sickness yourself?"

Anne shook back the ropes of her hair and smiled at her man.

"No," she said. "He is truly mending, and I am only spent. What were you going to tell me?"

"Gandulf is back from Pont-de-Foy. Gaston de Volsberghe is there, and the Barberghes, father and son. They seek me.

To-night I meet them also. The chaffering begins. Saulte and the prince's folk have kept their counsel well, but Gandulf heard a muttering of truth in the yard of the Inn of Harmony."

"Beware of those lords," counselled Anne. "It might serve *them* to take you or to slay you, and declare Ivo dead."

"*Ivo!*" growled Joris, in bleak astonishment. "Lass, are you out of your wits?"

"Very nearly," admitted the woman, with a strange dark flush overspreading her haggard face. "I should have said, and declare Thorismund dead. But I need not teach *you* craft. I only need sleep awhile, whose tongue plays tricks with my meaning."

"An ugly sounding trick," said Joris shortly. "Is it not time that poor fish had a nurse less strained and attentive?"

"Maybe," came the quiet reply. "But let not your craft spin webs for its own cleaving. By Mahound, Joris, the last man so to look at me was the Prior of Dor."

And despite her flush, Red Anne's blue eyes were amused; Joris even found time to feel that they looked through him rather than at him. The Devil of her choice was farcical and slain, but her beauty masked a demon that vexed him at such odd moments. Since her tale of Ivo's death she had not breathed the boy's name to Joris; why should it slip from her in an hour of black fatigue?

"Greatness is surely upon you," continued Anne. "Would Gandulf or Madoc themselves have tended your prize as I did? Or Romarec, the clumsy fool, or any other? You know they would likely have drunk your best wine, and left you a bundle of bones to consider. There is not much more there now; and what there is you owe to *me.*"

"How soon will he sit a pony again?" demanded Joris harshly, unwilling as ever to admit himself in the wrong.

"In a week at least," said Anne, rising to stumble away into the chief's own cave.

Joris stood still for a space, and then strode up to the entry of the lesser cave beside it. Plucking aside the screen of canvas that hung between two stakes set up in the sand, he peered beneath the mounting smoke at the red-haired shape beneath the wolf skins.

Thorismund seemed asleep; his head was bent away, and the only movement about him was that of the pulse in his thin stretched neck. But presently he stirred and turned a feebly inquiring face that was hollow-cheeked and gray and disguised by a first faint growth of red-gold beard. His great eyes, blue as Anne's own, were insolent with utter weakness; but Joris, who had seen him half a dozen times during the worst of the sickness, could tell that the latter was fast abating.

For a moment captor and captive stared at each other. Then the violet eyelids drooped in the half darkness, and Joris dropped the canvas and paced away.

"You tadpole of a sovereign," he muttered, "when Anne is My Lady indeed I shall keep her out of your way—if in fact you attain your growth; but that depends on your sweet cousin the Duke Conrad."

*   *   *

"Beware of those lords," Anne had said; but Joris required scant advice of that kind from her or anyone else. Twenty picked men of his following bent bows in the thicket when he moved forward to meet the three conspirators at sunset in the woods near Pont-de-Foy. The Barberghes eyed him with interest, but the Sieur Gaston only smiled, taking in dark-tipped beard and water-stained boots and scabbard with a quick professional glance; Joris had lately stood in the water to give an appearance of having crossed the river.

"Well met, good Dietrich Halbern," was the tall Vols-berghe's greeting. "To-day you have more than leather to sell. Are prices easy?"

"Easy for me," replied Joris coolly. "Do you want your man held, or handed over—and handed over dead or alive?"

"Handed over," said Gaston, "and very much alive. But

also, while we hold him, we want you still to bear the credit of his keeping until such time as may later be decided."

"But that delays my payment past the return of my security."

"Not it. The cardinal count shall deal with your excommunication, my lord and father the constable with your outlawry. You shall have letters of peace with Church and State, and five thousand gold nobles, before your prisoner leaves you; and with them a patent of nobility——"

"Hey?" interrupted Joris roughly.

"Your pardon if I spoke with indistinctness. A patent of nobility, already signed and sealed, to take effect from the moment of the crowning of Duke Conrad. He offers you the Barony of Thierne in Basse Honoy, and with it a free pardon for all offences past against the peace of the realm—*his* realm. Including"—and Gaston de Volsberghe's thick lips twitched in a cordial grin—"including the theft of a mare from the constable's son, some sixteen years ago."

Joris nodded, unsmiling, and eyed the nobles in turn. The Fox of Barberghe raised his eyebrows, as though in surprise at the outlaw's hesitation. The Viscount Robin fingered his riding switch, creasing his dark handsome face to a leer that could not hide excitement. Gaston de Volsberghe stood with arms folded and features as still as the forest darkening around him.

"These are fair terms, my lords," said Joris at length. "Add a pair of gilt spurs, and the right to wear them, and I think our bargain is made. But all that applies to my safety must apply to those with me, male and female alike. Also I need meat and corn."

"That is well understood," droned Gaston softly. "And as for chivalry, I but forgot to mention it. And for King René, be sure he will not last long."

They discussed times and places, and Joris smiled at last, feeling the iron of his will draw honours and gold toward him.

"Farewell till our next meeting," said Gaston when they

parted. "And know that your place is among us, you who bear the shape and bleed the blood of Montcarneau."

At sunrise Joris flung himself down beside his drowsy Anne, taking her in his arms to tell her all that had befallen.

"Whom do you cheat in the end?" she asked, holding him gladly and close.

"Nay, I know not yet," he muttered. "Suffice it that all goes well with us. The Barony of Thierne . . . my runes . . . *Anne* . . ."

Anne gave herself fiercely, and then stared out into the morning with Joris fast asleep against her breast.

*　　　*　　　*

"Conrad has it," said Joris, when he had made up his mind. "Fatten our prince for his journey; on Saint Andreas' Day I deliver him up and gain the first fruits of power."

"He will do well enough by then, at the rate he goes," said Anne. "But let not cross-eyed Romarec keep such frequent guard; he offends the lad beyond measure."

"A plague on your mercy," laughed Joris in great good humour.

"Had I chosen the other course, maybe I would listen to you. Yet you yourself seem very tired of our princeling. Is his hair too nigh the colour of your own?"

"His temper, as he grows stronger, is something too waspish. Nay, Joris, do not visit it upon him; what kind of a life will his be henceforth?"

"That is no affair of ours. For what you have just now said, he shall have Romarec for guard all night. What, shall he air his whims in the shadow of the Rock? Not he, by the chimes of hell! I have half a mind to break his knees; so long as his head and hands are hale Duke Conrad should be served. Nay, I cannot sit here like a slug. Gandulf was going to receive the cattle which Gaston sends for our winter provision; but I shall go myself, or little Thorismund will rue it."

Red Anne shrugged her shoulders and smiled, reaching out

for her lute. With voice pitched low as an oboe she sang a little song, watching the rain slant down beyond the cavern entry.

"When Merlin brought him to the lake,
  To take the brand Excalibur
Pendragon seemed but half awake
When Merlin brought him to the lake
The brand Excalibur to take;
  But lo! The shining steel astir
  When Merlin brought him to the lake
  To take the brand Excalibur!

"But little thought had Arthur then
  Of Guendolen or Guinevere.
He heard the thunder of his men,
And little thought had Arthur then
Of Guinevere or Guendolen.
  The witch-prow cleft the haunted mere;
  But little thought had Arthur then
  Of Guendolen or Guinevere!"

Joris sat with hands cupped beneath his pointed beard, and eyes hard and contented under their heavy lids.

"'He heard the thunder of his men,'" Anne quoted softly when she had done. "'Thousands of slain in the meadows, and the royal standard taken . . . Joris laughing amain at the end of a great battle . . . ay, and ten thousand men shall follow Joris.'"

"A strange and partial prophecy," said Joris, remembering. "Nothing of this our means of success, or of the Barony of Thierne. But the promise of my runes was misty enough in places; maybe the effort of welding a rhyme corrupted their message. And so, in your foreseeing, with Ivo's mind for your mirror. A mirror distorted—or so Lys had it—by Ivo's love for you."

"You speak his name kindly at last," muttered Anne, pressing queer chords from the lutestrings. "If—when—we are shriven, Joris, I will have masses sung for his soul."

"By the chimes of hell!" grunted the outlaw. "Are you

going over so far? Are you through that fog I might not know
—the bitter fog beyond the striving gods?"

"Not I," responded Anne, grown suddenly sullen. "But
if—*when* we are churched again it were well that one of us
had honesty in his heart."

Joris chuckled and spat, gaining a man's amusement from
the literalness of a woman. To him the coming ceremony
was a thing of convenience only; so far he had prospered apart
from God and in spite of a devil made manifest.

"Take it not too hard," he advised. "There are queer read-
ings of honesty in that galley. Nay, what if your Ivo were
right—what if Judas Iscariot were indeed a very godly man?"

Anne was silent for a moment, and when she replied her
voice was grim.

"Ivo's heresy bites deep," she said. "In faith I believe it
hard to come at Christ through his Church. But why did you
remember what Ivo said about Judas Iscariot?"

The laughter wrinkles deepened upon the cheeks of Joris.

"They say red hair is unlucky," he intoned. "Judas Iscariot
had red hair."

Red Anne grinned and threw her hood at him.

*　　　*　　　*

Bellowings far in the forest, and a tossing of black horned
heads against the stormy sunset. Laughing men on ponies,
shaping with shout and spear butt the course of that brown
unruly herd across the hills to the Rock. Every westward-
facing valley filled with a red light and a clamour of driving
wind. Hawthorns stripped and frantic against the slate-gray
cloud wrack, heather and bracken scourged and whistling,
tarns flailed to a furrowing glitter of saffron, rose, and
steel. . . .

It was as though the moors cheered Joris at his first harvest-
ing of fortune. Riding ahead of the tumult, he scanned the
forward slopes, permitting himself from time to time a little
choking sound of laughter. . . .

"You will have the beasts between Pont-de-Foy and Ververon?" Gaston had asked at the parley; and Joris had shaken his head.

"Give them to me to eastward of Mamion," he said. "*I will see them across Varne.*"

But since Mamion lay south of the Rock, there was no need to cross the river at all; and as Joris breasted a gentle slope and watched his shadow—a blue-gray centaur—climbing over the fading ling-tufts, he broke into his favourite song and boomed down-wind the name of Fastingal.

His life as he had made it was a brutal affair enough, but when he was alone—when he lacked that lust for domination which servile blood inflamed in him—his heart still held a boy's awareness of splendour incommunicable. So, for a long moment, he was at one with hills and wind and sunset. To himself the ringing song seemed shorn of spoken meaning; it voiced some exultation that burned with the burning western sky, yet gathered force from the sweaty reek of the sturdy beast between his knees.

"By God, I am alive!" he swore when his song was ended.

And with a great contentment he rode into the western end of the defile that deepened to the chasm of his home.

Fires sparkled, smoke bellied gray-white in blue gloom, but men stood at gaze without approaching their leader. The echoing uproar of driven cattle aroused the jackdaws from their winter nests among the limestone crannies; and the mingled din of bird and beast played Joris up to the door of his cave.

There by a newly kindled fire stood Madoc, fully armed, and very white beneath the tan of his hatchet face.

"Where is Anne?" demanded the chieftain.

"Gone," said Madoc tensely. "Taking with her the prince."

"Taking—with—her—*who was on guard?*"

"Romarec. He also is fled. And had it been my fault I too should have gone by now."

Joris looked his lieutenant up and down, and slipped from

the pony's saddle. The very wings of his nostrils were pinched and white with rage; he clapped one hand on his sword hilt and made a little clawing gesture with the other.

"When—when——" he croaked.

"The night before last," responded Madoc. "Romarec knifed the sentry at the top end yonder; the fool was asleep, I believe. Easy enough to get away if they had ponies hidden; no one counts the ponies these days. I had twoscore men ranging wide all day yesterday, but they saw nothing."

Joris wheeled, and lurched into his cave. His groping hands touched something in the darkness—the canvas cover of Red Anne's lute, that hung on a peg from one of the posts set up in the sandy floor. The strong fingers gripped the lute neck, feeling the inner cover of velvet rasp on the tautened strings before they whirled the thing aloft and crashed it against the wall. Other gear clanged and tumbled with it; Joris caught at his head with both hands and uttered a long howl of baffled fury. Then he pitched forward on to his blankets—biting, snarling, blaspheming alone in the darkness, with all his glory shredded and spent like the glow of the dead sunset.

"You hag of hell!" he groaned aloud; and then his words spread chokingly amid the names of Anne and Ivo, of Rufin and long-dead Tiphaine de Ath.

Once he began to laugh; but that was after he had found a wine skin. Then he paused and filled his lungs for a jest.

"Judas Iscariot had red hair!" yelled Joris of the Rock.

XI. THE CAUSEWAY AT MARCKMONT

"IT IS like the edge of the world," said Juhel, staring out of window to where, above the last hovels of the hamlet, the land split into long shoals and the sedge-brown marshes widened eastward beneath low-dragging cloud.

"The bright water beyond is the Lake of Cremalvay," said Piers beside him. "On a clear day, and especially when the light is low, you can sometimes see the further shore. When hawking is in season again we shall have rare sport—if we are still here."

Four towers, wide for their forty-foot height, and linked by stout curtain walls, composed the Castle of Marckmont. They stood on a low mound at the southern end of the long stone causeway which carried the northward road. This barony, indeed, was two parts water, and the third part the poorest lowland corner of the realm.

"If we are still here," repeated Juhel softly, his mind ranging backward over autumn, winter, and spring, with their alarms and journeys and the stormbound months on the crags of Ger above the northern sea. There Juhel had come to a new conceit of womankind; the Countess Reine could be stern enough, but her frank brown beauty went with a generous humour that the boy found worshipful and strange. Also he had a scar on his hand and a sweet memory in his heart— a memory of humming sea wind and upborne crash of waves, of sunlight pale on the clean brown rushes of the floor of the winter parlour.

In the great painted cradle beside the hearth had lain the baby Viscount Lothair, cooing contentedly to himself, weav-

ing a slow infinity of gesture with tiny helpless hands. Came a
sudden howl in the passage, a shouting, a padding rush—and a
boarhound, crazed and slavering, thudded against the jamb
of the half-open door and hurtled sideways into the room
where only Juhel stood. Over the arm of a chair beside the
cradle hung a new crimson cloak of the count's; as the great
brindled brute hunched his body and turned, Juhel leaped
in front of the baby and snatched up the garment in both
hands. His cry chimed with the snarl of attack; backward and
sideways he stumbled, bowled over into the scattered fire
ash by the weight of the hound's spring. But the red eyes and
the murderous jaws were whelmed in crimson velvet; a half-
gagged snap ripped the ball of Juhel's right thumb, forcing
a louder yell from him as Nino Chiostra's sword blade flashed
a foot from his face.

The velvet had drunken the venom, and the wound healed
cleanly; but Juhel would never forget the shock and scent
of the scalding wine, the intent scowl of John Doust bending
above his hand, the strong arm of the Countess Reine about
his shaken body and her hoarse words in his ear: "Juhel, brave
Juhel, God give you your due, for never can we." Also there
was the fair face of the Lady Dionysia de Saint-Aunay, ward
to my lord, who held the steaming bowl for Captain John;
yet best of all were my lord's own eyes, raised from the
frightened child in his arms to look at his faithful page.

All that was six months past, for it happened between
the escape of Prince Thorismund and the fall of the first
snow. Now full summer filled the land, and still the old King
René clung to life, fretting the nerves of great lords who
feared for plot and counterplot. The Count Raoul had brought
to Marckmont two thirds of the fighting men of Ger; the
little castle held only half of them, the rest being quartered in
log huts by the windmill. But Juhel had only just arrived, having come with Nino Chiostra by way of Hastain, Olencourt,
and Belsaunt; and joyfully he dropped his gear in the little
room he was to share with Piers.

"In faith I am glad to be here," he said. "And so, I believe, is Master Nino."

For in the next room sounded a great splashing, and the Tuscan's merry tenor lifted in cynical song.

"Observe Francesca, how she stands,
  Carim-cara, cara-carim;
As lithe a maid my heart demands
Without Francesca's clawlike hands,
  Carim, cara, carissima.

"Giovanna's eyes are kind and sweet,
  Carim-cara, cara-carim;
But tho' my word be indiscreet
Giovanna has enormous feet,
  Carim, cara, carissima.

"Yet this my lay I'll not prolong,
  Carim-cara, cara-carim;
Lest Cupid's hour should strike, ding-dong,
And prove me altogether wrong,
  Carim, cara, carissima!
  Carim, cara, carissima!"

Piers looked sideways at Juhel, and Juhel shrugged his shoulders.

"At most times he seems very gay," murmured Juhel, "yet once I heard him weeping in the night."

Piers nodded gravely. The little Lady Dionysia was heiress of Saint-Aunay, a proud fief in Nordanay; her father was that luckless count slain three years previously by Lorin de Campscapel. Sixteen and blonde and lovely, she did not lack for suitors among the proudest in the land; and whatsoever private equality was kept between Raoul of Ger and his comptroller, the Tuscan was nevertheless a landless foreigner, a nobleman's bastard whose sword was quick but whose first tool was a graver. The Lady Dionysia liked him, jested with him; but she cried scorn of his ungallant song without dreaming of the pain behind it.

"Greeting, my Tuscan mandrake!" boomed John Doust's voice beyond the half-closed door.

"Well met, old bear from foggy England!" carolled Nino Chiostra.

"You come to Marckmont and speak of fogs? By the scabbard of Michael Archangel, lad, I can count your ribs as never before. The remedy is copious inward application of baked heron, garnished with mallows, and weighted with a multitude of chopped eels."

"*Per Bacco!* The water was cooling, but a sight of your red jowl sets it steaming anew. To-night I thrash you at chess; to-morrow will do for accounting."

"What news of the king?"

"Dying, they said in Belsaunt. But that we have heard before."

"And of Ger?"

"All is well enough there. The lord viscount has six teeth and crawls about the floor."

"He will take kindly to swordplay, that one. Let me have the training of sons of lovers of peace. With five hundred of them I would make cold meat of the Soldan and tumble every city in Cathay."

"There, there," crowed Nino. "Lothair shall conquer Muscovy, and I shall be receiver general of taxes paid in amber. Amber to the ceiling, John, and I will go about to carve it with an ax. Or he shall plunder the Indies, and all your points be strung with pierced gems."

"Damnably uncomfortable when you came to buckle your sword belt."

"No need for sword belts those days; our peace should quarter the earth."

"Good Saint George deliver me from a day that needs no sword belt."

"Ay, you are right, war dog. Sword time takes the mind away from baying of the moon, giving a zest for little else but wine and puddings and sleep. But care killed the pig, and

there is in one of my packs a lump of rock crystal sweated
by Vulcan himself at the forge of the old gods. It will serve,
it will serve . . . ten thousand little fleeting devils, cannot
someone hammer flat the nails in this bathtub? No, I err;
it is a pebble, fallen out of my riding boot. So fast we rode,
John, the gravel flew over the treetops. Name of a name of
a dreadful name, bring me towels or I perish!"

Piers ran to obey. Juhel stood a moment alone beside the
unglazed window, sniffing the lazy summer air of the great
marshes.

"Nothing can beat the coast," he mused, "but this is very
fair."

*   *   *

So it proved in the weeks that followed, when Piers taught
Juhel to walk on stilts between the silvery sand spits. Sometimes they poled a boat, pausing to snatch up bow and shaft
and let fly at the waterfowl. Wild swans furrowed the mere,
riding in kingly files and squadrons; once the boys heard a
commotion and found a young swan slaughtering ducklings
with poignard thrusts of his orange beak and cruel stamping
of webbed feet, while the mother duck cried to unheeding
heaven, tearing a circular trail in the reeds, whipping the
water with frantic breast and wing.

Piers fended the destroyer off, while Juhel rescued the
sole survivor—a pitiful brown-gray fluffy thing, that twitched
and squeaked and fouled his hand in its terror.

"Here, duck," cried Juhel softly, floating the mite away
on a tuft of grasses; and when the fugitive pair had vanished
his eye fell on the three plump bodies fallen to arrows that
afternoon and now lying in the bottom of the little barge.

"Why should we kill them if the swan may not?" he mar-
velled. "What if a water sprite jumped like a fish and flung
us in to drown? The swan was doing it for fun, of course—
hey, but so were we."

He stretched himself in the blunt bows and let Piers

propel them forward. Rags of blue sky grew between cloud packs, and the dull steely water responded with innumerable shades of blue and green and shining gray. Sedges and half-drowned willows, and above them the faintly stirring poplars, whispered to a first breath of morning wind; eels twirled ghostly dark in the brown water beneath his nose, and a low hum of countless insects swelled from the shore a dozen yards away.

"I do not *really* want to kill anything," said Juhel to himself. "Or anyone—unless, perhaps, it were Joris of the Rock."

When they had landed and moored the barge, Piers and he walked slowly homeward in the growing heat of noon. The hamlet was all but deserted, for serfs were getting in the hay beyond it, and John Doust had marched the men-at-arms across the causeway for a mock battle in the foothills to the north. But by the door of one hut a sturdy peasant girl sat shelling peas; the pages passed close by her, and Juhel saw that she had very light blue eyes and very long dark lashes in a sunburned face. Juhel was big for his age now, with comely rounded features; he felt the pale eyes on him, and wondered, not for the first time, what such a creature might be thinking as she sat there like a cat in the bright sunlight. Part of him claimed disgusted knowledge; the Marckmont wenches preened themselves these days, with so many tall soldiers thronging the mean street; why should she challenge a page's eye unless she could not help it? Did she ogle the haystacks thus, or sweep her lashes up so proudly for the nanny goat she milked of a morning? Part of him vowed she did, and mocked her for a fool.

A week later he came on her gathering sticks in the oak glades toward the village of Olvay. Boldly she stood in his path, bare-armed, with her ragged skirt kilted above her strong brown knees. The moment slid out of time, and there was no past or future; Juhel felt he was damned for a coward if he did not clip and kiss her soundly. She feigned to avoid the caress, but at the last her mouth met his own squarely.

His grasp, that had been gingerly, tightened with sudden fury; hands and feet of this brown supple thing might be hard and earth-stained, but there was much beside that flowered smoothly from her rags beneath his fingers. The girl knew no subtlety; a hint of practice in her giggling surrender dug at his half-scared joy, yet could not uproot it.

But carnal triumph grew suddenly foul and spoiled and evil. With barely a word spoken between them he stood at length above her, loathing her body and his own, swept by a flood of despairing rage that baffled him with its blackness. One hand clutched his dagger hilt, the other groped in his purse; better to press the affair to one limit of baseness now, before he sounded a beastlier depth and struck what he had fondled.

A florin flashed in the flattened grasses; the girl snatched it and grinned up at him with the silver coldly bright between her white teeth. With a sound between a groan and a curse he turned on his heel and shambled away, utterly wretched, almost physically sick, yet aware of a dumb protest in his heart—a protest that what was accounted gay should prove such a bleak misery.

"Saints forgive me," he muttered; "I do not even know her name. And forgive her too—but *she* is like an animal— which makes it seven times worse."

Everything seemed different, yet everything was the same, from the banners of Ger and Marckmont that drooped above the distant towers, to the faint squealing of children in the hayfields a quarter of a mile away. The sameness itself abashed him, the difference being his own; he was vaguely surprised that no one read his sin from his unhappy face, or that Piers should sleep so soundly that night while he lay awake and stricken with remorse.

Early next morning he confessed, alone in the cold gloom of the chapel with kind old Father Paul, who was village priest and castle chaplain in one. A light burned on the altar, another by the door; in the white mist beyond the window slits the pigeons whirred, cooing as though appalled by this enormity of wrong.

"Boy, I can see you are shaken by honest repentance," came the mild voice from above Juhel's head. "But do not magnify your sin to gratify your pride. The one is grievous enough without its giving rise to the other. Now you are in this danger—that having lost bodily innocence, you may next be tormented with lecheries of the eye and of the mind. If this befall you, seek cold water, and if you cannot bathe, then dip your head in wholly, saying inwardly an *Ave* and a *Paternoster,* and thinking of the corruption and stench that attend the brightest flesh in death. . . ."

Somehow Juhel felt that the old priest dismissed too lightly his yesterday's impulse toward murder. A miserable conviction shook him; surely he was accursed, whose desires were brutally commingled.

"Is that also a vanity?" he wondered when he was alone. "Shall I gradually forget my horror, and in a month or two months seek her, or another, away in the quiet woods? I did not think Marckmont to be a place of peril."

Place of peril or no for Juhel, it was now a place of moment to all the realm; for early on that morning had died King René in Hautarroy.

At dusk of the same day three horsemen came full tilt up the road from Olvay. A single clang of the alarm bell brought Count Raoul out above his castle gateway. Leaning between two merlons beside his lord, Juhel saw the Barberghe red-and-black and felt his pulses quicken.

"Who is he?" demanded the count.

"The Chevalier de Medrincourt, my lord. He holds my own tower for my lord of Barberghe."

Men at arms clustered below on the drawbridge; half-armoured De Medrincourt wasted no time in formality.

"Bid your lord make ready!" he shouted. "Say to him from his friends: *Down portcullis!*"

Then he was wheeling his mount on the cobbles below the

castle mound; and with a wild clatter he rounded the nearest angle of the incline and was spurring along the causeway, followed by his two men. The racket of horses' hoofs waned and died in the excited stir below, and Raoul of Ger crossed himself.

After a moment Juhel crossed himself also, realizing that King René was dead, and that this must be Gaston de Volsberghe's signal to strike for Conrad of Burias.

The count turned to a rampart door as John Doust lumbered out of it. The Englishman's blue eyes twinkled, and he pursed up his slit of a mouth.

" 'Down portcullis,' " he quoted jovially. "And stand from under," he added for himself. Then, Juhel being there, he spoke with more ceremony: "My lord, shall we begin?"

"Yes, Captain," said Raoul of Ger, with the smile that had lately grown infrequent. "If further messengers find us at work, they must not pass northward. Since De Medrincourt asked for no change of horses, I suppose Gaston has set relays in the villages. Well, first for a muster of boats; the list is with Nino."

In the last light the fishermen of Marckmont dragged their little vessels, of hollowed wood or wickerwork and hide, into a row along the sandy beach beneath the castle mound.

"No man," commanded the count, "must use or take away his boat without leave from myself or from Captain John Doust."

But his own two flat-bottomed hunting barges he set in charge of picked men-at-arms, and east and west from the causeway they began to patrol the marsh, each bearing peasants to row and archers and crossbowmen to enforce the injunction that none should traverse the main water. At the far end of the causeway six men watched all night by threes in the darkness; but the strip of shore at the near end, between the hold itself and the three tall poplars which stood above the cobbled road at the mere's edge, was clear as day with firelight and torchlight.

Juhel and Piers, ordered to bed, fell asleep to a sound of hammering and knocking. When in the morning they awoke and peered out, the causeway was already stoutly defended; on the masonry itself, a score of yards from land, stood a *chevaux de frise* of heavy timber, railed and chained to a framework of stout trestles, and presenting a northward bristle of iron spikes and jags. A few paces behind the *chevaux de frise* two rows of barrels, filled with sand and standing five abreast, were set between the low stone parapets, and buttressed and locked in place with logs and sacks of earth. Mantlets of wood and hide were being fastened in front of them, and planks nailed across their tops; there half a dozen archers could find room.

More mantlets were set up along the sand, so that other archers in perfect safety could shoot obliquely along the flanks of the causeway; and as the sun came up a mangonel was wheeled from its lean-to shed in the gloomy courtyard and halted on the paved strip of ground between the priest's house and the water's edge.

There, with its throwing lever like a great iron-bowled wooden spoon, the engine rested until every other defence was completed. Not until late in the afternoon did the sweating men cease from toil and stand to watch the trial shooting.

The mangonel's crew strained at their levers; back and back leaned the tall spoon until it gaped at the cloudy sky. Then a round stone was placed in the bowl—"as though an archangel had laid an egg," said Nino Chiostra—and John Doust, standing on the causeway barricade where no one else dared go, waved a hand for the discharge.

With a dull thudding impact the spoon sprang upright against the padded crossbar; the stone whizzed in a wicked curve toward the causeway. The Englishman's fair hair gleamed strawlike in the westering light as he turned his head. Juhel, staring from the ramparts, saw the stone skim the further parapet by a yard and strike the water with a mighty splash.

"Well placed," roared John Doust down the rising wind. "Her tail six inches to your left, and try again."

At the fourth shot a stony smack resounded; a multiple splash and a serration in the parapet proclaimed a hit, and a cheer went up that scared the wild duck from the reeds for two hundred yards each way.

That night twin cressets burned on the marshward towers, with iron shields behind them that their flames might not dazzle the watchmen; and on the causeway itself an iron-screened brazier stood beyond the outermost defences, casting a flickering glow along the narrow way, filling the wind-whipped water beneath it with uneasy startings of reflected flame. From time to time a boat put out with fuel for its replenishment; then a steel-capped figure would swarm dimly up a ladder, and a shower of sparks would slant to perish out along the mere.

Dawn came on with a spatter of blown rain; the smoke from cressets and chimneys flattened out and whirled amid the bending willows. Piers shook the sleeping Juhel's shoulder, and Juhel awoke with a start, finding himself afraid. To-day he must help to confront, and maybe to withstand, Gaston de Volsberghe and Gaston's embattled host.

It troubled Juhel not at all that his beloved master had betrayed and was now more actively to betray the traitorous lords who trusted in him; indeed, it amused him to know that Gaston de Volsberghe and the Count of Montcarneau were wasting a fifth of the rebel power by marching it down toward Belsaunt, believing Marckmont unguarded and the Count of Ger their friend.

And again, although for a new reason, the boy found everything strange. Armour and gear, the simple furniture of his chamber, stood aloof from him; as for his leaders and comrades, they seemed of a different race. There was the Sieur Count, whistling as he combed his thick brown hair, and

Captain John playing with two deerhound puppies while he waited to break his fast. Master Nino, yawning as Juhel unarmed him, turned aside, before he stumbled to bed, to scowl at his lump of rock crystal, which now began to take the shape of a stretching leopard. Grave Master Hubriton, the secretary, irked by an unfamiliar corselet, grinned at himself in a mirror before he sat in to the board. And Piers was content as usual, serving as deftly as though this war were a holiday.

Juhel himself was dry in the mouth and scarcely able to eat. His fingers were thumbs for battle harness, but no one troubled to chide him. Up got the sun, out went the candles, down slid the broth and venison and wine. . . .

One of the barges moved away and landed two men at arms, with their horses, as scouts on the opposite shore; and all the morning scores of eyes scanned the well-known sandy spits, the swaying poplars and clumped lesser trees, beyond the brown expanse of reed-patched rippling water and beneath the dark foothills of the Forest of Nordanay.

By Marckmont the windmill sails went creaking round, and the ox-drawn wains hauled home the last of the good hay. Swine grunted as they were driven out to near pasture; cowbells tinkled, and cocks crowed, behind the cottages and barns. Men listened to these sounds as though they heard them for the first time, then forgot them as the sharp note of a horn from a turret was answered by the sombre boom of the gateway bell. Not for forty years had Marckmont looked upon the face of war.

"My helmet, Juhel," said Raoul of Ger.

When that duty was accomplished a glad excitement shook the boy, so that he almost ran down the steep stair and out of the courtyard. Somewhere above him he heard Nino Chiostra bawling for Piers to arm him; men who had watched in the night were tumbling from their quarters. When Juhel reached the barricade John Doust was calmly posting the archers, while serfs, handling leathern buckets, drenched wood and hides and timber with water. With Gaston de Vols-

berghe you never knew ; he might bring Greek fire on a wagon,
or any other devilish invention.

On the opposite shore the scouts were coaxing their horses
on to the barge ; one animal refused to board, and was dragged
into the water by its bridle, thereafter swimming dutifully
astern as the oars flashed and fell for safety.

There came a stir and a sparkle amid the distant trees.
Horsemen galloped out upon the sandy margin, their voices
faint but clear as they hallooed to the unanswering crew of
the returning barge. Presently half a score came pounding straight along the causeway, checking their gallop to a
trot as they saw the obstacle before them, checking the trot
to a walk as they took in the steel-clad shapes of count and
captain on the barricade, the glittering caps of archers and
pikemen, the crossbowmen behind the mantlets of the second
barge, now moored to flank their approach—and last, the
laden spoon of the mangonel reclining for its spring.

At a distance of a hundred yards the leader of the group
drew rein and barked an order. Immediately his men and he
turned about and clattered back along their path; and now
the sandy reaches behind them were alive with shifting
spears. There was hurried conference at the far end of the
causeway : then, at the head of a score of riders in full panoply
of plate, there loomed along the stony track a mighty figure
in gilded armour, astride a huge black horse. With gray eyes
steady and cool beneath a lifted visor, Gaston de Volsberghe
halted his troop and rode alone to the *chevaux de frise*.

"In God's name, my lord," muttered an archer, "bid me let
fly."

"It were as well," counselled John Doust on the count's
other side.

But the count stood and waited, with his own visor cocked
aloft; and above the mass of timber and pointed iron the
leaders met and held each other's stare.

"So Ger has changed his mind?"

The great bass voice boomed crisply, almost jovially, in the windy marshland silence; and rapidly the even tenor answered it.

"Ger changes mind less easily than Volsberghe changes surcoat."

For Gaston's short coat was not the azure of his house, charged with its golden gryphon, but the sable of Hastain, bearing the golden portcullis.

"What of your bond, you rat?"

"Oy, let me split his face!" groaned the kneeling archer; but the count lifted a gauntleted hand in restraint, and Juhel, close behind him, heard his teeth snap shut before he replied.

"What of your loyalty, you wolf?"

"Then you refuse allegiance to our lord King Thorismund?" roared Gaston, his gaze leaving Raoul's to sweep the line of defence.

"That trick is useless, De Volsberghe; for one here heard you plot his ruin in the Hotel de Ahun at Belsaunt."

The eyes of the Sieur Gaston widened, narrowed, and grew terrible; for the first time the deep voice jarred on a note of fury.

"Think on this day when I impale you, sorry little wasp!"

Then, clashing down his visor and featly whirling his destrier, the constable's son spurred back along the causeway in a hail of bolts and arrows that rang and bounced and turned aside against his plate of proof.

John Doust bellowed; the crash of the mangonel came a second too soon, the great stone thudding between Gaston and his wheeling troop, to roll along the causeway in front of the black stallion until flying hoofs could overpass it.

"Never mind," said the count to the downcast archer nearest him, "I warrant you have another chance before long."

All afternoon there was smoke and movement on the opposite shore, and the patrols of Marckmont ranged a league to east and west, knowing the marshes impassable save by treachery. At sunset the cressets were augmented by six great fires along the edge of the main water, and men lay under arms in boats that passed with muffled oars amid the reeds and dangerous banks, watching and listening for any sign of an attempted crossing by hastily built rafts where the meres grew wider. Near the far end of the causeway twenty campfires twinkled, but at midnight Nino Chiostra took a small boat right across and landed to reconnoitre, returning with the news that of a dozen spied upon, two only of the fires had men about them.

"We have given the king another three days for the mincing of Barberghe," said Raoul of Ger.

But Gaston de Volsberghe and Alain, Count of Montcarneau, had hurried northward with their horsemen, turned back the foot that followed, and hurled the whole fifteen thousand of them westward in a forced march over the wild moors of Nordanay. Near Hastain they fell like a cloudburst upon the king's own army, saving the pounded Barberghes and driving Thorismund back in retreat that was half a rout, on Rambard and Ververon and toward the loop of Varne, where the Inn of Harmony stood up amid the willow holts beneath the edge of the forest.

Thitherward also, from the south, retreated Saulte and the castellan, with Conrad and the constable pressing after, commanding double their numbers. The burghers of Alanol joined the king as he fell back past Ververon; the burghers of Belsaunt joined Raoul of Ger, when at length he left his inviolate barony and marched to reënforce the royal armies as the rebel pincers nipped them to a junction on the field of Pont-de-Foy.

XII. PONT-DE-FOY

S OMEHOW it was nightfall. Juhel turned slowly, conscious of terror and despair and a great heaviness of body.
Ahead the muddy road ran grayly into half darkness—yes,
it had rained this side of Belsaunt—and behind, the puddles
caught a weird gleam from the last opal bars of afterglow.
There the trees moved hideously—the goblin traitor trees;
all the deepening dusk was full of the wrack of a routed army.
Try as he might, Juhel could not remember one detail of
manœuvre; but he knew that his dear lord count was slain,
with Saulte and the Castellan and many more—that the young
king was taken and every hope destroyed. Master Nino
Chiostra had shrieked and drowned in Varne; only Captain
John Doust had somehow rallied a grim company, driving into
the forest through swathes of rebel dead. Hubriton, the glum
clerk, had halted to lean against a tree, and as he stared
at Juhel his eyes grew blank and his mouth fell open.

"Piers!" bleated Juhel, and remembered a heap, a nothing
with a flattened skull, half hidden in long grass beneath the
trampled falcon banner.

"Why am *I* not dead too?" demanded Juhel, blubbering
miserably in the twilight. "I am all alone—ah, who are you?
Oh, just and holy God!"

For sliding through the forest beside him he saw his own
white face and faintly gleaming corselet.

"It is time," said a great voice from the sky. Then he
was gripped by an invisible hand, and all about him was smitten to murk shot with the colour of blood.

His eyes were open before he awoke, but in a second or
two the murk was resolved into the canvas wall of the count's

tent, and the blood colour to the light of the campfire beating upon it from outside.

"It is time," repeated Piers, moving aside so that candle-light from behind him dazzled the younger boy.

Suddenly trumpets shrilled far off; Juhel sat up, his face wet with tears, his heart still sick and weighted with the burden of the evil dream.

"Now, plague me if *my* soul is left alone on the field when all the rest troop off to Purgatory," he thought indignantly. Then he grinned with relief to find himself yet alive, to see the count's head stir beside a tent pole, to hear John Doust blowing like a whale as he washed outside the tent, and to smell the unforgettable mingled odour of wood smoke, burned frying pan, and sizzling bacon.

This, then, was the morning, not the night, of Pont-de-Foy.

*   *   *

Thorismund's rear was to the forest, Conrad's to the river. Thorismund had the rising ground and the interior lines, but Conrad had the advantage of numbers and space in which to move them. Instead of four armies there were now two, for the young king had abandoned the Ververon road and the bridge head of Pont-de-Foy rather than risk a battle back-to-back with Saulte. The northern rebels had joined forces with their chief; it was plain to both sides that neither could retreat without great slaughter. And when the sun dissolved the morning mist along the river banks there came a murmur and a shaken glitter as over a hundred thousand men rose armed from prayerful kneeling to the voices of their clergy, who from either side called out upon God for remission of sin and for just and merciful victory.

The royal standard carried before Conrad from Hautarroy drooped from the summit of a mound—the middle tumulus of three which stood amid the willow holts between Pont-de-Foy and Angmer. Over against it, on the first rise of ground behind the Inn of Harmony, rose Thorismund's banner; to avoid confusion in the field, the king had unfurled his own gay device, quartering the arms of Neustria and Franconia, with the portcullis of Hastain on an inescutcheon. And there through the sunlit morning they stirred to a rising wind, which in the early afternoon brought ragged clouds and a thin drizzle of rain.

The right wing of Thorismund's army was commanded by the gaunt Duke of Boqueron, with Raoul of Ger to second him; red scallop shells on white, with the black gerfalcon on yellow, confronted the Volsberghe gryphon, the Barberghe chevrons, and the wolf heads of Montcarneau. And from that angle of the field Juhel looked first on killing; the rumour and terror of the great battle rang faintly enough in his memory before he died, but when the first onset closed it seemed all things were come together with a clang.

One moment he heard a wood pigeon in the dark fringes of the Forest of Honoy; the next, the air was filled with shouting and trampling and the hum of longbows, while behind roped stakes and heavy shields the men of Ger stood fast with pike and guisarme amid the dew-wet grass and young green bracken.

Couched lances, slanted shields, bright helms whose shapes made of the charging chevaliers one snouted grinning family —all rocked upon them with the roaring Volsberghe war shout; and a sleet of arrows drove uphill and down to the first screams of wounded horses and the first metallic clatter of the fall of armoured men. Then a crash, and the front of the whole wing was a surge of criss-crossed thrusting steel.

Juhel watched rise and fall the estoc of John Doust; a stumbling charger flung its rider full against the Englishman, but the latter only crouched to the shock and a moment later swung up his weapon again, the solid ranks of yellow coats hiding from Juhel the fate of the fallen chevalier. To left and right the destriers were rearing, plunging, wheeling before the unbroken line; horsemen were dragged to earth with the hooks of guisarmes, or smitten through the armpit mail as they raised sword or mace to strike beyond the stakes. Presently a trumpet wailed, and all along the attacking front blue figures leaned away and reined their chargers back.

A curt cheer went up from the crest of the rise; the enemy were retiring, leaving a glittering fringe of fallen on the slope above them. A gust of arrows from below heralded the first upward roll of Gaston's bearded Franconian mercenaries; four free companies surged abreast toward the rough stockade. Close beside Juhel the trumpeter of Boqueron woke a double blast; in half-a-dozen places the pikemen loosed or dragged aside the stakes and ropes they had planted, while the duke waved his hand to the Count of Ger. Through the gaps went trampling six troops or horse—deploying as they emerged, linking up and fanning out to follow gray Safadin downhill. Three hundred lances sank to the charge; badges of Ger and Marckmont and Guarenal mingled with Boqueron's and with devices of individual chevaliers. With a drumming rush between the thickets the gay mass of steel and colour gathered force and hurtled against the dark advancing line; Juhel, with heart in his mouth, stood holding the bridle of the count's spare charger and calling silently upon all saints to uphold and defend Raoul of Ger.

The Franconian formations paused and stiffened, but even their quick bristle of pikes could not withstand that impact. They had no stakes to shelter their bodies, no ropes to entangle the pounding horsehoofs; by sheer weight their lines were crumpled and borne backward in struggling disarray. Behind them the mounted ranks were reforming; the mercenaries knew that if once they really broke they would be ridden down in Gaston's second onset, and in five minutes their trained valour cost them scores of lives. Then Ger and his men were wheeling and cantering away up the slope; Safadin halted at the side of Boqueron's white charger, and two riders who reeled from their saddles were dragged behind the rough stockade before the pikemen closed their gaps and waited for the reënforced assault.

Again a storm of long shafts sighed amid the shouting; in front of Juhel an archer sat heavily backward and doubled up, groaning and whipping off his shooting glove to clap hand to his smitten shoulder. Juhel glanced up at the count; Raoul of Ger had seen, and nodded to him. To tether the horse to a hawthorn bush was the work of thirty seconds; Juhel stepped forward and snatched up bow and gauntlet, tucking a fistful of arrows clumsily into his belt.

Then he was shooting hard just over the bright helm of Captain John Doust. The longbow was too big for him, but he slanted it a little, drawing feathers trimly to his ear. Seven shafts he loosed, and then lost count; horse and foot were pressing together against the quadruple line of his comrades, and thrice he saw his arrow rebound from casque or gorget or elbow cop of an advancing chevalier.

Piers was standing near him, also with a longbow; cooks and grooms and camp followers were dodging about in the long grass, picking up hostile arrows and crossbow quarrels to thrust them at beckoning bowmen who formed the rearmost rank.

Juhel's mind began to blur; he saw things and failed to understand them until they were altered or lost. Once he knew Piers was singing—he even caught the shrill words, that twisted in his own head for half an hour thereafter:

> "Spikes on your spurs are seven,
>   Stay, love, stay!
> The Plough is wheeling up the heaven,
>   Hey, now, and away!"

Once he heard a voice say that the Inn of Harmony was burning; and he noticed a great smoke blowing northward from somewhere beyond and beneath the Saulte banner that waved on Boqueron's left. Once he heard Nino Chiostra laughing . . . but that was before the fourth attack, when the royalist wing gave on the extreme right, where men were stumbling in locked groups through thickets of holly and

brier and thorn at the edge of the dense forest. Scores of fully
armed riders were dismounted, plying lances and pikes with a
will; horses seemed disappearing strangely from between the
battle and the row of tents that fringed the first beech glades.
The Duke of Boqueron himself went thundering to the end
of his line, and presently restored it; Juhel saw him riding
back with visor lifted and a great battle ax held crosswise on
his saddlebow.

My lord himself walked Safadin up and down where the
defending front grew thinnest, leaning now and again from
his saddle to deal a wicked lance thrust between the bodies of
his hard-pressed men. Juhel found he was gripping a guisarme,
but did not remember having dropped the bow; now he
stumbled over sprawling bodies, now jumped to catch a
charger's bridle with the hook of his weapon, hanging back
hard while stronger arms than his beat from the saddle a
smiting, cursing Barberghe chevalier—the only rebel of them
all to pitch to earth right through the ranks of Ger.

"Yield you, De Medrincourt!" shouted the Squire of Ger,
who kneeled beside him to twitch up the battered visor and
bring a dagger point against the rim of the gorget. But the
fallen warrior was fighting mad, and his gauntleted fist
flailed up from the grass to clash on the other's shoulder plate;
the squire lurched, and his red excited face went white and
wicked beneath the bascinet rim. Juhel saw him shut his eyes
and blindly press the dagger home; and the seneschal of the
Tower of Ath kicked and lay still at the feet of its lawful
lord.

Juhel felt a gray sickness springing and spreading under
his ribs, but it passed and died at a new shouting; there
seemed a sudden access of daylight, although the clouds were
leaning low above the loop of Varne. Again the attacking
masses were falling back from before the shattered stockade; where Juhel had seen only steel and faces and bright
colour, were now the pine-clad bluffs beyond Pont-de-Foy,
darkling-clear a mile away above the welter of withdrawal.

Grunting men leaned on each other and wiped their sweaty faces; a few whom battle fever had sustained sank down with suddenly discovered injuries. The Count of Ger cried strongly out to summon his English war captain; and from the centre of the line John Doust came thrusting toward him, raising visor with one hand and using the great two-handed sword as staff in the other.

"Wounded, John?" called the count from his saddle; and the Englishman's little mouth twitched in his red good-natured face.

"Winded," he answered wheezily. "But by the harrowing of hell, my lord, this is the trimmest fray you have yet shown me."

"Scant credit to me, John," said Raoul of Ger above him, "but wait awhile, for I believe these two armies will destroy each other in the field."

For a moment they talked together, and then were interrupted by a horseman galloping upon them from the centre—a horseman who flung down his shield because it was riven in twain, and bared a heavy-featured brown face above a coat of checkered white and blue.

"How goes it, Enguerrand?" demanded the count; and Juhel saw that the newcomer was Piers's cousin, that Sieur du Véranger who had fought by my lord at Karmeriet and Alanol and Gramberge.

"Ding-dong," replied the portly vavasor, saluting the duke as he drew rein. "The castellan presses hard upon Camors and Ahun, but the fighting abbot is slain and the Inn of Harmony twice retaken; the constable has it now, and Conrad and he have brought up all reserves against the king. Saulte holds Queranay, but we can do no more. The King's Grace bids me say: *If the Count of Ger be alive, let him risk that folly he spoke of.* Am I understood?"

"Well enough!" grated Boqueron, eyeing the Volsberghe banner on the level ground below. "So be it, Ger; when strength and craft fail it is time for madness. Take your chosen men and adventure it; and God go with you—sparing an Eye for us, for we shall need it. Must you have your Captain Doust?"

"Ay, that I must," said the young count soberly. "Up on my spare charger, John, and summon those we prepared."

Along behind the line rode the big Englishman, calling out upon this man and that of the archers and men at arms of Ger. By twos and threes the latter left their comrades, striding back between the tents to where some sixty horses waited.

"A dozen are done for," grumbled John Doust. "I bade them keep the rear rank till we needed them; I doubt if even the words *I* know can reach them now in Purgatory."

Juhel and Piers stepped forward together; the count frowned and looked over their heads.

"Enguerrand!" pleaded the older boy, turning to his kinsman. "Ask my lord to take us with him!"

"In faith, Raoul," smiled the Sieur du Véranger, "my lord Duke here believes you good as dead; a dead count needs no pages any more."

"Off with you, Ger!" barked tall Boqueron. "Gaston is trying again. Lift your shield from the bridge, and I will come down on them with all my force. Farewell!"

"Come then, boys," rapped out the count. "Bring arrows, each of you, quickly, and follow us."

Truly, Gaston was trying again; but for Juhel the roar of battle thinned and died, for presently he was urging his mount through the gloomy forest in the wake of disappearing Safadin. "Spikes on your spurs are seven—stay, love, stay . . ." For the first time he noticed that a thin rain was falling; beech boughs glistened gray, and toadstools shone demurely amid the sodden mast. "The Plough is wheeling up the heaven— hay, now, and away!" Horse hoofs rasped in the rank grass of little tumbled glades; birds called and fled, and pine trunks showed on the higher slopes, processional against red earth or wet gray sky. All the air was laden with the tireless murmur of rain on leaves; that sense which noticed such things, awoke in Juhel, finding suddenly absurd this stiff and weary boy's body that rocked above and through them from butchery to butchery.

Somewhere ahead of all rode Master Nino Chiostra; for Nino, it seemed, knew of a secret ford whereby a wide detour would bring swift-moving men to Pont-de-Foy itself, full in the left rear of the rebel army.

Once, on that difficult ride, the gray curve of river below him bore to Juhel's ears the shredded tumult of the battle two miles or more away; but at the ford itself was only silence of wet summer afternoon until the calling and splashing began in the wake of Nino's charger. It was nearly an hour after leaving the tented hilltop that Raoul of Ger checked Safadin amid the pines on the low crest behind Pont-de-Foy.

Below lay other tents, revealing the camps of Barberghe and Montcarneau. Beyond them was the hamlet, and the high-arched bridge itself; and Juhel's pulse galloped as he saw the great fight unfolded from Angmer to the high woods where Boqueron's line still held.

"Now, Nino," said the count, "I and John will take twenty ahead and seize the bridge; do you trickle the others madly after, roaring all of you as though a thousand followed."

And like a volley of slung stones the first score of mounted men at arms plunged down the quarter mile of sloping ground upon Pont-de-Foy.

The villagers had mostly fled into the forest, but a huddle of camp followers broke yelling from the crazy street toward the rear of the battling array. Half a dozen Barberghe men-at-arms guarded tents and baggage, but they ran or were cut down, and when two farm wagons were dragged to form a barricade a third of the way across the bridge, the count swung his shield aloft on the head of an upthrust lance.

Dimly on the opposite hill, beneath the edge of the forest, the red and white of Boqueron's banner dipped in ready reply.

Juhel and Piers were among the first to break downhill as reënforcement. Side by side, and shrieking their loudest, they hurtled into the narrow street, leaping to earth and crowd-

ing their mounts into the hedged churchyard, where already
Safadin and a score of other destriers trampled uneasily to
and fro or cropped grass amid the little mounds.

The count and John Doust and four more stood upright in
the wagons; the rest were stretched or crouched or kneeling,
with weapons poised over shafts, between wheels, or beside
their comrades' legs across the width of the clumsy carts.
Half a dozen wielded bows, and for an age-long moment
they waited, hearing first the bellowing of their own slender
reserves, and then the swelling battle cry of down-charging
Boqueron.

Juhel slid beneath a wagon, and wriggled until he could
draw string sideways, with one horn of his weapon beyond
the thick spokes of a forewheel and the other almost touching the stones of the parapet. Sheltered above and in front,
he knew a moment's hard amusement; then he was only aware
of a darkening rush of horsemen against the barricade.

A medley of stamping hoofs that blotted out the meadow—
galloping legs stockinged with white, or richly black or brown
or gray between back-blown caparisons—lance points promising ugly· death, swords swinging out of sight—Barberghe
colours·everywhere, red and black and cloaking polished steel.

Crash! They were at it over Juhel's head before he had twice
let fly. Wood splintered to smashing horseshoes; shreds of the
wicker wagon side rained down upon the slippery stones,
a shard of yellow-painted shield dropped and bounced; a horse
screamed dreadfully and slithered against the parapet. Thinly
from a closed helm rang the curses of Barberghe; the Fox
himself had headed this rush, and the Fox himself was the
first to fall to the sweep of John Doust's estoc. Down clanged
the bulk of steel; blood welled beneath the riven gorget and
soaked the red shoulder of the short surcoat. The bow was
beaten from Juhel's grasp by the whirl of a pointed solleret;
the boy gasped and bunched himself backward and a man-at-
arms stooped behind him and thrust the haft of a great
pike beneath his empty hand.

"Make sure of him, lad!" boomed the man-at-arms. "Have at him while you may!"

But the groaning struggling Count of Barberghe was already pinned to the cobbles and whelmed and lost beneath two of his fallen followers; Juhel screamed with excited dismay and fumbled with the heavy weapon, fearing to strike at dying men, shamed by his fear and angered by his shame.

"Horses off the bridge, you dolts!" thundered a voice beyond the immediate tumult; but a fourth figure blocked Juhel's view—a figure with brown boy's hands that clutched at the great wagon wheel, and loosened grasp, and fell, while a steel cap clashed on the wet stones, and a face that grinned in agony slewed down as though to peer between the spokes.

It was Gavin, once page to the Viscount Robin—Gavin, leaping to rescue the Fox with the rash fury of seventeen years—and the end of all his boasting was a death wound in the breast and a fainting fall across the Fox's dead charger. With Gavin's wide glazed eyes a yard from his own knee, Juhel pointed the pike and gave his mind blankly to battle; chevrons and wolf's heads crowded together as the tall Count of Montcarneau led a savage rush to clear the bridge of this impudently lodged defence.

Abreast on the wagon above were now Raoul of Ger, John Doust, and Nino Chiostra; three such swords gave sufficient reason for no one to heed the boy crouching half hidden below them. The barricade was covered with swarming grappling men; Juhel never knew what part his own thrusts played in that last desperate issue. He only knew that before the end the bodies were piled so high that he could barely see in front of him; and by the war shouts from above, the three still kept their places in the midmost heart of the shambles that was Pont-de-Foy.

At length: *"By God we have done it!"* screeched Master Nino Chiostra; and suddenly all the living in front of Juhel seemed running, and all behind him cheering and shouting one to another.

"Boqueron breaks them—a Boqueron, ho-ho!"

"Gaston is thrashing his own pikemen—no, it is useless, they scatter in spite of him—look, look, my lord!"

"Hey, by the harrowing of hell, the whole wing melts like snow—ay, chevaliers and all—Saint George! Saint George!"

The voices rang and jarred and exulted; Juhel scrambled from under the wagon and tottered to his feet. Half dazed, he stared for a moment at the flats where panic spread—at the northward road alive with scurrying fugitives, at the Barberghe banner reeling amid the thickets, at the steel-gray sweep of river toward Angmer, where already scores of rebels were wading, swimming, drowning. Then he looked for Piers, and saw him, and with a wail lurched forward upon bended knees; for Piers lay staring skyward, with a long shaft driven through his smooth extended throat.

"Juhel, bring Safadin hither!" were the next words he understood. The count's mailed hand fell on his shoulder; the count's eyes narrowed with pain as he looked from one lad's still face to the other's that ran with tears.

"It is not yet done, boy," said the count. "Time for our sorrow later. Now go."

When Juhel brought up the great charger the wagons had already been tugged apart. Barberghe and Montcarneau lay straightened out in their gilded armour; the one had stifled where he fell, the other had died upright with the broken blade of John Doust's estoc fast in his riven helm. Gavin's body and many another were tumbled more hurriedly aside; there was trampling and laughing on Pont-de-Foy, and Raoul of Ger turned in his saddle and gestured to the Englishman.

"Your bridge, John," he said. "The king shall know we owe it to you. Stand fast for the present—Boqueron drives them northward, and I drive to the centre, so that none should trouble you here."

John Doust lifted a puzzled face that glistened with sweat.

"What is the bell?" he demanded, glancing oddly around him.

"What bell? I hear none."

"Nor I," added Nino Chiostra, wheeling his mount close by them. "In faith, John, you are dreaming. The bell chimes only in your head . . . belike the mace of Montcarneau awoke it before you finished him."

"Nay, nay . . . I know it . . . it rang as for a passing even now. It is the Minster bell."

"What minster, man?"

"The great Minster of York . . . hey, you are right, I dreamed it. God speed you both. I keep the bridge behind you. I must get me another sword. . . ."

Then count and comptroller were away with Juhel and thirty more crowding behind them; for in the mid-field, near the smoking ruins of the Inn of Harmony, the great fight rolled toward the river—a crazy welter of death whose result still seemed to hang in the balance.

"Ha! Robin Barberghe!" cried Raoul of Ger grimly; and Juhel looked aside to see the signs of a past eddy of strife— churned earth, splayed grasses, hacked willows, a score of dead around the torn chevron banner that once darkened a page's ride from Saint-Eloy-over-Hardonek. And in the midst a propped corpse, unhelmed, with dark head bowed as though in meditation.

"Titles to spare this night," commented Nino Chiostra; and Juhel felt a dull amazement at this deadly twining and cutting of so many threads of life.

But when they came to the centre they found the tumult slackened; on the middle mound of three, beneath his royal father's banner, that had been his own for a week, Conrad of Burias stood bareheaded and haggardly at bay. His charger he had scorned to use for flight; his power had flaked away on either hand, and beside him were now the constable and most of his other chief supporters who had not yet gone down. Two or three hundred were gathered with them—chevaliers and squires for the most part, who had chosen their game and would play it to a finish.

On three sides of them closed their foemen; the young king flung up his visor and showed a chalk-white face as he rode up to the ranked rebels.

"Bid these your men surrender, Conrad," he shrilled. "Six heads shall pay the score for all."

"What say you, lords and chevaliers?" demanded Conrad loftily of them around him.

A short and angry roar of refusal beat in Thorismund's face.

"Better die with Burias than live with Hastain!" shrieked the daft Count of Lestembourg; and Conrad smiled at his royal cousin and one-time friend.

"You hear?" he thundered. "Let loose your hounds, good kinsman; we take a relay of them where we go!"

Thorismund tightened rein and waved a savage command. A flung spear rebounded from his shoulder plate, and he snapped his visor down. Behind him the Saulte and Olencourt lances sank for the last time; and on the western mound Raoul of Ger set Safadin in motion.

"Hey, there is little Judas Ger!" yelled Conrad. "Come hither, Judas, and share the sport you planned!"

"I come," cried the young count deeply; and Juhel followed him in the trampling rush which made safe Thorismund's throne.

Half an hour later the sunset of Pont-de-Foy flared redly through the drizzle to show the six heads Thorismund had claimed, with ten more added as an afterthought, laid in a grisly row for swift conveyance to the principal cities of the realm; and Nino Chiostra looked from them to the group about the king's pavilion, and spoke in the ear of Raoul of Ger the only jest which Juhel heard that day.

"Now they are all at peace together, tenants *in capite* and tenants *sine capite*."

But the count caught his friend by the arm and pushed him forward to kneel before the weary sovereign, who struck with a hacked blade upon shoulder after plated shoulder of those who had well served him since the dawn.

"My liege, this is Nino da Chiostra, who guided us over the ford."

"So. It was well done. Rise, Chevalier Nino, and serve as you have served before. Raoul, good cousin, where is your English captain? Boqueron here has told us of the bridge you held, you two and he together."

"He is still posted there, guarding the bodies of Barberghe and Montcarneau. He slew them both beside our barricade."

"Send him to us when you can. You are well served, cousin —yet God may witness, no better served than we are. Only Gaston is fled, and only Camors and Ahun are taken. The rest—are here."

Juhel turned from the victor groups to scan the field below him. Already scores of campfires twinkled between the forest and the river; smoke circled and blew beneath the purple clouds that drifted together and whelmed the sun. The thin rain ceased, and out of the woods came damp scents of summer evening, contending with and cooling the sharp odours of camp and horse lines and stale carnage. Already monks from Angmer were dotted over the fields, helping the tired men-at-arms who sought the wounded among the slain.

"That was a strange dream," mused Juhel. "I must tell Piers about it."

Then he remembered, and groaned aloud; but again his grief was checked by action, for a horseman in a falcon coat came charging up the westward slope, and away behind him men were running as though upon Pont-de-Foy.

"Where is my lord?" shouted the messenger; and king and commanders and chevaliers turned behind Raoul of Ger.

"What is it?" demanded the count.

"My lord, I have sent what men I met—Joris of the Rock with near a hundred thieving rogues is broken out of the woods; they are knifing the hurt and stripping the slain and pressing Captain John Doust on the bridge—he bade me find you quickly—and I——"

The horseman stopped and leaned from his saddle, clutching

at the arrow which had him in the thigh. Down he crashed
before they could catch him; amid the running and the shouting Juhel saw the king's physician waddling over the wet
grass.

Then there was only the scramble of mounting—each man
on the charger first to hand—and the singing of air in Juhel's
ears, that thinned the tumult of that second headlong ride
toward the twilit hamlet by the river.

*   *   *

*Thousands of slain in the meadows . . . the royal standard
taken . . . Joris laughing amain at the end of a great battle.*

The heavy-lidded eyes were rimmed with red, the eagle face
was lined with a new savagery, the golden beard half gray now,
and no longer trimmed to a point; but Joris could still achieve
a shout of honest mirth as he sat in a high beech fork and saw
that rearward threat of threescore men plunge Conrad's whole
left wing into dismay and panic-stricken rout.

"By the chimes of hell it *is* ill work to cross the viper of
Ger!" he said.

Then his face chilled with anger; *she* had said that—the
woman whom he now called Thorismund's harlot, the creature
who had brought him within grasp of power and then thrust
him back upon his old wolfish life. No word of her had reached
him in the eight months newly past; but Thorismund took his
loves lightly, and Joris thought of Anne as maybe fallen to
some lesser paramour in Hautarroy. And Gaston's forced
march—possible only by grace of that year's dry spring, which
gave footing for men and beast in moorland ways at most
times impassable—had sent Joris southward only to find the
realm in arms between himself and his Rock.

"This for our entertainment," he said to his staring men;
and all day long they had gazed from the trees and thickets,
their view raking the line of fight from Pont-de-Foy to
Angmer. Ger and his troop must have circled their lair; and
Joris swore in surprise when he realized the use to which

they had put the ford he deemed his secret. He pondered rushing across behind them and adding a grimmer surprise to the day's chances; but Gaston was not the man to reward him with anything but a hempen noose. It was better to wait and watch what befell, with men unwearied in case of need.

So, when the end was apparent, when Ger rode off to the centre across the littered levels, Joris climbed down from his wet perch and threaded a way to the edge of the deep thickets. Brightly the last light was reflected in steel and gilded armour of the fallen; less than a score of yellow surcoats moved on Pont-de-Foy.

"Raoul of Ger I will not encounter," said Joris between set teeth, "but these his men make a mouthful too tempting to pass by. Madoc, take ten and have the ponies ready; when we have cleared the bridge, drive straight across it. We will empty those tents beyond—if my kinsman of Montcarneau be down, I am as good an heir as any. *Haro!*"

And he broke out into the open, with his followers at his heels.

"There is that damned English captain," came Gandulf's warning word; but Joris only laughed again, content with speed and odds and prospect of some small revenge.

The half of his men charged with him, the others spreading out to begin their grisly work among the helpless fallen. On the bridge the little group of yellow coats had stirred to rapid action; one man leaped on a horse and spurred obliquely across the line of attack before the outlaws were within fair bowshot. Nevertheless Joris himself sent an arrow true to its mark; the man at arms dropped the ax he carried, but held to his place and rocked away on the trail of his vanished lord.

"Now we must hasten," cried Joris. "Stand and let fly— forward—stand and let fly again—down bows and at them all together—this for the belfry at Gramberge!"

One of the wagons once more half blocked the bridge; John Doust stood forward with three more heavily armoured

companions; their plate of proof protected them and helped
to shield the others, of whom four wielded bows and the
rest pikes or guisarmes.

"This for your whole foul fame, you rat from the sewers
of hell," said the Englishman quietly; and a whirled blow of
his snatched-up sword split the buckler on the outlaw's lifted
arm and beat Joris flat on his back. Across their leader dived
and pressed the first stout rogues of the wolf pack; left and
right swung John Doust's weapon, slaying one and stunning another, who dropped like a log on the chieftain's knees,
while Gandulf's sloped shield took a pike thrust aimed at the
chieftain's head.

Joris heaved himself back and away, stumbling amid the
throng of assault; a second buckler was thrust to his hand,
and with three long forward strides he plunged into the fight
of his life.

A mace had beaten awry the Englishman's visor point; his
armour was dinted and riven in places, but he seemed to
have taken no hurt. Nevertheless he was tired, and his heavy
strokes were mistimed; this, and the quickness of Joris,
balanced the strength of plate, so that he dealt one blow
for every two he received. Also he raised no war shout against
the bark of Joris, but kept his breath for hewing and thrusting, and gave not an inch of ground.

In brief, for the second time that day John Doust was holding Pont-de-Foy; and beside him fought and fell and died
the men who survived the earlier onset—each slaying an outlaw or two before he dropped in the wagon or on the narrow
way.

"Hurry, hurry!" screamed Gandulf, cautious even in mid-
battle; and as John Doust split the second buckler and gashed
the shoulder of Joris beneath it, Gandulf shore the steel knee
cop from the Englishman's fore-bent leg. John Doust staggered and swore, and ignored recoiling Joris to whirl out
a terrible back-handed blow that split the face of Gandulf
and dropped him dead in his tracks.

Wounded Joris took his chance, and thrust, instead of striking, over the chopped shield rim; beneath the rent and flapping falcon a battered breastplate gave to his point. With four inches of steel in him, John Doust grunted and reeled, his harness bumping against the wagon, his shield drooping, his sword wavering up for a last flat ill-aimed smack that laid the outlaw's jawbone bare and spun him half round to the parapet.

"To hell yourself, you English hog!" he grated, wrenching his own blade back and smiting hard; but this time plate repelled the edge, and the yelling and tumbling of his men told Joris of flight and danger. He glanced round in the sudden twilight, and saw coloured coats converging toward the bridge—and behind them others, mounted, gaining swiftly upon them.

Last of all his band, Joris turned and fled the way he had come, heedless of wounds or of plunder, or of the fallen men of his own who squealed for help as he passed. And on the bridge John Doust slid to a sitting posture, back to the wagon wheel and feet among the dead; his empty sword hand wavered up to the flattened visor, but one of his three surviving men had to open it for him, while another hobbled down the bank to fetch water in a bascinet.

Out of the twilight drummed the last charge upon Pont-de-Foy. Juhel, being light in the saddle, had gained the van of that company; when he leaped to earth he ignored the horses, stumbling forward, plucking out of his wallet the pliers used with armour. But Raoul of Ger and Nino Chiostra were first of all on the bridge; brushing aside the men at arms, they knelt beside their friend.

"John," croaked the young count; and to Nino: "Quick, his breastplate. I will unhelm him."

"Juhel, here . . . take hold."

The little blue eyes of John Doust went twinkling from one to the other; he gave a curious short cough, and his great face was not now very red.

"Lung," he muttered quickly. "Nay, you can do no good. Praise to Saint George, I pinked the wolf and broke his ugly jowl . . . but a man cannot fight all day and all night too. If I had not smashed my estoc . . ."

Nino was slitting leather and linen; Juhel, turning aside to lay down the pierced breastplate, all but set it on the steel shoe of the young king. Thorismund stood at the feet of John Doust; behind or about him were great commanders—Saulte, Boqueron, the grim castellan—and among them stood forward the portly Bishop of Belsaunt.

"One moment, my lord Bishop," came the sharp royal command; and Thorismund once more dragged out his sword.

"We must keep our promise," he said. "We dub you Chevalier John. God lift you to your feet ere long, brave Englishman, and give us other such swords among our friends."

John Doust smiled at the king, and shook his head slightly. The Bishop of Belsaunt clanked to his knees beside the Count of Ger; *Paternoster* and *Ave Maria* boomed to the work of reddened fingers whose skill availed nothing.

John Doust smiled at the bishop, with a little nod of thanks; he had taken the Bread and Wine at dawn and seemed in no dismay. The armoured group around him burred the last *Amen;* then, falling silent, they heard his words to his own comrades.

"I knew it was the Minster bell. My lord, you will tell your valiant imp I would have taught him swordcraft fit for a paladin . . . great times we would have had . . . amber out of Muscovy. . . .

"*Trust in God and mount your archers.* Nay, Nino, it was to be. . . . I have mounted my last archer and now can only trust in God. Michael Archangel has His ear, and my own good Saint George, and by them have I sworn, and in them greatly confided.

"The—the men—they fought like the brave rogues they are. Which of them live?"

Neither the count nor Nino could speak; Juhel got the names out somehow, and the pale slit of a mouth moved again.

"Give each of them some gear of mine . . . it was a good fight. Let little Juhel have my dagger. Hang the hilt of my estoc in the hall at Marckmont."

John Doust's face was gray now; his voice that had gained a little in strength sank low again. For the last time his blue eyes went from the face of the Count of Ger to the face of the Chevalier da Chiostra; then they closed, and he spoke as though to himself, three several times.

"Nino, Herluin, good lads both."

For a moment he paused, and then, in a kind of bewilderment, entitled himself quietly in his own tongue.

"Sir John Doust."

Then he gave the ghost of a chuckle, and spoke from past to future with sudden tender reproof.

"Nay, mammy, all will be well."

The heavy head with its straw-coloured hair drooped childishly against the Tuscan's gorget. King and nobles crossed themselves, turning aside with a rattle of steel, averting their eyes from the face of the Chevalier Nino.

But Raoul of Ger stood upright and cried out in a choked and dreadful voice upon his royal kinsman.

"My liege, lend me—lend me——"

"Lend you what, Raoul?"

"Lend me the quarter of your army, with horses to mount each man of them, and by the living God I will track that hell dog down and send you his head at last. If we are swift, we can ring him round. I hoped I might see you crowned, but better a gap by the throne than Joris still at large. See, he is in this angle of the hills. Men racing north and east must partly enclose him. . . . Alanol and Belsaunt will contribute. . . ."

Thorismund pondered, and next to speak was the Castellan of Montenair.

"It is no bad plan, Your Grace. The hills will be full of broken and lawless men for months or years to come, unless you give word to purge them now. The company of Joris will itself grow to an army; we must root him out in the end. Ger shall have half my swords: my brother will command them."

"Gladly will I," said tall Rogier de Olencourt.

Thorismund nodded and looked again at Raoul of Ger.

"From any other man, for any other purpose, we should require more argument," he said. "But there is virtue in your imaginings; witness this bridge where now we stand. And Joris merits a peculiar attention. For six months we create you our Lieutenant in the North; choose men to help you, of rank beneath your own. Go now if you will; your commission shall follow this night. And this your Chevalier John shall rest by the old abbot in Saint Austreberte's of Belsaunt."

Around Raoul of Ger crowded the lesser noblemen; besides Rogier de Olencourt he chose for his chief lieutenants Serlo de Saulte, the duke's youngest brother, and Enguerrand du Véranger, his old comrade-in-arms. Within the half hour men who had hoped for sleep were riding north and east to bear the news of battle and rouse the moorland and forest folk for the hunting of Joris of the Rock.

XIII. THE BEATING OF THE HIGH HILLS

"AT LEAST I am partly quit of my debt to little Ger," thought Joris with satisfaction when the clamour of instant pursuit was shaken off behind him. "If the ford be henceforth useless, I will steal boats and swim the ponies across. I give their host a week to disperse; meanwhile there are the fugitives. Some will come in, and some be easy prey. But I would I had the pretty gear of kinsman Montcarneau —yet Gandulf alive were worth a score such suits to me."

By the light of his little campfire, far in the forest depth, he sat that night alone with Madoc, and with the silver-hilted dagger that once was Rufin's he made a new nick on the bone hilt of his long sword. The nicks were tokens of eight killings that had given Joris peculiar satisfaction, whether or no the weapon itself had achieved them; the first was for the fat sub-prior of Medrincourt, the second and third for a blacksmith and a chevalier who had crossed him in early days of outlawry, the fourth for Ursin, the fifth for Rufin himself, the sixth for Guy de Saulte, the seventh for Yaan the mock fiend, and the eighth for Captain John Doust.

"Six of them very stout swordsmen," Joris reflected with grim relish. "I might have had Gaston de Volsberghe too—and girl-faced Thorismund—and wildcat Ger himself, at Gramberge or in Hautarroy. But I am here, my lords, not finished yet. Wait until you are parted again, and you shall hear of me."

He stared into the leaping flames, recalling his runes and Ivo's vision, the double tangle of vague prophecy that had so long upborne him.

"Anne's fate I cannot fathom," he mused, almost without anger. "But for myself there is yet the boy—the son of Joris of the Rock. Whose lad could that be? There was Marie, and Jehane, and Jolette at Montcarneau—two of them pupped, but I cannot remember which. And at Medrincourt the innkeeper's wife—by the beard of Goliath of Gath, she was a fat rascal. And what was the wench named whose milk pail rolled in the quarry? Then there were two or three not so pleased—Tiphaine de Ath whom I saved from Gaston—but she and her token of unwisdom perished in the Jacquerie. Nay, I give it up, unless Anne—no, that were unlikely."

Joris rolled himself up in his cloak and presently fell asleep. Every triumph now was over all his enemies; Anne's desertion had blasted in him a last emotional check on his lust for power, and it seemed to him as though he injured Gaston, and even Red Anne herself, when he dealt a death wound to the English captain upon Pont-de-Foy.

*   *   *

For three days the outlaw company lay hidden in the forest between Alanol and Olencourt. Their numbers were augmented by a score and more of lost and half-starved men who wore, or had already cast aside, the device of one or other of the fallen rebel lords. From such recruits Joris learned of the swift-riding conquerors who swept the main roads toward Hastain and Belsaunt; and not until he ventured a cattle raid did he begin to realize his own danger.

Then, bandaged and cursing, he fled from a hamlet whose defenceless-looking huts had disgorged Saulte archers; and on that same night a neighbouring hilltop suddenly sprouted flame. Joris, already miles away, frowned and then chuckled at that untoward apparition.

"That is the first time I have been honoured with a beacon," he said.

Also it was the first time in the year that his men had gone hungry for twenty-four hours at a stretch; and in the early morning they trotted their ponies out of the thickets toward a larger village on the road between Alanol and Ververon.

The village lay in a gorge; a horn brayed on the opposite slope, and scores of armed and mounted men broke shouting into view, taking line to await any attack. Joris swore and counted them; Madoc exclaimed and pointed to a height toward Alanol, where a puff of smoke appeared and grew and slanted gently away to the eastward.

"Now, now," growled Joris, "I will have good measure for this interference. Whose are the colours yonder?"

"Blue and white check are Le Véranger," affirmed one of his men, "but the tawny are townsmen of Alanol. On their way home, belike."

"Maybe. But that damned Sieur du Véranger is far enough from his home, unless he be sent to hold the castle of Camps-capel. And they were not in the village; they were waiting on the hillside. Well, they may wait, and we will go hunting."

"They do not pursue," commented Madoc. "But see, there goes another cursed little balefire, westward."

"They think us stragglers," suggested another beside Joris.

"Back into the forest," was the leader's curt bidding, and back they went, to chase red deer and boar and shoot at birds and rabbits.

That evening Joris sent out spies to examine the south-ward and eastward roads; in two more days one party returned with news that the ford and all the angle of the forest above Pont-de-Foy were held by groups of soldiery, while the Belsaunt way was constantly patrolled by the green coats of Olencourt. As for the other party, no more was seen of it; and Madoc himself went eastward alone, leaving Joris amused yet thoughtful in the densely wooded highlands south of Alanol.

"I could do with rain," thought Joris; but the weather was fine and frequently cloudless, and Madoc came again with a rueful grin on his hatchet face, and a tale of proclamation cried at every market cross in the fringes of moor and forest.

"First," he announced to his leader, "free pardon to all

rebels beneath chevalier's rank who come in within two weeks. Then, a thousand gold nobles for *your* head, and the same free and unconditional pardon for any outlaw or rebel—or any party of either kind—which brings that head to chevalier or nobleman. Ger is Lieutenant of the North, commissioned to receive submission of all rebels and to break up the company or companies of outlaws in the hills of Honoy and Nordanay."

"You heard this where?" demanded Joris.

"At Montenair."

Joris looked narrowly at his lieutenant, and his eyes twinkled.

"You are slow to seize your advantage," he gibed. "What is amiss with a thousand gold pieces, and pardon to put in your pocket?"

Madoc's hatchet face grew red beneath grime and sweat and sunburn; Madoc's quick brown eyes were veiled, and Madoc's hand went out to the horn of clear brook water beside him.

"But if you are slow," went on Joris, "some others may not be. How many men has Ger to track us?"

"It is said, ten thousand."

"Chimes of hell! You remember lad Ivo, in the cave beneath the Rock?"

"Ay."

" 'Ten thousand men shall follow Joris' . . . as fugitive, it seems. Well, little pick-lock Ivo did not promise they should catch me. Now, Madoc. South of Angmer, near the road from Hautarroy, I buried once a little coffer of gold—good monastery gold—Saint-Eloy's-over-Hardonek, if truth were known. But until you and I come reasonably near that coffer, it were perhaps wise to keep about us what swords we can. Then, with such spoil to claim and share, we two can slip through any net and swim Varne under cover of night. Once across, we may settle what comes next. The Rock awaits us if need be—hey?"

Madoc nodded, but sat silent, staring away between the oaks of the Forest of Honoy.

"You think the band is doomed in any case?" he ventured at length.

"As a band, yes; I am sure of it. Only dissension among the lords has saved it thus far. Our chance as a free company was lost when Thorismund escaped us. A hundred thousand men might never find us, but they can find and drive the game, and guard all cattle and corn within our reach. And these who are now assembled against us are hunting, so to speak, for love; each man of the leaders has a private grudge, unless it be that Olencourt—and he is of a family damnably addicted to law and order. And since I once caused to be kicked the behind that now warms the throne, I think it time for private abjuration of the realm."

"Eh, Joris," said Madoc, "I could not be so merry in your shoes."

"Nor I so glum as you with fortune at my dagger's point."

But even as Madoc laughed again there came, in hot haste on a pony, one of the scouts whom Joris now threw out on all sides of his camps. Olencourt men were five miles distant, driving straight through the forest as though from Montenair to Alanol.

"Two hundred at the least," the fellow affirmed, "and with them many great dogs."

"And the green of their coats so bright," jeered Joris, "that even now its reflection abides on your countenance. What, man, have we no arrows? Be sure, if other meat fail, hound's flesh is none too sorry fare."

Then he gave orders to mount and ride, and in a quarter of an hour was jogging southward toward Belsaunt at the head of his hundred and ten men.

Once, as he rode, Joris handled his sword hilt, and smiled to feel the eight nicks in the smooth surface of bone.

"A pound or two of steel is worth a ton of prophecy," he mused. "Yet I would hear more of my son who is to be in the hills. What thinks he of himself, that son of Joris of the Rock?"

*   *   *

Juhel, sitting at that moment in the keep of the great hold of Ger, thought of himself again as accursed and damned. The lovely Lady Dionysia de Saint-Aunay had bidden him play chess with her, and valiantly he set his mind to the ivory warriors sharply white and red upon cream and crimson squares of the old ivory board; but more sharply to his senses shone the grave blue eyes, the fluffy golden hair, the pearly throat and dimpled rosy cheeks and fingers of the Lady Dionysia. The dark remembered impulse stirred in the boy's blood; it seemed that neither battle, nor fatigue, nor the death of dear companions, nor yet instinctive gentleness and proud habits of duty, could still its faint appalling voice that bade him violate and slay.

No matter that the prompting was grotesque, that Juhel formed a willing link of the armed might of Ger that would have held the king himself from offering one harsh word to little Dionysia; he felt it there—the poisonous ferment of a wrong unknown to him—and sank into a dream of self-loathing.

"Your move, Juhel."

"My—my lady, I beg you will pardon me!" he muttered, blushing for his discourtesy.

Dionysia smiled, but her smile was wan.

"I thought you were not pondering a check," she said. "Yet you would growl if I should say—lie down on the window seat and go to sleep."

Juhel looked at her with a sombre gratitude, and slowly moved a white pawn. Nino Chiostra was closeted with the countess, having brought letters from her lord, and the young pages of Ger were shy of this silent page of Marckmont, so that Juhel had sat alone among the seniors of the household until Dionysia found him.

"At times like these," went on the girl, almost as though she spoke to herself, "women who live on flattery find mighty thin fare. Men look through them as though they were ghosts. Maybe they *are* ghosts—the misty tallies of a man's pride in his own nobility. Maybe men have no true life but in warfare."

Juhel summoned no pretty speeches. He knew she gibed at herself a little, and counted him as a man; but also he saw that her real thought was of Chevalier Nino.

"No true life but in warfare?" he repeated, watching the dainty fingers nip away one of his bishops. "God forbid that, Lady Dionysia."

He castled behind his screen of pawns, and glanced up from the red attacking queen to make a little sound of shocked distress; for down the pink cheeks of the heiress of Saint-Aunay stole two enormous tears.

"Oh, Juhel," came her shaken whisper, as impatiently she brushed them away, "Oh, Juhel—Nino and his big Captain John—you and your dark clever Piers—such a mighty victory won, and all the king's foes slain or scattered, and you with nothing but pain in your faces and in your hearts."

"Not only pain," murmured the boy. "We will have the head off that ravening wolf before my lord has done."

"Small joy will be yours of that revenge," said Dionysia flatly. "Ay, if your own sword achieved it. What can women do that men should find in them at last the spirit they seek in comrades of war?"

He was fifteen, and she a year older, but they looked at each other with fair if uneven understanding of the violent life of their day.

"I do not know," mumbled Juhel, hanging his head; for he knew that he himself would never seek from a woman what he had sought and found in Folquin de Forne and Piers du Véranger and the Count Raoul of Ger.

"But whatsoever it is, my lady there has done it," he added, boldly grinding heel into the corpse of a slain jealousy.

Dionysia nodded, and eyed the door of the adjoining room.

"Therefore it may be done by others," Juhel ventured just above his breath.

A rose flush swept the girl's forehead, and Juhel was aware that grief had aroused what mirth left slumbering.

Later, when it was time to leave, he saw through a half-open door the curly head of the Chevalier Nino bowed on the silken lap of the Lady Dionysia. It was plain the pair were lovers declared, and utterly miserable; beyond them the dark girl countess Reine had turned away to a window, scorning to fashion comforting words that had no hope behind them.

Nino had lost his best friend, and might not aspire to the maid of his choice; that was how true men were often rewarded. Whereas a villain such as Joris ran wild for twenty years. Piers, with all his delicate chivalry, lay buried by Pont-de-Foy; Juhel was spared to glance evilly sideways at women who honoured and trusted him. What had the Sieur God in mind when He made an eye to gladden at tender beauty, and then soured all its gladness with inward adulteries?

Perhaps it needed some terrible effort to appease this God, who seemed to demand that every man should either crucify Christ anew, or be somehow crucified with Him.

How would it be, thought Juhel, to pray each night and morning for a thing quite apart from himself? Say, for comfort of all whom Joris of the Rock had wronged, be they dead or alive. How would it be. . . .

*   *   *

At that moment Joris was losing many men, but not in the way he intended. Orderly beating of forest fastnesses he was more or less prepared for, but the straight march of compact forces took him by surprise. Destriers and nags made slow going compared with the hill ponies, but once he was face to face with Olencourt, the latter's arrows flew fast as his own. Avoiding one plodding troop, he stumbled across another; for ten minutes a heady fight raged in a sun-flecked beech glade.

Three or four greencoats paid no heed to anything but their war horns, spurring this way and that to wake a summoning clamour. Whether they were heard or not, that hint of near assistance broke the outlaws; and behind the fleeting ponies were launched a dozen hounds of chase, abler to pull down men than stags, and willing to pull down anything that breathed.

By twilight Joris and seventy men had reached the edge of the true forest between Alanol and Cape Conan. Behind them the dozen hounds were slain, but still the distant horns resounded; before them humped and rolled the heather, rising in endless crests and ranges to the great central ridge, that lay in two provinces and linked the mountain Dondunor with the mountain Dondonoy.

Pine woods and gorse and bracken awaited the coming of night. Joris and his following ate oat cakes made with the flour that each man carried in a sack on his saddlebow. Joris found that the wound in his shoulder had broken with new bleeding, and Madoc bound it up anew when they slunk to moisten their oatmeal beside the Conan Beck. Nothing stirred in the silent hills; red-brown dusked into sable and the sky filled with stars; Joris lay breathing evenly, awake but unperturbed, when he heard the movements and muttering which told that some of his men were deserting him.

"Let them rat," he whispered, when Madoc dug him in the ribs. "The fewer we are, the more easily we go, and the risk of treachery grows less."

In the morning his band numbered fifty-three, and once a faint clamour of horns to southward hinted misfortune for those who had bolted. Thousands of men in scores of companies might plunge about for a year and never find outlaws who kept their heads; hounds might be baffled or slain, if you knew the lie of the bogs that threaded the hills, but Joris thought of the proclamation and of the little desperate knots and groups of battle fugitives who would not hear of it until too late. Scattered behind him in the woods, they were a peril in themselves; winter, and wolves of the four legged kind, would finally clear them away. Joris lay from sun-up till noon, watching for movement that did not come, and then decided to leave the forest and take to open moor.

"No soldierly concerted plan would hurtle columns of men through the glades and leave this glen unpicketed," he thought. "Or do they think the place too near to Alanol for me to venture in it? Maybe each leader uses his own device. And that, too, may be awkward if I pass from one to another of their allotted districts. But this at least I know—the bulk of them are southward from here, and deer and grouse and pheasant abound in the empty hills ahead. If need be, I dodge until autumn, then break back toward Varne, and . . . farewell all old creditors in Honoy and Nordanay."

Leisurely, in the afternoon, he led his men across the rough hill road, across the bracken-filled ravine, and into the wine-red fastnesses where stood the broken march towers of Lorin de Campscapel. Alanol townsmen had battered them down lest Joris and his kind make use of them, but old precaution was observed, since watchers might lurk in the ruins. Joris, riding parallel with the rest, but on a higher slope, turned for a last glance at the Alanol way, and saw a horseman in a yellow surcoat trotting deliberately toward Capel Conan.

"Raoul of Ger is a fool after all," said Joris between his teeth. "Who but a fool would bid his men wear surcoats of that colour in clear summer weather—or indeed in any weather, on such an errand as theirs?"

Hard on his scorn came a discomfort; what if he had been seen, and in his turn were meant to see that twinkle of buttercup hue against the green of the pines? But while the outlaw observed him the rider never turned his head to glance northward into the hills; it seemed pure chance that he should cross the track of Joris less than half a mile in his rear. With pine boughs Madoc and another had effaced the crowded hoof marks from the dusty track; and the distant horseman was so unhurried it seemed an outlaw's shame not to send a man or two back to stalk and shoot him.

But as Joris watched, a second horseman, similarly coated, broke from toward Capel Conan and galloped to meet the first. The yellow specks made one for a long moment, then parted— each riding now his hardest; and Joris felt the breeze from the south play coolly on his scarred face, while over the green pine masses beyond the travelling riders came the first shouldering shapes of a mass of cloud.

"Rain before morning," said Joris, sniffing the air with relish; and he steered a craftily chosen course into the trackless central wastes, aiming for certain high and hidden grassland where ponies would find food and water.

The Conan Beck must be crossed again where it ran from the east as though to burrow into Dondonoy; and under a slowly clouding sky Joris rode into the shadow of the mountain. Southward for a couple of hours the wider views were hidden, but when he gained a low spur of the great massif, and turned to look back toward Alanol, he cursed at length and with precision.

In a rough line from east to west, six heathery hilltops bore dainty plumes of northward-driven smoke under gray sky.

For the first time since his early days of outlawry, so many years before, Joris knew a self-distrust that was not immediately overborne by habits of decision. Then he steadied himself with the thought of pursuers so scattered that they had not dared to attack him at the edge of the Forest of Honoy; and he turned his back upon Dondonoy and spent the remaining hours of daylight in driving northeastward toward the Forest of Nordanay.

Dusk found him out of sight of any beacon flame, with thin rain beating up on a wind veering to southeast. His men were sullen and jumpy, and to light a fire was forbidden; but Joris called them about him and raised a jovial voice.

"Mistake not chance for craft," he commanded. "Twice they have blundered upon us, but whom do you think they seek? Gaston de Volsberghe and others like him, although they may be willing enough to settle our score as well. Now, I mean to round Dondunor and work back toward Ververon across the naked moors. If any more wish to leave me, let them now go—on foot, for these ponies are *mine*."

No one stirred or spoke until Joris reached for his meal bag. Later the drizzle abated, and the wind shifted again; by midnight it blew from the northeast, rustling loud in the heather.

"Was I a fool at Pont-de-Foy?" Joris wondered sleepily. "No, this chase will tire the pursuers before it tires me. I have been down before, I shall be up again."

He cuddled his long sword under his cloak, and smiled into the wind-filled dark; as well (he thought) question the wind's will as that of this fate that stalked the fells—this man for whom the world was made.

Again the dawn was fine and clear; the wind sang chilly over the ridges and gave the foraging outlaws trouble in stalking a herd of red deer. But when they had slain seven and were feasting beside a tarn one man cried out and pointed eastward; over a sheltering brow came running the scout posted in that direction—and behind him, as though on his trail, were plunging a score more of the deer, the antlers of five stags leading and the females streaming behind.

"Who are they?" demanded Joris, getting to his feet.

"There is no one I can see!" spluttered the man. "But the heather is fired for miles, and the fire spreading this way."

Joris caught up a hunk of broiled venison, and, stuffing himself as he strode, mounted the slope to stand at the top and stare at his enemies' work. The northeast hills were clouded with no ordinary cloud; weeks of drouth were not to be remedied by one evening's drizzling rain. The white smoke shapes curled and checked and crept forward, sometimes stabbed with an unlikely looking tongue or two of orange flame. Thinly along the striving wind came the first pleasant odours of burning; and as Joris watched, the moors began to yield their frightened creatures. Pewits shrilled and hurtled zigzagging westward; grouse raised a panicky shouting chatter as they broke overhead or burst from nearer cover; pheasant and wild duck joined in accidental formation; a raven croaked as though in distaste of such mixed company; and high in the blue sailed hawks and a buzzard, observant of the rout.

Joris, no less observant, but seeking different knowledge, chewed calmly at his venison and saw that there was time to finish one meal and provide for several more. With bulging cheeks his men strung bows and slaughtered as they pleased; and every arrow used came back to its owner's quiver.

"Behold, the beaters are beaten," he jested half an hour later, when all were mounted and away with plump game at their saddlebows. But actually he was disturbed; the heather fire was a gesture both savage and methodical, and no bold words to his men could much longer reassure them.

Coolly he pondered taking Madoc and deserting the rest that night; for Joris carried logic of the sword to its honest and unheroic conclusion, believing that men banded together only when chances of shared gain outbalanced the hope of solitary plunder. Hence his word of the coffer to Madoc; Joris could barely fathom the feeling which brought the little hatchet-faced ruffian back with his simple news of the proclamation. Red Anne had commanded his own loyalty, but that was as it were a gamble of the flesh; her comradeship he valued, yet felt it thrown into her side of their gallant bargain.

But at last he had roused two warlike provinces to question the value he set upon himself; he who had lived by dissension forgot the danger of challenging unity. And in the late afternoon of that day, with a dozen miles of moorland smoking far behind him, he led his followers up the flank of the great ridge that linked the two mountains—to see, at the head of his chosen gully, a dozen men in yellow coats who kindled yet another fire and impassively watched the outlaws below them.

Shadows were gray on the eastward grit and blue on the westward limestone. The men-at-arms moved clustering round a boulder, tugging and straining and slipping, with a rapid twinkle of steel. Joris swung his pony about and crashed off through deep heather; down the gully snored the boulder, tearing heather out of the peat, snapping hawthorns amid the rocks, scoring a lane in the dense bracken before it came to a stop. Outlaws yelled and reined aside, a few escaping by yards only; then they were out of the gully and fleeing behind the fleeing Joris along the difficult slope.

The leader still could smile at himself for naming their enemies cowards; but one bully among his men was already losing nerve and crying out nonsense. Swift and adroit to rape or slay, he proclaimed that this rolling of rocks was unfair, and upbraided Joris for guiding them where such hellish practice was possible.

Yet in the last dusk, when the ponies began to fail, and white coats sallied from a pine wood to bar their stumbling advance, this same bully retrieved his courage in face of the weapons he knew. Joris saw him ringed around and fighting upon his knees; it was Joris himself who failed that time, for he had spared his own beast and now was well rewarded. His charge carried him through the line of mingled horse and foot; one man he struck down, and two or three more he wounded. Another cried out his name, and Joris turned face to the nearest upward slope and flogged his mount with the flat of his sword, leaving the wreck of his company to fight it out in the heather. Ahead was open country; behind him should be Madoc, but Madoc was not there. No one at all was there. Strange how it had happened! After eighteen years, to be alone again.

Something plucked at his attention—something he knew but did not wish to acknowledge—Madoc's voice that squealed a claim that he, Madoc, was Joris of the Rock.

"Daft comrade," said Joris kindly. "Well, I am through them and safe for a time—which is what he wanted. So Ivo saved Red Anne. It is strange, this itch for sacrifice. Now, where to sleep at the end of this tiresome day?"

That question was more or less answered by the pony between his thighs; for the creature suddenly grunted and staggered and fell dead amid bents and field rush.

Joris cursed its awkward manner, and fumbled for cloak and meal and ducks. Then he trudged back and forth awhile and finally found a gorse-screened hollow; and there he watched the distant ribbons of fire, and presently slept as soundly as Dondunor itself.

It was strange to wake in the morning with none to do his bidding any more, and stranger to see the raven that flapped up from the dead pony to see if fresher fare were ready. Joris picked up his bow and strung it, sending a shaft most sweetly through the ominous creature's gizzard. A helm cloud banked on Dondunor, but the rest of the heaven seemed clear; Joris sampled raw duck, and drank, and washed his face in a pool; and since he was suddenly lonely he addressed a remark to the mountain.

"Hey, Tooth of the North," he said, "I will live awhile in your caves. You at least will not betray me to the ax of Ger."

As though the monstrous crags had heard, the flat under side of the cloud rippled, and drove downhill long shreds and streamers that linked and pressed toward him.

"Thanks, my black-browed friend!" cried Joris—and turned, and stiffened where he sat, for far beneath him were little groups of white or yellow coats, that thinned into long single lines and crept across hill and hollow and along the edge and foot of precipitous crags.

"They are more deadly seen like this than at the point of one's own sword," he told himself. "But certainly they mean to clear the country. I wonder, do they think the Rock is north of Varne?"

He was momentarily sick for a sight of the wind-bitten limestone crag, for the drift and blur of his camp smoke in the depths of the winding ravine; but he checked the thought grimly.

"Nay, that is past now, and only Anne and I had ever

the fulness of it. Well, it is time to see the other side of the mountain."

Moving with caution and skill, he neared his old haunts at noon; and as he lay in the heather clumps five hundred yards above the highest cave, he saw horses tethered amid the hawthorns and a slim dark-haired young man in half armour who knelt with a bowl in one hand and seemed to be cleansing his teeth.

"Oh, dainty chevalier," said Joris, "I would gladly beat them down your gullet. If only you were alone I should try. But having arrived thus far, I mean to go on. As for *you,* old Tooth of the North, you are too big to knock down any-one's throat but God's. Now I wonder—nay, I have mocked at God in my prosperity, and will not whine to Him in danger. Two or three days will see me out of this."

*   *   *

But two or three weeks passed, or perhaps more—Joris did not know how many. Incidents ran together, gleamed sharply and faded again, when he tried to assemble them in any kind of order. From the time when he slew a boarhound by a tarn to the time when the little man in brown came on him in the birch wood he had lived in constant peril. There had been many welcome darknesses, but one long darkness was a faint, for he had slipped as he climbed down a crag and come to sprawling in dense alders that had broken his twenty-foot fall and saved his life. Again there had been fire—this time close to him, with smoke that choked and stung. Once he had crawled across ash and blackened roots and soil still hot from the burning; then he had hidden for hours in one place, with leisure to examine the sable and gray and silver wreck that had been a clump of heather. But its roots, he noticed, were of healthy wood, cream and orange up to the peaty surface; in a year or two the plant would sprout as though there were no Joris and no Count of Ger to send ten thousand swords in quest of him across the desolate hills.

Then there was dreadful baying of dogs, and a shivering hour in a stream; once the outlaw crouched beneath an overhang of clay and hawthorn roots while a mastiff snuffled and sneezed a yard above him. And there were chilled or sweating moments in a land of thin orchards and little limestone farmsteads—farmsteads with roofed towers and loopholed gateways, with curs rattling uneasy chains and poultry rousing a comfortable clack and chuckle that searched the belly of a famished hunted man.

Then the birches, silver and gray beneath their whispering green, and the mossed roots before your nose when you tried to rise and could not. And last of all the little man in brown woollen tunic and hose peering down with a face somehow familiar; but it was too much trouble to remember.

"Jesu!" the little man growled. "Joris, do you not know me? I am Flar, the smith from Alanol, whom once you saved in the snow. Listen! Lie here till dusk and I will come to tend you. There is a loft where you shall hide—what? A thousand gold . . . be damned to that! I will fetch wine and a snack of cold porridge as soon as I am able. And I will bring my dog that he shall know you. I am the blacksmith, now, in the village of Gomblay yonder. Be sure by midnight you shall lie in safety."

Safety! It smelled of tar and straw and rotting wood, the safety provided by Flar at the edge of the village called Gomblay. The loft had a shuttered window, but that Joris kept closed; knotholes in its wood, cracks in the hard mud walls, and the "owl's postern" beneath the thatch, gave ragged and partial light upon Flar's corn sacks and a few old broken barrels and boxes. Below was Flar's cowshed, empty now; the floor of the loft had a great trap door for entry, but Flar kept the ladder in his forge. Also, immediately above the cowshed door was a smaller uncovered opening, through which Joris could peer down on anyone standing in the doorway; but this aperture he generally shrouded with sacking left over from his rough bed.

And there he lived for nearly a month, while his face and shoulder healed and his strength came slowly back to him. Quickly he learned which floor boards creaked, which spyhole gave completest observation in any direction, and which way quicklime must be scattered to give some pause to the rats. By the end of his first week he knew the village of Gomblay—knew when the cattle were watered, when the miller's wife beat clothes on the bank of the brawling stream, when the bailiff and the old priest would meet near the packhorse bridge, and when the sturdy hayward would slouch past with his long bow and short sword. And as party after party of men at arms and archers passed this way and that, or paused for clanging ministration of the smithy, Joris came to accept Flar's action as nothing very remarkable.

At dawn, and sometimes after vespers as well, the smith would slip from the door of the forge and unlock that of the cowshed adjoining it. Then the foot of the ladder would rasp on the cobbles, and its head bump violently beneath the trap. Joris would raise the heavy door, and the two would whisper together, passing up and down the evidences of that close concealment. Flar would tell of the ceaseless search which still went on in the uplands—of three men taken here, and four men taken there, some being hung and some sent to the king's galleys.

"The hills are black with the burning," said Flar. "The searchers are very weary now, but their leaders give them no rest. Yesterday—you saw?—I shod the horse of the Sieur du Véranger."

"I saw him, the fat ox," growled Joris between his teeth. "What was that outcry later by the Church?"

"Ah, that is new vagabond law. There are three here who have sometime seen you, or say they have sometime seen you, besides myself, who say I have not. And Dodart the hayward and the bailiff's two constables must detain each wanderer on this road until one of these three has taken oath the fellow is not *you*. Yesterday's catch was a swart Jew who was flogged for bidding the bailiff admire his golden hair."

"They spare no pains," breathed Joris; and Flar nodded and left him alone in the gloom and silence of the loft.

"If I were in Flar's place," mused Joris, "I would have that thousand nobles. Yet what would the poor oaf do with it? He is only good for the work he has. But I—eh, wait for me snugly, you little chest of Saint Eloy's gold near the road to Hautarroy!"

XIV. THE SON OF JORIS OF THE ROCK

H ARVEST time at Gomblay. The double daily procession
to the cornfields—the men with scythe and sickle soon
after dawn, the women and children a few hours later. Laughter and shouting, dying down to expectant silence; then the
clang of the gleaning bell, and slow hours of peace in the
empty village, until the loft was riddled with low sunlight
and a second clang stayed what the first had begun. After
that, the returning processions of tired folk, whose hearts
were not so sluggish but that they would have missed a beat
to know what cold blue eye observed them from the blacksmith's loft.

An afternoon drowsier than any, when Joris sprawled on
his sacking, watching the ducks manœuvring in the pond
beneath the windmill, while he traced each sound he heard to
its indubitable cause. Rats stirred, as ever, in thatch above
and manger below him; gusts of cooing rose and subsided
from the priest's pigeon cote, and now and again strong
pinions whined and fluttered past the owl's postern. The
forge was fallen silent, for Flar had gone to the gleaning
and taken with him his deaf assistant; and no creak from the
mill came down the windless air. A cur trotted snarling up to a
recumbent cat, adventured too close, and fled yowling toward
the distant fields, whence came the faintly waxing, faintly
waning murmur of an active throng. Once a barefoot child
padded up the street, bearing an empty jug to the stream; and
young Dodart, the hayward, clumped solemnly from hiding,
combing with brick-red fingers his dusty mop of hair.

By the door of Flar's cowshed Dodart paused; there was
a *montoir* there for use of those who patronized the forge and

were too old or fat to climb unaided to saddle. Joris heard
Dodart seat himself and sigh and spit with the resignation of
one whose night's work lay before him; and presently the summer hush was lightly jarred by an approaching rhythm of
clog and crutches.

Joris twitched the canvas from the hole above the cowshed
door, and lay with his ragged beard cuppèd in his hands, gazing down at the worn threshold stone and the sun-drenched
cobbles beyond it; and Dodart raised a genial hail of welcome
to the one-legged newcomer.

"Ho, Gleeman Ingolard, are you here in time for our
harvest home?"

"That am I," came the silvery piping answer, "since none
on my way could be found to swear that I am Joris of the
Rock."

"Bah, that folly! They will never catch the knave alive."

"True, Dodart—not though they shear and comb the
heather as if the fells were sheep's fells. But why are you
not in the fields to-day?"

"I am hayward now, bending my bow by night instead of
my back by day. But I take a turn at the threshing when it
comes. Now sit you down awhile; it needs two hours until
gleaning time is over."

"Gladly. Nay, the *montoir* is too high for me."

Ingolard swung into the outlaw's sight, turning in the doorway below and shifting grip on his crutches to slide deftly into
a sitting posture, with back against the doorpost, stump
sticking straight ahead, and thin white curls the brighter for
the faded scarlet hood and multiplicity of patched and tattered
tunics beneath it.

"Are you from Rambard?" asked Dodart.

"Ay," said the silvery voice. "A league on such a day is
worth three in a frost. Phew! It is good to be still."

"How have you fared of late?"

"Times are hard—as Adam was wont to say, and as that
man will be saying whose voice is quenched by the Doom

Trumpet. There are still those who lend an ear to tales of love
and war. Nor do I grudge a yawn in the midst if they part
with a coin at the end. But war in these parts is a stale delight,
and love is more easily come by now than in the winter evenings."

"Brr! Keep your winter evenings!"

"I hope to, Dodart, for another year or two. Ay, times
are hard—although I did well enough at Hastain Midsummer
Fair."

Hastain Midsummer Fair! Joris counted the years since
Ingolard sold him runes by the limestone market cross and
made them eighteen.

"I was there once," said Dodart. "I watched the archery
all day. Good work, by the Mass!"

"Ay. Time was when *I* fancied my shooting. And even now
contentment pricks my very bones to see the quiver of a cloth-
yard shaft in the bull's eye."

"Ingolard, where lies your other leg?"

"Three leagues across the frontier, beyond Volsberghe."

"Lost in battle?"

"Ay, if you call it battle. Volsberghe—the late constable, I
mean—raided the Gothmark forty years gone by. I was a
foolish clerk with a mind for war. On our way back the saucy
Gothmarkers took heart; it seemed they did not like our just
and gentle raid. It was midsummer, hotter than to-day; our
wagons laboured in dry water courses, and a mule was struck
by an arrow, and screamed so that I yet can hear it, and over-
turned a wagon laden with wine. My leg was under the
wheel when it came to rest. Monks hauled me out as I lay in a
swoon. Their infirmarian had my crushed bones off me before
I woke therefrom. He was greatly addicted to surgery, and
bartered a cask of the recaptured wine for my poor carcass;
else I had died with the rest who fell by the way. Very seldom
do I tell *that* tale, and never for gain. Most men and many
women had rather you were butchered than befriended by the
enemy."

The gleeman's voice, still musical, had sunk a tone or two, as though bells of silver had become bells of bronze. Joris listened, half lulled and half contemptuous; no doubt this crippled manikin must have his hours of candour like any other.

"What is your farthest journey nowadays?" asked Dodart after a pause.

"Hastain to Dunsberghe and back. Sometimes to the coast, and very seldom to Belsaunt; for either way is very hilly, and I love not great hills, neither the going in them, nor their shape and shadow."

"Why, man, what ails the shape and shadow of a hill?"

"The memory of that dreadful day which saw its first uprising. Wind and sea are forever in motion, but the hills stand tranced and *waiting*. I would not be thereamong when Gabriel wakes them."

"Gleeman, you dote with monkish fancies."

"Maybe. But yonder, in the twilight"—Ingolard gestured eastward toward the higher uplands of Honoy—"I have seen the long woods crawl and hang upon the crests like the stark brood of Jormungand——"

"Nose of the Pope! Who was he?"

"The serpent that lay coiled beyond the ocean, the serpent that would one day rise and slay the gods. It is old foolish legend—the terror with which Satan smote the heathen. Yet when storm clouds veiled the height of Dondunor I, a good Christian according to my strength, have walked backward, watching until rooftree or stack or church tower should conceal them, fearing always lest they rise and show . . ."

"Show what?"

"I do not know. Lest they show That Which Is Among The Hills. Something is there which draws me and threatens. What it is I know not, save that it is not the Sieur God. I am no Moses; Canaan is not Nordanay."

"Perish your folly, gleeman. A hill is a hill, from which you may spy your quarry, or maybe your foeman. If whimsies such as these invade your stories, what wonder your purse goes empty?"

Ingolard laughed a tinkling laugh.

"Nay, Dodart," he rejoined, "I know you for a lad of discretion. Such whimsies are not allowed to interfere with life as it is lived in my romaunts. *There* is balm for any woe, and sharp swords in the nick of time for every desperate occasion. Ay, time is nicked most gloriously for the contentment of my lords and ladies. Ho, I have dealt with Arthur Pendragon, with Paladin Roland and Theseus Duke of Athens, so that those heroes must have smiled in pains of Purgatory! True, when I first began I told what tales came in my head. But no, that would not do at all."

Ingolard chuckled and paused and then went on.

"Each has his dream of how life may be good, and if I pierce his dream my own will quicken it. Then a face lights up in the crowd, and I know why I was born. Also I learned very long ago to bend a story as I fashion it, so that most of my tales have endings two or three or four—for castle hall, for abbey guest house, for farmstead, and for tavern of the town. Many a lesson took Ingolard while he wetted his whistle with ale. To keep the sneer from the almoner's lips and the fog from the eyes of the swineherd—there is craft in the ploughing of that furrow. Or again, to stir the mirth in a priest, yet touch the chivalry in a man-at-arms—that chivalry which the strong use toward the weak who do not cross them."

Joris, listening above, found something distasteful in this do-nothing's claim to conjure with deeds impossible of his own bodily achievement. But Ingolard seemed intent on purging his mind, for an hour at least, of syrup by which he lived; and his practised voice ran mockingly on in comment and quotation.

" 'That is too grim for truth,' said one—too grim for truth, with the Franconian wars not five years ended. 'La, what a tide of gore,' quoth a maid. But if the fighting languished, a man would mutter: 'We know how winds go whistling and how the primrose blooms; when is the rogue to flesh his steel again?'

"So at it once more with sword and buckler, and for reward a goodwife's sigh: 'Mercy upon us, who would hear tell of such a brute?' Then: 'I,' spoke up her little husband in the corner. 'And I,' chirped a boy whose bedtime was forgotten. 'And I,' blew out the blacksmith, fingering his muscles with a grin.

"Why, if my chevalier should pause in slaughter or reveal compunction, there would be a voice to jeer: 'Bah, he was made for a monk, that one.' Thus it went on. Some would have dragons, which must infallibly perish; *they* were fools who knew not the dragon in their own breasts. Some—in the towns —would have witches to be merry old women on broomsticks; and never a witch must kiss the face beneath the Devil's tail. If truth be harsh, avoid it!

"Also there were the loftily ignorant, who drawled: 'Who is this Lancelot of the Lake?' As though to say: 'He could not be, since I have never heard of him.' Then again, there were those who wondered what manner of troll you were that had learned all these things; those were they who pass blind and deaf and stupid through war and childbed, pestilence and famine.

"Eh, that reminds me of an anchoress near Volsberghe—a · dear and saintly soul, with whom I sometimes talked through the window of her cell. I, being young, let fall some heedless word concerning an archer who strode past us and doffed his cap. I knew him bound for a coppice where a bright-eyed girl waited; but still I treasure the gentle reproof that smote into my sinful ear: 'I would have you know, Master Ingolard, there is no wenching in this parish!'

"And her window upon the world was just a foot square. . . .

"But most of all in my early days I learned to beware of the shepherd who, knowing each one of his twenty sheep apart, grumbled most vilely if more than six people came into any story. My hero wandered far from place to place? No matter, he must meet the same folk everywhere. He might have one or two lovers, one friend to talk to, and one enemy to kill. A king might command two courtiers, a queen two demoiselles, a captain two lieutenants—but all was dire confusion if the number grew to three.

"The fault lay partly in the telling, if partly in the thickness of the shepherd's skull; so although it went against my conscience I pared my tales to the bone. And still sometimes I saw the flame of a secret dream wake sweetly in the eye of Sixty or Sixteen. Or pride of guarded knowledge, or memory of joy and power. . . .

"Ay, Dodart, you yawn. But I warrant *you* also know a thing or two that for strangeness or sorrow or laughter would well adorn any tale. Now, is it not so? Have you not listened to me or to another, thinking the while in your heart: 'Ah, but he does not know what I know about'—whatever it may be?"

Dodart chuckled, and Joris curled his lip to hear the flattering twist of talk recapture the youth's attention.

"Well, now you say it——" blurted Dodart, and stopped importantly.

"Nay, do not tell me and be ashamed thereafter," chided the old man gently. "I have listened to queer things enough in my time, and do not seek to know any more."

"Ashamed to hell!" protested Dodart. "And it is not about myself, save that he lay in my cradle when I first learned to crawl. He whom they call the Sieur de Ath is not the Sieur de Ath at all, but the true heir's baseborn cousin, begotten in rape by Joris of the Rock. When the Jacques stormed the Tower of Ath my father, who was miller there, rescued the one baby, and hid it till the end of the revolt, and said it was the other, and so saved his own neck and the keeping of the mill. He and my mother died in a week of the sweating sickness; my father told me before he passed, in case the knowledge should one day prove useful. Useful, by the Mass! Useful when I want to lose my ears."

"Ay," agreed Ingolard placidly. "Such things are best forgotten. And as for the Tower of Ath, one lord is there if another is not. What became of the little sieur?"

"Barberghe had him in ward, but lent him to Ger before war broke out. So he is page to Ger,.I was told. Maybe squire by now. I never saw him. But is it not strange?"

"Yes."

Joris thought so too, as he lay motionless in the gloom above Ingolard's head. So there *was* "a boy in the hills, the son of Joris of the Rock."

But while the faint memory of that far-off violence stirred in him Dodart uttered his name again, and the pitiful wraith of Tiphaine was presently swept from his mind by a storm of emotion.

"Joris, too, is a bastard. Did ever you see *him*, Ingolard?"

"Not that I know of. They say he has the face and stature of the house of Montcarneau. No mistaking *that* in a crowd. Ay, there is often torment in the blood of noble bastards. Witness Conrad of Burias, God rest his traitor soul—for him I *have* seen, and he was as nobly dark as the king is nobly red. . . .

"Dodart, have you heard the prophecy made when Thorismund was born? It came from near Hastain, and it was a fair shot on the target, for I myself peddled it before the little prince was Duke of Hastain, and before the old king built the castle there."

"No. What was it?"

"Thus, in runes, if I rightly remember:

> "Black and gold
> Red shall hold.
>
> "Gold and red
> At hand are led,
>
> "Yet separatèd
> Till years be sped.
>
> "Red shall sin
> For black to grin;

"Black and red
In the same bed.

"Gold shall sunder
And black shall blunder;

"Red shall run
Ere all be done.

"Black shall be riven
And gold given
To red new-shriven."

"There! You follow the marvel of it?"

"I follow not at all," was Dodart's grumpy confession. "What is it about, that tangle of red and black and gold?"

"Listen, and I will expound it, phrase by phrase. I knew the old seer who forecast it, and twenty years after his death I honour him afresh. . . .

"*Black and gold red shall hold.* Red-haired Thorismund shall hold Hastain, whose ducal device became a golden portcullis on a sable field. . . .

"*Gold and red at hand are led, yet separatèd till years be sped.* Thorismund was only a child when he first stood heir to the crown, but he had ten years to wait while René wore it. . . .

"*Red shall sin for black to grin.* Black-haired Conrad encouraged his cousin in all demeanour unworthy of a prince. . . .

"*Black and red in the same bed*—the bed of the Lady Yolande de Volsberghe. Her, too, I have observed, and by the Rood I blamed not her or either of the lads, for all were very fair to see. Then: *Gold shall sunder and black shall blunder.* The crown came between Thorismund and Conrad; and Conrad trusted Raoul of Ger.

"*Red shall run ere all be done*—and run it did, in torrents on the field of 'Pont-de-Foy.

"*Black shall be riven, and gold given to red new-shriven.*

Plain enough, is it not? And they say Thorismund spent two nights upon his knees before the crown was set on his red head, God bless and guard him!"

"Amen to your prayer," said Dodart, "but that was a very grand prophecy! Are you sure it is not made up since the great battle in June?"

"I am sure," replied Ingolard, scratching himself gravely.

"And I also am sure," thought Joris, trembling to a silent storm of mingled rage and laughter.

Anne was gone, and his men were gone, and his runes were proven a mockery. This miserable crutched maggot, this piping vendor of ghostly adventure, had fooled *him* as he fooled the silly country wenches at any fair in Basse Honoy. It was true that he, Joris, had not only imagined, but also carved with his sword, another interpretation to that jangle of rhymed couplets; it was true that Anne's face would have haunted him without the gleeman's assistance. But that his strength and purpose should have bowed to Ingolard's fantasy, to Ingolard's turning of a silver coin—it was not even now to be borne.

It should not be borne—but how to—ah, Dodart was moving.

"Time to cease talking of marvels," said Dodart. "I must get my horn and my bow. Wait you there, Ingolard; Flar will be coming soon."

"Wait you there, Ingolard," mocked Joris with silent intentness. *"Dodart has heard your gleeman's confession; death will be coming soon."*

Dodart's shuffling tread grew soft and died away. Joris lowered his breast to the sacking and reached out both hands to the corner beyond him. There had long lain three heavy flattish stones, of the sort used for weighting thatch. One he seized and softly drew to him; his body writhed to the effort, and a floor board creaked sharply beneath the altered strain.

Ingolard's white head moved, and the lips of Joris curved in a savage grin. He poised the stone over the hole, and spoke a hoarse summons.

"Ingolard! Gleeman Ingolard!"

The cripple started and turned where he sat, twisting aloft a brown and wrinkled and inquiring face.

"Yes?" he inquired, sharply. "What is it? Who are you?"

"That Which Is Among The Hills," laughed Joris, and dropped the heavy stone.

Then he reached for his sword belt, stuffed food into his wallet, looked at his hunting horn and slung it, snatched up his cloak, and tore at the trap to swing himself to the floor of the cowshed. Out rasped his sword; Dodart was coming back at a shambling trot. The blurred thump of stone on stone had punched a strange hole in the silence; one of Ingolard's brass-ferruled crutches had clattered in the cobbled roadway.

Dodart cried out and pounded up to the door; Joris had no space for a blow, so sped a fierce thrust, and broke out between the collapsed bodies, tearing his weapon free and loping away into the thickets toward the wood where Flar had found him.

Sweat sprang quickly to his face; his legs were stiff and weak with inaction, and his first score of footprints stamped the sand with red. A dog saw him and gave tongue, but drew near to the cowshed and fell suddenly silent. Fortune favoured the brave, and Joris was nearly a league away before the second gleaning bell heralded wild tumult in the little street of Gomblay.

Twice he waded along a stream, in case hounds should track him. Curled up in deep bracken, he slept a sleep of exhaustion, and only woke to blink at a sun already high in the heaven.

Having eaten, he climbed a beech tree, and made sure of his whereabouts. Deep forest was near, and half-wooded land lay between. Nevertheless he had now no bow, and foraging would be difficult. Also his muscles were lax and he soon tired of running; but he was still Joris, and he spent a pleasant moment or two nicking his hilt a ninth time in honour of Gleeman Ingolard.

That night he slipped over the Ververon road, crawling flatly across wayside clearings when clouds hid the harvest moon. Morning found him observing a gibbet from bushes by a crossroads; the dreadful thing that swung therefrom had certainly once been known as Madoc, and Joris grimaced and turned away, and found "The Lay of Fastingal" careering through his head:

> Here spins he by the gallows-tree
> Whom shadows long befriended,
> Stiff and stark at the edge of dark
> With all his cantrips ended.

For a moment Joris had a desolate picture of the past month in the hills—of the dwindling handfuls of hopeless fugitives, the tightening coils of famine and fire and steel, the mad breaks for safety, the baying and whooping and hallooing, the flurry in the heather, and the stoop of raven or hooded crow when the bright coats were gone. And he unslung his great horn with its mouthpiece of chased silver, and flung it into the next forest pool; no use to burden himself with that, for those whom it once summoned were past all rallying now.

Next he looked angrily round, for it seemed as though Dodart and Ingolard spoke of him, softly and near at hand. But nothing was there beneath the oaks—nothing, not even a chattering squirrel or any kind of bird.

Joris swore and headed southward, talking to himself aloud lest he hear those mocking voices again; but three days passed before they ceased to trouble him.

*　　　*　　　*

A nun, gray-robed, with huge starched coif of spotless white, bore an empty basket through a beech wood on the wide estate of the great convent of Vautrem. She had taken alms to the squalid village where lived the convent serfs, and now, in the last light, she picked her way with bent head amid moss and beech mast and the gray roots splashed with sunset gold.

She was sturdily built, and valiant apart from any confidence in her cloth; for when she saw the ragged scarecrow stealing upon her between the trees she paused and turned to take a step toward him. And her blue eyes, set widely in a worn but still enchanting face, focussed with directness startling as a squint.

"Why, Joris," she exclaimed, her deep voice muted with caution. "I heard you were slain three days gone by; each night and morning since have I prayed for your soul—but your body is not safe here!"

Joris leaned against a tree and bent a wolfish glare upon her. His mind reeled to the shock of encounter, but past brooding quickened his speech.

"And think you that yours is safe here?" he demanded, grinning with rage.

"Safe as anywhere else," returned the nun, drooping her basket in front of her.

Her gray sleeve, caught up on the wickerwork handle, revealed the end of a ghastly weal on one strong cream-white forearm. Joris felt his eyes swell and heard himself utter a groan; Herodias at Hastain had become Diana in the deep forest, and now was changed again to Magdalen at Vautrem.

"You—you——" he stammered, and then achieved a difficult control of his astonished wrath, and took a stride toward her.

"So Thorismund hid you here when he turned you out of his bed? How long was it before he tired, that royal rider of so many shapely mares?"

"Avaunt your foulness and folly," said she who had been Red Anne. "The prince had nothing of me, save that he wept in my arms from weakness and shame of his sins; and I had nothing of him save entry into the convent and a shortened term of novitiate. Believe it or no, Joris; I swear it on my rosary."

She loosed the basket with one hand, and caught at beads and crucifix. And there was that in her gesture, in the strange and implacable gentleness of her vivid fearless face, which twisted the outlaw's heart to belief and brought him a crippling pang of despair. For all his pride in evil living, all dark self-righteousness of men for whom the world was made, could not reconcile Joris to sight of another's escape out of wickedness by a path hidden from his own understanding.

"And what—what wrought this change in you, whose bully was Grand Master of the Covens of Nordanay, whose lovers were Lorin de Campscapel and Joris of the Rock?"

"Maybe I had played long enough at being a man, who in the end am only a barren woman. And remember, I too had a prophecy—a prophecy no less strange than your runes."

"You knew my runes were a sham?"

"I knew they were told in Hastain when I was a child; I know they are told again since Pont-de-Foy. You had your truth of them; let Thorismund have his. But how can I tell you what befell me, before I passed into the shadows of the Hill with its three Trees? Lys had her share in it, and Ivo who died for me, and Thorismund himself, who in his deadly sickness forgot all light loves and cried only upon his mother—ay, in his raving he took *me* for herself."

"You have hair much of a colour, you and he and Judas Iscariot. But it is true I shall not be edified to learn the manner of your conversion. What do you think to do in the convent there?"

"Work, and fast, and pray for a measure of forgiveness. It is true my offerings are damnable, but all damnation is not so deep as the mercy of that central Tree. And if the Anne you know still fights, and is conquered by inches only, be sure that the peace I sometimes grasp is a more fearful thing to know than all delight of body and mind."

"Ha! There spoke Red Anne indeed, who, having squeezed both earth and hell, takes Paradise in greedy hands and will have the last of that also! You would be abbess, would you not?"

"No, Joris. Henceforth I school myself to obey the word of others to my life's end."

She stood gravely before him, looking steadily into his eyes.

The great white headdress dusked her face, the stiff linen cupped her strong round chin, the gray robe hid the gracious body whose curves his hand once knew as it knew the hilt of his own sword.

"To your life's end, hey?" he rasped, with all the serf's blood in him curdled to venom. "That schooling should not be too hard. I pass your betrayal of our old companionship, for at least you led no foemen to my Rock. But I for eighteen years have had no benefit of clergy, and never shall Holy Church have any gift of me. If she be the Bride of Christ on earth, she shall lack to-night a gem of her arrayment—a tarnished gem, I grant you, but one she will mourn to lose."

With that, and wilder comment beside, he tore his blade from its scabbard. If Anne prayed, her prayer was silent; she did not even drop her basket, but lifted her chin a little, and almost began to smile.

"I wear a corselet of penance," she warned him; and that was the last thing she said. Indeed, the iron turned a thrust and for a moment her eyes daunted him; but hardship and loss, and corruption of power, whipped up the wolf whose dearest lust was only to destroy.

Presently very few could have told that even the uncoifed hair was Anne's, for it had been trimmed like a boy's, and moreover was streaked with gray. The vesper chime stole out across the fields, staying the hand of Joris to loosen a tongue that gibbered a moment before he could command it.

"You will be late!" he snarled—and turned and blundered away, between the beeches that struck at him as he passed, toward the westward shapes of cloud that dabbled beastlike in the lifeblood of the sun.

*   *   *

It was true they believed Joris dead. A tall rogue late of his company, with beard and colour not unlike his own, had been trapped in a burning hut near Santloy. Between the fire and the fallen ridge beam, the fellow's head was charred and flattened beyond recognition; but most of Ger's army were heartily sick of that prolongation of arduous service, and no one grudged the men who claimed it their share of the king's reward.

So Joris lay for two days more half crazed and very hungry in the woods near Ververon, and watched his former pursuers march up or down the roads toward their homes. When he ventured forth the country seemed empty; he robbed a forester's hut of food and pressed southward toward Pont-de-Foy.

He came out on the river bank in a misty mid-morning, when pale sunlight began to find the first yellows of September foliage. Varne rippled beneath the willows, banding the dim woods with a curve of brown and silver; fifty yards away from silent-stepping Joris, a young stag glided into the water, dipping an antlered head to its blurred reflection, drinking swiftly but placidly, and finally turning to regain the bank and vanish like a ghost.

The outlaw examined the ford's approaches, and found no recent footprints of man or beast. The white of broken branches was dimmed; the bracken and grasses had repaired the trampling havoc of Ger's passage in the previous June. Joris had been prepared to wait until dusk and swim for it, but his secret seemed his own for the day; nothing stirred on the opposite bank, that cleared a little as he watched it.

Presently he was up to his armpits, grimacing at the chill of the stream, prodding with his sword point to hold to the narrow way. His late killings had ceased to trouble him; given respite from fatigue and hunger, Joris was always able to find ease in doing the next thing. He had long ago wrested a trick of religion to simplify his problem of conduct; he had not so much forgotten God as become a god to himself. That any within his power should dare withstand him seemed to him almost blasphemous. True, there were shreds of a mad misery floating about in his mind, but freedom of action and

stress of river passage combined to restore a gleam of bleak
contentment to the haggard aquiline face that moved slowly
forward above the whispering tide.

At length he was climbing the sandy margin of the southern
bank of the river. His clothing clung and gleamed and dripped;
his naked sword, that was slightly oiled, shed a shining
slackening succession of fat drops beside the firm damp im-
print of his striding brogues; and there were now ten nicks
upon the hilt of horn.

On the brow of the first slope, when his footfall crackled
among pine needles, he halted and turned and shook his
glittering blade at the shore he had abandoned.

"Hey, by the chimes of hell," he laughed, "I have fooled
the armoured lot of them."

A sound fell on his quick ear, and he spun round on his
heel. A dark boy, bow in hand, with a black gerfalcon on his
yellow tunic, was trotting a pretty chestnut nag toward him
between the sun-kissed trunks of the pines.

*   *   *

"Before I leave for Hautarroy," had said the Count Raoul,
"I will set in train at Pont-de-Foy the buiiding of a chantry
chapel for John Doust."

A monk from the Priory of Dor, a famous architect, rode
south with the count to Angmer, and lodged there in the inn
with him, talking little but sketching a lot. So that Juhel
found black lead and paper once more at hand, and knew a
rewakening of that deep satisfaction in drawing which he had
almost forgotten. Each day he rode past the blackened ruins
of the Inn of Harmony, whose master had lately thriven for
all that he lived in his own stable that had escaped the fire;
and by learning the ground of the great battle and going over
in his mind the many stories he had heard from men who
fought in the left and centre, Juhel made many crude pictures,
some of which he gave to the count's secretary Hubriton—who

oiled them cunningly to fix the smudgy lead, and pasted them into his chronicle which Juhel loved to read.

The boy was now legal ward to Raoul of Ger, and once, during that late summer's work of ranging through the hills, he had ridden to his own Tower of Ath with the gray-headed chevalier whom the count had sent as seneschal until Juhel should be of age. That day Juhel was very silent; he looked askance on his serfs, and they on him. When the seneschal and he came together to the gloomy little chapel, Juhel asked to be left alone; and there for a long time he knelt and prayed, or simply listened to the wind that sang quietly in the worn stone. The future, not the past, oppressed the latest Sieur de Ath; his overlord would be Ger, not Barberghe, but the thought of his own wide powers-to-be brought anything but pleasure. He had no desire to command men, or to obey any lord because he was a lord; he wanted somehow to live to himself, with employment peculiar to his own hands, and without the disturbances raised by women.

He was glad to leave Ger that last time, and more glad to leave his domain of Ath; but at Angmer he found a deeper content than any he had known since Piers fell. Raoul of Ger, and Nino Chiostra, and Hubriton the secretary, and Dom Blaise the architect of Dor were each of them men to be served with respect and listened to with pleasure. And on the day before their intended departure Juhel rode westward along the river bank to revisit the scene of that last gallop before the holding of Pont-de-Foy.

His bow he took from habit, and a pheasant hung at his saddlebow before he wheeled the chestnut for return. Sitting motionless among the pines, he stared awhile at the ford, meaning to make a drawing that night of the crossing he remembered. And so he saw the solitary figure whose beard shone faintly in the sunlight.

"Some forester of the Duke of Saulte's," he reflected, watching the slow-moving head and shoulders with their attendant ripple. Then: "Saints, but he is tall. Too ragged for a Saulte man. Besides, he bears no badge. Now, is he an outlaw, so far escaped and chancing the unlikeliest way for any of his kind? I think I had better see him close at hand.

"And I wish I were not alone. But it cannot be helped."

He flicked an arrow from his quiver, gripped it against the bowshaft with a doubled forefinger, and jogged sturdily forward to do his duty.

*   *   *

"Stand, fellow!" he called. "Tell me, who are you?"

Joris regarded him and his bow and judged it best to dissemble; here at least was a horse, and no other rider in sight. Juhel observed one great red hand tip the last water from a leathern scabbard, while the other swung a long blade into place and drove it home. The matted gray-and-gold head came up; Juhel drew rein and gasped to see the red-rimmed heavy-lidded eyes, the weathered savage face and tangled beard.

"Dietrich Halbern!" he cried sharply. *"I know you—you are Joris of the Rock!"*

He dropped rein and bent his bow. Joris laughed and tore out his dagger, dodging aside amid the pine trunks to leap diagonally forward. His aim was at once to frighten the horse, to keep its head in the rider's way, and to lessen the twenty yards between them for surety of a throw. But the brown-eyed boy with the sunburned face was not to be fooled that way; he danced his mount on its white-stockinged legs, but his sighting and hands were steady.

The fierce twang, the streaking shaft, the splitting lancing pain as he sprang, were all one to Joris; ducking to let the arrow pass over, he met it, and stumbled on his face, with the feathered butt sticking out of the hollow behind and above his right collar bone.

Stamping of hoofs as he rolled in the pine needles, stamping of spurred boots as he wrenched himself up on one hand. The boy was running upon him with a short sword lifted high; there was still time to grope for the dagger and fling it left-handed, but the silver hilt clashed flatly against the trunk of a tree.

On his knees, with half-drawn blade, Joris suffered the first of a rain of clumsy blows. He leaned backward, shielding his face, and felt a breaking in the breast even as screamed words reached his consciousness.

"I am Juhel de Ath, you dog! *That* for my kinswoman Tiphaine—and *that* for Captain John Doust—and *that*—and *that*—and *that* for every other foul crime of your whole filthy life!"

Lying flat on his back now, the groaning Joris opened his eyes; he was still, as it were, surprised that this should have happened to *him,* and although he knew his life ran redly he still had skill to remember Tiphaine. And Juhel lowered his point, struck still with fascination to see beneath the heavy eyelids a flame of hideous and unconquered glee.

Joris lifted a maimed and wavering paw; if God had played this trick on Joris, there was still a trick to play on the lad. With his last breath he still could blast—as Rufin once had striven to blast—the life and fortune of his slayer.

But when he tried to speak he could not, for his mouth was full of blood. To Juhel the pale staring eyes lost glee and took on agony and horror; Joris spat and choked and spat again, clutching his great chest and writhing, bowing his crimsoned head in a last feral effort to spur his voice at will.

Dodart and Ingolard knew, and he had slain them both. Not the Church with its ban, or Red Anne with her treachery, or Raoul of Ger with ten thousand men and fire and famine to help him, could have brought this end upon Joris if he had not helped them to it. A spark of pride in grim achievement glowed in his head and was gone; power left his limbs, and the boy's face faded in a mist that whirled from red through brown to billowing blackness. Lungs and windpipe fused in a column of frantic pain, yet a trickle of breath obeyed him, and he spent it before he knew.

"*God knows,*" he gurgled, and began to choke again. Blinding lights burst in the blackness, and a far-off booming shook the void. God knew; and the last thought of Joris was that he heard the laughter of God.

*   *   *

"Ten thousand little fleeting devils!" cried Nino Chiostra from his saddle. "Lad, you have made a mess of him. Who in the name of——"

"This is the real Joris of the Rock," said the boy, lifting a white and wretched face. "I shot him down with the arrow, and then—and then—he was nearly helpless—and——"

"Ay," cut in the Tuscan crisply. "I know how it feels the first time."

"This is the last time too," muttered Juhel between clenched teeth; and turning about he swung his wet sword back and hurled it hard and high into the air. Twirling lazily as it fell, the weapon splashed in the waters of Varne; and Nino got to the ground.

"I never saw Joris but once," said Nino, "and then he was running away. But no doubt you are right, and my lord Count will confirm your judgment. Finish what you began, boy; off with his villainous head. The reward is given in error, but I doubt not you will reap another. Why did you throw your sword away? Here, take mine—or his own."

"I will not touch him again," muttered Juhel sulkily.

"Well, I must see you righted," said Nino with tranquil amusement; and stepping forward, he hacked off the wolf's head and cut a piece of the outlaw's sopping cloak to carry the grisly prize.

Juhel watched him oddly, with colour coming back into his face; and when the Tuscan had cleansed his sword and picked up the uncomely burden, the boy moved and spoke.

"Chevalier Nino."

"Hey?"

"You—*you* have taken the head off Joris. Will you take upon you my slaying of him, too? *I* want no credit or reward—

whereas if you—if my lord—if the king hear that you had done it——"

"Well?"

"There—there is a matter in which I—we, all who know you—wish you great fortune, and would—would do what little we can to—to help——"

"Juhel, dear knave, have done. I would have given much to be the slayer of Joris, but think you, even for that other matter, I could accept such a fantastic gift of fame? And Juhel, keep you this secret, for now it rests only between my lord Count and Hubriton and you and myself. This morning, after you were gone, a post rode in from Hautarroy. When I had read one letter, I took a horse to cool my blood a little, and that is how I am here."

"Ah, Chevalier Nino, tell me!"

"You will lately have noticed in this realm a thinning of old nobility. Maybe the king is ill-advised, or maybe Count Raoul, God have him in keeping, has sworn to revolt if it be not done; but in any case *I* am count-designate of Saint-Aunay, the only condition being that I marry the late count's heiress."

"Chevalier—I mean my lord Count—I—I——"

"Nay, lad, no need to say these things, with such an offer as yours scarce cooled upon the air. I am not yet a lord; but when I am one there will always be honour for you at Saint-Aunay. And now—come away from this carrion. Is that his dagger, with the silver hilt?"

"Yes. Now I think *I* will take his sword—and offer it upon my knees, for I believe it will please Heaven to know it can do no more wrong. Will *you* not keep the dagger, Chevalier Nino?"

"Gramercy. Gladly will I. When I think of John Doust it will not be unpleasant to look up and see the silver hilt and remember this day by my ford—by *our* ford—by the ford that Joris may have used for many a bloody raid. . . .

"You have the sword? And I the dagger. And the Fiend his black soul. King Thorismund shall have his golden head, and the crows and kites the red rest of him. And now we will find my lord Count."

"Ay, that is Joris," said Raoul of Ger, when Nino slit the cloak for his inspection. "So I may keep my promise to our lord the king; for the head we thought to belong to this rogue was not worth sending to Hautarroy. . . .

"So, Juhel, *you* have purged the realm and quitted me of my task. God knows I owe you enough already; but what can I give you now?"

"A blade, for one thing," smiled Nino. "And a rap on the shoulder therewith, for another."

Juhel went very pale, and crossed his hands on the nicked hilt of the long sword he carried. From the golden-brown face of Nino Chiostra he looked to the brown-ivory face of Raoul of Ger.

"My lord Count," he said simply, "you can give me one thing only."

"It is yours—but what may it be?"

"Your leave to enter Holy Church," said the son of Joris of the Rock.

THE END

www.ingramcontent.com/pod-product-compliance
Lightning Source LLC
Chambersburg PA
CBHW021456240626
47154CB00002B/387